CHILDREN OF THE NIGHT

Swinging her into his arms, Logan drew back the covers and lowered Mara onto the mattress. After sliding under the covers beside her, he gathered her close. The night was beautiful, and so was the woman nestled in his arms. He had dreamed of this moment many times over the years, but he had never believed it would happen, and now she was here. He had never put much stock in fate, but he couldn't help thinking it was more than co-incidence that had brought them together at a time when she desperately needed help. Exactly what kind of help, he wasn't sure, but he was prepared to do whatever was necessary, up to and including sacrificing his own life for hers.

"Logan . . ." Her hands moved restlessly up and down his back. "Kiss me," she murmured. "Kiss me . . ."

"That's it, darlin'," he said, his hand caressing the silky length of her thigh. "Just tell me what you want."

She locked her hands behind his nape. "I want you. All of you." A seductive smile tugged at her lips. "Every inch."

D1167891

Other titles available by Amanda Ashley

A WHISPER OF ETERNITY

AFTER SUNDOWN

DEAD PERFECT

DEAD SEXY

DESIRE AFTER DARK

NIGHT'S KISS

NIGHT'S MASTER

NIGHT'S PLEASURE

NIGHT'S TOUCH

IMMORTAL SINS

EVERLASTING KISS

EVERLASTING DESIRE

BOUND BY NIGHT

BOUND BY BLOOD

HIS DARK EMBRACE

DESIRE THE NIGHT

BENEATH A MIDNIGHT MOON

AS TWILIGHT FALLS

Published by Kensington Publishing Corporation

Night's Mistress

AMANDA ASHLEY

East Baton Rouge Parish Library
Baton Rouge, Louisiana

ZEBRA BOOKS
KENSINGTON PUBLISHING CORP.
http://www.kensingtonbooks.com

ZEBRA BOOKS are published by

Kensington Publishing Corp.
119 West 40th Street
New York, NY 10018

Copyright © 2013 by Madeline Baker

All rights reserved. No part of this book may be reproduced in any form or by any means without the prior written consent of the Publisher, excepting brief quotes used in reviews.

If you purchased this book without a cover you should be aware that this book is stolen property. It was reported as "unsold and destroyed" to the Publisher and neither the Author nor the Publisher has received any payment for this "stripped book."

All Kensington titles, imprints, and distributed lines are available at special quantity discounts for bulk purchases for sales promotion, premiums, fund-raising, educational, or institutional use.

Special book excerpts or customized printings can also be created to fit specific needs. For details, write or phone the office of the Kensington Special Sales Manager: Attn.: Special Sales Department. Kensington Publishing Corp., 119 West 40th Street, New York, NY 10018. Phone: 1-800-221-2647.

Zebra and the Z logo Reg. U.S. Pat. & TM Off.

ISBN-13: 978-1-4201-3041-6
ISBN-10: 1-4201-3041-2

First Printing: August 2013

eISBN-13: 978-1-4201-3042-3
eISBN-10: 1-4201-3042-0

First Electronic Edition: August 2013

10 9 8 7 6 5 4 3 2 1

Printed in the United States of America

*For all the readers who have
waited so patiently for
Mara's story . . .*

Chapter One

Mara stood on the balcony of her home in the mountains of Northern California. Staring out over her domain, she lifted her gaze to the endless indigo vault of the sky, to the moon that had been her sun since the night she became a vampire so many centuries ago. Even though she could now walk freely in the light of day if she was so inclined, she was still most comfortable in the darkness she had inhabited for thousands of years.

In the silvery wash of the moon's light, the world around her looked peaceful. The people who lived in the small town located in the shallow valley below were all sleeping now, dreaming their innocent mortal dreams, blissfully unaware that one of the Undead lived in the sprawling old house near the top of the mountain. The War for supremacy waged between the vampires and the were-wolves had ended, and most humans were content to pretend it had never happened.

After a time, she let her mind expand, homing in on the few people in the world that she cared for.

Roshan DeLongpre and his witch wife, Brenna, were on an extended vacation in Venice. Vince Cordova and his pretty blond, blue-eyed wife, Cara, were at home in Porterville. At the moment, they were sitting outside, enjoying the quiet of a star-studded Oregon night. Their son, Raphael, and his bride, Kathy McKenna, were in bed, wrapped in each other's embrace. Mara wondered how Kathy was enjoying her new life as a vampire.

Mara had once offered to bequeath the Dark Gift to Kathy. As Mara's fledgling, the girl wouldn't have been affected by the Dark Sleep, but Kathy had wanted Rafe to be her master. Mara couldn't blame the girl; after all, if one had to be bound to a master, it was always more pleasant if it was someone you loved and trusted, someone who would guide you patiently, and gently teach you all the things a new vampire needed to know in order to survive. Someone who would never abandon you, or betray you. Not long after being turned, Kathy had sold her bookstore in Oak Hollow, and she and Rafe had moved to Porterville.

Raphael's twin brother, Rane, had finally made peace with what he was. He and his wife, Savanah, had also bought a place in Porterville. Just now, Rane and his bride were at home, sitting on the floor in front of the fireplace, their three-month-old daughter, Abbey Marie, sleeping peacefully on a blanket between them. Savanah had not yet accepted the Dark Gift her husband was so eager to give her. They had both agreed it would be best to wait a few years, until Abbey was older.

Mara told herself she wasn't jealous, that she didn't envy any of them the love or the happiness they had found, but deep within the hidden recesses of her heart where she didn't look too often, she knew it for the bald-faced lie it was. She was Mara, the oldest and most powerful of her kind. Vampires, male and female, envied her. Men sought her favors, willing to do anything she asked just to be near her. She should have been blissfully happy and content, and yet her existence lacked any real purpose or meaning. She was finding it more and more difficult to find a reason to rise each night; she was growing increasingly weary of her self-imposed lonely existence.

She had taken mortal lovers from time to time, but she had loved none of them. Afraid to fully trust any man, be he mortal or vampire, she had always withheld a part of herself, never letting any of the men she had known get too close, or see too much.

Until she met Kyle Bowden. She had been captivated by him from the moment she first saw him standing at the foot of the Sphinx with a sketch pad in his hand. He had been hatless in the sun; his short brown hair highlighted with streaks of gold. The sleeves of his white shirt had been rolled up, revealing suntanned skin and muscular arms. She had watched his hand, quick and confident as it moved over the paper, and wondered if he possessed that same confidence with women.

Eager to meet him, she had purposely bumped into him with a murmured, "Sorry."

He had turned toward her, stared at her a moment, and then blurted, "Good Lord, but you're beautiful."

Before meeting Kyle, she had intended to find a place to go to ground, to bury herself deep in the earth in the Valley of the Nile and sleep for a year or two, perhaps ten, but with Kyle at her side, the world no longer seemed like such a dreary place; the lethargy that had plagued her disappeared, and she found herself wanting to travel the globe again, to see it anew through his eyes.

As giddy as a schoolgirl with her first crush, she had quickly fallen head over heels for him, charmed by his innate sweetness, by the sincerity and adoration in the depths of his deep gray eyes. For the first time in her existence, she had given her heart to a man, something she had sworn she would never do.

But then she had foolishly trusted him with the truth of what she was, and seen the look in his eyes turn from love to revulsion. She remembered that night so well. They had been reclining on the loveseat in his studio, their arms and legs intimately entwined . . .

Kyle reached for a bowl of black grapes and offered her one. With a slight smile, she shook her head. "No, thank you."

"You never eat with me," he remarked, popping the grape into his mouth. "Why is that? Are your table manners so terrible?"

"Of course not," she replied. "I'm quite tidy."

"Tidy?" he repeated with a grin. "That's an odd way of putting it."

"I have odd tastes."

He ate another grape. "Odd? How so?"

"You don't want to know."

"I love you, Mara, with all my heart. I want to know everything." He set the bowl aside and traced the curve of her lower lip with his forefinger. "Everything. I want to know what makes you laugh and what makes you cry, and why you sometimes look at me strangely, as if . . ."

"As if I want to eat you up?"

"Yes, something like that." He withdrew his hand, his brow furrowing. "But that's not the only thing."

"No?"

"I don't know how to explain it, how to put it into words . . ."

She ran her fingertips along the side of his neck, her nostrils flaring. "Try."

"Your eyes . . . sometimes, like now . . . they change . . ."

Her eyelids fluttered down and she drew a deep breath. She was getting so comfortable in his presence, she sometimes let her guard down. Especially at times like these, when they were lying close together, when the scent of his blood was almost overpowering. She had to be more careful, had to remember that he didn't know what she was.

"Mara? What are you keeping from me?"

Back in control, she opened her eyes. "Trust me, Kyle, if I tell you, you'll never look at me the same again."

"Trust you? It's you who doesn't trust me. If you did, there wouldn't be any secrets between us."

He was right, of course. She didn't trust him. She didn't trust anyone, but maybe he was right. Maybe it was time to find out if he truly loved her, or if they were only empty words.

"Fine." She rose to her feet. "You want the truth? Don't say I didn't warn you." And so saying, she unleashed her power and let him see her for what she was. Lips drawn back, fangs extended, her eyes blazing red, she towered over him.

It was a mistake, just as she had known it would be.

He had jumped off the loveseat and practically flown across the room in his haste to put some distance between them. "Get away from me, you bloodsucking fiend!"

His words had shocked her, her insides going cold as the love in his eyes swiftly turned to revulsion. She could have mesmerized him, made him forget what he had seen, but she had been too proud. He couldn't accept her for what she was, and she couldn't accept that . . .

* * *

She shook the unpleasant memory from her mind. She loved being a vampire, loved everything about it. She wouldn't have gone back to being mortal again even if it was possible. Not for Kyle. Not for anyone, or anything, else. She had seen the world change and grow through the centuries, witnessed the rise and fall of kings and queens, of kingdoms and nations, observed the Dark Ages and the Industrial Revolution, seen the birth of innumerable inventions that the people of her day would have hailed as miracles—things like space travel and the automobile, iPads and Kindles, satellite television, wireless computers, Twitter and Facebook, and cell phones that did everything but cook and clean house. She grinned wryly. In her day, a roll of toilet paper would have been acclaimed as a miracle.

For the first time in her long existence, she felt the weight of past centuries sitting heavily on her shoulders. These days, there was little in life that surprised her; few things that she hadn't seen or done a hundred times. Twining a lock of hair around her finger, she wondered if perhaps it was time to end her existence, to find out what, if anything, waited on the other side.

It would be a new adventure, she mused, a place she had never been before. Was there another life, another existence, after this one? She had seen no physical evidence of an afterlife. If one did exist, would her soul find rest in some heavenly paradise? That seemed doubtful. It was far more likely that she would be tossed into a sea of endless damnation, forced to spend eternity in the deepest pit of a cruel and unforgiving Hell.

With a sigh of resignation, she closed her eyes as thoughts of her past washed over her.

She had been raised a slave in the house of Chuma, one of Pharaoh's trusted advisors. She had been a month shy of her fifteenth birthday when Chuma presented her to Shakir, a wealthy ally, as a reward for a service well done. Perhaps that had been hell enough. Mara had not taken kindly to being a slave in Pharaoh's household, but she had been treated well enough. Captivity in Shakir's household was another thing entirely. He had been a cold and cruel man, one who demanded instant obedience, one who did not hesitate to wield the lash at the slightest provocation, real or imagined. Shakir had allowed only female slaves under his roof. Many in Chuma's household had mocked Shakir behind his back, saying it was unseemly for a man of Shakir's position to have women working in his stables, caring for his armor, preparing his meals, acting as his butler, driving his chariot, but Shakir had ignored their taunts. He refused to share his quarters with male servants. There were no eunuchs in his household staff, no stallions in his stable.

Shakir claimed to love women. Old and young and in between, he professed to love all the female slaves in his household. And he bedded them all, from the oldest to the youngest, whether they were willing or not, eager to prove his manhood by the number of children he sired. His touch had made Mara's flesh crawl. For some reason she never understood, her blatant distaste for Shakir's touch soon made her his favorite. At first, he had found her loathing amusing, her temper tantrums entertaining.

Desperate to escape both his bed and his whip, she had run off many times in the ensuing five years until, finally wearying of her constant attempts to leave him, Shakir had put her in chains.

Mara had thought her life a hell before, but now it was much, much worse. Shakir kept her chained in a small cell in the bowels of his residence. Food was delivered once each day, unless the wrinkled old slave, Kesi, forgot. Shakir refused Mara the ease of a pallet, the warmth of a blanket, the comfort of a light. He even denied her the opportunity to bathe except on those nights when she was brought, still in chains, to his bed-chamber. Once she was bathed and powdered and perfumed, he chained her to his bed and used her as he saw fit. She would never forget his cruelty or the humil-iation of being bound and helpless, forced to submit to whatever he demanded of her.

She had begged Kesi to kill her, or to bring her a knife so that she might take her own life, but the old woman had feared Shakir's wrath too much to help her.

And then, late one night, when she was huddled in a corner of her cell, her back raw from the lash, the candle outside her cell sprang to life and a shadowed figure ap-peared beside her. One minute she had been alone in the dark, the next he was there, a dusky-skinned man of medium height. A long black cloak fell from a pair of broad shoulders, the hood pulled low over his face, shad-owing his features, save for his eyes, which seemed to glow with some dark inner fire.

"Who are you?" She had scrambled as far away from him as her chains would allow, the pain in her back forgotten. "How did you get in here?"

"I go where I wish," he had replied. "No one can keep me in. Or lock me out." He took a step toward her. "Tell me, my raven-haired beauty, are you happy here?"

"Of course not." She recoiled when his hand snaked out from under his heavy black cloak to brush her cheek. "Leave me alone!"

"And if I refuse, what will you do? Cry for help? Who is going to hear you down here, I wonder?"

"Who are you?"

"I am Dendar, master of the night."

He moved closer. She could see little of his face or form in the near darkness of her cell. But she could see his eyes, red and glowing now, like Hell's own light.

When he put his arms around her, she struggled for a moment, and then went still. She had prayed for death, and now Death stood before her.

With a sigh, she closed her eyes and waited. Soon, her misery would be over. Soon, she would discover the Great Mystery that awaited everyone.

There was a moment of pain, and then there was pleasure beyond anything she had ever known. She felt weightless, as if her spirit had left her body far behind and was now floating effortlessly in the air. She had no fears, no worries. There was only a deep, sensual pleasure she hoped would last forever.

And then he was gone, and she was alone in her cell, confused by what had happened. Had she imagined him? Had it all been a dream? She lifted a hand to her neck, shivered with revulsion when she felt two tiny puncture wounds. When she licked her fingertips, she tasted blood. Was it hers?

Near dawn, pain unlike anything she had ever known engulfed her body. Moaning softly, she writhed in agony on the cold stone floor until, after what seemed like an eternity, she pitched headlong into a chasm deeper and blacker than anything she had ever known or imagined. Her last conscious thought was that, at last, death had found her.

When next she opened her eyes, she was lying naked on a slab, about to be mummified, no doubt to be put into Shakir's burial chamber where, upon his death, she would serve him throughout all eternity. She didn't know

who was more surprised to find that she was alive—
herself, or the handful of men who ran screaming out of
the chamber when she sat up. She had looked around,
confused, her senses reeling under a visual and aural as-
sault unlike anything she had ever known. Heedless of
her nudity, she had leaped lightly from the slab, hungry
in a way she had never been hungry before. The frantic
beating of many hearts drummed against her ears.

She hadn't known what she wanted until, in his haste,
one of the fleeing men tripped and cut his hand on a
sharp stone.

The warm, coppery scent of fresh blood wafted
through the air, sweet, tantalizing. She had pounced on
the luckless creature before he'd had time to scream.

Other men had come, armed with daggers and spears.
Impervious to their puny weapons, she had effortlessly
swatted them all aside and left the building.

Filled with power, she had gone to Shakir's residence.
She had found him reclining on a pile of furs, a woman
at his side. He had stared up at her, eyes wide, mouth
open in a silent scream for mercy. She had advanced on
him slowly, eyes burning, fangs bared. The woman had
run screaming from the room, but Mara had no interest
in the female. She had pinned Shakir to the floor, buried
her fangs in his throat, and slowly drained him dry. After
she had avenged herself on him, she had freed his slaves,
and then she had burned his house to the ground.

She had found the vampire who had turned her against
her will the next night. Still in the throes of acclimating
to her new life, nearly mad with her hunger for blood,
she had attacked Dendar without mercy.

Mara shook her head at the memory. She had prayed
for death and the Fates had granted it to her, only not
quite in the way she had imagined.

"Be careful what you wish for," she murmured to the man in the moon, "lest you get it."

Thinking of Dendar now, she regretted destroying him. But, back then, angry and confused, afraid of the changes his bite had wrought, her only thought had been to kill him. Had she known how much she would glory in being a vampire, she might have kissed him instead.

Chapter Two

Kyle Bowden stood in front of the canvas, the paint drying on the brush in his hand as he looked at the portraits of the woman he had drawn from memory. The first canvas, painted in the first blush of new love, depicted Mara as she had looked when he'd met her—beautiful, exquisite, almost ethereal, with her glossy black hair and flawless, alabaster skin.

The second canvas, the paint still wet, showed her as she truly was—a beautiful monster with bloodred eyes, and sharp white fangs.

Mara, the vampire.

Even now, months after she had told him the truth of what she was, he found it hard to believe that the woman he had adored, the exquisite, sensual creature he had taken to his bed, wasn't a woman at all, but a soulless creature like the one who had killed his father and left his mother barely alive. His mother, may she rest in peace, had lingered between this world and the next for almost a month before death carried her away. He had been a week shy of his thirteenth birthday when she breathed her last. There followed one foster home after another until he turned sixteen and took off on his own.

For a time, Kyle had tried to find the vampire who had killed his father during the War, but by then, it was too late. The War for supremacy that had raged between the Vampires and the Werewolves was over and finding one particular vampire had been virtually impossible.

Kyle blew out a sigh. He had tried to put Mara out of his mind, tried to forget the halcyon nights they had spent in each other's arms, but to no avail. He imagined he could still smell her scent on his clothing, on his sheets, his pillows. He told himself it was impossible and yet, each night when he climbed into bed, her essence seemed to surround him. The merry sound of her laughter echoed in his mind; his skin tingled from the memory of her touch. She had been an incredible lover, unlike any woman he had ever known. He grunted softly. A foolish statement, that, when she wasn't really a woman at all.

This morning he had risen early and put brush to canvas, hoping that by painting her as the monster she truly was, he could somehow excise her memory from his mind and heart, but to no avail.

Vampire or temptress, her portrait only made him yearn for her all the more. He moved to stand in front of the first painting. He had captured her likeness, but not her spirit, nor the true look in her eyes. She had often seemed older than she looked, wise beyond her years; now he knew why. Her physical appearance had belied her age, but the truth had lurked in the depths of her eyes, those incredible emerald green eyes that had watched centuries come and go.

He swore a vile oath. If he lived to be a hundred, he would never forget her. He laughed humorlessly. If he lived to be a hundred, he would still be an infant compared to her. Little wonder she had known so much about Egypt's history, he mused glumly. She had lived it.

As for being an incredible lover, he thought bitterly, that was to be expected. She'd had hundreds of years of practice.

And probably hundreds of lovers, as well.

The thought of her with other men tied his insides in knots.

Dammit! How was he ever going to forget her?

Chapter Three

Needing a change of scenery, Mara decided to return to Southern California and mingle with the Hollywood crowd. In days past, she had met a movie producer or two, a star or two. It had been easy enough to charm the rich and the famous, to finagle an invite to a cocktail party here, an opening night there. Not only was she a beautiful woman, but she possessed the innate charisma of a vampire, something few men, rich or poor, old or young, could resist. Movie star and star maker alike, they had showered her with gifts—jewels, stocks and bonds, automobiles, vacations in exotic locales. Thanks to their generosity through the years, she now owned a fabulous home in the Hollywood Hills, a house in the mountains, and a sumptuous villa in Italy. She had always enjoyed mingling with the famous and the infamous; on occasion, she had thrown a few lavish parties herself.

Of course, the Hollywood of today was nothing like the Hollywood of the thirties and forties. Movie stars had truly been stars back then. There had been a mystery about them, a larger-than-life presence that had projected beyond their screen image. Stars like Gable and Bogart, and her favorite, the ever-appealing bad boy, Robert Mitchum. He had smoked too much, drunk too much, and she had adored him. She had been on the set when he filmed *Out of the Past,* totally captivated by his performance, by his broad shoulders and heavy-lidded eyes. She had once overheard him remark that acting "sure beat working." He had been a star who defined cool. How she missed him.

Mara shook her head. Movie stars today . . . they just weren't cut from the same cloth. Only a few of them were even worthy of the name. Most were just celebrities, rising out of nowhere, shining brightly for a few brief moments, and then disappearing just as quickly, unremarked and soon forgotten.

Mara had been in town less than a week when she heard that one of the major producers was hosting a little get-together at his palatial estate in Brentwood. Knowing she would be welcome, Mara donned a slinky white gown that was slit provocatively up one side, stepped into a pair of silver, spiked heels, and arrived at the house, unannounced and uninvited, just after ten.

The producer, Sterling Gaylord Price, welcomed her with his usual lecherous smile. Sterling was pushing seventy if he was a day, but you would never know it to look at him. No doubt a skilled and expensive plastic surgeon was responsible for shaving ten years off Price's appearance. And everyone knew sixty was the new forty.

"Mara!" he gushed, kissing her soundly on both cheeks, "it's been too long. Too long. Where have you been keeping yourself?"

"Wouldn't you like to know?" she replied with a saucy grin. She linked her arm with his as they moved from the foyer to the front parlor. "I love what you've done to the place."

He beamed at her. "Alison's a whiz at decorating." He gestured at a tall, slender young woman with bright blond hair. "She did the whole place herself."

"Amazing." Mara glanced at the scantily clad Mrs. Sterling Price, who was holding court amidst a group of suntanned young men. By Mara's reckoning, the girl, who couldn't have been more than twenty-two, was the fifth Mrs. Price. Like all the others, she was no doubt a whiz at calling a decorator, writing checks, and bleeding Price for everything she could get before he tired of her and moved on to the next overeager starlet who was willing to trade favors for fame and fortune.

"I'm so glad you're here," Sterling said, giving Mara's arm a squeeze. "Maybe we can get together for drinks, just the two of us, sometime next week."

"Maybe," Mara replied with a coy smile. *When Hell freezes over*. Sterling was a notorious playboy, always on the lookout for the next future ex-Mrs. Price.

She chatted with him another few minutes, relieved when some pouty-lipped starlet with flaming red hair and cleavage she hadn't been born with called him away.

Mara spent the next hour flirting with several young men, all of whom were movie-star gorgeous, even though none of them truly appealed to her. They were too young, too pretty, too eager.

A handsome waiter bearing a candy-laden silver tray paused to offer her a truffle. Lost in thoughts of Kyle, she took it without thinking and popped it into her mouth. Dark rich cocoa and chocolate liqueur flowed over her tongue like liquid silk, followed by a rush of panic. What had she done? She hadn't eaten mortal food in over two thousand years. She had thoughtlessly nibbled on a fig soon after she had been turned, and been violently ill.

Not wanting anyone to see her, she hurried toward the

double doors leading to the veranda. Outside, she took a deep breath, her hands clutching her stomach, and then she frowned. She didn't feel sick at all, didn't feel anything except a strong desire for another chocolate truffle. Maybe two.

"How can that be?" she muttered. "Mortal food is like poison to us." Curious, she went back inside, her gaze darting around the room until she spied the same waiter.

He smiled knowingly when he saw her hurrying toward him. "Delicious, are they not?" he asked with a wink.

"Very." Mara picked a plump one from the tray and carried it outside. She ate it slowly, savoring the way the chocolate melted on her tongue, the way it flooded her senses with an odd sense of euphoria.

Nothing in all the world had ever tasted so good.

Or scared her so much.

What was happening to her?

Mara noticed several other changes in the course of the next few weeks. Although she could be active during the day, she had always preferred the night. Now, she found herself spending more of her waking hours in the daylight, resting more at night. In the past, she had, on various occasions, been tempted by mortal food, mainly items that were unheard of when she had been mortal— things like ice cream, cheeseburgers, hot dogs smothered in mustard and onions, caramel popcorn, thick-crust pizza topped with ham and pineapple. But she had never dared satisfy her curiosity.

Three nights after the party at Sterling's, Mara went to a formal sit-down dinner at the home of a well-known director. Indulging her curiosity, she sampled every course that was placed before her—Maine lobster served on a bed of fluffy, long-grain, white rice, broccoli smothered in butter, a warm fudge brownie topped with vanilla ice cream and drowning in chocolate sauce.

Later, back at home, she paced the floor, her thoughts in turmoil as she tried to understand what was happening to her. No matter how often she contemplated her burgeoning appetite for mortal food, her diminished lust for blood, and her sudden preference for taking her rest at night, she always reached the same conclusion. Like it or not, she was becoming less vampire and more human with each passing day.

Was such a thing even possible? And if so, how long would it be until her preternatural longings and abilities were gone and she was once again mortal, subject to all the frailties and weaknesses of the human race?

She told herself it was inconceivable. She had been a vampire for thousands of years. Once a vampire, always a vampire. It wasn't a sickness, but a way of life. There was no cure, no going back, even if one wished it. And she most definitely did not. She scarcely remembered what it had been like to be mortal, nor did she have any desire to experience it again. She was Nosferatu, the oldest and most powerful of her kind.

Any other way of life was out of the question.

And even as the thought crossed her mind, she found herself craving the taste of a hot fudge sundae like the one she had seen advertised on the satellite screen earlier that night. It would take only a moment to will herself to the nearest restaurant . . .

Muttering an oath, she slammed her palm against the doorjamb, grimacing as the wood cracked beneath her hand.

She would not be human.

She would not be mortal.

It was unthinkable, impossible. It was simply that she had gone too long without feeding, too long since she had taken a life and savored the strength and vitality that flowed into her and through her as her prey's heartbeat slowed, and then stopped.

Tonight, she would hunt, and heaven help the first healthy, attractive mortal male who crossed her path.

Mara stalked Hollywood Boulevard, bypassing the men dressed as women, the women dressed as men, the prostitutes, the drug addicts, the pimps. There had been a time when she would have taken the first unattached mortal she saw, but not now. She wanted only the best this night, a virile, healthy male in the prime of his life.

She found what she was looking for a short time later—a young man exiting a movie theater. He was tall and tan and beautiful. She followed him to the parking lot across the street, her footsteps making no sound on the pavement, her nerves singing in anticipation.

He was reaching for his keys when he suddenly realized he was no longer alone.

Hands clenched, he whirled around to face her. "Why the hell are you following . . . ?" His voice trailed off when he saw her, the fear and anger in his expression replaced by a sheepish grin when he realized that what he had first perceived as a threat was only a slender young woman clad in tight designer jeans and a hot pink turtleneck sweater. "Sorry about that," he said politely. "Can I help you?"

"Yes, indeed." She took a deep breath, inhaling his scent. Young and healthy and strong, she thought, noting his flat stomach and broad shoulders. He didn't smell of tobacco or drugs or alcohol. No doubt he ate right and worked out every day. Perfect.

"Just name it, honey, and it's yours." The words were innocent enough, but there was no mistaking the lustful gleam in his eyes.

"You," she said with a smile. "I want you."

"All right by me, babe. Your place or mine?"

"Right here," she murmured, moving closer. "Right now."

Before he could reply, her gaze trapped his. "Unlock the door, *babe,* and get into the backseat."

Face slack, eyes blank, he did as she asked without hesitation.

Climbing in beside him, she closed the door and then drew him into her arms. She ran her tongue along the strong column of his neck, savoring the taste of salt and fear, the scent of warm, living blood flowing just beneath his skin. Too long since she had fed, she thought, too long since she had filled herself with the crimson elixir of life.

She closed her eyes, letting the anticipation of the pleasure that was to come wash over her—the heat of his skin, the thrill of that first warm coppery taste sliding over her tongue, the sudden rush of power, the almost sensual satisfaction when she had taken her fill.

And on that thought, she sank her fangs into his throat, only to recoil as her mouth filled with his blood. Instead of experiencing a sense of warmth and pleasure, she felt only revulsion.

Overcome with confusion, she pushed him away, then stared, horrified, at the blood that oozed from the two tiny wounds in his neck, trickling down to soak into the collar of his pale blue shirt.

Murmuring, "What's happening to me?" she released him from her thrall and fled the scene.

She stopped when she reached the outskirts of the city. Something was wrong. Very, very wrong.

She could feel it deep inside, and it felt like death.

Chapter Four

Rane Cordova stood in the shadows, his back resting against a tall tree as he enjoyed the quiet of the night. Much had changed in his life in the last few months. After years of estrangement from his family, he had finally gone home. His bride, Savanah, was partly responsible for the changes in his life and his attitude. Soon after their wedding, she had sold her father's house and they had moved to Oregon to be near Rane's parents and his brother. Although Rane had never voiced his concern aloud to Savanah, he'd had some reservations, not only about how she would fit in with his relatives, but how they would react to her. He knew it couldn't be easy for Savanah, being the only mortal in a family of vampires, but she was holding up pretty well so far, all things considered. It helped that his family genuinely loved her; hopefully, in time, she would agree to accept the Dark Gift, as had his mother and his sister-in-law.

Yes, life was good. He had returned to the stage, performing his acts of magic and sleight of hand under the name of Iago, the Illusionist. In the last month, he had done a dozen shows in the surrounding cities. Of course, what he did wasn't magic at all, merely an overt display of his preternatural powers. Savanah had taken a job as a columnist for the local newspaper. Occasionally, she played the part of his assistant on stage. A beautiful woman was always a welcome distraction.

Pushing away from the tree, he strolled around the yard. Even now, three months after the fact, he found it hard to believe that he was a father. Of course, the child sleeping peacefully in the nursery on the second floor wasn't his. Vampires couldn't create life, so Savanah had gone to a doctor who specialized in artificial insemination. Rane hadn't been sure how he would react to being a father, or how he would feel about a child not of his own flesh and blood, but one look into Abbey Marie's angelic face and all his doubts had fled. Savanah had given birth to the child, and that was all that mattered.

Rane shook his head. It was easy to care for an infant, but what kind of father would he be when his daughter was five, ten, a teenager? Knowing it was impossible for him to have a child, fatherhood was something he had never contemplated.

They owned the right kind of a house for raising children, though. They had bought it soon after Savanah learned she was pregnant. It was a quaint-looking, two-story blue-gray house with bright white shutters, and a backyard he was already picturing with a puppy and a swing.

He grinned into the darkness. Becoming a father had been quite a shock to his own sire. Vince Cordova had been a vampire only a short time when he'd met Cara DeLongpre. After a rather torrid and dangerous courtship, the two had married. Rane and his twin brother, Rafe, had arrived shortly thereafter. To Rane's knowledge, his father was the only vampire who had ever fathered children.

With a sigh, Rane turned and walked back toward the house. He had almost reached the back door when Savanah stepped outside. It still amazed him that she was his. His gaze moved over her as she walked toward him. Her hair was the color of liquid moonlight, her eyes as clear and blue as a mid-summer sky. He felt a familiar warmth envelop him as she went up on her tiptoes and kissed his cheek.

"What are you doing out here?" she asked.

"Just enjoying the night. What are you doing up at this hour?"

"I woke up and you weren't beside me."

"You should be sleeping." Taking her by the hand, he led her to the wrought-iron bench situated under a flowering peach tree. Sitting beside her, he slipped his arm around her shoulders. "Abbey will be waking in an hour or so. You should rest while you can."

"I know, but it's lonely in that big old bed without you."

"Is something troubling you?"

"No."

He looked at her, one brow arched. "Finding me gone in the middle of the night is nothing new for you. Tell me what's wrong."

"Nothing. I'm just being silly, but you've been a little distant lately and . . . well, you're not sorry about the baby, are you?"

"Of course not. Why would you think that?"

"Well, I know you weren't thrilled about the idea at first."

"Savanah, you asked if I was against it. I said no. I meant no. You didn't ask me if I liked the idea, but none

of that matters now. I couldn't love our Abbey more if she
was my own flesh and blood. I love you both, and right
now I can't imagine my life without either of you.
Okay?"

"Okay."

Rane drew her closer. "This whole parent thing takes
some getting used to, you know? I never expected to be
a father. I'm not sure I'll be any good at it."

"Well, I've never been a mother, either," Savanah said
with a rueful smile. "I'm not sure I'll be any good at
parenting, either."

"One of us had better be good at it," Rane said, kissing her lightly. "We can't send her back now." He gazed
into the distance. "Do you think it will upset her when
she's old enough to be told what I am?"

"No. By then, she'll know what a good man you are.
Look at your mother. She was upset when she first
learned her parents were vampires, but only because they
had kept it a secret for so long."

"I hope you're right."

"Little girls always love their daddy best of all,"
Savanah said, thinking of her own father. "I know I did."

Rane squeezed her shoulder. "I know you still miss
him." Savanah's father had been killed by a vampire
almost two years ago.

With a sigh, Savanah rested her head against his
shoulder. They sat there for several minutes, enjoying the
quiet of the night, before Rane said, "Your daughter is
calling you."

Savanah pressed a hand to her breast as it filled with
milk. "Right on time," she said, rising. "Are you coming in?"

Rane was about to say yes when he sensed a familiar
presence lurking in the shadows. Brushing a kiss across

Savanah's cheek, he said, "I'll be along in a few minutes. Warm up my side of the bed, will you?"

With a little "humph," Savanah hurried into the house.

As soon as the door closed behind Savanah, Rane turned to face the woman who stepped out of the shadows. She wore a long, hooded black cloak over a pair of black jeans and a bloodred sweater. Though he was happily married, Rane couldn't help but admire his visitor. There was no one else like her in all the world. He doubted any male over the age of twelve could look at her and not want her.

"Good evening," she murmured. "I didn't mean to intrude."

"Mara, when have you ever been an intrusion?" he chided softly. "We don't see you nearly enough, although I am surprised to see you here. I thought you were going back to Egypt."

She lifted one shoulder in an elegant shrug. "I changed my mind."

"Always a woman's prerogative," he replied, noting her sober expression. "Is anything wrong?"

Mara paced a few steps away from him, then turned and paced back. "Yes, very wrong, but I don't know what it is, or how to explain it." She glanced around the yard, as if to make sure they were alone. "I'm changing," she said, her voice low, as though she feared someone might overhear, "and it scares me."

"Changing?" His gaze moved over her. She looked as young and beautiful as ever. Her hair, as black as ink, fell in waves over her shoulders. Her skin was like alabaster, her eyes as green as new grass. Save for Savanah, he had never known a more beautiful, vibrant woman. "Changing how?"

"I've been getting tired at night and I'm having trouble

sleeping during the day. The last time I fed, it made me sick. I've been craving mortal food. My powers are weakening. I'm afraid I'm losing them."

"I've never heard of anything like that happening before. What do you think is causing it?"

"I don't know!"

She looked up at him. For the first time that Rane could remember, he saw fear in the depths of her eyes. "Have you talked to Roshan?"

She shook her head. Roshan had been a vampire for over three centuries. Years ago, Mara had given him her blood, increasing his preternatural power, and allowing him to walk in the sun's light. He was Rane's grandfather and the head of the Cordova family. "No, I haven't told anyone else."

Rane swore softly. "Maybe you should talk to him. He's been a vampire a lot longer than I have."

"No."

"Why not?"

"Because I'm . . . I'm too vulnerable."

"What the hell does that mean? You don't think he'd . . ." Rane shook his head. "You don't honestly think he would try to destroy you?"

"No, but . . ." She crossed her arms over her breasts. "Like you said, he's been a vampire a long time. We're all predators at heart, Rane, and predators prey on the weak, even among their own kind."

"I don't believe this! Dammit, Mara, you're my godmother, and Abbey's, too. We're family. If you're in trouble, you need help. I can't give it to you, but maybe Roshan can."

"Maybe, maybe not." She stared past him into the darkness. "When I was first turned, I heard an ancient legend that said if a vampire survived for a hundred years, he would be restored to mortality. I didn't believe it, of course, and when I turned one hundred, nothing happened, but"—she lifted her troubled gaze to his—"what if it's happening now?"

"Is that what you think is going on?"

"I don't know!" She made a vague gesture with her hand. "What other explanation can there be?"

Rane shook his head. "Beats me."

Seeing the fear in her eyes, he drew her into his arms. How could this be happening? Mara was the oldest, the strongest, of their kind. Was it possible she was reverting to mortality or, worse, dying? And if so, what had caused it? And what did it mean for the rest of them? Everyone knew vampires were virtually immortal. But what if they were wrong? If something like this could happen to Mara, it could happen to any of them.

Mara took a deep, calming breath. "I should go. Savanah is waiting for you."

Rane glanced up at the house. Savanah stood at the bedroom window with Abbey Marie cradled in her arms. Even from a distance, he could see the curiosity in his wife's eyes.

"We haven't solved anything," Rane said. "Maybe you should stay with us for a few days."

Mara shook her head. "No."

"Dammit . . ."

She cupped his cheek in her palm. "I'll be all right."

"You'll keep in touch? Promise?"

"Of course. Don't worry about me."

Rane grunted softly. "If you didn't want me to worry, you shouldn't have said anything."

"I'd appreciate it if you wouldn't mention this to anyone else, and that includes Savanah."

"Mara . . ."

"Take care of yourself, Rane."

"Yeah, you, too."

She nodded; then, with a graceful wave of her hand, she was gone.

Rane stared into the darkness. What would it be like, to not only consume mortal food again, but to crave it? How would he feel if he lost the urge to hunt? Would he miss it? What would it be like to keep the same hours as the rest of the world? It was obvious that Mara wasn't happy about the prospect of being mortal again. He couldn't blame her. He didn't think he would be too keen on the idea, either, but then, being a vampire had been in his blood since birth; he couldn't imagine any other way of life.

With a shake of his head and a hope that Mara would be all right, Rane went into the house.

Savanah was waiting for him in the kitchen. "Was that Mara? What's going on?"

"She asked me not to talk about it."

"About what? Is something wrong?"

"Savanah . . ."

"Oh, that's not fair! She comes here in the middle of the night to tell you something, and you won't share it. Was it bad news? At least tell me that."

"Oh, yeah," he said, slipping his arm around her shoulders. "It was bad."

Chapter Five

Logan Blackwood stood on the corner of Sunset and Vine, his arms crossed over his chest as he watched the late-night crowd drift by. The world had changed considerably in nine hundred years and yet, in many ways, it remained the same. Much like himself, he mused. He'd had many personas in the last nine centuries, but none suited him quite so well as the role he played now—that of an eccentric millionaire who liked to dabble in financing movies and hanging out with the slick Hollywood crowd.

He got quite a kick out of being around movie people, with all their odd little quirks and their need to forever be in the spotlight. It made hunting ever so much easier, especially among starlets who were willing and eager to do anything to get a foot in the door. It wasn't really hunting, he thought with a grin. More like shooting fish in a barrel. All he had to do was mention that he knew famed director Sterling Price and a bevy of beauties surrounded him, each one anxious to do whatever he asked in hopes of an introduction to Price. In one instance, Logan had actually had a hand in paving the way for a talented young actress to make her film debut. Years later, she had won an Academy Award. Logan had been immensely pleased, and more than a little surprised, when she mentioned him by name during her acceptance speech.

He was about to call it a night when a woman clad in a pair of black stretch pants, a white silk shirt, and high-heeled black boots stepped out of a late-night boutique. Logan stared at her. It couldn't be, he thought, but it was. Mara, the vampire who had turned him over nine hundred years ago. Though he had not seen her in centuries, he recognized her instantly. But that was understandable. Having once seen her, no man on earth, living or Undead, would ever forget her. She looked just as she had that fateful night centuries ago, slender with lush curves in all the right places, her hair like a waterfall of gleaming black silk, her eyes as bright and green as emeralds. Mara.

She turned his way just then and he inclined his head in greeting, wondering if she even remembered him, and then he saw that she was wearing the heart-shaped ruby pendant he had given her so long ago. If she wore the ruby, she hadn't forgotten him. Had she ever wondered what had become of him after she walked away without a word? Would she acknowledge him now?

She stared at him for a long moment, her eyes widening in recognition, and then, with a toss of her head, she glided toward him, as lithe and beautiful as he remembered.

"Mara."

"Hektor. This is a surprise." She experienced a warm rush of excitement at seeing him again, but then, how could she not? He was gorgeous, by far the most handsome man she had ever known, with his thick, wavy black hair and deep brown eyes. A supple black leather jacket caressed his broad shoulders, faded blue jeans encased his long legs. The boots he wore were scuffed but expensive. He looked fit and prosperous and as sexy as the devil on a Saturday night. The dimple in his left cheek winked at her when he smiled.

"I go by the name of Logan now," he said. "Logan Blackwood." His gaze swept over her in a long, assessing glance. "So, how have you been?"

"The same as always. You're looking well."

"So are you." And yet, there was something different about her, though what it was, he couldn't say. But something wasn't right. He took a deep breath, and then frowned. "Do I smell onions on your breath?"

She shrugged. "Perhaps."

"How is that possible?"

"I'm Mara," she replied with an enigmatic smile. "Anything is possible."

Grinning, he said, "Ah, girl, you don't know how much I've missed you." He hadn't meant to speak the words aloud. Knowing that she didn't want entanglements of any kind, he had never confessed his love for her. When she left him, he had told himself that it didn't matter. In the years that followed, he had convinced himself that he was over her, that he had stopped loving her centuries ago, yet one look and he knew he had been kidding himself. He would love her until the day he ceased to exist.

"Have you?" Her gaze searched his, as if she were trying to decide if he was telling the truth. "Missed me?"

"Every night of my life."

"You never came looking for me."

"What was the point?" he asked, unable to keep a note of bitterness from creeping into his voice. "You made it clear that you wanted a clean break." He would have followed her to Hell and back if he had thought she cared at all. But he had his pride. He had been nothing more to her than a momentary diversion; the fact that she had severed the link between them had proved that.

"It seems fate has decided we should meet again." She started walking, confident that he would follow. "What have you been doing since we parted?"

Logan fell into step beside her, shortening his naturally long stride to match her much shorter one. "Trying to keep busy," he said with a shrug. "Always looking for something I haven't experienced before." Which, after nine hundred years, wasn't easy to find. "How about you?"

"The same."

"I was on my way home," he said casually. "Would you care to come along?"

She hesitated a moment, and then nodded. It had been a long time, after all. She was curious to see how and where he lived. There had been many men in her life, but none like Logan. The fire between them had burned brighter than the sun. His power, even when first turned, had been stronger than that of any of her other fledglings. Perhaps it was because he had been arrogant, self-confident, and strong, even as a mortal. It had been those very characteristics that had drawn her to him. He had burrowed deep into her heart. When she found herself caring too much, willing to surrender her will to his, she left him.

Logan's home proved to be a mansion in the hills not far from her own. The large, two-story white house was set behind a tall wrought-iron fence amid well-tended grounds. Sycamore trees lined the long, winding driveway.

A veranda spanned the front of the house; wrought-iron bars covered the windows.

"You've done well for yourself, I see," she remarked as he unlocked the front door.

He shrugged. "Well enough."

He led the way into the house. A large stone fireplace dominated the living room. The furniture was modern and expensive. Her feet sank into the plush dove-gray carpet.

"Very nice," she murmured.

"I like it." He stood inside the doorway, his arms crossed over his chest, while she wandered around the room. She paused to browse the titles on the bookshelf, moved on to examine a small marble statue of Venus that sat on a low table next to a ruby sphinx.

Moving to the fireplace, she ran her hand over a gold statue. "An Oscar?" She glanced at him over her shoulder.

"I produced the best picture last year," he said, a trace of pride in his voice.

"Really? That's wonderful, but . . . when did you get into the movie business?"

"A few years ago." He gestured toward the sofa. "Please, sit down."

She sat at one end of the sofa and he sat at the other.

"I was bored," he remarked, picking up their conversation. "I started hanging out where the stars congregate. One night I overheard some guy saying he had this great idea for a movie but it was so off the wall that no one in the business would give him the time of day. I told him I'd finance him. He made four movies with my backing. The fourth hit the jackpot."

"Congratulations."

"Thanks."

"What did you do before that?"

He draped his arm along the back of the sofa. "I was a dealer in Vegas for a while. I worked as a bartender at a fancy singles' club in Chicago. I tried my hand at being a night watchman for a big corporation in Manhattan, but that didn't last long."

Mara nodded. She tried not to stare at him, but she couldn't seem to help herself. He truly was a magnificent-looking man. She had met him in Crete in 1109. He had been twenty-six at the time. Despite the fact that he had been betrothed to another, they'd had a torrid love affair. One night, caught up in the heat of passion, she had bitten him and accidentally taken too much.

Rather than let him die, she had brought him across.

Rather than face his family, he had fled the country.

Mara had stayed with him for a time, but when she found herself caring for him more than she wanted to, she had fled without a word. Though she had never admitted it to another soul, she had cared for Hektor—Logan, she reminded herself—in a way she had never cared for any of the other men she had turned.

Truth be told, she still cared. There was something about him that set him apart from the rest, something more than his chiseled good looks and deep-set brown eyes. Even though she had turned Logan against his will, he had never berated her for it, never cursed her or tried to destroy her as she had destroyed Dendar. He hadn't bewailed the loss of his humanity; instead, he had accepted his new way of life, and her, without reproach. She had always admired him for that.

She couldn't help wondering now if leaving him had been a mistake.

She thought fleetingly of Kyle Bowden, who had professed he would love her as long as he lived, until the night she revealed her true nature. She supposed she could have better prepared him for the truth, but it didn't matter now. He was a part of her past, as were so many others.

"So," Logan said, "tell me about you."

For a moment, she was tempted to confide in him, to pour out her fears as she had to Rane, but it would be foolish to do so. For all that she and Logan had once been lovers, it would be unwise indeed to let him know that her powers were weakening.

"Mara?"

"I recently returned from Egypt. Before that . . ." She made a vague gesture with one hand. "What does it matter?"

"You were heavily involved in the War between the Vampires and the Werewolves, weren't you? I heard your name mentioned from time to time."

"Really. I didn't see you."

He grinned at her. "I got my licks in, so to speak."

She lifted one brow. "Indeed?"

"Some of us fought quietly on the sidelines."

She smiled. "You never did like taking orders."

"Nope. Not even from you."

"I remember." She suddenly remembered so many things. The nights they had hunted together, the way he had treated her, as if she were some fragile creature made of glass instead of the most powerful vampire in the world. The times they had made love . . .

Her breathing quickened; her body tingled with the memory of his hands on her skin, his mouth on hers, the way she had responded to his caresses, the husky sound of his voice murmuring love words to her in his native tongue.

Mara saw the subtle change in his expression and

knew that he, too, was remembering the good times they had shared. Why had she ever left him?

"Are you involved with anyone?" Logan asked.

She thought fleetingly of Kyle, then shook her head. "No, are you?"

"No." His heated gaze trapped hers. "There's been no one for me since you."

His words, the seductive tone of his voice, made her insides quiver with pleasure. "No one? In nine hundred years? I can't imagine you living as a monk."

"I didn't say I'd been living as a monk, but there's a big difference between scratching an itch and what you and I had. I think you know that."

Mara nodded. She had been lying to herself and others for centuries. When asked, she had always answered that she had been in love many times when, in truth, she had never truly loved anyone with her whole heart and soul, not the way Rane loved Savanah, or the way Rafe and Vince loved their wives. True, she had fallen hard for Kyle Bowden. Foolish as it had been, she had convinced herself that she had finally found a man she could love with no reservations, a man she could trust with the truth. She would not make that mistake again.

"I'm forgetting my manners," Logan said. "Would you care for a glass of wine?"

Mara licked her lips, thinking she would rather have a soda. She had developed quite a taste for sugary soft drinks in the last few weeks, but she couldn't ask for a Coke, didn't want to answer the questions that would surely follow such a request. "Yes, thank you."

"Coming right up."

Rising, he left the room, only to return a few minutes later carrying two crystal goblets.

She accepted one with a murmured, "Thank you."

"Are you going to be in town long?" Logan asked, resuming his seat.

"Perhaps. I have a home not far from here."

"You mean we're neighbors?"

"It looks that way, at least for the time being."

He smiled at her over his glass. "That's the best news I've had this century."

Chapter Six

As was his wont, Rane stood in the shadows outside his house, enjoying the touch of the night air while Savanah put their daughter to bed. He shook his head, bemused. It was still hard to believe he was a father, or that he had grown to love Abbey Marie so deeply in such a short time. He had discovered there were many kinds of love—that of a son for his parents, that of one brother for another, that of a husband for his wife, and that of a father for his child.

He smiled into the darkness. Life, as he knew it, was good. And only promised to get better.

He glanced up at the second floor as the lights went out. In a few moments, he would go inside to find Savanah waiting for him in the living room. It was his favorite time of the night, sharing a few quiet moments with the woman he loved above all else.

He was about to go into the house when a movement to his left caught his eye. Lifting his head, he sniffed the air. "Bowden, what the devil are you doing skulking around out here in the bushes?"

Looking somewhat sheepish, Kyle stepped out of the

shadows. "I was hoping you could tell me where to find Mara."

"Why would I do that? From what I heard, you told her you didn't want anything to do with a . . . how did you put it? A 'bloodsucking fiend.'"

Bowden waved a dismissive hand in the air. "I didn't mean it."

"No? She was pretty sure you did."

Kyle shrugged. "What did she expect? I mean, sure, I knew vampires existed. One killed my father, after all. I was around during the War. I heard my share of horror stories, but I never expected to meet one, much less fall in love with one."

Rane grunted softly. "Doesn't sound much like love to me."

"Okay, I behaved badly, I admit it, but she caught me off-guard. When I asked her to tell me what she was hiding, having her go all vampire on me was the last thing I expected."

"So, what's changed? She's still a vampire."

Kyle ran a hand through his hair. "I can't eat. I can't sleep. I can't stop thinking about her." He didn't sound at all happy about it.

Rane understood what Bowden was saying, feeling. He knew all too well the effect vampires had on unsuspecting humans. All too often what mortals believed was love was nothing more than attraction to the supernatural glamour common to all the Undead.

"So, where is she?" Bowden asked.

"I can't tell you."

"Why the hell not? We were more than just friends, you know, not that it's any of your business."

"I know exactly what you were," Rane said, his voice

cool. "Just like I know you hurt her. I'm not about to give you a chance to do it again."

Bowden took a step forward, his hands clenched at his sides, his eyes narrowed. "Listen here . . ."

"No, you listen. I'll tell Mara that you're looking for her. If she wants to see you, she'll find you."

"But . . ."

"No buts," Rane said tersely. "This conversation is over."

"He was there?" Mara sank down in a chair in front of the hearth. "And he wants to see me?"

"That's what he said."

She tapped one finger against the edge of her cell phone. Kyle had gone to Rane's house looking for her. "Did he say anything else?"

"He said he misses you, and that he behaved badly. Do you want me to tell him where you are?"

Mara stared at the flames dancing merrily in the fireplace. Did she want to see Kyle again? What was the point? Nothing had changed.

"Mara?" Rane's voice brought her back to the present.

"Tell him . . . tell him I'll think about it."

"How are things in Tinsel Town?" Rane asked.

"Fine." She smiled, thinking of Hektor . . . no, not Hektor. He was Logan now. She had to remember that. "How's Abbey Marie?"

"Beautiful, like her godmother."

Mara laughed softly. "Flatterer."

"It's true."

"You like it, then, being a father?"

"Yeah. It's amazing. Abbey's amazing. I can't believe how much she's changed in just the last few weeks, or how much she's changed our lives."

"How's Savanah holding up?"

"She's terrific," Rane said. He paused a moment. When he spoke again, his tone was suddenly wistful. "I just wish Abbey was really mine. It's not that I don't love her," he said quickly, "but . . ."

"I understand," Mara said, though she really didn't. She had never wanted children, and then Dendar had brought her across and motherhood had no longer been an option.

"So," Rane said, "I take it Hollywood agrees with you."

"Yes, very much." She had seen Logan every night for the last three weeks. Later tonight, they were going to yet another Hollywood party to dance, and dine. "I'd better go. Tell everyone hello for me."

"Will do."

After bidding Rane good night, Mara ended the call, then sat there, her fingers beating an impatient tattoo on the arm of the chair as she waited for Logan to arrive.

The party was in full swing when Logan and Mara made their entrance. As Logan passed his overcoat to the butler, he noted that Sterling Price had pulled out all the stops for this shindig. The mansion was lit up like a Christmas tree. A full orchestra played in the ballroom. Men clad in Armani suits danced with women elegantly attired in fashionable evening gowns by Dior, Versace, and Galliano, and sporting enough diamonds to rival the number of stars in the sky. But Mara put them all to shame. She wore a floor-length emerald gown that clung to every delectable curve. The heart-shaped ruby pendant he had given her was her only adornment. Nestled in the hollow of her slender throat, it glittered like a drop of fresh blood.

They had timed their arrival so that they arrived well after dinner had been served, but a dozen round tables dressed in fine linen were laden with platters of sliced meats, fine cheeses, iced shrimp, and caviar. Baskets and bowls held a wide variety of breads and fruit. There was imported wine and champagne, of course, and a fully stocked bar.

Logan frowned at Mara when she nibbled on a slice of rare roast beef. "How can you do that?"

"Do what? Oh." The cat was out of the bag, she thought, then shrugged. "I'm not sure, but I think it has something to do with my longevity as a vampire."

"What's it like?" he asked. "I can't remember the taste of solid food."

"It's very good. A little salty."

"So, what else can you eat?"

"Any red meat that's rare." She hadn't tried chicken yet, or pork, or fish.

Logan glanced at the platter of meat, a look of longing in his eyes.

"Try it," Mara urged, curious to see his reaction. "You've been around quite a long time yourself."

Looking dubious, Logan speared a slice of roast beef with a toothpick. He eyed it suspiciously, sniffed it, and then took a bite. One swallow, and he bolted from the room.

Murmuring, "Ah, well," Mara followed him outside. She found him on the balcony, one hand clutching his stomach.

He slanted a look in her direction, then doubled over with a groan.

Murmuring, "I'm sorry," Mara patted him on the back.

When he straightened, she turned her head to the side and bared her throat. "Here, drink. Perhaps it will help."

She closed her eyes as he ran his tongue along the side of her neck, sighed with pleasure as he drank.

Muttering an oath, Logan recoiled from her. Turning away, he spat her blood from his mouth.

"What's wrong?"

"You taste like . . . like . . . hell, I don't know. Poison!"

She stared at him in horror. For centuries, those of her kind had sought to drink from her. Her blood had strengthened the weak, healed wounds . . . but not Rane's injuries, she recalled with a frown. It had taken Savanah's blood to heal him.

Logan grabbed a glass of red wine from a passing waiter and downed the contents in a single swallow. After wiping his mouth with the back of his hand, he tossed the glass over the rail of the balcony onto the grass below.

"If that's what eating human food does to you, maybe you shouldn't eat any more." He shook his head. "Damn, that was vile."

"I . . . I'm sorry, I don't know what . . ." Bewildered, she looked up at him. "I'm sorry."

Logan drew in a deep breath and let it out in a long sigh. "All right, Mara, what the hell's going on?"

"I don't know." Tears burned her eyes and wet her cheeks. "I'm changing, and . . ." She turned away from him, her voice little more than a whisper as she admitted, "I'm scared." She hadn't been this afraid since the night Dendar had appeared in her cell. "I think . . ." She loosed a long, shuddering sigh. "I think I'm dying."

Since becoming a vampire, she had never contemplated her own demise, but now she was overcome with a sudden fear of death. The ancient Egyptians had believed that their time on Earth was only a step toward a better life in another world, and so they made extensive preparations to assure the comfort of their spirits, hence the lavish tombs filled with everything one might need in the next life. If she was dying, as she feared, who would see that her body was properly prepared for the afterlife? She had long ago turned her back on the religion of her ancestors, but now, facing the very real possibility of her own demise, she found her thoughts returning to the old ways, the ancient beliefs. And they were more frightening than anything she had ever known in this world. The wicked were tormented in the Netherworld, compelled to swim in their own blood, which was squeezed out of them by one of the gods of the underworld. A rather ironic punishment for a vampire, she thought morbidly.

Muttering an oath, Logan drew Mara into his arms. He had never known her to be afraid of anything. He had seen her outraged, angry, defiant, belligerent. On rare occasions, he had seen her pensive, and on even rarer occasions, sad or depressed. But never frightened, he thought as he stroked her hair.

He had sensed something different about her the last time they were together; tonight, to his chagrin, he realized what it was. She had always exuded an aura of preternatural strength unmatched by any other vampire, but he had no sense of it now. Whatever was ailing her had undermined her supernatural powers, leaving her weak and vulnerable. And that could be dangerous, because she had made a lot of enemies in the last three thousand years, and not all of them were dead.

"Here now," Logan said, "crying won't help." He pulled a handkerchief from his back pocket and dried her eyes, noting that her tears were no longer tinged with blood. Not a good sign. There was definitely something amiss, though he had no idea what it could be. "What do you say we get out of here?"

When Mara nodded, Logan wrapped his arms around her and willed the two of them to his place. They materialized in the living room. A wave of his hand lit a fire in the hearth.

"Can I get you anything?" he asked.

She shook her head. "I should go home."

"Is that what you want?"

What she wanted was to curl up in his arms, to lose herself in his touch, to see if his lovemaking was still as explosive and satisfying as she remembered. She knew he desired her. The yearning was always there, in his heated glances, in the husky timbre of his voice when he spoke her name. Thus far, she had kept him at arm's length, but looking at him now, she could feel the walls of her resistance crumbling.

"Mara?"

She looked at him, mute. What was wrong with her? Men had always bent their will to hers. She had bestowed her favors on those who pleased her and callously cast the others aside. But tonight, all she could do was wait and hope that Logan could read her mind.

He ran his knuckles lightly over her cheek. "Do you want to stay the night?"

Weak with relief, she nodded.

His hand slid around her nape, coaxing her back into his arms. "Remember that night on the river?"

"Yes." How could she forget? It had been the first time they made love. Even after all these years, that night remained vivid in her memory—the yellow sand beneath them, a blanket of twinkling silver stars overhead, the moon's light reflected on the black ribbon of the Nile, the night wind whispering secrets to the trees. She had seduced him until he turned the tables on her, his mouth capturing hers, his body young and firm, his arms strong around her. She would never forget the sound of his voice, husky with desire as he tucked her beneath him, the way the curves and hollows of their bodies had fit together perfectly, the taste of his warm, living blood on her tongue.

"It was like magic." He dropped a kiss on her forehead, the tip of her nose, her cheeks. "It was magic."

She nodded, her breath catching in her throat as his hand slid ever so slowly and seductively down her side to rest on her thigh.

His free hand captured one of hers and he brought it to his lips. "Let's go make magic again."

Feeling as though she were dreaming, she followed him down the hall.

His bedroom, with its pale gray walls, black furniture, and red accents, suited him perfectly. Heavy drapes hung at the windows. The bed, covered with a black satin quilt, was fit for a sultan.

Mara sat on the edge of the mattress. After removing her shoes, she dug her toes into the thick gray carpet. When she looked up, Logan stood at the foot of the bed, watching her, his eyes hooded.

"My feet hurt," she remarked with a shrug.

Logan nodded. Rounding the bed to where she sat, he knelt before her, a willing supplicant before his queen. Lifting her foot to rest on his thigh, he began to rub her instep.

Mara watched his hands move over her foot. Large hands. Gentle hands that were familiar with every inch of her body. She had never thought of a foot massage as being sexy, she mused as she stared at his bowed head, which just proved that even a three-thousand-year-old vampire could learn something new.

Her insides curled with pleasure as his hand slid under her skirt. She could feel the latent strength in his fingers as his hand moved up, massaging her ankle, her calf, her thigh, and then moved down to her foot again, easing away the pain.

Her breath left her lungs in a long shuddering sigh as his hand slid slowly, sensuously, up her leg again, and then, gifting her with a wicked smile, he began to work his magic on her other foot.

By the time he finished, she was aching with need, trembling with desire.

Rising, he sat beside her, then drew her into his arms. "Don't be afraid, love." His fingers sifted through the heavy fall of her hair. "I don't know what the devil is going on with you, but whatever it is, I won't let you face it alone."

"Logan . . ."

"Hush, love. We'll worry about it tomorrow, but tonight . . ." He stood in a lithe movement. Drawing her to her feet, he turned her around and unzipped her dress. "Tonight is just for us."

Taking her by the shoulders, he turned her so she was facing him again, and then he eased the dress off of her shoulders and let it fall to the floor. Her bra and panties quickly followed.

Logan whistled softly. She was as exquisite as he remembered. Standing there wearing nothing but the ruby pendant he had given her and an uncertain smile, she looked like every man's fantasy come to life. But she was real and, for tonight, she was his.

Mara couldn't take her gaze from Logan as he undressed, revealing the same bronzed, hard-muscled body that she had once known so well.

Swinging her into his arms, Logan drew back the covers and lowered Mara onto the mattress. After sliding under the covers beside her, he gathered her close. The night was beautiful, and so was the woman nestled in his arms. He had dreamed of this moment many times over the years, but he had never believed it would happen, and now she was here. He had never put much stock in fate, but he couldn't help thinking it was more than coincidence that had brought them together at a time when she desperately needed help. Exactly what kind of help, he wasn't sure, but he was prepared to do whatever was necessary, up to and including sacrificing his own life for hers.

"Logan . . ." Her hands moved restlessly up and down his back. "Kiss me," she murmured. "Kiss me . . ."

"That's it, darlin'," he said, his hand caressing the silky length of her thigh. "Just tell me what you want."

She locked her hands behind his nape. "I want you. All of you." A seductive smile tugged at her lips. "Every inch."

His gaze burned into hers, his voice low and husky as he confessed, "I'm yours, Mara. Don't you know I've always been yours?" And lowering his head, he claimed her lips with his own.

She moaned softly. His kiss, gentle at first, grew deeper, more impassioned. This was what she wanted, what she had always wanted. Why had she denied it for so long? She had flitted from man to man, searching for someone to take Logan's place when she could have had Logan the whole time. Why hadn't she realized it sooner?

The thought gave her pause. She was supposed to be in love with Kyle Bowden, so why did it feel so right to be in Logan's bed, in Logan's arms? If she truly loved Kyle, would she even want to be with another man?

She pushed the thought away as Logan caressed her, his hands strong and sure, his mouth hot on hers. His familiar touch quickly aroused her, taking her back to that first night they had made love, back to a time when she had been sure of herself, in command of her world and everything in it, including the man rising over her.

She surrendered with a sigh, willing, for this night, to follow where he led, to pretend that nothing had changed.

Much later, lying side by side, Logan said, "Tell me what you've been doing since you left me."

"Didn't we already talk about that?"

"You never really answered me. How many others have you brought across? How many men have there been in your life since you walked away from me?"

She gestured at the two of them, lying entwined in each other's arms, the perspiration still cooling on their flesh. "Do you really think this is the time or the place to discuss that sort of thing?"

He nibbled her earlobe. "I can't help it. Not knowing is eating me alive."

"I've never kept count of the men in my life. As for others I've turned"—she shrugged—"I really don't remember."

"I've heard it was no more than a handful."

Vince Cordova had asked her the same question. She

remembered the conversation well. It had taken place shortly after she'd brought him across.

"Am I the only vampire you've made?" he had asked.

"No. There were five before you."

"Are they still alive?"

She made a vague gesture with her hand. "I don't know. I don't care."

"Then what are you doing here? I mean, if you didn't give a damn about them . . ."

She laughed softly. "Why do I care about you?"

"Yeah."

"I don't know. That's why I came."

She had asked Vince about his relationship with Cara. He had asked if she had ever been in love . . .

"Many times," she had replied. "But it never lasts. Mortals are such fragile creatures, and they live such a short time."

"The ones you made, were you in love with them?"

"No."

"Why did you bring them across?"

She shrugged. "It's been so long ago, I don't recall. Curiosity, I suppose. Or maybe boredom."

"Is that why you brought me across?" he asked bitterly. "Because you were bored?"

She remembered laughing as she said yes.

She hadn't been completely honest with Vince when

he'd asked if she had been in love with those she turned. True, she had been fond of them all in varying degrees, and Vince most of all, but it had been only Hektor, now Logan, that she loved.

So many years since she had brought anyone across, she thought, and now the power to do so was lost to her.

She was supposed to be immortal, but she couldn't shake off the feeling that the existence she had so taken for granted for centuries was rapidly coming to an end.

She moved closer to Logan. If her days were indeed numbered, then she wanted to spend whatever time she had left here, in Logan's arms. She had often pondered whether it was better to love or be loved. It was the one question for which she had never found a satisfying answer but, for now, she would gladly take all the love he could give.

With a sigh, Mara closed her eyes.

Propped up on one elbow, Logan studied the woman resting beside him. Centuries had passed since he had last seen her, and yet being with her now made those lost years unimportant. He had asked her how many men she had been with, how many fledglings she had made. Not surprisingly, she hadn't answered him. She had professed that she couldn't remember, but somehow he doubted that. More likely, she just didn't want him to know. She was a lusty wench. No doubt there had been hundreds of men in her life since they'd parted. If he had his way, he would be the last.

He brushed a lock of hair from her neck, then bent down and ran his tongue over her skin. Her scent aroused his hunger, but as his tongue brushed his fangs, he had a vivid recollection of drinking from her earlier that night. She had told him she was changing. He hadn't really believed it until he had tasted her blood. Instead of being sweet and satisfying, it had been sour. He would have thought she was ill, only vampires didn't get sick. She feared she was dying. Maybe she was right. But how was that possible?

Mara was the oldest of their kind. Maybe, contrary to vampire mythology, they didn't live forever. Maybe they were subject to old age and death like every other living creature. Maybe people believed vampires lived forever simply because vampires existed for an incredibly long time, outliving the mortals around them.

"Logan?" She frowned at him in the darkness and he wondered if, along with her other weakening senses, she had also lost her preternatural vision.

"Yes, love," he murmured, and switched on the light.

"Why are you staring at me?"

"Because you're beautiful." He stroked her cheek. "So damn beautiful." He took a deep breath. "Why do you think you're dying?"

"I told you. I'm changing. And tonight . . . tonight you said my blood tasted like poison." She placed her hand over her stomach. "There's something wrong with me, I can feel it inside."

"Maybe you need to see a doctor?"

She looked at him as if he had lost his mind.

"There are a few vampire doctors," Logan said with a shrug. "I don't know if there are any in California, but I can check around."

"I don't know . . ."

"What could it hurt? Wouldn't you rather know what's happening than spend all your time worrying and wondering?"

"I guess so."

Her indecision, her vulnerability, worried him more

than anything else. She had always been strong, decisive, often blunt to the point of rudeness.

Cupping her face in his hands, he said, "Whatever's going on, we'll see it through together."

Tears burned her eyes and brought a lump to her throat. "Thank you, Logan."

"Hey, I'm not going to let anything happen to you, not now, when I've just found you again."

Chapter Seven

Kyle stared at the painting above the mantel. He had painted it in Egypt, during happier times, before he knew what kind of creature Mara was. He took a step closer, his eyes narrowing. Was she looking back at him? Laughing at him? Damn her! What evil magic had she worked on him that he couldn't get her out of his mind?

He should burn the painting, burn her out of his heart and his mind. But he couldn't. Not that he hadn't tried. He had lost count of the number of times he had tossed the painting, frame and all, into the fireplace and lit a match, only to watch the tiny flame flicker and go out. Destroying the painting wasn't the answer. He had to see her again, he thought. It was the only way to get her out of his system.

And if that didn't work, what then?

He swore softly. If he couldn't forget her, he would have to join her, become a vampire himself. But first, he had to find her. Maybe if he went back and talked to Cordova again, or maybe one of the others . . .

He snorted softly. Like that would do any good. Since Rane had refused to help him, he wasn't likely to get any answers out of the rest of the Cordova clan, so what hope did he have? None, he thought bleakly, and then he frowned.

He was going about this all wrong. Mara was a vampire. Who better to help him find a vampire than a vampire hunter? Of course, that was the answer.

Moving to the table in the corner, he poured himself a glass of red wine.

In the room's dim light, it looked like blood.

Chapter Eight

It took some doing, but after numerous inquiries, Logan managed to find a doctor who belonged to the community of the Undead. Logan called and made an appointment and a week later, he drove Mara to a small town in Northern Nevada to meet with Dr. Thomas Ramsden.

From what Logan had been able to learn about the man, Ramsden had been a doctor with the Union Army during the Civil War. The doctor had been searching the battlefield for wounded late one night when a hungry vampire found him. The vampire had also been a Yankee and rather than kill a compatriot, he had turned the good doctor. Ramsden's wife had been less than thrilled when she discovered her husband had become a vampire, and from what Logan had ferreted out, had been even less thrilled when the doctor brought her across.

Thomas Ramsden's office was located in a three-story red brick building. Logan noted there were no windows on the second and third floors.

"Are you sure we should be doing this?" Mara asked as they exited the elevator on the second floor and entered the reception area.

Logan shrugged. "I'm not sure about anything, but we've got to start somewhere."

In truth, he was more worried than he had let on. For the first time since Mara had brought him across, he had no sense of her as a preternatural being. She no longer smelled like a vampire. Even more unsettling, the two-way blood link that had bound them together for over nine centuries no longer existed. He could still sense her presence when she was near, but the bond that had allowed them to communicate telepathically was gone. He wondered if she had noticed.

There was no one else in the well-appointed waiting room. A receptionist, whose name tag identified her as Cindy, handed Mara a double-sided form to fill out.

Mara glanced at the paper. The doctor knew she was a vampire. Why did she have to fill out a form? What the heck, she could play along. Maybe there were humans in his employ who would ask questions.

She looked at the form again. Last name? She frowned, then wrote the surname Logan was currently using. Date of birth? She felt a bubble of hysterical laughter rise in her throat as she imagined a human doctor's astonishment if she jotted down her real age.

Sobering, she did some quick figuring in her head and wrote the year she would have been born if she were a human twenty-year-old. Address? She thought a moment, then made one up. Phone number? She made that up, as well. She didn't have a Social Security number, so she left it blank. There followed a long list of ailments with instructions to check the boxes that applied: Whooping cough. Measles. Mumps. Chicken pox. Polio. High blood pressure. Syphilis. The list went on and on.

She left all the boxes blank, then signed and dated the bottom of the form and returned it to the receptionist.

Tapping her foot nervously, Mara glanced around the room. A number of abstract paintings adorned the walls, a brass pot held a ficus tree, several magazines were scattered across a large square coffee table which was located amidst a grouping of chairs upholstered in a dark blue print. Water bubbled from a fountain in one corner, no doubt meant to soothe the nerves of waiting patients.

It wasn't working.

Moments later, a nurse with curly blond hair and brown eyes called Mara's name, then led her into an examining room. Was the nurse a vampire? With her weakening powers, Mara couldn't tell.

"Make yourself comfortable," the nurse said with a friendly smile. "I'll be right back."

Mara glanced around the room, noting that the walls were bare save for a painting of a sailboat on a storm-tossed sea. With a sigh, she sat on the foot of the examination table.

"I've got a bad feeling about this," she muttered, and wondered why she had let Logan talk her into coming here.

A short time later, the nurse returned. A name tag identified her as Susan. She took Mara's blood pressure, made a notation on a chart, and then handed Mara a paper gown and a covered plastic cup.

Seeing Mara's confused expression, the nurse said, "We need a urine sample. The bathroom is the first door on the left at the end of the hall. Just leave the cup on the sink, then come back here and put on the gown."

Mara blinked at the woman. Did she seriously expect her to pee in a cup?

"Is there a problem?" the nurse asked.

"I don't have to . . . to . . ." She held up the cup.

"I'm sure you can, if you try."

"I. Don't. Have. To," Mara said, speaking each word clearly and distinctly.

"Oh, well, maybe later. Doctor will be right in," Susan said, and left the room.

Muttering, "A really bad feeling about this," Mara placed the cup on the counter. After undressing, she slipped the flimsy paper gown over her head and sat on the edge of the examining table again. In all her life, she had never been examined by a doctor, and she had no idea what to expect. She jumped when someone knocked on the door.

"Mrs. Blackwood?"

"Yes. Come in."

The door swung open and a tall man with graying brown hair and brown eyes entered the room, a clipboard in one hand.

"Mara," he said, his tone respectful. "I never thought I would have the opportunity, the pleasure, of meeting you."

She smiled, unsure of how to respond. She was unsure of so many things these days, she hardly felt like herself anymore.

"So," Ramsden said, scanning the form she had filled out, "what brings you here?"

"I'm not sure. I just feel, I don't know, strange."

"In what way?"

"I can't explain it. More and more, I'm taking my rest at night instead of during the day. I can consume mortal food and drink. I'm gaining weight, something I've never done before. Sometimes I feel sick to my stomach. My breasts are tender."

He looked at her, his eyes widening as she described her symptoms. "Is it possible . . . no, of course not, but . . ."

He shook his head, his eyes narrowing thoughtfully. "Have you been intimate with a man lately?"

"Of course." Vampires were notoriously sensual creatures.

Ramsden tapped his fingers on the clipboard, then laid it aside. "Lie back on the table and put your feet in the stirrups. I'm going to examine you."

"What do you mean?"

"I'm going to give you a pelvic exam." Opening the door, he called for his nurse, then dragged a stool up to the end of the table. After sitting down, he pulled on a rubber glove. "Have you ever been examined before?"

"Of course not. Will it hurt?"

"No. But there might be a little discomfort."

Susan entered the room and took a place behind the doctor.

"What's she doing in here?" Mara asked. "Does it take two of you to do a pelvic exam?"

Ramsden and his nurse both grinned, as if she had said something funny.

"It's customary to have a nurse in the room for something like this," the doctor explained.

Feeling scared and vulnerable, Mara lay back on the table, placed her bare feet in the cold metal stirrups, and closed her eyes while the doctor examined her. Discomfort really wasn't the right word for it, she thought, gritting her teeth. Aside from being uncomfortable, she didn't know which was more humiliating: having a strange man examine her so intimately, or having the nurse standing by, watching. Fortunately, it didn't take long.

"You can sit up now," Ramsden said. Scooting back from the table, he removed his glove and tossed it in a waste receptacle.

Sitting up, Mara smoothed the paper gown over her hips. "So?"

After dismissing his nurse and closing the door, Ramsden said, "I don't quite know how to tell you this, but . . . you're pregnant."

Mara stared at the doctor as if he were speaking a foreign language. "What?"

"You're pregnant. You know, in the family way. With child. A little over four months along, I'd say."

She could only stare at him. "Pregnant?" She shook her head. "Are you sure?" She shook her head again. "It's impossible!"

"I know." He stared at her a moment, his expression distant. Rising, he picked up her chart. "Nevertheless, it's true."

"But . . . how can that be?"

Ramsden made a vague gesture with his hand. "I have no idea. Is Logan the father?"

"No."

"I see." He pulled a pen from his pocket and jotted a few things down. "Do you know who the father is?"

She hesitated a moment before shaking her head. "No." She no longer had the power to read minds, but there was something about Dr. Ramsden that made her wary of sharing too much information about the baby's father.

"Too bad." Ramsden made another note on her chart, then regarded her thoughtfully for several moments. "You're losing your powers, aren't you?"

She started to ask how he knew, but the answer was obvious. Any vampire worth the name could sense the power another vampire possessed, just as they could detect the presence of another of the Undead, whether the other was in the same room or a mile away.

Ramsden made another notation. "How did this weakening of your powers happen?"

"I don't know, but I'd appreciate it if you wouldn't spread it around."

"Yes, of course, I understand." Such knowledge could put her life in danger. "Did you lose your powers all at once," he asked, "or gradually?"

"Gradually. What does any of this have to do with my being pregnant?"

"I'm not sure, but that's something I hope to discover."

"Do you think my powers will return after the baby is born?"

"I don't know. I'm not sure there's any connection between your being pregnant and the loss of your powers. At this point, I'd say it was doubtful. In my opinion, if you lose your powers entirely, you probably won't get them back."

"Why not?"

"It's just my opinion, you understand, but I think you'll probably be immune to becoming a vampire again, sort of like humans are immune to the chicken pox once they've had the disease. Of course, I could be wrong. Only time will tell."

"So, if I was to ask someone to turn me again, you don't think it would work?"

"No, in fact I believe it would most likely be fatal for you and the baby." Eyes narrowed, Ramsden stroked his chin, his attention momentarily focused elsewhere.

"Fatal?" A sudden coldness engulfed her as she repeated the word. And then she shook it off. As far as she knew, no vampire had ever reverted before, therefore Ramsden had no more of an idea than she did about what would happen if someone worked the Dark Trick on her a second time. Still, he was a doctor. His opinion, and the possible risks, were something to consider.

"Perhaps," Ramsden said. "There's no precedent for any of this, no way of knowing for certain what the consequences might be. We're breaking new ground here. I want you to go down to the lab and let them take some blood." He handed her the cup she had left on the counter. "And give them a urine sample."

Ramsden pulled a pad from the pocket of his lab coat, scribbled a few lines, and tore off a sheet of paper. "Give this to the technician downstairs. Seeing as how you're able to digest mortal food with no ill effects, I want you to stop at a drugstore on your way home and buy some prenatal vitamins. Since I've never looked after a pregnant vampire before, we'll handle this as we would any other pregnancy and see how it goes." Patting her on the shoulder, he said, "I know this is hard to accept, but stars above, it's a miracle."

Or a curse, Mara thought bleakly. "The . . . the baby, will it be a vampire?"

"There's no way to know for sure one way or the other." The doctor took both of her hands in his. "I'm sorry I can't be more helpful, but we're both breaking new ground here. There's nothing about this kind of thing in Doctor Spock." He grinned at her, then grew serious once more. "I think we need to discuss the possibility that you might not be able to carry the child to full term. To my knowledge, no vampire has ever given birth or sired a child."

Mara thought of Vince Cordova. He had sired twins, but he had been a new vampire at the time. If she was still a fledgling, it would be easier to understand how she could be pregnant, but she had been a vampire for centuries . . .

Getting pregnant should have been impossible. She must have been gradually losing her powers without being aware of it while she and Kyle were together. It was the only answer that made sense.

"We'll have to monitor your progress very carefully," Ramsden was saying. "It might be necessary to hospitalize you during your last trimester."

"My what?"

"During the last three months of your pregnancy."

"Why?"

"Simply as a precaution."

Mara stared at him, a thousand questions running through her mind. A child! She didn't want a child. Rane and Rafe had grown and aged like normal mortal children until they turned thirteen and their vampire natures had taken over. Would her child react the same way? If not, if it was born a vampire, it would never grow up. It might age mentally, but physically it would always be an infant, dependent on her for its every need. What kind of life would that be for either of them?

"I know you must have a number of questions," Ramsden said, chuckling. "I have quite a few myself, but at the moment, I don't have any answers. I'll need to see your bloodwork, and then examine you again. Come back in six weeks. You can make an appointment at the desk on your way out. And don't hesitate to call me if you need to talk, or if you experience any contractions or bleeding."

She stared after him as he left the room, her mind whirling. Pregnant! How on earth could she be pregnant? What would Kyle say? Should she tell him? And what about Logan? Pregnant! It just wasn't possible, and yet the doctor seemed convinced that she was expecting.

Feeling numb, she wadded up the paper gown and

tossed it into the trash. She stood there a moment, her fingers splayed across her belly, and then shook her head. She couldn't be pregnant. Ramsden had made a mistake—that's all there was to it.

After dressing, she went out into the reception area.

Logan was pacing the floor. He came to an abrupt halt when he saw her, then hurried toward her. "What did the doctor say?"

"I'll tell you later. I have to go downstairs so they can draw some blood."

Logan lifted one brow. "Are you kidding me?"

"That's what I said." Turning back to the receptionist, Mara made an appointment for her next visit.

"A blood test," Logan muttered as they took the elevator down to the lab. "What's the cup for?"

"You don't need to know."

The elevator doors opened into a large room that reminded Logan of a bank vault. "Do you suppose he has vampires working down here?"

"How should I know?" Mara replied irritably. There could be a hundred vampires in the building and she would never know it. When they passed a wastebasket, she tossed the cup inside.

"You know, this might not be a bad place to work," Logan remarked as they walked down a long gray corridor. "You could draw blood for lab tests, and take a little extra for yourself."

"Very funny."

A heavy-set woman with orange hair smiled at them when they reached the lab. "May I help you?"

Mara handed the woman the piece of paper the doctor had given her.

The woman glanced at it and wrote something down

on a clipboard. "Just follow me. This will only take a minute."

After sending a worried look at Logan, Mara followed the woman into a small room. The walls were pale green, lined with glass-fronted cupboards. Mara sat in the chair the woman indicated and rolled up her sleeve.

"Here," the woman said, giving her a square of foam rubber. "Squeeze that for me."

"Why?"

"It'll bring your veins up. That's right." The technician wrapped a strip of rubber around Mara's arm, then inserted a needle.

Mara stared at the blood that began to fill the syringe. In the past, her blood had always been dark red; now it was a much brighter hue. Mortal blood. Feeling suddenly queasy at the sight, she turned her head away.

"You're not going to faint on me, are you?" the woman asked, worry evident in her tone.

"No."

"We're just about done," the woman said. "You're not allergic to paper tape, are you?"

"I don't know."

"Well, I guess we'll find out, won't we?" the woman said cheerfully. After removing the needle, she placed a cotton ball over the tiny wound, then covered it with a strip of tape. "Doctor will call you with the results in a few days."

With a nod, Mara left the room.

"How was it?" Logan asked curiously.

"Horrible, like everything else."

He slipped his arm around her waist and gave her a sympathetic hug as they headed for the exit. "Sorry, love."

"It's not your fault. Was she a vampire?"

"Yeah, a fairly old one."

"And the receptionist upstairs?"

"No, she's human. The nurse was a fledgling, not more than a few months old." He glanced at her, frowning. "Couldn't you tell?"

"No." She stared into the distance a moment before asking, "Have you ever wanted to be human again?"

He considered the question a moment, then shook his head. "No. So, what did the doctor say? What's making you sick?"

"I'll tell you in the car. You'll never believe it." She couldn't believe it, either.

Neither did Logan when she told him.

"Pregnant?" He pulled out of the parking lot and onto the street. "How in the hell can you be pregnant?"

"I don't know. Neither does the doctor." She gazed out the window. "Logan, I've lost most of my powers. When I was with the doctor, I couldn't tell if he was human or one of us. Even with you . . . I can't feel the bond between us anymore."

His hand tightened on the steering wheel. "I know." The bond no longer went both ways, but because of the blood they had shared, he could still read her mind if he chose to do so, could sense her proximity even when they were apart.

"I don't want to be mortal again!" she exclaimed. "I don't want a baby. A baby! What do I know about taking care of a baby?"

"You don't have to have it if you don't want it."

She stared at him. He was talking about an abortion. It was an ugly word, and an ugly deed. She knew little about childbirth, but she had watched a documentary about abortion and wondered how anyone could kill a living fetus. She had done some brutal things in the course of her existence, but she had never preyed upon the young or the helpless. Or the unborn.

Placing her hand over her stomach, she tried to imagine a child growing inside her womb. Kyle's child. A little boy with her black hair and Kyle's gray eyes. "No, not that." She couldn't kill her own child.

"What are you going to do, then?"

"I don't know."

She didn't want to be human again, didn't know how to be human. She knew there were vampires who hated what they were, who spent their entire existence lamenting their lost humanity. They were among the most miserable creatures she had ever known. She had never been one of them. Once she'd accepted what had happened to her, she had made the most of it. True, she had killed her sire, not for turning her against her will, but for abandoning her once the deed had been done.

Human again. How could she survive without her preternatural powers? Others of her kind had envied her strength and her longevity. In the course of her existence, she had made a good number of enemies. Secure in her strength, knowing she was virtually indestructible, she had blithely said and done as she pleased and to hell with the consequences. But now . . . now she had little supernatural strength. She was nearly as vulnerable as any mortal female. Even Ramsden had sensed it. In time, would she lose what little preternatural power she had left?

She glanced at Logan. Should she have confided in him? Was she being foolish to trust him? She had never trusted anyone. How could she start now, when she was weak, helpless? If she wanted to survive, she was going to have to consider everyone her enemy. And what about her doctor? Dared she trust him? Vampires were notoriously suspicious of their own kind, jealous of their hunting grounds, protective of their lairs.

She wondered how many of those she had turned were still alive, how many men she had thoughtlessly offended might still carry a grudge.

She shrugged off her fears. Worrying wouldn't solve anything. The world was a big place. She had rarely run into any of the men she had turned.

Logan pulled into her driveway and cut the engine, then turned to face her. "Do you know who the father is?"

"Of course!"

He lifted one brow. "So, are you gonna tell me his name?"

She shook her head. "You don't know him."

"But he's human?"

"That's a stupid question! Of course he is."

"So, where is he?"

"I don't know."

"Does he know about the baby?"

"No. And I'm not going to tell him," she said, anticipating his next question. "Can we not talk about this right now?"

Even though the bond between them was gone, Logan had no trouble reading her thoughts. She was worried, confused, and more distrustful than ever. He could hear the rapid beat of her heart, smell the panic she was trying to hide. He supposed he couldn't blame her. She was treading where no vampire had journeyed before. It was bound to be disturbing. As for losing her powers, he couldn't begin to imagine what that would be like, could scarcely remember what it had been like to walk the earth as a mortal man.

Resting his arm along the back of her seat, he lightly

stroked her hair. "You've nothing to fear from me. You know that, don't you?"

"I don't know anything anymore," she replied sullenly. "I just want this to be over!"

"Come on, let's go inside."

Taking the key from the ignition, Logan got out of the car. Opening her door, he offered her his hand, felt a brief flare of annoyance when she hesitated before placing her palm in his. He told himself to be patient. He had loved her from the moment they met, and that hadn't changed. He knew she was fond of him; in her own way, she might even love him. But things were different now. For the first time in their long acquaintance, *she* needed *him*. And she didn't like it one little bit.

"Are you going to be all right?" he asked.

"How should I know? This has never happened to me before."

"Maybe you should come home with me."

"Not tonight."

"Are you sure?"

"Yes." She needed to be alone, to come to terms with what was happening to her. Mortal. Pregnant. Impossible. "Thank you for your help."

"I still think you should come home with me tonight."

"I need some time alone, time to sort all this out."

Logan nodded. He could understand that, but he didn't like the idea of leaving her alone, not now, when she was as vulnerable as a new fledgling. "I'll see you tomorrow night. If you need me before then, give me a call."

"Yes, I will." She stood on the front porch, watching as he got into his car and drove away.

She was pregnant. It had never occurred to her to ask Kyle to take precautions, but why would it? Vampires couldn't reproduce. Everyone knew that. Only, she wasn't a true vampire anymore.

She went inside, careful to lock the door behind her. Fear was a new emotion, one she instantly despised. But she was safe in her house. She had never invited any of the Undead into this place. As long as she stayed inside at night, she would be safe from most of the vampire community. To her knowledge, there was only a handful of vampires who were old enough and strong enough to endure the sun's light. She didn't think she had anything to fear from Roshan's family, but what if there were others who could walk in the daylight that she didn't know about? Secrets were hard to maintain in the vampire community, but not impossible. Gossip spread like wildfire. She didn't know how many of her enemies still existed. If any of them learned of her vulnerability, she would be helpless to defend herself.

Maybe she was worrying for nothing. Maybe she wasn't losing her powers. Going into the living room, she stood in front of the hearth and willed the fire to light. Nothing happened.

She closed her eyes and tried to find her link to Rane. Nothing. It was the same with Rafe and Vince and Roshan. She didn't know why her failures surprised her. If she could no longer feel her bond to Logan, a connection that was older and stronger than her bond to any of the others of her kind, then it was a safe bet that her link to the Cordova family had vanished, as well.

She tried to dissolve into mist, only to blink back tears of bitter frustration when nothing happened.

Going to the window, she stared out into the night. Without her preternatural powers, the world seemed dull and quiet. As a vampire, she had seen colors and textures clearly. Day or night, it didn't matter, the world had been bright, the colors vibrant and alive. Once, she had been able to hear the flutter of a moth's wings, the stirring of birds in their nests, but no more. She felt empty, adrift, cut off from all that had once been familiar.

Mortal, she thought. *I'm a pregnant mortal woman with no family, and no one I dare trust, including the baby's father!*

Sinking down on the floor, she folded her arms over her belly and rocked back and forth. If only she had never revealed her true nature to Kyle. She could have stayed with him until the baby was born, and then, with him none the wiser as to her true nature, she could have moved on and left him to raise the baby. Kyle was a good man, strong yet gentle. He would have made a good father.

She wiped the tears from her eyes. Maybe it would still work. If he had truly loved her, he would be happy that she was now mortal, she thought, and then frowned. Maybe without her vampire allure, he would look at her and feel nothing at all.

She remembered the way he had stared at her when she'd told him what she was, the revulsion in his eyes when she revealed her true nature. Did she want to bind herself to a man who had looked at her like that? Would she ever feel safe with him? Would he even consider caring for a child he had created with a woman he thought of as a monster, a child that might be half vampire?

A baby . . . She moaned in despair.

What was she going to do with a baby?

Chapter Nine

It took Kyle three weeks to find a vampire hunter. It would have taken a lot less time if he had just looked online, but he was an artist, not a computer geek, and searching the Web hadn't occurred to him until he had exhausted all other search avenues.

The hunter agreed to meet him at his place the following night. The doorbell rang at seven o'clock sharp.

"Right on time," Kyle murmured as he opened the door.

Kyle wasn't sure what a vampire hunter should look like, but he had never expected a woman. Especially a woman who stood five-foot-nothing, with pale blond hair, deep blue eyes, and a beguiling dimple in her right cheek.

"You're the hunter?" He doubted if she weighed a hundred pounds soaking wet.

"Lou McDonald at your service, Mr. Bowden. May I come in?"

He blinked at her. Clad in a pair of loose-fitting gray trousers and a bulky white sweater, she looked completely harmless. "You're Lou?"

"Short for Louise." She lifted one brow. "May I come in?"

"What? Oh, sure." He stepped back so she could enter the apartment, then closed the door behind her. "Make yourself at home."

She glanced around the room before taking a seat on the sofa. He wondered what she'd expected to find, then decided that, considering her line of work, she was probably just naturally cautious.

"Can I get you anything?" he asked. "Coffee? Tea? Soda?"

"Nothing, thank you."

Kyle sat in the overstuffed chair across from the sofa. This had to be a joke. She couldn't be more than twenty-five years old.

Lou reached into her bag and withdrew a small red notebook and a pen. "You said you're looking for a vampire. I'll need a name, if you have it."

"Mara."

Lou's eyes widened. "Mara? You don't mean the one they call the Queen of the Vampires?"

Kyle stared at the hunter. Queen of the Vampires? Was she kidding? "Do you know her?"

"I know of her. Why are you looking for her?"

"Does it matter?"

"Not really. Do you have any idea where she might be?"

He rubbed a hand across his jaw, suddenly conscious of the fact that he hadn't shaved in days. "Last time I saw her, she was in Oregon. How old are you?"

"I beg your pardon?"

"You heard me."

"I'll be twenty-nine next month."

"How long have you been a hunter?"

"Ten years. I've made twenty-eight confirmed kills, and I don't come cheap."

"I was expecting someone a little older and more experienced . . . a little more . . ."

"You were expecting some kind of big macho man," she said dryly, "just like everyone else."

"That's why you list yourself as Lou, isn't it? So people will think you're a man."

She didn't deny it.

"Can you find Mara?"

"I won't know until I try."

"I don't want her dead."

"Excuse me?"

"I don't want her dead. I just want you to find her."

"I'm not a private eye, Mr. Bowden, I'm a hunter. I hunt vampires and I destroy them."

"I'm willing to make it worth your while. Anyway, from what I hear, she can't be destroyed."

"Yes, I've heard that, too," Lou replied. "But every living thing can be killed, one way or another."

"I thought vampires were already dead."

"Dead or destroyed, it means the same thing. No more vampire."

"Yeah, well, like I said, I want her alive. So if you want to work for me, it'll have to be on my terms."

"Very well, but it will cost you double my usual rate, and I'll be wanting half up front."

Kyle nodded. "All right."

She held out her hand. "Looks like we have a deal."

Chapter Ten

Four weeks had passed since Mara's first visit to the doctor. Her nausea had passed, and now she was hungry all the time, but instead of craving blood, she was craving the oddest things, like potato chips and pizza. And chocolate—the darker, the better. She couldn't seem to get enough of it, had never tasted anything so wonderful. She loved the way it melted on her tongue, the almost sinful pleasure it gave her.

She looked up when Logan entered the living room.

"The word on the street is that someone is looking for you," he said, sitting beside her. "I think you'd better stay here, with me, from now on."

"Do you know who's looking for me?" She popped another dark chocolate truffle into her mouth.

"I couldn't begin to guess. What about you? Any ideas?"

"No, it could be anybody." During the War, she had made enemies among the werewolves as well as the Undead. None of them would spare her just because she was pregnant. Of course, she had made a lot of other enemies in centuries past. Who knew how many of them were still carrying a grudge?

"Ramsden called me last night," Logan said. "He wanted your phone number. Said he needed to reschedule your appointment."

"I'm not going back there. I'm not sure I trust him."

"Why the hell not?"

"I don't know."

"Mara," he said patiently, "you need to see a doctor. All things considered, we agreed a vampire doctor would be the best."

"I think I'll go to a mortal physician from now on," she said, although she wasn't sure she wanted to put herself through another pelvic examination. And then she frowned. If a routine exam was so embarrassing and uncomfortable, how would she ever endure childbirth?

"What do you think about staying here, with me?" Logan asked. A muscle throbbed in his jaw when she didn't say anything. "Or don't you trust me, either?" he asked, his voice tight.

"If I stay here with you, it's like admitting that I'm afraid."

"You are afraid! I can smell it on you."

"Oh, I hate this!" She didn't understand how it had happened, and happened so quickly. It just wasn't fair. She ate another truffle. These days, nothing was quite as comforting as rich, dark chocolate.

Logan frowned at her as she licked a bit of chocolate from her lower lip. "You look like you're having great sex," he muttered.

Mara grinned. "I heard a woman on a talk show remark that good chocolate was better than sex."

Logan quirked a brow at her. "Is it?"

Mara licked the last bit of candy from her fingers. "Try it for yourself and see." She unwrapped another truffle and offered it to him.

Logan eyed it the way Adam must have looked at the apple; then, remembering what had happened the last time he partook of human food, he shook his head. "No, thanks. Once was enough."

Unable to help herself, Mara burst out laughing.

"Think it's funny, do you?" he asked with a growl.

Impulsively taking him by the hand, she led him into the bedroom. She might be losing her preternatural abilities, but she had powers of her own that had nothing to do with the supernatural—feminine wiles as old as Eve's. She pushed Logan toward the bed until the backs of his knees hit the mattress and he sat down, and then she began to move. She had once danced for Pharaoh; now she danced for Logan, her body dipping and swaying slowly and provocatively to music only she could hear.

He whistled softly as she began to undress, each move sensually tantalizing as she removed one piece of clothing after another, each inch of bared flesh more provocative than the last, until she stood naked before him, a goddess clothed in mortality.

"Beautiful," Logan murmured. He held out his arms in invitation, eager to touch her, to run his hands over her alabaster skin, to nuzzle her breasts, to bury himself in her warmth.

Instead of moving into his embrace, she crossed her arms. "Now you."

"What?" He shook his head in disbelief. "You don't expect *me* to do a striptease, do you?"

"Why not?" She closed the distance between them and ran her fingertips down his cheek. "I did."

"Mara . . ."

She retreated when he reached for her. "Don't tell me you're shy?"

"Maybe." His voice was a low growl of frustration.

"I don't believe you."

"If you want me naked, you'll have to undress me."

She canted her head to the side, a seductive smile teasing her lips. "Think I won't?"

"I'm hoping you will," he said, his dark eyes filled with mischief.

"Are you going to help me?"

"Nope." He flopped back on the bed, his arms outstretched. "How much do you want me?"

She climbed on the bed and straddled his hips. "How much do *you* want *me*?" It was a foolish question. His desire was readily apparent.

He laughed softly. "Are we making a contest out of this? 'Cause you're not really dressed for a fight."

"And you're over-dressed." Taking hold of the hem of his sweater, she eased it up, revealing a hard, flat belly. He wasn't wearing an undershirt and as she lifted his sweater higher, she rained kisses on each inch of newly exposed skin.

After tossing his sweater aside, her hands made quick work of his belt buckle. She tossed his belt on the floor, along with his shoes and socks, and after gaining her feet, she stood at the end of the bed and slowly tugged his trousers off and flung them aside. The black briefs he wore did little to hide his erection.

"You're quick," he said with a grin.

"And you're horny," she remarked as she relieved him of his briefs. "Now we're even."

"You think so?" In a blur of movement, he sat up and wrapped his arms around her. Falling back on the bed once more, he rolled over, carrying her with him, so that she lay beneath him. "What are you gonna do now?"

"Anything I want," she murmured, and locking her hands

behind his neck, she drew his head down and kissed him, a long, lingering kiss that left both of them breathless.

She ran her hands over his face, his shoulders, his chest, his taut buttocks, and each caress reminded her of days gone by, of endless nights of lovemaking along the banks of the Nile. She hadn't intended for things to go this far. She was in love with Kyle. But what had started out as a little harmless flirting with an old flame had quickly gotten out of hand. She knew she should tell Logan to go, but, somehow, she couldn't summon the words. It felt good to be in his arms, like returning home after a long vacation.

He murmured to her in his native tongue, making her wonder if he, too, was recalling those halcyon days gone by. She moaned softly as his hands worked their familiar magic, cried his name as the tension built deep within her, built until she thought she would explode with need, until, thrusting deep, he brought her to fulfillment.

Sated, she closed her eyes, but he wasn't done with her yet. Holding back his own release, he aroused her again, more slowly this time. Her nails raked his back as she writhed beneath him, mindless with wanting. Her skin was slick with perspiration, her body arching upward as he continued to move deep within her, his own climax coming quickly on the heels of her own. Breathless, she lay spent beneath him, trembling with little aftershocks of pleasure as he held her close.

"So," he said, his voice a low rumble in her ear, "do you still think good chocolate is better than great sex?"

Later, after they had showered and dressed, Logan again brought up the subject of her moving in with him.

"This is a big place," he said. "You can have your pick

of the bedrooms. Hell, you'll have the whole house to yourself during the day."

He was very persuasive. Staying here was tempting, so very tempting. Living with Logan wouldn't be a hardship. He had a house that was even bigger than her own, with a lovely view, an Olympic-sized swimming pool, and a Jacuzzi. Best of all, she enjoyed his company. Still, if she agreed to move in with him, she wasn't just admitting she was afraid, she was surrendering a portion of her free will. The thought rankled.

"If you won't come here," Logan remarked, playing his ace in the hole, "then I'm moving in with you."

"You can't come into my house unless you're invited."

He lifted one brow. "Can't I?"

She stared at him uncertainly. Thresholds had a mystical power of their own. They repelled vampires and other supernatural creatures. Had Logan found a way to nullify that power?

"The bond between us may be broken, Mara, but you're forgetting one thing. I'm still a vampire."

The threat was clear. If she refused to move in with him, or refused to allow him to move in with her, he could forcibly bend her will to his. Without her supernatural powers, there was nothing she could do to stop him. She probably wouldn't even be aware of it. Not only that, but he had tasted her blood, which meant that no matter where she went, he would always be able to find her, a power she had once used to her own advantage without wondering or caring what mortals thought about her invading their privacy.

"You're not playing fair," she said petulantly.

Logan shrugged. "You know what they say about love and war."

"Are we at war?"

He trailed one finger down her cheek. "No, darlin', but one of us is in love."

She had no answer for that. She cared for Logan deeply, but she wasn't in love with him. And then, in the back of her mind, came that troubling question again: Was she?

Knowing Logan wouldn't relent, Mara agreed to move into his house, at least until the baby was born.

Logan did his best not to look smug, but he failed miserably. It made her want to smack him.

The following evening, Logan arrived at her house with a small moving van. "I would have hired someone to help out, but the fewer people who see you, the better."

With Logan's supernatural strength, there really wasn't any need for help. In addition to her suitcases, he easily managed the few large items she wanted to take with her.

Two hours later, Mara had settled into the upstairs master bedroom in Logan's house. It was a spacious room, but it was definitely masculine, from the heavy dark furniture to the gray walls and carpeting. She blew out a sigh as she opened one of her suitcases. The room was nice but not to her liking.

Logan stood in the doorway, watching her unpack. "So, what color are you going to paint it?"

Mara looked up. "What?"

"The room. What color are you going to paint it?"

"Are you serious? You'll just have to paint it again when I leave."

He shrugged. "The colors don't suit you." She was never meant for insipid shades of gray. "I'll run down to the paint store and get some samples while you unpack."

Before she could assure him that it wasn't necessary, he was gone.

Fighting the urge to cry, Mara sat on the edge of the bed. She hated being so weepy all the time, but she couldn't seem to help herself. Was it because she was becoming more human every day? Or just because she was pregnant? Pregnant! No matter how often she said it, she couldn't believe it. All these tears made her feel weak and foolish.

With a shake of her head, she resumed unpacking. Logan had thoughtfully emptied the large walk-in closet and the six drawers in the dresser. He really was a sweet man, she thought, and wondered again why she had left him. Boredom, perhaps, or maybe just her lifelong fear of letting anyone, mortal or vampire, get too close, see too much.

She was hanging the last of her clothes in the closet when Logan reappeared with two dozen color samples. He spread them out on the top of the dresser. "Take your pick."

She moved up beside him, frowning as her gaze moved over the small colored paper squares. Looking at them made her yearn for the preternatural sight she had once taken for granted. As a vampire, she had seen colors with more clarity. When she looked at fabric, she had seen each individual thread. Now, the various shades of blue, green, pink, lavender, and yellow looked faded, washed out.

Her preternatural hearing was gone, too. As a vampire, she would have been able to hear the traffic noise from the street below, if she wished, the tick of the clock downstairs, the whisper of a moth's wings. But no more. It was as if she had lost half of herself.

"Mara? Hey, if you don't like any of these, I'll go get some more."

Blinking back her tears, she said, "You pick one."

Logan slipped his arm around her waist. "Listen, we're gonna get through this, okay?"

"We?"

"I'm in this for the long haul, darlin'. However long it takes. I love you," he said, kissing her cheek. "I've always loved you. Human or vampire, it doesn't matter. I'll be here as long as you need me."

"Logan, you're so good to me."

"Geez, woman, cheer up. Come on," he said, grabbing her by the hand. "Let's go for a swim."

"I don't have a bathing suit."

"Good, neither do I."

The pool was lovely in the moonlight. Logan flicked a switch on the patio and the backyard turned into a fairyland. Twinkling colored lights shone in the shrubs and the trees, and glowed from the bottom of the pool.

Mara sat on the edge of the deck, dangling her bare feet in the water.

Logan, never big on modesty, shucked his clothes while she watched. He was beautiful, a young Greek god come to life, Adonis and Apollo all rolled into one.

He winked at her; then, striking a bodybuilder pose, he flexed his muscles. "Impressed?"

Before she could answer, he dove into the water, then surfaced in front of her. "Come on in. The water feels great."

"In a minute."

With a nod, he pushed away from the edge and began to swim with long, even strokes that quickly carried him from one end of the pool to the other, and back again.

He was a delight to watch. He swam effortlessly, his

body barely making a ripple as he moved smoothly through the water. Moonlight dappled his long black hair.

After a hundred laps or so, he swam up to her again. "I think it's been a minute."

Rising, she undressed, then dove into the pool. He was right. The water felt wonderfully erotic against her bare skin. She shrieked with mock terror when Logan came up behind her and wrapped her in his arms.

She leaned back against him, loving the feel of his body against hers, the sensuous slide of wet skin against wet skin as she turned in his arms to face him.

Excitement stirred deep within her as his hand cupped the back of her head. His kiss, when it came, sent fingers of flame shooting through her. Good thing they were in the pool, she thought, or she might have gone up in smoke.

She ran her hands restlessly over his back and shoulders, groaned softly as her need for him intensified.

Backing up against the side of the pool, he wrapped her legs around his waist and made love to her, there, in the shallow end of the pool, with the crickets singing a serenade and the moon smiling down on them.

She was dreaming. Even in sleep, Mara found the idea astonishing. She had not dreamed since Dendar brought her across, yet she was dreaming now, of people she had known down through the ages, of cities and towns long gone.

As if watching a movie in her mind, she saw herself walking along a dusty boardwalk in some nameless town in the Old West . . .

* * *

She smiled inwardly, pleased by the looks the men cast her way as she passed by. She wore a yellow dress with long sleeves and a full skirt over several petticoats. High-button shoes encased her feet; white gloves protected her hands, and she carried a white parasol to shade her from the desert sun. And a hat, of course. A lady never went outside without a hat. This one sat at a jaunty angle; colorful streamers trailed down her back.

She winked at a cowboy as she strolled by, grinned as he quickly removed his hat. She loved the cowboys. They treated her as if she were made of spun glass even though she worked in a saloon. It was the perfect place to find prey. Starved for female attention, men practically fell at her feet if she so much as looked at them. It was all too easy to take them upstairs where, instead of satisfying their lust, she satisfied her hunger, then sent them on their way, none the wiser about what had really happened.

It was an amazingly realistic dream. She could feel the sun's heat on her back, smell the dun-colored dust that choked the air, hear the out-of-tune notes of a distant piano.

At the end of the street, she entered the Calico Saloon. It was her favorite haunt. She smiled at Ed Rogen as he shambled toward her.

"Mara." He embraced her. "Remember, you promised me the whole night."

She batted her eyelashes at him. "Why, Ed, how could I forget? My room, nine o'clock?"

"I'll be there."

The scene changed quickly, as dreams were wont to do, and she was in San Francisco, strolling along the waterfront in the dark of night, searching for prey, mesmerizing *a young prostitute, taking the life of some thug who tried to steal the girl away from her.*

She was bending over the girl, savoring the thick, rich taste of her blood, when, abruptly, the scene changed again and now she was back in Egypt with Logan soon after she had brought him across. Such a glorious time, when he had been a new vampire. They had spent his every waking moment together as she helped him adjust to his new life. They had spent hours in each other's arms, two supernatural creatures who never grew weary. Not surprisingly, he had reveled in his newfound ability to make love all night long. He had been an incredible lover, young, tender, eager to please her . . .

Mara woke, her desire unfulfilled, her body bathed in perspiration. Damn, why couldn't she have slept for another few minutes? It had been such a wonderful dream, so real she could almost feel Logan's hands on her flesh, his breath hot on her skin, his tongue laving her breasts. Filled with yearning, she sat up and reached for her robe. She didn't have to settle for dreams, not when Logan was just down the hall.

She frowned, the robe in her hand forgotten. Was it Logan she wanted, or Kyle? She had thought herself in love with Kyle, so why was she dreaming of Logan? Of course, she couldn't control her dreams, but she was awake now, so why was it still Logan that her body burned for? Maybe indecision was a part of being mortal.

Confused, she fell back on the bed and closed her eyes. Maybe, if she was lucky, she could recapture her dream . . .

She woke in the morning to discover that, while she'd slept, Logan had painted the bedroom. How had he managed it without waking her, she wondered, and then shrugged. He was a vampire. He wouldn't need a light to see by, and with his preternatural speed, it wouldn't have taken him more than a few minutes to paint the whole room.

Sitting up, she glanced around. The room, once pale gray, was now a lovely shade of sage green with sparkling white trim. Logan's black bedspread was gone, replaced by a luxurious satin quilt that was green on one side and white on the other. New drapes hung at the window. A beautiful, old-fashioned, full-length mirror stood in one corner of the room, a note taped to the top.

Rising, she unfolded the sheet of paper and read the message scrawled in Logan's bold hand: *So you can see how beautiful you are.*

Staring at her reflection, she wondered if it was possible to be in love with two men at the same time, and what she would do if she couldn't make up her mind.

Chapter Eleven

Lou McDonald sat at her desk, quickly scanning through her e-mail. Since putting out the word that she was offering a reward for information on Mara, her inbox had been flooded with mail. It seemed every contact she had from Alaska to Mexico and in between had seen the Queen of the Vampires. Unfortunately, none of the leads had panned out.

Lou leaned forward, her eyes narrowing as she read an e-mail from her sister in Nevada. She read it again, and yet again, and then, shaking her head, she leaned back in her chair.

"Very funny, Cindy," she muttered as she typed her response. Mara, pregnant in Northern Nevada. That was very funny indeed. But then, Cindy had always had a twisted sense of humor. They had been partners in the vampire hunting business since a vampire had killed their younger brother eleven years ago. Cindy didn't have the stomach for staking hearts or taking heads, but she was aces at undercover work and ferreting out the lairs of the Undead. Working for Ramsden gave her access to his records and other valuable information. It was the only reason he was still alive.

Lou glanced at her watch, and swore softly. She was late for her two o'clock appointment with Kyle Bowden. He was an odd duck. She had never had a client who wanted a vampire found but not destroyed. She wondered if he wanted to destroy the vampire himself or if, poor fool, he had fallen under the creature's spell. Lou had been hunting vampires for ten years and had yet to find one who didn't deserve a stake in the heart. But Bowden wasn't paying her for her opinion.

After shutting down her computer, Lou left her office. She didn't for a minute believe that Mara was pregnant.

But a little voice in the back of her mind kept asking, What if it's true?

"Pregnant?" Kyle stared at Lou. "Is that even possible?"

"No. Vampires are unable to create life." Lou wasn't sure why she had even mentioned it to Bowden, except she had been curious to see his reaction.

"So, the only lead you have is that she might be in Nevada?" Gaining his feet, Kyle paced the floor. "It's been weeks!"

"I'm sorry, Mr. Bowden, but looking for a vampire isn't the same as trying to find your average woman. Mara doesn't have a Social Security number. As near as I can tell, she doesn't have any credit cards or bank accounts. If she has a residence, it's not in her name. The same goes for a cell phone. She doesn't show up on any census rolls or tax records. To my knowledge, she's not on Facebook or any of the other social networks. Vampires tend to be very protective of their identities. But I'll find her."

Kyle dropped back down on the sofa. "Anything else?"

"No. I'll be in touch."

"Yeah, thanks."

After walking Lou to the door, Kyle poured himself a shot of whiskey. The hunter claimed it was impossible for a vampire to get pregnant, but what if she was wrong? What if Mara was carrying a child—his child?

Dammit, he should have asked for the doctor's name, but learning that Mara might be pregnant had thrown him for a loop.

Grabbing his cell phone, he dialed McDonald's number, muttered an oath when he got a busy signal. Too restless to sit still, he paced the floor, then picked up his keys and left the apartment. He needed a drink, and he didn't like to drink alone.

Lost in thought, Lou sat at the curb in front of Bowden's apartment while she accessed the messages on her office answering machine. A call from her mother, a wrong number, an inquiry about her services. Nothing urgent.

Dropping the phone on the seat, she tapped her fingertips on the steering wheel. Whatever had possessed her to agree to find Mara and not destroy her? The so-called Queen of the Vampires had been alive for centuries. No doubt she had killed thousands of helpless mortals. If any of the Undead deserved to be destroyed, it was Mara.

What if she was really pregnant?

Lou shook her head. It was impossible and yet, what if Cindy had been telling the truth? There hadn't been any smiley face at the end of the e-mail, nothing to indicate that Cindy was pulling her leg. So, what if it was true, and Bowden was the father? Did he have some special DNA that enabled him to impregnate the Undead?

She swore softly. Now that was a scary idea. There were already too many vampires in the world without some foolish mortal going around making more.

She glanced out the window as the mortal in question emerged from the apartment building, got into his car, and pulled away from the curb.

Being curious by nature, and having nothing better to do, Lou started the car and followed him down the street. When he pulled into the parking lot of a tavern a few blocks away, she drove on by. What if Bowden knew Mara was pregnant and that was why he was looking for her? She shook her head. No, his surprise had been genuine.

"Well, hell," she muttered. She wasn't getting anywhere here. Picking up her cell phone, she noticed a missed call from Bowden. Ignoring it, she punched in Cindy's number.

After listening to the recorded message, she said, "Hey, Cin, this is Lou. Just thought I'd let you know I'll be in town tomorrow night."

Chapter Twelve

Mara hadn't been inside a grocery store more than a dozen times in her existence, and then only when she was following some tasty-looking mortal. But today she wasn't looking for prey, she was shopping for food. Mortal food to ease the odd cravings she was experiencing, cravings made harder to fulfill because she wasn't really sure what she was hungry for other than chocolate. She never tired of it, but, according to some prenatal guidelines she'd read on the Web, she knew she needed to eat fruits and vegetables and drink lots of milk for the baby's sake.

Thinking of the baby brought Kyle to mind. What was he doing? Did he miss her? She didn't miss him as much as she'd thought she would, but then, Logan was responsible for that. He was good company, always there to cheer her when she was down, to assure her that everything would be all right.

Earlier in the week, she had gone shopping online and bought a stove and a refrigerator. Logan had looked at her askance when the appliances were delivered.

"I was getting tired of going out for food three times

a day, or having it delivered," she had explained with a shrug. "Besides, if I'm going to be mortal, I need to learn how to cook, not only for me, but for the baby."

Mortal, she thought as she moved slowly up and down the aisles. Why did anyone want to be mortal? It was tiring, it was messy, and so far, it hadn't been much fun. She picked up one item after another, studying the pictures on the cans and the boxes, reading the directions on the packages. She knew, of course, that hot dogs weren't made from real dogs, and that Goldfish crackers weren't made from goldfish, but what on earth was tofu?

She bought chocolate milk and bread sweetened with honey, several bags of miniature chocolate candy bars, chocolate-flavored cereal, and even chocolate-flavored coffee. Not exactly the kind of diet a pregnant woman was supposed to eat, she reminded herself, and with that thought in mind, she added some fruit to the cart—oranges because they smelled good, red apples because she liked the color, watermelon and peaches and pears, lettuce and tomatoes. She picked up a couple of thick steaks, and added a bottle of red wine for Logan. Lastly, she bought half a pound of rare roast beef and some cheese for sandwiches, and then headed for the checkout counter where the clerk and the box boy both flirted with her. She flirted back shamelessly, pleased that men, old and young, still found her attractive.

She was still smiling when the taxi pulled into Logan's driveway. No doubt both the clerk and the box boy would have been shocked to know just how old she really was. The thought wiped the smile from her face. She had lived for thousands of years. How many years did she have left, now that she was becoming mortal? One? Ten? Twenty?

She didn't want to die—not in twenty years, not in a hundred.

Blinking back tears, she paid the driver, then carried the groceries into the house. Why was this happening to her? And why now? Damn Kyle Bowden and his puppy dog eyes and his sexy smile. It was probably all his fault, she thought, putting the last of the groceries away. She had been fine until she met him.

"Hey, what's this?" Logan asked, coming into the kitchen. "Why are you crying?"

Mara wiped the tears from her cheeks as Logan came up behind her and slid his arms around her waist. "I'm not."

He kissed the side of her neck, then turned her around to face him. "Come on, tell me what's wrong. The cost of groceries too high? They were out of Midnight Milky Way bars? You broke a fingernail?"

"Logan . . ."

He kissed the tip of her nose. "I've been online, reading up on what we should expect during your pregnancy."

"Oh?"

He nodded. "It said pregnant women tend to be overly emotional. You know, hormones out of whack and everything."

"I don't want to be pregnant," she wailed. "I don't want to be mortal." Mortals were weak, subject to illness and death. She could be hit by a car, struck by lightning. She could die in childbirth. Was death the end, or was there truly a life beyond this one? The thought of eternal damnation was even more frightening than the thought of dying. Not for the first time, she realized that if there was an afterlife, she was surely bound for Hell.

"I think we've covered this before."

"I know." She sniffed back her tears. Maybe Logan

was right. Maybe she was just behaving this way because she was pregnant. Once the baby was born . . . She blew out a sigh of resignation. Once the baby was born, she would still be mortal. But Logan could fix that. Or could he? It was Ramsden's opinion that she couldn't be turned a second time.

No. She refused to believe that. It was just his best guess. She had to hold fast to the hope that Logan could bring her across once she got rid of the child. Even with the Dark Gift restored, she probably wouldn't be the same as she had been before. She had been the most powerful vampire in the world, but she hadn't gained her incomparable power overnight. No, it had taken centuries before she could walk in the sun's light, centuries to gain the strength and abilities she had once possessed.

What would it be like, to be a fledgling again? To be under her master's control? At least Logan loved her. He wouldn't be cruel or condescending. He would treat her as an equal. Soon the baby would be born and she could put an end to this wretched existence. She just needed to be patient and all this would be over. If being a vampire had taught her anything, she thought as she rested her forehead against Logan's chest, it was patience.

"You were thinking about me this morning," Logan said, stroking her hair.

Startled, she looked up, her gaze searching his.

"Weren't you?" He ran his knuckles over her cheek, his touch tender, sensual.

"Yes." The word was little more than a whisper. She had been disturbed by her dream about Logan. Did he also know there were nights when she dreamed of Kyle? She felt discomfited, as though her mind had been violated. Had mortals felt this way, when she divined their thoughts? She wanted to be angry with him, but she couldn't, not when he was stroking her hair, not when his gaze rested on her face.

"I'm here now," he said quietly, and kissed her brow.

"Logan . . ." Why couldn't she love him instead of Kyle?

"I'm here," he murmured. "I'll always be here." And cupping her face in his hands, he kissed her gently.

She moaned softly as she leaned into him. His mouth was as warm and firm as she remembered. Why did she continue to think about a man who had scorned her? To wonder if things would have turned out differently if she had kept the truth to herself? Logan was worth a dozen Kyle Bowdens. So why did thoughts of Kyle continue to plague her? Maybe it was normal, all things considered. After all, she was carrying his child.

Logan's arms tightened around her as his hands skimmed up and down her back, pressing her body closer to his. "Is this what you want?"

"Yes. No. Oh! I don't know what I want anymore!"

"No?" He lifted one brow. "It's what you wanted last night."

She didn't deny it. It was what she wanted now, too, but how could that be when she was in love with Kyle? Wasn't she?

Logan brushed a kiss across her lips. "Past or present, it doesn't matter. We were always good together."

She stroked his cheek. "Yes, but . . ."

He took a step backward, his expression hardening. "You don't want to get too involved."

Mara folded her hands over her stomach. "It's not that."

"It won't hurt the baby."

Last night, swept up in a firestorm of passion, she

hadn't been thinking about the baby. "Are you sure? How do you know?"

"I told you, I've been reading about pregnancy, what to expect, what to do, and what not to do."

She found it endearing, knowing he cared enough to read about her condition. She closed the short distance between them. Why not make love to Logan? He was here. He wanted her. And if she was going to be honest with herself, she definitely wanted him. "Are you sure it's safe?"

A smile tugged at the corners of his mouth. "Very sure. I don't have any diseases, and you're already pregnant. What else is there to worry about?"

Kyle's image flashed through her mind, and with it the memory of the last time they had made love. He had been so tender, so gentle. He had given her a bouquet of red roses, spread a furry blanket on the floor in front of the fire. He had undressed her, his gaze filled with adoration, his hands sure as they aroused her. Had their child been conceived that night?

Logan blew out a sigh. He didn't have to read Mara's mind to know she was thinking of someone else. "Why don't you get some rest?" he suggested, reining in his jealousy. "I need to go out for a while."

"I'm sorry I can't go with you."

"So am I. It's been a long time since we hunted together." He kissed her cheek. "I won't be gone long."

After leaving the house, Logan fed quickly, then strolled down Hollywood Boulevard along what was known as the Walk of Fame, which stretched from Gower Street to La Brea Avenue. From time to time he glanced down at one of the pink five-pointed stars rimmed in bronze that were embedded in the sidewalk. He had read somewhere that the Walk of Fame had been created in

1958. The first honoree had been Joanne Woodward back in 1960. Now, there were stars honoring over two thousand artists of radio, television, theater, and the recording industry. So many names—Houdini, Greta Garbo, Boris Karloff, Bob Hope, Elvis Presley, and Johnny Cash shared space with Walt Disney, Mickey Mouse and Snow White. There was even a star for Lassie.

He paused at the forecourt of Grauman's Chinese Theatre, where famous celebrity handprints were preserved in cement. He wondered idly what it would be like, to be famous, to know that people would come to this place long after you were gone and stare at your handprints. He had outlived most of these famous folks, yet only a few people knew his name. Ah, well, fame, like life, was fleeting. The stars on Hollywood Boulevard, the handprints at Grauman's, served to remind those in the present of those who had gone before. So many famous people, now mostly gone, and yet he remained, unchanged for centuries.

Moving on, his thoughts returned to Mara. He pictured her, resting back at his house. She had certainly changed. How was it possible that the world's oldest vampire had metamorphosed back into a human? In time, would it happen to him, as well?

The thought was not a pleasant one. He enjoyed being a vampire, enjoyed the strength and power that came with being Nosferatu. He loved the night, the taste of warm, living blood on his tongue, the enhanced senses that made the world around him more vibrant and alive.

His thoughts returned to Mara. She had apologized for not being able to hunt with him. She was finding it harder to stay awake after midnight, she who had once prowled the shadows long after most mortals had gone to bed.

She was vulnerable now, needy. He had never known her to be anything but invincible. She had always been the bold one, the strong one. But no more. For the first time in their relationship, she needed him. But she didn't want him. The thought burned like sunlight on preternatural flesh. She wanted the man who had used her. From thoughts he'd read in her mind, it was apparent that the man, Kyle, had turned away in revulsion when he discovered her true nature.

Anger erupted through Logan. With a savage cry, he slammed his hand against a brick wall. It crumbled beneath his fist.

Muttering an oath, he found himself thinking of the baby she carried. Would it be human, or vampire, or some bizarre combination of the two? He couldn't imagine Mara with a child. Couldn't imagine having a baby in his house.

A baby. Young. Innocent. With blood that was pure as only the blood of the very young could be. His tongue brushed his fangs at the thought. He had never killed a child though he had, on one occasion, dined on one. It had happened shortly after Mara left him. Angry and confused, wanting to hurt her, he had decided to end his existence. If she didn't want him, then he had no reason to endure. And so, on a night in early spring, he had gone outside to wait for the rising of the sun. That sunrise was forever imprinted in his mind—the beauty of the sky as it lightened from indigo to gray to blue, the brilliant slashes of crimson and ocher that had streaked the heavens. The pain—he would never forget the pain as the sun's bright golden light scorched his preternatural flesh. With an anguished cry, he had burrowed into the blessedly cool arms of the earth, deep into the welcome darkness, where he had slept the healing sleep of the Undead. When he rose the following night, he had found a young family on their way to the city. The man and the woman had been his dinner, the infant his dessert. It was his first taste of innocent blood; it was a taste he had coveted ever since. Ah, the warm, sweet nectar, now but a distant memory. He had avoided infants ever since, afraid he might succumb to the temptation, afraid that the next time, he wouldn't be able to stop at a taste.

How could he have a child constantly underfoot, constantly tempting him? Once again his thoughts turned to Mara. She needed him now, but for how long? Would she stay here, with him, once the child was born? Or would she leave him again? Could he bear to let her go?

He had known many women in the course of his existence, more than he could count, more than he could recall. But Mara . . . He had never forgotten her. He remembered every moment they had spent together, every word she had spoken, every look, every gesture, every touch. Dammit, he couldn't lose her again, he thought bleakly.

And then he smiled. He didn't have to. If she wouldn't stay with him of her own free will, well, there were ways to make her stay, ways to make her believe staying was her own idea.

Whistling softly, he headed for home and the woman he loved.

Mara sat on the sofa in front of the fireplace, a book of baby names open in her lap. Of course, before she made a decision, she would need to know if her baby was a boy or a girl. And then she wondered why she was even worrying about it. There was no room for a baby in her life. She knew nothing of being a mother. A baby, she thought. A boy, with Kyle's eyes . . .

She glanced at the book again. So many names to choose from—common names, like John and Mary, exotic names like Kamenwati and Cleopatra. She sighed as she thought of Egypt's ancient queen. She had been with Cleopatra in the throne room when Octavian came to tell the queen what her fate would be. Later, Cleopatra's ladies-in-waiting had hovered around their queen, their expressions anxious. That had been the night Mara had offered to work the Dark Trick on the queen of Egypt, but Cleopatra had refused.

"Antony is dead," the queen had murmured. "My son is dead. Why would I want to live forever?"

Mara hadn't pressed the issue. Cleopatra had set her face toward death and she had accomplished it with the same flair she had exhibited in life. In dying, she had robbed Octavian of his prize. It was her last victory over a hated enemy.

Ah, Cleopatra, one of the few women Mara had considered her equal. If her child was a girl, she would name her after the Queen of the Nile. And if it was a boy . . . ? She turned to the section listing boys' names again and thumbed through the pages. Aaron, Benjamin, Clyde, Daniel, Ezekiel. She shook her head. Nicholas, Obadiah, Parker, Quennel.

"Quennel?" she muttered. No way. If it was a boy, she should probably just name him after his father.

Blowing out a sigh, she rested her head on the back of the sofa and closed her eyes. She wasn't fit to be a mother. She had never been around children, or wanted any. She supposed she took after her own mother, who had given birth to Mara and abandoned her five years later. If one of Pharaoh's servants hadn't found Mara scavenging in the marketplace, she probably wouldn't have survived. She had been strong once, indomitable, always in control. Now she felt helpless, awash with doubts. Not for the first time, she asked herself how she could take care of a child when she couldn't take care of herself. She was just now learning to cook, and not doing a very good job of it.

She couldn't even drive a car, but then, she had never felt the need to learn. As a vampire, she had been able to move faster than any motorized vehicle. But those days were gone. Perhaps, when she felt better, she would ask Logan to teach her. How hard could it be, anyway? After all, she couldn't expect him to drive her everywhere, nor did she like being dependent on him, or anyone else. As a vampire, she had done as she pleased, when she pleased. She had been self-sufficient then; it was time she regained her independence. Being able to drive would be a step in the right direction. Everyone did it, from pimply-faced teenagers to white-haired octogenarians. And she was going to be a mother now. Mothers drove their kids to the doctor, to school, to soccer games. She shied away from those images. She wasn't planning on keeping the baby, but she definitely needed to learn to drive. But not today.

Lost in an abyss of self-pity, she wasn't aware that Logan had returned until he sat down beside her. That, too, was scary for someone who had once been able to sense another's presence before they appeared.

"Are you all right?" he asked. "You look like you're about to cry."

The word *again* hung, unspoken, in the air between them.

"I am."

"What's wrong? Are you sick?"

"No, I'm just . . ." She shrugged. "Just hopelessly helpless."

"You're not hopeless. As for helpless . . . Honey, you just need to learn how to be human again." He lifted both hands in a gesture of surrender when she glowered at him. "I know, I know, you don't want to be human, but you'd better get used to the idea, at least for the time being. Are you taking your vitamins like a good girl and drinking lots of milk?"

"Yes," she replied sullenly.

Logan laughed. She sounded more like a petulant child than a woman who had lived for thousands of years, and then he sobered. Even though she had lived for centuries, she had been turned while she was still a young woman. Now that her powers were gone, she was that young woman again. Wiser than most, to be sure, but with the loss of her powers, she had also lost her arrogance. She was human now, with all the female ailments and foibles that Mara the vampire had shed years ago.

With a thoughtful sigh, he gathered her into his arms. Stroking her hair, he couldn't help missing the spoiled, strong-willed woman he had fallen in love with so many centuries ago.

Chapter Thirteen

Lou was waiting outside Ramsden's office building when Cindy got off work. Lou gave her sister a quick hug, and then they walked across the street to Cindy's favorite steakhouse.

"How was the drive?" Cindy asked after they had been seated.

"A breeze. How's Dwayne?"

"Working late, as always. I think I saw him more before we got married." Cindy's husband was a detective for the local police department. He had no idea that his fair-haired, diminutive wife was a vampire hunter, or that her employer was a vampire.

"Sorry, sis. So, what's the low-down on Mara? Is she really knocked-up, or were you just pulling my chain?"

"No, she's definitely pregnant," Cindy said. "About five months along by now. Amazing, isn't it? Ramsden's so excited, he's almost bouncing off the walls."

"I'll bet."

"He's fixing up a room in the basement. At first I thought it was a nursery, but now I think it's a delivery room. He hasn't confided in me, but I caught a few bits and pieces of a conversation he had with Susan before I left tonight. I think he's planning to keep the child for himself, if it lives."

"That doesn't bode well for the mother, does it?"

"No. I can't be sure . . ." Cindy fell silent as a waitress came to take their order. When she left, Cindy leaned forward. "As I was saying, I can't be sure, since I'm not privy to Ramsden's private files, but something's not right with Mara. I'm not sure what it is."

"What do you mean, not right? Is she sick?"

"I don't know. But something's out of whack, or she wouldn't be pregnant, would she?"

Lou nodded. That was true enough.

The waitress arrived with a basket of warm bread and their drink orders. "Your steaks will be right up."

Lou nodded her thanks as she buttered a slice of bread. "I could make a meal out of this."

"You and me both. So," Cindy said, reaching into the basket, "who do you think the father is? It can't be another vampire, can it?"

"I doubt it. It's got to be a mortal, and I think I know who he is."

"Who?"

"His name is Kyle Bowden. He hired me to find Mara. Just find her. Not stake her."

"You didn't agree to that, did you?"

"As a matter of fact, I did . . ."

"Lou, what were you thinking?"

"I was thinking that once I reunite him with Mara, the job is over and it's open season on Mara. It would be quite a coup, to take her head. And if it turns out that Bowden really is the father, then I'm thinking he'll have to be taken out of the picture, too."

"Of course," Cindy said. "But, well, what about the baby? You don't mean to kill it, too?"

Lou squared her shoulders. "A vampire is a vampire."

"But, Lou, a baby . . . I don't think . . ."

"Yeah, yeah, it's the old 'would you have killed Hitler when he was a baby' argument. I don't have an answer to that one, either." Lou blew out a breath. "I've got to find Mara first . . ."

"Lou, I know how you hate vampires. I do, too. But you can't kill an innocent child. It might not even be a vampire . . ."

"All right, all right!" Lou threw up her hands in surrender. "I won't do anything until the brat's born. But I'm not promising anything after that."

Chapter Fourteen

Mara sat on the sofa, watching a cooking show on the satellite screen. The chef was a plump, middle-aged woman with poufy brown hair and a strong New York accent. Judging from the woman's behavior, one would think that her every thought was about food and food preparation. In the last month, Mara had watched a number of cooking programs and home decorating shows in an effort to learn how to behave like a mortal woman. The truth was, as much as she enjoyed mortal food, she hated cooking, probably because she wasn't very good at it. So far, practically everything she had tried to prepare either came out woefully undercooked or burnt to a crisp. She didn't think she would ever get the hang of baking or frying or broiling. Of course, some of the directions and ingredients remained a mystery to her, reminding her that she needed to download a cookbook.

Logan watched her culinary attempts with amused forbearance. He praised her few successes and politely ignored the stink of her failures.

No, she definitely didn't like cooking. Far easier to order in, or go to one of the fast-food places for take-out.

Strangely, even though she no longer had a taste for blood, she missed the thrill of the hunt, the rapid beat of her prey's heart, the sense of power that came with holding another's life in her thrall.

With a sigh of exasperation, she switched off the screen. Was this how mortal women spent their days: cooking and cleaning and watching silly soap operas? She didn't like being human, didn't like being awake and active during the day. The sun was too bright, its light too warm. She had tried sleeping during the day so she could stay up late into the night and early morning with Logan, but her body refused to adjust. By midnight, she could scarcely keep her eyes open.

And she was bored. Even though Logan had a large house, it didn't take much effort to keep it clean. He was very tidy, for a man. He didn't leave his dirty socks on the floor, didn't expect her to pick up after him. Not that she would have minded, she thought wryly. It would have given her one more thing to do.

She glanced at the clock. It wasn't even four o'clock. Logan wouldn't be up for another two or three hours. Maybe she needed a mortal friend, someone to talk to. It was a totally foreign concept. Except for Cleopatra, she had never had a female friend. She'd had acquaintances, of course, but for most of her life, Mara had preferred the company of men.

And now she was living with one of the most handsome creatures—man or vampire—she had ever known. When she had been a vampire, mortal men had been drawn to her without knowing why. Attracting them had never been a problem. A smile, a come-hither look, and they had hurried to her side, eager to do her bidding, grateful for a kind word, a touch. Would men find her equally attractive now that she was human? She smiled, remembering the clerk and the box boy at the market. They had certainly enjoyed looking at her.

Curious, she went upstairs. In the bedroom, she removed her clothes and studied her reflection in the full-length mirror Logan had bought her. She was pretty, her skin clear, her hair long and thick and black, her eyes a deep, dark green beneath delicately arched brows. She fisted her hands on her hips and turned from side to side. Her figure, always slim, was just beginning to show the signs of pregnancy.

Was she as pretty as she had been when she wore the glamour of a vampire? Would Kyle think so?

Not wanting to dress again, she slipped into a pair of pajama bottoms and a soft cotton T-shirt and went downstairs. In the living room, she switched on the satellite screen, thinking how tiresome it was to have to use a remote device when she had once been able to operate the screen with little more than a thought.

She flipped through the channels until she found a romantic movie. She watched intently for several minutes and then turned it off. None of the silly ploys used in the movie would ever work on Logan. He wasn't a mortal man who could be manipulated by feminine wiles, but a powerful vampire. A vampire who was almost as powerful as she had once been.

Going to the window, she pulled back the heavy drapes and studied her reflection in the dark glass. The one thing she hadn't liked about being a vampire was her inability to see herself in a mirror. Now, she found herself staring at her image at every opportunity. As a vampire, she'd had her portrait painted every twenty-five years or so. The artists changed. The backgrounds changed, fashions changed, but she had always looked the same.

Lifting a hand to her cheek, she murmured, "I'm still pretty."

"You're more than pretty," confirmed a deep voice from behind her. "You're beautiful. More beautiful than any woman I've ever known."

His words filled her with warmth. "Thank you, Logan."

He moved closer, his arms sliding around her waist as he nuzzled the side of her neck. "So beautiful. I can't look at you without wanting to touch you, taste you, make love to you."

She leaned against him. There was something reassuring about the strength of his arms around her, something comforting in the way his breath caressed her cheek, the hard wall of his chest at her back. His hand slid over her hip, his fingers splaying over the swell of her belly.

"I've never been with a pregnant woman before," he said, his voice husky. "I find it incredibly sexy to think that you're carrying a new life. Think of it, Mara. You're doing something none of our kind has ever done before. I wish . . ."

She turned in his arms to face him. "What do you wish?"

"I wish it was mine."

She stared up at him. "Logan . . ."

"Pretty silly, huh?"

"No." Rising on her tiptoes, she kissed his cheek. "I wish it was yours, too," she whispered, and at that moment, she meant it. Logan wanted her. He didn't care if she was vampire or mortal. He had loved her when she was the world's most powerful vampire; he loved her now, when she was weak and helpless and afraid of what the future might hold.

She gazed deep into his eyes, eyes that smoldered with desire. He wanted her and right or wrong, she wanted him, needed him to restore her faith in herself. She thought briefly of Kyle. What was the point in yearning for a man who didn't want her? Would she be yearning for him if she had been the one to walk out? Maybe, like Scarlett O'Hara's determined pursuit of Ashley Wilkes, she only wanted Kyle because she couldn't have him.

Logan caressed her cheek, calling her back to the present. He was here now, and he loved her, had loved her for centuries. She didn't know what she would have done without him these past months. True, he could be bossy and overbearing, but no matter what she said or how badly she behaved, she knew Logan would never turn his back on her.

"Mara." His gaze searched hers. Slowly, giving her plenty of time to turn away, he lowered his head and claimed her lips with his. His kiss was tentative. Not a demand, but a request. When she didn't pull away, he deepened the kiss, until his need, his desire, were her own. His tongue tangled with hers, sending heat straight to her very center.

She groaned softly. She should pull away, tell him no, but her body refused to obey her mind. She tried to summon Kyle's image, but the touch of Logan's mouth on hers drove away every other thought, every other desire except her need for Logan. His hands spanned her hips, drawing her against his erection and she leaned into him, her breasts crushed against his chest, her arms wrapped around his neck. Like a bit of flotsam caught in the ocean at flood tide, she was helpless to resist the desires of her own heart, the longing that burned away every thought but one.

Swinging her up into his arms, he carried her into his bedroom, his mouth never leaving hers. Placing her on the bed, he continued to kiss her as his hands, his quick clever hands, made short work of their clothing.

And then he was lying beside her, his dark eyes burning into her own. "Do you know how many times I've dreamed of this? Of having you here, in my bed, in my arms?"

His hand slid beneath her head, his fingers threading through her hair as his mouth descended on hers once again. There was no gentleness in this kiss, only the hunger of a man who loved a woman to distraction and was afraid he would lose her again, all too soon.

His mouth plundered hers. He was the predator and she was prey and he drank from her lips as he longed to drink her life's essence. His body trembled with the effort to hold back. Reining in his desire, he kissed and caressed her as he murmured love words to her in a dozen languages.

Mara moaned with pleasure as his touch reawakened places within her that no other man had ever stirred. She murmured his name, her hands skimming restlessly over his back, his shoulders. She ran her teeth along his neck, tears burning her eyes as she trembled on the brink.

"Logan . . ." She whispered his name. "Now, Logan . . ."

She clung to him, weeping softly as his body merged with hers, sweeping her away to another place, another time, when he had been her willing slave and she had been the queen of her world . . .

She came back to earth slowly, her face buried in the hollow of Logan's shoulder, more confused than she had ever been in her life. If she truly loved Kyle, how could she find such pleasure, such contentment, in Logan's arms? Of course, Logan wasn't an ordinary man. She tried to tell herself that she had been helpless to resist him, that he had seduced her with his innate charm and preternatural power, but she knew it wasn't so. He had wanted her and she had wanted him. It was as simple as that.

She stared up at the ceiling, wondering again if it was

possible to be in love with two men at the same time. It wasn't, she decided. It was just that Kyle's leaving had wounded her pride, made her doubt her femininity. She had been feeling vulnerable and alone and she had turned to Logan for comfort and reassurance, or maybe making love to Logan was her way of getting back at Kyle for leaving her. Whatever the reason, it had been wonderful, comfortable, familiar. No doubt she would feel guilty tomorrow, she thought, but for now . . .

"Oh!" Sitting up, she splayed her fingers over her belly.

"What is it?" Logan asked. "Are you in pain?"

"The baby . . ." She looked at him, her eyes wide with wonder. "It moved." She grabbed his hand and placed it over her stomach. "Can you feel that?"

Logan swore softly as he felt a faint flutter beneath his hand. Mara's child, alive and kicking. It was the most miraculous thing he had ever experienced. "Does it hurt?"

"No," she replied, her voice tinged with awe. "It feels . . . amazing."

She had never looked more beautiful to him than she did in that moment, with her cheeks flushed with excitement and her eyes filled with wonder. And he had never been more envious of a mortal than he was of Kyle Bowden.

"I'm really pregnant," she said, slipping back down beside him. "Logan, I'm going to be a mother."

"Yes," he muttered dryly. "I know."

She had bought a calendar a few days ago and penciled in the due date the doctor had given her. Until now, it had stood for the day when this part of her nightmare would be over and she could pursue her dream of becoming a vampire again. But now it meant so much more. For the first time, the child she carried was more than an inconvenience. It was real, a living being growing inside of her.

Logan put his arms around her and drew her close to his side. Gazing into her eyes, he felt his throat thicken with emotion. In all the years since she had turned him, he had never looked back, never lamented the life he had lost. The most miserable people he knew were those who were forever looking backward, longing for something they could never recapture. He had accepted being a vampire along with everything it entailed but now, seeing the joy in Mara's eyes, he regretted the fact that he would never know the thrill of holding a child of his own.

"A baby," she murmured. "We'll have a baby in October."

Logan grunted softly, and then he chuckled. "If it's a vampire, it's gotta be born on Halloween."

"I don't see how it can be a vampire," Mara said, her brow furrowed. "Kyle is human, and I must have been more human than vampire when I conceived."

"I guess so," Logan said. "But I'm still hoping she comes on Halloween."

"She?" she asked, poking him in the ribs.

Logan shrugged. "Or he." He kissed her, his hands delving into her hair, loving the way the silky strands curled around his fingers. He had never known a woman with such beautiful hair. He took a deep breath, inhaling the musky scent of her skin. That quickly, he wanted her again.

"It's a boy. I just know it," she said, smiling. "Can we go to the bookstore?"

"Why?"

"I need to buy some books on child rearing and cooking and . . . everything!"

His hand slid along the curve of her breast. "Now?"

"Yes, now! I have so much to learn."

"You can find it all online tomorrow."

"I don't like reading on the computer."

"Mara . . ."

But she wasn't listening. She was already out of bed, pulling on her discarded clothing, looking for her shoes.

With a sigh, Logan went into the bathroom. Before they went anywhere, he needed a shower. The colder, the better.

Chapter Fifteen

Rane paused in the shadows, taking a moment to enjoy the quiet beauty of the night before he returned home. It was late. Savanah and the baby had been sleeping peacefully when he'd left the house to go hunting. His prey had been a woman in her mid-forties. He had found her walking aimlessly down a dark, deserted street, the picture of despair.

Her grief-stricken countenance and slumped shoulders had tugged at his heart. After mesmerizing her, he had eased his hunger, then escorted her into a bar where, after releasing her from his thrall, he had bought her a drink and listened to her tale of woe. She had recently lost her teenage daughter in a car accident. Her husband had left her for a younger woman. She was contemplating suicide. Though he rarely interfered in the lives of his prey, he had mesmerized her again; then, speaking to her mind, he had assured her that her life wasn't over, that, in time, her pain would ease, that the day would come when she would be able to smile again when she thought of her daughter. He assured her that she was better off without her husband, that she would find love again. Searching his pockets, he had given her all the money he had, released her from his spell, and sent her on her way.

He was almost home when a ripple in the air told him he was about to have company; moments later his brother and his father materialized on the street beside him.

"Looking for me?" Rane asked.

"As a matter of fact, we were," Rafe said. "It's been a long time since the three of us spent any time together without our womenfolk."

"So, what's wrong?" Rane asked.

"I heard a rumor about Mara," Vince said.

Rane glanced from his father to his brother and back again. "What kind of rumor?"

"That she's no longer one of us," Vince said.

Rane swore softly. "Where did you hear that?"

"A friend of mine heard it from a friend who heard it from someone in Nevada. I guess it's supposed to be a secret, but you can't keep a secret like that."

"No longer Nosferatu," Rafe muttered with a shake of his head. "How could that happen?"

"Beats me," Rane said.

"You don't suppose Edna and Pearl are working on another cure, do you?" Rafe asked, referring to a couple of elderly female vampire hunters. During the War, they had concocted a drug they had hoped would cure the werewolves and restore the vampires to their human state whether they wished it or not. He and his wife, Kathy, had been a part of those heinous experiments. They had escaped with their lives. Others hadn't been so lucky. It had been in Rafe's mind to kill them both when he found them, but he just couldn't bring himself to kill two old ladies. Instead, he had forced the Dark Gift on Edna and Pearl. At the time he had thought of it as poetic justice.

"Hell and damnation, I hope not," Vince said.

"Well, they weren't happy when I brought them across," Rafe said, remembering how they had struggled against him when they realized what he intended to do. "Could be they've come up with another cure. One that works."

"Well, at the moment, that's neither here nor there," Vince said. He started walking, and Rafe and Rane fell in on either side of him. "We need to find out if the rumor about Mara is true." He shook his head. "How could it have happened?"

"I don't know how it happened," Rane said. "And I don't know if she's human again, but she came to see me a few months ago." He paused, knowing he was about to betray a confidence. "She told me she was changing, losing her powers. She was scared."

"Mara, scared?" Rafe shook his head. "I don't believe it."

"And you didn't think that little piece of news was important enough to share with the rest of the family?" Vince asked.

"She made me promise not to tell anyone."

"Well, I can understand that," Rafe said. "She must be feeling vulnerable as hell."

Rane nodded. "She was supposed to keep in touch with me, but I haven't heard from her since."

"Have you tried calling her?" Vince asked.

"No."

"Why the hell not?"

"He's been busy, what with Savanah and the new baby and all," Rafe said, coming to his brother's defense.

Vince shook his head. Practically from the day they had been born, his sons had stood up for each other. Adulthood hadn't changed that.

"I think the rumors must be true," Rafe said. "I tried to find her not long ago, but the bond between us was gone like it never existed."

Vince swore softly. "I only told you half of it. There's more."

Rane frowned. "What do you mean, more?"

"I also heard she's pregnant. The idea is ludicrous and I dismissed it out of hand, but now . . ."

"If she's human," Rafe said, "she could be pregnant. Shoot, if it's true, anything is possible."

Vince nodded. "We need to find out, one way or the other. I'll talk to my friend and see if he's heard any more."

Rafe grunted thoughtfully. "If it's not just a rumor, I'll bet Edna and Pearl would love to know how Mara regained her humanity."

"I don't think so," Rane said. "Last I heard, they were both pretty happy about being vampires."

"Really?" Rafe asked. If Kathy hadn't been there at the time, he likely would have killed the two women when he'd had the chance. Bringing them across had seemed a fitting punishment for their crimes at the time. He hadn't figured on their embracing the vampire lifestyle.

Rane shrugged. "It happens."

"I guess it's not surprising," Rafe mused. "If I hadn't brought them across, they'd most likely have died of old age by now."

"We need to keep this business about Mara under wraps as best we can," Vince said, getting back to the subject at hand. "Mara's made some enemies in her time. If she's lost her powers, this would be the perfect time for those who hate her to try to get even. If either of you hear anything, let me know."

Rafe nodded. "Will do."

Rane blew out a ragged breath. Why was nothing in life ever easy? Some days, he wished he could mutter a few magic words and make the rest of the world disappear.

Chapter Sixteen

Mara sat on the examining table while Dr. Ramsden listened to her heart, then took her blood pressure. Earlier, he had examined her and ordered more blood work.

"So, is everything all right?" She had intended to make future appointments with a human doctor, but Logan had talked her out of it. Even if she was fully human, he'd argued, the baby might be a vampire. No human doctor would be prepared for that. After thinking it over, she had agreed with him.

Ramsden nodded. "So far, so good. Your vital signs are normal."

"For a mortal, you mean?"

He smiled sympathetically. "Yes, for a mortal."

"And the baby?"

"Growing as expected."

He glanced at her chart. "You, on the other hand, are growing a little more than you should," he remarked, flipping through his notes. "You shouldn't be gaining more than a couple of pounds a week."

Mara shifted on the edge of the table. She had been eating way too many sweets, but she couldn't seem to help it. Whenever she was worried or depressed, which was often, she reached for something covered in chocolate.

"What's your diet like?" Ramsden asked.

She shrugged, too embarrassed to tell him that she favored chocolate over broccoli, and cheeseburgers and fries over salad.

He frowned thoughtfully. "Eating must be an interesting experience after so long."

"Yes, it is."

"I don't even remember what food tasted like," he mused. "Are cheeseburgers as good as they look?"

She nodded.

"Tell me, what it's like, eating solid food again? My last meal as a human was black beans and brown bread. Hardly noteworthy."

"It's . . . I guess 'interesting' would be the best way to describe it. There's so much to choose from, so many textures and flavors unheard of in my time, or yours." You could spend thirty minutes in the store just trying to decide on what kind of bread to buy—white or whole wheat, potato or rye, cinnamon with raisins, or Hawaiian. Not to mention bagels and buns and muffins in mind-boggling varieties.

"I should have thought to recommend a book on nutrition." Ramsden pulled his prescription pad from his coat pocket and jotted down the title of a well-known book on dieting and pregnancy. "You might want to pick up a copy of this on your way home, or look for it online. And try to get some exercise." Tearing the sheet from the pad, he handed it to her. "I'll want to see you again in six weeks." He made a notation on her chart. "Have you given any thought to moving here, at least for the time being?"

"No, why?"

He lifted one brow. "Because your doctor is here."

Of course. Why hadn't she thought of that?

"You remember I told you it might be necessary to hospitalize you during the last trimester?"

She nodded, though spending three months in bed was the last thing she wanted. Of course, if she could spend it in bed with Logan, it wouldn't be so bad. "Do you think that's going to be necessary?"

"No, but I'd like you close by, just in case." At her worried expression, he patted her arm reassuringly. "I don't want to worry you unnecessarily, but you need to be prepared for . . ."

"For what?"

"For complications," he said. "As far as I can tell, everything is as it should be, but due to your past, there could be problems. You understand?"

She placed her hand over her stomach, reassured when she felt the baby move.

"The way things look now, I don't see any need for bed rest. Assuming nothing changes, I'd suggest you arrange to be here no later than the end of September. I'd like you close by during that last month. First babies often come early, and with your history"—he shrugged—"better safe than sorry."

Mara nodded. She had hoped to find a doctor in Los Angeles, but qualified vampire doctors were few and far between; in case of an emergency, she wanted a doctor who knew about her preternatural background.

"So, how'd it go?" Logan asked when she entered the waiting room.

"He said everything's fine." She refused to think that something might go wrong. With every day that passed, the baby she carried became more real, more important.

"How would you feel about moving to Nevada in a month or two?"

Logan frowned, then grunted softly. "I guess it would be a good idea, wouldn't it? I'll see about finding us a place to live."

Mara stared at the date on the newspaper. July third. It was her birthday, an event she hadn't thought of or celebrated since Dendar had brought her across all those centuries ago. Counting only her mortal life time, she was twenty-one years old today. Twenty-one, unmarried, and pregnant. It would have been a scandal in days gone by. She remembered when girls who had the misfortune to get pregnant out of wedlock were locked away, or sent out of town to stay with a relative until the baby was born. These days, it was no big deal. Girls went to school pregnant; they even took their babies to school with them. Morality seemed to have gotten lost somewhere along the way, along with so many other values that were now viewed as old-fashioned and out-of-date. All in all, she thought mankind had been more civilized back in the early twentieth century. Certainly human values today were not what they once had been.

Mara placed a hand on her swollen abdomen. What kind of world would her child grow up in? She had been excited the night she felt the baby's first kick. She had gone to the bookstore and bought a dozen books on childbirth and child rearing and read them avidly, her excitement waning from one page to the next as the reality of what she was facing dampened her enthusiasm. Parenting was an awesome responsibility. She could barely take care of herself these days. How could she raise a child? She had never had a loving home, but she wanted one for her son or daughter. Perhaps Dr. Ramsden could help her find a suitable couple to adopt her child.

With a sigh, Mara gazed out the window. Her son or daughter would never know her. Perhaps she could write a letter to be given to her child when it was old enough to understand why she'd had to give it up. Or, better yet, perhaps she would write the story of her life. If it did nothing else, it would provide her with something to do until the baby was born.

Excited by the idea, she booted up the computer, then sat there, staring at the blank screen. How to begin? At the beginning, of course. The words flowed as she described her early years, the time she had spent as a slave in Pharaoh's household, Dendar's appearance in her cell, her awakening in the *per nefer*, the room where mummies were made.

Mara paused, wondering if she should describe the process used for making mummies. It was a rather grisly undertaking, one that took seventy days to complete. The chief embalmer, known as the *hery seshta,* wore a jackal mask to represent Anubis, the god of mummification. He had assistants known as the *wetyu.* After the organs were removed from the corpse and dried, they were placed in special containers called *canopic* jars. In the afterlife, the various parts of the body would come together again and the deceased would again be whole. Once all the organs were removed, the body was washed with wine and rubbed with spices and then it was left to dry for forty days. After the body was fully dried, it was adorned with jewelry and then wrapped in a linen shroud and bound with strips of linen.

After the mummy was wrapped, it was fitted with a mask fashioned in the likeness of the deceased so the *ka,* or spirit, would recognize itself in mummy form. The masks of kings had been made of gold; the masks of lesser mortals had been made of wood and painted gold. Slaves weren't customarily mummified, but Shakir had been a wealthy man and he had wanted to take his slaves, all of them, into the afterlife with him. If it hadn't been for Dendar, she would now be lying in Shakir's tomb.

Mara glanced over her shoulder as Logan entered the room. He had fed recently. It showed in the lingering glow in his eyes, the added color in his cheeks.

He smiled when he saw her. "What are you doing there?" Coming up behind her, he placed his hands on her shoulders and looked over her head at the screen. "What is this?"

"I'm writing my life story. I thought I'd give it to whoever adopts my baby and . . ."

"You've decided not to keep it?"

"Yes. As I was saying, they can give it to him when he's grown. Maybe it will help him understand who I was and why I had to give him away."

"It might be a girl, you know."

"No, it's a boy. I'm sure of it. Do you think Dr. Ramsden could help me with the adoption?"

"Are you sure about this? I mean, it's kind of sudden, isn't it?"

"I think it would be best for the baby. Don't you?"

"I don't know, Mara. This has to be your decision, but if you're sure it's what you want, why not ask Rane and Savanah if they'd like to adopt him? That way you could see him—or her—whenever you want."

"Of course," Mara said, wondering why she hadn't thought of it herself. She considered Rane and his kin as family. Who better to raise her child? Her son and Rane's daughter would grow up as brother and sister. "I'll go see him tomorrow night . . ." Her words trailed off. She could no longer will herself to Porterville. She looked up at Logan. "Will you drive me?"

"How about if I take you there, vampire-style?"

"I'd like that," she said wistfully. She missed her preternatural powers more with every passing day, missed her old life and all that it had entailed.

"Tomorrow night, then," Logan said. "Will it be a problem, my being there?"

"I don't think so." Vampires were notoriously territorial, but she was sure that, since Logan was her friend, he would be welcome in Cordova territory.

The thought of seeing Rane again filled her with excitement, but it was short-lived. She had always been the strong one, the Queen of the Vampires. How would Rane and his family feel about her when they learned her powers were gone? Would they look at her with pity, or with contempt?

Rising from the computer, she looked up at Logan. "I don't think I can face them."

"Why not?"

"Because I . . . because he's . . . they're . . ."

"Ah," Logan murmured. "You're embarrassed because you're no longer one of them." He stroked her cheek. "One of us."

She nodded. "I was always the one in control. Now I'm . . . prey."

Muttering an oath, Logan drew her into his arms. "Stop that! I've never met any of the Cordova vampires, but from what you've told me, they're not going to feel any different about you. And I'll be there to protect you, just in case I'm wrong."

Mara wrapped her arms around his waist. "You're so good to me, Logan, and so good for me," she murmured, and wondered again why she had ever left him.

* * *

Logan and Mara left for Rane's home just after dusk the following evening. For Mara, being whisked through the air while under someone else's power was a new experience. As a vampire, it was exhilarating; as a human, it made her feel queasy and a little dizzy. She added it to the long list of things she didn't like about being human.

When they arrived at Rane's house, Mara took a deep breath, then knocked on the front door, wondering what Rane and Savanah would think when they saw her. The fact that she was pregnant was clearly evident now.

Rane smiled when he saw her standing on the porch. "Mara! This is a surprise," he said enthusiastically.

Rane's expression sobered when he saw Logan standing behind her and recognized him for what he was. Even without her preternatural senses, Mara was aware of the way the two men sized each other up, like two feral wolves meeting for the first time.

"This is my friend Logan," Mara said quickly. "I hope you'll make him welcome."

Rane nodded. "Of course. I'm pleased to meet you. Come in." Rane tried not to stare at Mara as she entered the house. It had been one thing to hear she might be pregnant, quite another to see the truth of it with his own eyes.

Mara preceded Logan and Rane into the living room. Savanah was sitting in a rocking chair with Abbey in her arms. The baby looked pink and perfect.

Rane introduced Logan to his wife and invited Mara and Logan to sit down. Mara didn't have to be a mind reader to know that Rane and Savanah had both noticed she was pregnant but were too polite to mention it.

"So, Mara," Rane asked, taking a seat across from the sofa, "what brings you here?"

Mara placed her hand over her stomach. "I need to ask you a favor," she said, "a rather large favor."

"Sure, anything," he said. "You know that."

"I'm going to have a baby at the end of October, and I'd like you and Savanah to adopt it."

So, Rane thought. It was true. Frowning, he looked at Logan. "Are you . . . ?"

"Of course not," Logan replied.

"How did this happen?" Rane asked, unable to hide his astonishment.

"The usual way," Mara replied dryly.

"But . . ."

"I don't know how it happened. The doctor doesn't know. It just"—she made a vague gesture with her hand—"happened."

Rane looked thoughtful for a moment, then said, "It's Kyle's, isn't it?"

"Yes, but he doesn't know, and I don't want him to."

"Don't you think he has a right to know?" Rane asked. "I'm not sure what went wrong between the two of you, but he's been here a couple of times trying to find you. I think he still loves you."

"He thinks I'm a monster."

"Well, you're not anymore," Rane pointed out.

"I don't want to talk about Kyle," Mara said flatly. "He has no part of this."

"Why don't you keep the baby?" Savanah asked, hugging her daughter closer.

Mara shook her head. "I don't know how to be a mother."

"No one does, until it happens," Savanah said, smiling. "You should at least give it a try."

"I don't know." Mara's gaze settled on Abbey. She had never wanted children, never thought to have any of her own. Just then, her baby gave a lusty kick. Placing her hand over her abdomen, Mara felt the first stirring of love for the child she carried. Maybe she could be a good mother. And she didn't have to stay mortal forever. Once her baby was grown, she could ask Logan or one of the Cordova men to make her a vampire again.

"If you decide motherhood isn't for you, Rane and I will be happy to raise your child, won't we, Rane?"

"Sure." He smiled at his wife and daughter and then returned his attention to Mara. "I think Savanah's right. You should at least give it a try before you decide. Have you told anyone else?"

"No."

"All right, then," Rane said, "we'll keep it that way if it's what you want."

"I suppose you can tell Rafe and the rest of your family, but no one else."

"A baby," Savanah said, smiling. "I think it's wonderful. Oh, we'll have to give you a shower! I'll talk to Kathy . . ."

Mara stared at Savanah. "No. I don't think . . ."

"Just for our immediate family," Savanah said. "It'll be fun. Maybe we'll even let the guys come and we'll make a party out of it. What do you say?"

"I don't know. I'll have to think about it."

Later that night, back at Logan's house, Mara weighed the pros and cons of keeping the baby while she lingered in the bathtub. The more she thought about it, the more excited she became. Maybe keeping the baby wouldn't be such a bad thing. She had spent most of her life alone, afraid to trust anyone, afraid to let anyone get too close. But the baby, *her* baby, would be a living, breathing part of her, someone she could love unconditionally. Someone who would love her in return. Someone who would need her day and night for years to come. Years ago, she had asked Roshan what it had been like, raising a human child. He had thought about it for a moment, and then said, "Interesting."

Mara grinned as she reached for the soap. Right now, interesting sounded pretty darn good.

Mara grew more and more dependent on Logan as the days went by. She had no mortal friends and even though she had known Roshan and Brenna for years and considered them and their descendants as family, she couldn't help feeling inferior, and even embarrassed, when she was with them. She knew it was foolish, but she couldn't help it. Strangely, she didn't feel that way with Logan, probably because she had known him for so long, or maybe because he made her feel safe, protected. Loved.

Mara thought of Kyle from time to time. Too bad she hadn't met him now, when she was mortal. The cad. He had said he loved her, but it had been a lie. Far better to be loved than to love, she mused. It certainly hurt less.

She shook his image from her mind. She would not think of him now.

Earlier, Logan had dropped her off at the mall to shop while he went hunting. She had bought some much-needed maternity clothes and then wandered through the baby section of a department store. She hadn't meant to buy anything, but the blankets were so soft and pretty, the sleepers so cute, the booties so tiny, she just couldn't resist, and before she knew it, she had spent over three hundred dollars.

Logan whistled softly when he picked her up half an

hour later. "What'd you do, buy out the store? How many maternity outfits can one woman wear?"

"It's not all for me, silly. I bought a few things for the baby."

"A few!" he exclaimed as he stowed her bags in the trunk of the car. "Looks like you've got enough junk here for a dozen kids."

"I couldn't help it. Everything was so cute and"—she shrugged—"I never did have any willpower when it came to shopping."

"I found a place for us in Nevada," Logan informed her on the way home. "It's in a little town called Tyler, about ten minutes from Ramsden's office. It's not as big as my place, but it'll do for a few months. We can move in anytime you're ready."

They moved into the house in Nevada the first week in September. Located at the end of a quiet, tree-lined street, it was probably the last place anyone would think to look for her. Not that there was anything wrong with the house. It was just so ordinary, from the bland beige walls and carpets to the unremarkable furnishings, but these days she didn't take much interest in her surroundings. Logan had offered to redecorate the place, but she lacked both the desire and the energy.

Logan had been the soul of patience since they had moved. He put up with her moods and her bad temper, rubbed her aching back and her feet, held her when she cried, and assured her that everything would be all right.

One Friday night in late September he decided she needed to get out of the house. Turning a deaf ear to her protests, he gathered her close to his side and transported them to Reno. The arch over Virginia Street proclaimed Reno to be "the biggest little city in the world."

Mara frowned at him as they materialized at the end of the town. "What are we doing here?"

"I thought we could both use a change of scene. Come on." Taking her by the hand, he led her down the street.

Reno, which was named for Union officer Major Jesse L. Reno, had started life as a mining community back in the 1800s. Mara recalled spending a few days in the town back in the 1930s. At that time, the city had been famous for its liberal divorce laws and legalized gambling, both of which had helped to create its economic boom. At one time, it had been the gambling capital of the country, but that had changed with the growth of Las Vegas and casinos owned by Native American tribes. Still, it was an exciting place.

The city had certainly changed since the last time she had seen it. The casinos she had once visited, like the Nevada Club, Harold's Club, and the Palace were gone; the Comstock, the Sundowner, and the Virginian, were closed. Some had been turned into condos. Now, there were newer, larger, grander hotel/casinos like the Atlantis and the Peppermill. Even without her preternatural senses, she could hear the excited cries of gamblers hitting the jackpot as she passed by one of the smaller casinos.

"Care to try your luck?" Logan asked.

Mara shrugged. "Sure, why not?"

They decided on the El Dorado Casino, simply because Mara liked the name. Hand in hand, they walked through the casino, trying to decide which game to play.

Logan's hand tightened on hers as they passed a blackjack table. She looked up at him and then, following his narrowed-eyed gaze, felt a shock of recognition when she locked gazes with the dealer. Ed Rogen. She hadn't seen him in over a hundred and fifty years, but there was no mistaking him for anyone else.

Rogen recognized her, as well. Hatred flared in the depths of his pale blue eyes. Leaning forward, he whispered something to a voluptuous red-haired woman sitting at the end of the table. The woman glanced over her shoulder, looked Mara up and down, and then said something to Rogen.

"Is he someone you know?" Logan asked quietly.

"Yes."

"Not a friend, I take it."

"No." She tugged on Logan's arm. "Let's go."

Out on the sidewalk, her heart pounding, Mara took several deep breaths. Ed Rogen. The last thing he had ever said to her was that, one day, he would destroy her. Judging by the ominous glint in his eyes, he hadn't changed his mind.

"What the hell did you do to him?" Logan asked, and then answered his own question. "You turned him against his will, didn't you?"

"Yes." Looking back, she realized how thoughtlessly cruel and heartless she had been. She had never asked any of her fledglings if they *wanted* the Dark Gift. She had bestowed it upon those she cared for and when she tired of them, she had severed her connection to them and moved on. How many of them still existed? As a vampire, facing her enemies hadn't been a matter of concern. Confident and uncaring, she could have easily destroyed them all. It hadn't mattered how many were left; now, stripped of her powers, she had no way of knowing which ones still existed. In the way of vampires, they would have changed their names through the centuries. She was the only one, of all the vampires she had known, who had stubbornly and arrogantly refused to change her name. She had been Mara, Queen of the Vampires. Back then, it had been a name to be reckoned with. Now, for the first time, she wondered if she should take on a new identity.

"You're trembling," Logan said. "Are you cold?"

"No." Not cold, she thought, only afraid. Not for her own life, but for that of her unborn child.

"Come on," Logan said, "let's go get a room."

After registering at the Peppermill, Logan settled Mara into a hot bath, hoping it would relax her. He had been a fool to bring her here. This close to the baby's birth, he should have known better. She tired easily these days. He could have just taken her to a movie, but no, he had wanted to take her out and show her off. Pregnant or not, she was the most beautiful woman in the world, and he was proud to be seen with her. One thing he had never expected was to run into one of her fledglings. He had seen the hatred in the other vampire's eyes, smelled it on his skin.

Logan swore softly. He could understand the other vampire's hostility. It was a terrible thing, to be turned against one's will, to lose everything you knew, everything you loved, to a woman's whim. He, himself, might have hated Mara if the circumstances had been different, if he'd had a decent life, a home, a family. But even as the thought crossed his mind, he knew it wasn't true. It wouldn't have mattered. Even knowing how quickly she would tire of him, he would gladly have given up anything, everything, to be with Mara. It had been true then; it was true now.

He would order her something to eat and then take her home, where she belonged.

* * *

Mara reclined in the tub, her eyes closed. She didn't think she would ever get over the shock of seeing Rogen, or forget the hatred smoldering in the depths of his eyes. The last time she had seen him, he had been mining for gold in Virginia City. Back then, Reno had been nothing but a small community that had grown up alongside a toll bridge that connected Virginia City and the California Trail. The bridge had been built by Charles Fuller in 1859. Two years later, Fuller sold the bridge to Myron Lake, who added a kiln, a grist mill, and a livery stable. When he wasn't mining for gold, Rogen had worked at the stable.

Mara recalled deciding to take a moonlight ride late one summer night. She had cajoled Ed into lending her a horse, and then invited him to come along. She'd had her eye on him for weeks, admiring the flex of his muscles as he curried the horses or mucked the stalls, wondering what it would be like to feel his strong, work-roughened hands moving over her flesh.

Like all men, he had been powerless to resist her once she had decided she wanted him.

They had ridden out under the stars. Later, they had stopped alongside the river and there, in the lush grass in the light of a full moon, she had let him seduce her. He had been boyish and charming and completely smitten with her, totally unaware that it was she who was doing the seducing.

One night, when she was bored and hungry, she had brought him across. When he rose the next night, he had been confused by what had happened, and then furious. Overcome with rage and a hunger he couldn't control, he had vented his anger on the town, leaving Mara to clean up the mess he left in his wake. When his temper was again under control, she had tried to appease him and when he refused to listen, she had turned her back on him, as she had so many others.

Thinking of it now filled her with guilt. How could she have been so callous? With a sigh, she stepped out of the tub and reached for a towel. Would he listen to her now? Would he accept her apology? Recalling the animosity she had seen in his eyes, she thought it unlikely.

She was drying off when Rogen materialized between her and the bathroom door. With a startled gasp, Mara hugged the towel to her chest.

"I see you remember me," Rogen said, his pale eyes glinting malevolently.

"Of course." She glanced past him to the door, wishing her mind was still linked to Logan's. If she called for him, could he make it into the bathroom before Rogen killed her?

Rogen took a step forward. "I knew if I survived long enough, one day I'd find you again."

She opened her mouth to speak, but he clapped his hand over it, forestalling her.

"Shut up!" he hissed. "I don't want to hear anything you've got to say. You took my life, and now I'm going to take yours." Frowning, he leaned closer, his nostrils flaring, his eyes filled with confusion. "Mara?"

She felt a rush of hope. Since she no longer smelled like a vampire, he wasn't sure of her identity. She thought of lying, of telling him that he had the wrong woman, but her pride wouldn't let her. Instead, she lifted her chin and squared her shoulders, wishing, as she did so, that she was wearing something more dignified than a towel.

Dropping his hand from her mouth, Rogen took a deep breath. "What's happened to you?"

"Nothing," she replied imperiously. "Get out of my way."

"What are you gonna do if I don't?" Rogen asked with a sneer.

"Maybe you should ask what *I'm* going to do."

Rogen tensed visibly at the sound of Logan's voice coming from behind him. Hands clenched at his sides, Rogen slowly turned around. "Are you the poor fool who's fighting her battles now?"

"Sure looks that way."

"Okay by me," Rogen said, cracking his knuckles. "First you, then her."

Logan snorted softly. "You think you can take me?"

"Damn right!"

Mara glanced from one man to the other. Rogen had always been quick with his fists. In the old days, he'd had quite a reputation as a bare-knuckles boxer. He was perhaps two inches taller and fifty pounds heavier than Logan, but it wasn't size that made the difference when vampires fought. It was age. Vampires grew stronger and more powerful as they grew older. Rogen had been a vampire for a hundred and fifty years; Logan had seven hundred and fifty years on him.

"Let's take it outside," Logan said, jerking his chin toward the door. "I don't want to have to clean up the mess."

Rogen made a derogatory sound deep in his throat. "When I get finished with you, there won't be anything left to clean up."

Mara laid her hand on Logan's shoulder. "Logan . . ."

"You'd better kiss your pretty boy good-bye," Rogen said, "'cause after tonight, you'll never see him again." His gaze moved over her. "After I settle this, you and me are gonna have a little talk."

Rogen's gaze swung to Logan. "I'll be waiting out back," he said, and vanished in a cloud of dark gray motes.

Logan drew Mara into his arms, his hands sliding up and down her bare back. "I won't be gone long." He kissed her once, hard and quick, and then he, too, vanished from sight.

Mara pressed a hand to her heart. Logan was older, stronger. There was nothing to worry about. So why was she suddenly so afraid?

Chapter Seventeen

Logan faced Rogen across six feet of barren ground on the outskirts of the city. He couldn't remember the last time he had battled another of the Undead.

Logan circled Rogen warily, all his senses alert. His tongue brushed his fangs. He wasn't afraid for his own life. He wasn't afraid of whatever fate awaited him on the other side of eternity. He had lived a good long life, and lived it on his own terms. He had no regrets. But this was a fight he had to win, not for his own sake, but for Mara's, and for the sake of the baby she carried. He had no doubt that if Rogen were victorious, he would go back to the hotel and kill Mara without a qualm, and her child with her.

And with that thought in mind, Logan summoned his power, lowered his head, and attacked.

Fangs bared, nails like claws, Rogen met him head on. The coppery scent of fresh blood rose on the night wind as they slashed at each other.

It was a quiet and bloody battle, one Logan knew could last well into the night unless one of them suffered a killing wound. Rogen's minor injuries healed almost immediately, as did Logan's.

Despite his size, Rogen was light on his feet. And he was eager for battle, certain of victory.

Logan danced sideways as Rogen darted toward him, his fangs bared. Spinning around, Logan grabbed Rogen by the back of his shirt and gave a good, hard yank. Rogen stumbled backward, momentarily off balance. Moving swiftly, Logan kicked out, sweeping Rogen's feet out from under him. With a startled cry, Rogen fell backward and hit the ground, hard.

Logan was relishing an imminent victory when he sensed the approach of others. Out of the corner of his eye, he saw a dark swirling mist moving rapidly toward him. A low growl rose in his throat as the mist got thicker, darker, taking on shape and substance, until four men materialized in its place.

Vampires all. Their combined power charged the air like the electrical energy that preceded a storm.

Rogen scrambled to his feet, a smug expression on his face.

Logan glared at him. "Afraid to fight me on your own?" he asked, his voice laced with contempt.

"I came to win." Rogen wiped the blood from his face and licked it off his hands.

Logan swore under his breath. One on one, he could whip any vampire who came against him, but five to one?

He backed away as the five Nosferatu stalked toward him. It was like a scene from some bad horror movie: five fanged, red-eyed monsters advancing toward the hero. Logan grunted softly. In a movie, someone would have come to the hero's aid. In his case, no help would be forthcoming.

He could have vanished from their sight, but he stood

his ground. Leaving now might save him for the moment, but he knew that, sooner or later, there would be another confrontation. Now that Rogen knew Mara had lost her powers, he wouldn't rest until he had avenged himself on her, or he was dead.

Deciding to carry the battle to the enemy, Logan bared his fangs and charged. It startled Rogen and the others, but only for a moment.

Logan's last thought before they surrounded him was for Mara, and then there was no time for thought as they tore into him, literally and figuratively.

Logan summoned every ounce of strength he possessed but it wasn't enough. Would never be enough. The five vampires circled him, growling like rabid wolves. Singly and in pairs, they darted in to bite and slash, and while he defended himself against those in front, others attacked from his rear, gradually wearing him down. One of them, a vampire wearing a bright red shirt, came in low and fast, his fangs opening a long wicked gash down Logan's left side. Blood gushed from the wound, running down Logan's thigh, staining the earth at his feet. Red Shirt's fangs were still embedded in Logan's flesh when a fair-haired vamp rushed Logan from the other side, his fangs scraping along Logan's throat.

Weak from the blood he had lost, Logan dropped to his knees, snarling defiantly as four of the vampires fell on him, pinning him to the ground.

Rogen stood over him, a sinister smile on his swarthy face. He lifted one hand, bloody claws extended. "I'm going to enjoy this."

Logan glared up at him, his whole body tense as he waited for Rogen to rip his heart from his chest. He wasn't afraid of dying, only of never seeing Mara again.

Rogen took a step forward and then, with a strangled

cry, he stared in disbelief at the stake protruding, point first, from his chest, before he toppled to the ground.

Logan grinned faintly when he saw Vince Cordova standing in the moonlight, flanked by his two sons.

The cavalry had arrived, just in the nick of time.

The remaining four vampires closed ranks and stood behind Rogen's body.

The tallest of the four gestured at the dead vampire. "It's over as far as I'm concerned," he muttered, and vanished from sight.

"What about the rest of you?" Vince asked. "You three up for a little one on one?"

Red Shirt and the other two vampires exchanged glances.

Rane took a step forward. "Come on," he said, motioning them closer. "Let's do it."

"I'm right behind you, brother," Rafe said, baring his fangs. "It's been a long time since we fought side by side."

"Hey, now, hold on a minute," the fair-haired vampire said. "We've got no quarrel with any of you. As for him . . ." He gestured at Logan, and then shrugged. "Rogen's past caring if your friend lives or dies. And I sure as hell don't care."

Vince looked at the other two vampires. "You boys feel the same way?"

"Like Murray said, we've got no quarrel with you," Red Shirt muttered, and one by one, the three vanished from sight.

Logan blew out a shaky breath. "How'd you guys know I was in trouble?"

"Mara called us," Vince said.

"On the phone," Rane added. "You look like hell."

"That's about how I feel." Logan pressed a hand to his injured side. Blood leaked between his fingers. "I can't believe she didn't think I could take Rogen."

Rafe shrugged as he grabbed hold of Logan's forearm and pulled him to his feet. "She said she had a premonition that you were in danger. I would say she was right."

"Can you make it back to the hotel on your own?" Vince asked. "Or do you need some help?"

"I can get there under my own power," Logan said gruffly. He ran a tentative hand over his face, wondering if his nose was broken. "I guess I owe you guys a favor, big time."

"Just take care of Mara," Rane said. "That's payback enough. How's she getting along, anyway?"

"She's doing all right, I guess. I think she's starting to like being mortal. She's even learning to cook."

Rafe muttered an oath. "Cook? Mara is cooking?" He shook his head ruefully. "Next thing you know, the rivers will be turning to blood."

Grinning, Rane slapped his brother on the shoulder. "Hey, that wouldn't be such a bad thing, now, would it?"

Mara was pacing the floor when a sudden coldness whispered past her. Whirling around, she came face-to-face with a woman who looked vaguely familiar.

"Who are you?" Mara asked. "How did you get in here?"

The woman smiled, displaying even white teeth. And fangs.

Mara stifled the urge to make a run for the door. The worst thing you could do when faced with a predator was show fear. She remembered all too well the thrill of the chase. "Who are you?" she asked again.

"Sasha. I'm a friend of Ed's."

"I see." Mara knew now why the woman looked so familiar. She was the redhead who had been sitting at Rogen's blackjack table earlier.

"Ed told me you'd lost your powers. I didn't believe him." Sasha lifted her head and inhaled sharply. "But it's true, isn't it?"

Mara didn't say anything, merely stood there, her mind racing as she glanced surreptitiously around the room. If the vampire attacked, she had no way to defend herself. It suddenly occurred to her that if she got out of this alive, she needed to stock up on holy water and a couple of sharp wooden stakes.

The vampire laughed softly. "Ed said the three of us are going to party after he destroys your boyfriend."

Mara lifted her chin and squared her shoulders. "We'll have a party, all right," she said with more bravado than she felt, "only you'll be the main course."

The redhead snorted derisively. "I can't wait to tell my friends that we brought you down. Of course, since you've lost your powers, it won't be much of a coup. But then . . ." She fell silent, her eyes narrowing as she gazed toward the door.

"Then what?" Mara asked, stalling for time.

"Then we'd . . ." Sasha stilled, her words abruptly cut off as Logan materialized behind her, one hand locked around her throat.

"You wanted a party," Logan said, his voice gruff. "Are you ready to play?"

The redhead struggled in his grasp, her nails digging into Logan's arm, her breath coming in ragged gasps as he tightened his hold.

Mara took a step forward. "Logan . . ."

He glanced at Mara over Sasha's head. "Did she hurt you?" he asked, his voice silky smooth with menace.

Mara shook her head. "No." But she could see that Logan was hurt. His face was bruised and bloody, his clothing bloodstained and shredded. In the aftermath of the fight with Rogen, his eyes still burned red.

"Rogen's dead." Logan hissed the words in the red-head's ear. "You can join him, or you can get the hell out of town now, tonight. What'll it be?" He loosened his hold on her throat so she could speak.

Sasha took a deep breath, then cried, "Damn you! Let me go!" She clawed at his face, her nails raking down his left cheek, laying it open to the bone.

"Dammit!" Logan roared, and threw her across the room as if she weighed no more than a child.

Sasha landed against the wall, her head snapping back hard enough to crack the plaster, but it didn't slow her down. Fangs bared, she sprang toward Logan with murder in her eyes.

In spite of his injuries, he was quicker, stronger. Catching her in midair, he hurled her out the window. There was the sound of breaking glass followed by a horrible, blood-curdling cry, and then silence.

Mara stayed where she was, her arms crossed over her stomach, her gaze on Logan as he walked across the room and glanced out the window.

"What happened?" she asked, her voice little more than a whisper as that last, agonized cry replayed itself in her mind.

"There's a little white picket fence in the side yard."

He didn't have to say any more. A picket fence made a very fine wooden stake. She tried not to imagine Sasha's body impaled on the wooden spikes, but the harder she tried to ignore it, the clearer the image became.

Logan turned away from the window. "Who the hell was she?"

"A friend of Rogen's."

He snorted softly. "More than a friend, I'd say." He lifted a hand to his cheek. "Damn, that hurts."

Nodding, Mara went into the bathroom, turned on the taps in the tub, and dampened a washcloth. Returning to the other room, she pressed the cloth to Logan's cheek. "Hold that," she instructed, even though it wasn't really necessary. The nasty gashes were already healing. "I'm sorry you had to kill Rogen."

Logan lifted one brow. "You're sorry he's dead?"

"I didn't mean that. I meant, I'm sorry you had to fight him because of me."

"Well, I fought him, but I didn't kill him."

"Oh?" Her gaze slid away from his. "How did he die?"

"Old man Cordova drove a stake through his heart."

"Vince was here?" she asked, surprised.

"Yeah, and the twins, too. I should be angry with you, you know, thinking I needed backup. Even though I did," he added gruffly.

"What happened?"

He tossed the bloody wash rag on the dresser. "I was whipping Rogen's ass when he sent out a call for help and four other vamps showed up. Rogen was about to rip my heart out when the Cordova boys arrived on the scene." Logan cupped her face in his bloody hands and kissed her. "How'd you know I was in trouble?"

"I'm not sure." Taking his hand in hers, she led him into the bathroom. "I just had a feeling something was wrong." She unbuttoned his shirt, slid it over his shoulders and down his arms, and tossed it into the trash can.

"Hey, I paid over a hundred credits for that shirt!"

"Yeah? Well, it's beyond repair. Kick off your shoes. Anyway," she went on, unbuckling his belt, "I tried to sense your whereabouts. I couldn't, of course."

She unfastened his trousers and pushed them down

over his hips. Logan stepped out of them and kicked them aside.

"So I called Rane and asked him to find you. He wasn't supposed to let you know he was there, unless you needed help." She slipped her thumbs into the waistband of his briefs and slowly dragged them down his legs, chuckling softly as she did so. The man had just been in a brutal fight, had almost lost his life, but it hadn't affected his libido in the least.

Catching her amused gaze, Logan shrugged. "Hey, sex is life affirming. Everybody knows that."

"Maybe later," she said, turning off the water. "Right now, you need a bath."

"Are you gonna wash me?"

"I don't think so."

"You'd refuse me?" he asked with feigned astonishment. "Don't you know that in my weakened state, I could drown?"

"Oh, please," Mara said, fighting the urge to laugh.

He groaned softly as he sat on the edge of the bathtub. "I could have been killed."

"You're a vampire, remember? You'll be your old self by tomorrow night."

She was moving toward the door when he said, "My last thought was of you."

His words, quietly spoken, went straight to her heart. How could she refuse his request? Blowing out an exasperated sigh, she said, "Oh, just get into the tub."

Stifling the urge to gloat, Logan slid down into the water. Resting his head against the edge, he watched Mara through heavy-lidded eyes as she pulled a clean cloth from the stack on the sink. Dropping to her knees, she leaned forward and washed the blood from his face and neck.

Heaven, he thought as her hands moved over him. Or at least as close to it as he was likely to get. Closing his eyes, he surrendered to her touch.

Mara glanced at the water, which was turning bright pink with blood. She should have run the shower for him instead, she thought, but it was too late now. She washed him as gently as she could. So many bites and scratches, some of which would have been fatal if he had been a mortal man, while others would have taken weeks to heal. Yet even as she watched, the bruises and less serious gashes he had sustained were knitting together, fading, disappearing.

Logan opened one eye. "Why don't you join me?"

"I don't think so." She grimaced at the water, which was now an even darker shade of pink. "You'll need a shower when you get out of there."

"Yeah, I think you're right."

She ran the soapy rag over his broad shoulders and down his arms, over his flat belly and his long, muscular legs, and all the while, she tried to ignore the growing evidence of his desire and the rush of heat that pooled low in the pit of her stomach.

She wondered how many women had shared his bed. She wanted to hate them, all of the nameless females who had made love to him in the past, but it was impossible. How could she fault them for wanting him when she was aching for his touch, hungry for the taste of his kisses? When she yearned to feel the weight of his body on hers, to hear his voice whispering sweet love words in her ear?

She frowned when she met his knowing gaze.

"Aching for my touch, are you?" he asked with a roguish grin.

"Oh!" She threw the washcloth in his face. "Stop reading my mind!"

"Hungry for my kisses?" Laughing softly, he grabbed her wrist when she would have retreated. Rising to his knees, he drew her closer to whisper, *"Ti amo, il mio angelo, il mio cuore, la mia vita."* I love you, my angel, my heart, my life.

And then he kissed her.

Her eyelids fluttered down, all thought of resistance melting away as his mouth covered hers in a hot hungry kiss. His hand slid under her hair to cup her nape as he deepened the kiss, his tongue mating slowly, sensuously, with hers in an erotic dance older than time itself.

"Mara." His breath fanned the curve of her throat. "You make me weak."

She smiled inwardly, thinking that, in spite of his wounds, he was anything but weak.

In a single, fluid movement, he rose from the tub. Lifting her with him, he carried her into the bedroom. She didn't protest when, using his preternatural power, he bared her body to his gaze and then, murmuring her name, he lowered her to the bed and stretched out beside her.

"You're all wet," she murmured. "The bed . . ."

"Will dry." He nibbled on her earlobe, raked his fangs, ever so lightly, along the side of her neck. "Let me."

She had no thought to refuse. Whether he wanted to taste her or make love to her or drain her dry, she didn't care, so long as he eased the need burning deep inside of her.

He was the warrior, victorious in battle, and she was the prize. He claimed her boldly, his hands worshiping her beauty as he stoked the flame of her desire and then, feeling her shudder beneath him, he uttered a wild cry reminiscent of men going to battle as he thrust deep within her, felt her silky heat surround him, carrying him to victory yet again.

Some time later, Logan rained kisses along her eyelids, the tip of her nose, the point of her chin. "So, how's that ache?"

Mara punched him on the shoulder. "As if you didn't know."

He laughed softly. "I've got to say, this night ended up a lot better than it started." He placed his hand on her belly. "How many other enemies do you suppose you've got out there?"

"I don't know," she said, smothering a yawn, and then, as a new thought occurred to her, she sat up, her arms folded over her belly. What if she ran into others she had turned against their will? Or if some mortal man attacked her? In her current state, she was helpless to protect her baby.

"What's wrong now?" Logan asked, tugging her back down beside him.

"Maybe I'm making a mistake in keeping the baby."

Logan blew out a sigh. She was as changeable as the wind. "What brought that up . . . ? Oh, never mind. Meeting Rogen. Right?"

"If you hadn't been here . . ." She didn't want to think of what might have happened if she had been alone.

"Stop worrying, darlin'," he said, running his knuckles down her cheek. "I'll always be here."

Chapter Eighteen

Logan and Mara returned to the house in Tyler the following night. After seeing Mara safely inside, Logan kissed her on the cheek, then left to go hunting.

Mara curled up on the sofa. She was glad to be home again, away from the crowds and the lights. On her last visit to the doctor, Ramsden had advised her that he intended to induce her on the eighteenth of October. When she had asked why he thought it necessary to induce the baby, Ramsden had reminded her that he was a vampire and as such, he would have to deliver the baby at night, in his office.

"Don't worry," he had said, "I have a complete hospital room set up downstairs. And if there should be complications . . ." He made a vague gesture with his hand. "I think it would be better for all concerned that no one else be aware of it. It wouldn't be wise to have blood samples fall into the wrong hands, or for people to ask questions we'd rather not answer."

She wondered why he hadn't mentioned inducing her before, and why the idea of having the baby in his office filled her with such trepidation.

Four more weeks until she held her baby in her arms. She could hardly wait. She just hoped the next four went by faster than the last.

The sound of laughter drew her to the window. Across the street, a handful of teenage boys were playing basketball in the driveway. A couple of fathers sat on the front porch, watching. Her neighbors were friendly, nodding and waving whenever they saw her.

Soon after she and Logan had moved in, their next-door neighbor, Louise, had invited Mara over for coffee and donuts. Mara had been hesitant to go at first. Making small talk with human females was something she had rarely done. She was even more diffident when Louise invited her inside. In the big family kitchen, Louise introduced her to three other women who lived in the neighborhood. The women had welcomed Mara like an old friend as they introduced themselves. Sally Blankman had nine-year-old twin boys and lived across the street. Her husband, Terry, was a dentist. Judy Michaels lived next door to Sally. Judy had a three-month-old daughter. Her husband was an airline pilot. Monica Sorenson lived next to Mara. Monica had three teenage daughters. Her husband was a Marine.

As soon as Mara had settled at the table with a cup of hot coffee and a chocolate donut, the ladies asked about the baby. Was this her first? How far along was she? Did she know if it was a boy or a girl? Once she had answered all their questions about her pregnancy, they had shared their stories of childbirth with her, stories of eighteen-hour labors and emergency C-sections that had given Mara nightmares and made her wonder why any woman, having gone through childbirth once, would willingly do it again.

* * *

Now pressing a hand to her aching back, Mara went into the kitchen for a glass of milk, which led to a couple of cookies and another glass of milk. She thought about trying to write more on the story of her life, but she just didn't have the energy. Maybe it had been a silly idea. Who would believe it, anyway?

With a sigh, she put the glass in the sink, then waddled into the living room to watch TV. She had gained so much weight, she would probably never be thin again. Logan told her repeatedly that she wasn't fat, she was pregnant. Easy for him to say. She had weighed a hundred and ten pounds for as long as she could remember. Well, those days were long gone. The last time the doctor had weighed her, she had gained almost forty pounds. When she was standing up, she couldn't even see her feet anymore, which was just as well, because they were all fat and swollen, too.

Of course, she couldn't blame it all on the baby. Ever since she had discovered that mortal food didn't make her sick, she had devoured practically everything in sight, but after over two thousand years on a warm liquid diet, who could blame her?

Because she couldn't think of anything else to do, she went into the bedroom and booted up the computer, then called up her life story. She read it from the beginning, adding a few paragraphs here, rearranging a few sentences there, reliving each chapter as she read. It needed a lot of work, she thought, but then, she wasn't a writer, and if she decided to keep the baby, there would be no reason to hurry. She would have the next eighteen years or so to finish it.

If she decided to keep the baby. Logan had said he

would always be there. But would he? And if he left, how would she manage without him?

She tapped her fingers on the desktop as she gathered her thoughts, and then she began to write . . .

I moved to Georgia just before the start of the Civil War. It was an era I dearly loved, a time of quiet elegance and Southern charm, of chaperones and nannies. With its rigid rules about propriety and its quaint customs, it was like a make-believe world, so different from anything I had ever known before.

I bought a plantation, complete with a few servants who were warned of dire consequences if they intruded on my rest during the day. I knew they gossiped about my peculiar ways, about the fact that I didn't eat in their presence, but it was of no consequence. I treated them well and they had no reason to rise against me.

It was an elegant time. I loved playing the part of a Southern belle, adored the clothes of the period, the long dresses and longer courtships, the dainty hats and gloves, the enormous petticoats, the balls and cotillions, the country barbeques. And, most of all, the handsome young men clad in Confederate gray. What dashing creatures they were. Innately polite, they treated their women like porcelain dolls, to be displayed and treasured but never taken too seriously.

Life changed with the coming of the Civil War, a war the South embraced, but had little chance of winning. In spite of the War, the South clung to the old ways.

I especially remember Lieutenant Captain Jeffrey

Dunston. Ah, Jeffrey, with his hair like burnished gold and his blue, blue eyes. Clad in his uniform and plumed hat, he cut quite a gallant figure the evening he rode up to the plantation astride a big black horse.

Dismounting, he climbed the stairs, one hand on the saber at his side, his bright blue eyes twinkling when he saw me standing in the doorway. Of course, it was considered quite scandalous for him to come calling when I didn't have a proper chaperone, and even moreso to visit a lone female after dark. I was of the opinion that one of the reasons he enjoyed my company was my open disdain for propriety.

He bowed over my hand. "Miss Mara."

"Lieutenant, this is a surprise."

"A pleasant one, I hope."

"But of course. Please, come in."

After removing his hat, he followed me into the front parlor and, at my invitation, took a seat on the lovely, high-backed sofa.

"I'm afraid I have come to deliver bad news." His thick Southern drawl poured over me, warm and sweet, like summer molasses.

"Bad news?" I sat beside him, my hands folded primly in my lap. "Whatever do you mean?"

"The Yankees are coming. It isn't safe for you to stay here, with no chaperone and no one to protect you."

"You're very sweet to worry about me so, but I'm not afraid."

"I know you're not, Miss Mara, but I'm afraid

for you. Promise me you will leave tomorrow, while there's still time."

I placed my hand on his and batted my eyelashes. "I appreciate your concern, Lieutenant, but I assure you I'll be all right." I smiled inwardly. It was the Yankees who should be afraid.

"You are far too brave." Dunston sighed as he covered my hand with his own. "I'm afraid I have more bad news."

"Oh, no."

"My regiment is leaving tomorrow. I don't know when we'll be back."

"That is bad news," I said, and meant it. I had hoped to amuse myself with him for another few weeks. He was such a gentle, easygoing young man, it was hard to believe he was fit for battle. I couldn't imagine him riding off to war, enduring hardship. Taking a life.

"Will you . . . ?" He cleared his throat. "Is there any chance that you'd . . ."

"That I'd what?"

"Write to me." A blush reddened his cheeks. "Wait for me. I know we haven't known each other very long," he said, his words tumbling over each other, "but we'll whip those dirty Yankees in no time, and . . ."

"Don't go, Jeffrey."

"What?" He blinked at me. "I don't understand."

"Why don't you stay here, with me, instead of going off to war?"

"Are you . . . are you asking me to desert my regiment?"

It was exactly what I was asking. I looked up at

him through the veil of my lashes. "It sounds so awful, when you say it like that."

"But that's what you're asking?"

"Wouldn't you rather be here, with me?"

He sat up straighter. "Yes," he replied stiffly, "but I cannot bring shame to my family, or to myself. And I cannot help being disappointed that you would suggest such a thing."

"I'm sorry, Jeffrey," I murmured contritely. "But I simply can't abide the thought of you going off to war where you might be . . ." I sniffed loudly as I pulled a white lace hankie from my skirt pocket and dabbed at my eyes.

His expression immediately softened at my repentant look. "It's all right, Miss Mara. And I'm . . . I'm deeply touched by your concern for my welfare. Truly, I am. But I must go."

"Of course you must." I gazed up at him. "Kiss me, Jeffrey. Kiss me once, before you go."

"Miss Mara!" He looked as shocked as he sounded. Shocked and eager.

I seduced Jeffrey Dunston that night, promised him a new life if he would stay with me. Caught up in the throes of passion, bewitched by my preternatural power, he begged me to turn him so we could be together forever. It was a glorious night. I had seduced only a few virgins in my life. Their blood is the sweetest of all.

Jeffrey's friends came looking for him the next day, quite frantic because he hadn't slept in his bed the night before.

"Captain Cahill's furious," exclaimed a towheaded young man. "Iffen Jeffrey don't show up right quick, he's gonna be in mighty big trouble."

The other two men nodded in agreement, their expressions somber.

"I'm so sorry," I said, one hand pressed to my heart, "but I have no idea where Lieutenant Dunston might be."

"He wasn't here?" queried the towheaded young man. "He said he was a' coming here to say his good-byes."

"He did, indeed, come to bid me farewell, but he left soon after. He didn't say where he was going, but I assumed he would be returning to his regiment. I do hope no harm has befallen him."

"Obliged for your time and trouble, ma'am."

"I'm so sorry I couldn't be of more help."

I stood on the porch, my hand shading my eyes as I watched the trio mount and ride away. When they were out of sight, I went into the house, locked the door, and dismissed the servants for the night.

Humming "Rose of Alabamy," *I glanced upstairs. Come sundown, Lieutenant Jeffrey Dunston would rise, a newly made vampire. And like all of the newly Undead, he would be ravenous . . .*

With a sigh, Mara sat back in her chair. Poor Jeffrey. In the throes of passion, he had begged her to bring him across. When he woke as a vampire, with the hunger raging through him, he had begged her to make him mortal again. And when he learned it wasn't possible, he had turned away from her. She had tried to convince him that being a vampire wasn't a bad thing, but, alas, she had failed. The next morning, before the Dark Sleep claimed him, Jeffrey had run out of the house to meet the dawn. When she realized what he intended to do, she had hurried after him, but she had been too late. One touch of sunlight on newly made preternatural flesh, and he had burst into flames. It had been over in an instant, but the sight of his body being consumed by flames had haunted her dreams for months. Years had passed before she turned anyone else.

She was rereading what she had written when Logan came up behind her. "Still writing your life story?" he asked, dropping a kiss on the top of her head.

"Mostly jotting down memories. Once I get it all down, I guess I'll have to put it in some sort of order." She shook her head. "I don't know. Maybe this wasn't such a great idea."

Logan grunted softly. "Digging up some unpleasant memories, are you?" he asked, reading over her shoulder.

"A few."

"Well, come on, let's go for a walk."

Stretching, she ran a hand through her hair. "Now?"

"Why not now? Didn't Ramsden say you needed to get some exercise? Besides, there's nothing like a stroll in the moonlight to put your mind at ease."

That had been true once, she thought, remembering how she had always loved the night. "Let me shut down the computer first."

"I'll get your jacket. It's cold out."

Minutes later, they were strolling down the sidewalk like an old married couple. Logan wore faded blue jeans and a black T-shirt; Mara was bundled up in sweatpants, a long-sleeved shirt, a jacket, and fur-lined boots. She grinned inwardly, thinking they looked like ads for summer and winter.

She sighed as her thoughts returned to Jeffrey. He had been a bright young man, easy to talk to, with a dry sense of humor. She had been quite fond of him. His destruction had been such a waste, but some people just weren't cut out to be vampires. They hated their new existence, hated the one who had brought them across. Unable to embrace what they had become, they went out to meet the dawn and instant destruction. Others, unable to take their own lives, sought out older vampires and asked to be destroyed, or spent their lives trying to deny what they were. They refused to feed until the hunger became unbearable and then, almost mad with pain, they hunted. Driven by an insatiable need, they often ripped their prey to shreds, only to suffer nights of remorse afterward. Truly, they were the most miserable of all the Undead. Of course, there was no way to know how a person would take to being Nosferatu until it was too late.

After Jeffrey's death, Mara had sent her servants away and abandoned the plantation. She had taken to haunting the battlefields, where she ferreted out those who were beyond any hope of recovery. She soothed their pain and their fears, eased her hunger, and sent them peacefully into whatever lay beyond the grave.

"You're very quiet," Logan remarked.

"I'm sorry. I guess I'm not very good company tonight."

They walked in companionable silence for a time, and then Logan said, "I heard some disturbing news today."

"Oh?"

"Yeah. You ever hear of a vampire by the name of Travis Jackson?"

"Jackson, yes, I remember him."

"Someone took him out."

"Who?"

"I don't know. The vampire who told me about it heard it thirdhand. Happened somewhere in North Hollywood."

"Really? The last I knew, he was down in Texas with his grandmother." She had never been fond of Jackson. He had been a hunter before he was turned. At last count, he had destroyed thirty-six vampires, killed eighteen werewolves, and a were-tiger. During the War between the Vampires and the Werewolves, Jackson, his grandmother, Pearl, and Pearl's friend, Edna, had caused a great deal of trouble. Pearl and Edna had concocted a serum they had hoped would cure the vampires and the werewolves. They had rounded up a number of test subjects, Rafe and Kathy among them, and injected each one. Fortunately, it had had no effect on vampires or humans. Werewolves had not fared as well. The experimental drug had killed two of them.

"Do you think the Jackson killing was an isolated incident?" Logan asked.

"How would I know?" Mara replied testily. "I'm a little out of the loop these days. What do you think?"

"I'm not sure. It's the first killing I've heard about in quite a while. Well, except for Tasha."

"Yes, Tasha," Mara murmured. Tasha had killed Savanah's father, and Savanah had driven a stake through her heart.

"I hope Pearl and Edna have enough sense to lie low for a while," Logan said.

Mara snorted softly. She had no liking for either of the old biddies. Had it been up to her, she would have destroyed them both after the War. How like her softhearted Rafe to bring those two meddlesome old fools across rather than destroy them as he should have done.

Chapter Nineteen

The next morning after breakfast, Lieutenant Jeffrey Dunston was still on Mara's mind. Lingering at the table, she thought again how sad it was that he had taken his own life rather than accept being a vampire. She had intended to spend a few years with him, to teach him how to wield his powers, to take him to London and Paris and Rome, to see the world anew through his eyes. But he had been too weak to accept the gift she had given him.

After Robert E. Lee surrendered, Mara had stayed in the South for a time, but living through the reconstruction period had been no fun at all, and so she had headed West. With no particular destination in mind, she had traveled from town to town, staying in one place or another for a month or a year as the spirit moved her.

She had always had a thing for men in uniform, whether they were wearing Confederate gray or Army blue, and so it was that in 1876, she found herself in Dakota Territory at Fort Abraham Lincoln. Women had been scarce in the Old West, especially women with soft hands, and faces that weren't browned by the desert sun and lined by the stress of living on the frontier. The men she met treated her with the utmost courtesy, and if they weren't quite as refined as their counterparts in the South, they made up for it in enthusiasm.

But it had been a Lakota scout named Runs With Thunder who had captured her interest and her affection during that time. In all her travels, she had never met a Native American and Runs With Thunder fascinated her. He was unlike any man she had ever known, and perhaps that was his attraction. He wasn't the least bit interested in her, and that, more than anything else, had made her determined to have him.

She started her campaign slowly, asking questions about his people, how they lived, what they believed in, why he was working with the Army. At first, his answers had been cool, stilted, but her interest had been genuine and after a week or so, he began to answer her questions.

The Lakota were a proud race, their warriors fierce and brave. He told her of their customs, how the number four was sacred, how the tribe moved with the seasons, following the sun and *Pte*, the buffalo, how warriors went into the *Paha Sapa*, the sacred Black Hills, to ask the Great Spirit for a vision to guide them through life . . .

Rising, she hurried downstairs and booted up her computer, wanting to record her memories of Runs With Thunder while they were fresh in her mind.

"Have you sought a vision?" I asked. We were sitting on a blanket out on the prairie, away from the dust and distractions of the fort.

Runs With Thunder nodded. "When I was sixteen summers, I went to the Paha Sapa. *I had been there for three days, fasting and praying, when a red-tailed hawk landed on a tree branch above my head. He spoke to me, telling me to beware of a white woman with hair as dark as night and eyes like greening grass. I know now he spoke of you."*

"Me? Why would he warn you about me?"

"He told me you would bring change to my life."

"What kind of change?"

"Not in a good way. He said you would kill me but I would not die."

"This bird really spoke to you?"

"Ai."

"But you don't believe what he said?"

"My spirit guide would not lie."

"If you believe him, what are you doing here, with me?"

"I do not know. You are wasichu, *and yet . . ." He lifted a hand, as though to stroke my cheek, then curled it into a fist. "I should not be with you, but I cannot stay away."*

I knew it was my vampire glamour that drew him. I wondered if he would feel the same if I were human, and knew he would not. He was Lakota, I was a white woman, his enemy. But he wanted me, and that was all that mattered. Because I desperately wanted him. He was beautiful, with his long black hair and tawny skin. Clad in a buckskin shirt, trousers, and moccasins, he looked every inch the warrior that he was.

"What change will you bring to me, chikala?"

"Perhaps one day I'll tell you. What does chikala *mean?"*

"Little one."

"Little one," I murmured, smiling. "I like that."

"Are you going to change me?"

"Do you want me to?"

He regarded me through serious black eyes for

several moments, his expression thoughtful and then worried. "How can you kill me and yet not kill me?"

"Do you really want to know?"

"Ai."

"Your people believe in spirit guides. Do they also believe in vampires?"

He nodded. "There are stories of those who drink the blood of the living and walk in the night, but"—he stared at me, his eyes wide—"you cannot be one of them." He shook his head. "They are skeletal creatures, with long teeth and hairy palms, and they smell bad."

I couldn't help it. I laughed. "Perhaps there are vampires like the ones you describe, but I've never met any."

"This is a bad joke, Mara."

"It isn't a joke."

"Show me, then."

"Some other time, perhaps."

Now it was his turn to laugh. "I knew it was not true."

I saw him often in the next few weeks, and then, one night, he told me he was leaving the fort.

"Why? Where are you going?"

"Long Hair Custer is going to the Greasy Grass to battle against my people. I must go home to fight with the Lakota."

I tried to dissuade him, but, like Jeffrey Dunston, Runs With Thunder was a man of honor. His people were going to war, and he was determined to fight alongside them. I thought of forcing the Dark Gift on him, but I remembered Dunston's reaction all too well. The thought of Runs With Thunder meeting such a horrific end was more than I could bear.

After Runs With Thunder left the fort, I contemplated leaving as well. Instead, I followed Custer's regiment from a distance. What a grand sight they made, with Custer riding proudly at their head while the band played "Garry Owen."

I had met Custer at a dance at the fort shortly before he left. I had thought him an arrogant fool. He was so sure of victory, so certain that he was indestructible.

I trailed the Seventh by night and burrowed into the welcoming arms of the earth by day. Resting in the ground on June 25, 1876, I heard the sounds of battle as white man and red man met on the banks of the Little Big Horn. I heard the war cries of the Lakota and the Cheyenne, the bugle calls of the Seventh Cavalry, the gunshots and the sibilant hiss of arrows flying through the air, the screams and sobs of the wounded and the dying. Even buried deep in the earth, I smelled the blood as it soaked the ground. So much blood.

And later, I listened to the silence.

And then came the high-pitched keening of the Indian women as they grieved for their dead.

I rose with the setting of the sun. The battlefield was littered with corpses. The Indians had carried their dead away, but I prowled the battlefield, looking for Runs With Thunder.

I had been about to abandon my search when I found him, badly wounded. He had crawled away from the battlefield and lay in a shallow ravine, hidden behind a clump of sage. He smelled of blood. And death.

"*Runs With Thunder.*" *Calling his name, I sank to my knees beside him, shook him when he didn't answer. "Thunder, answer me!"*

Slowly, his eyes opened. He looked at me blankly for a moment, and then his lips formed my name, though no sound emerged.

"*I can't let you die,*" *I whispered, stroking his cheek. "Your spirit guide was right. I'm going to change your life. I hope you won't hate me for it."*

He tried to speak, but it was beyond him. His heartbeat was sluggish, heavy. His eyes filled with horror when I bent over him, my fangs extended. And then, smiling faintly, he closed his eyes.

His blood was warm and sweet as I drained him of what he hadn't lost in the battle, drank until he was a breath away from death, and then I bit into my wrist. When I held it to his lips and bid him drink, he did so greedily.

When I felt he had taken enough, I carried him away from the Little Big Horn into a cave high in the Black Hills. In the nights that followed, I taught him what it meant to be a vampire—how to feed, how to shut his mind to the barrage of sound that assaulted him on every side, how to call his prey to him.

I took him to New York and Rome, to London and Los Angeles. We hunted the nights together, and it was wonderful. But, after a year or so, he began to long for the Paha Sapa *and his own people.*

"*I must go home,*" *he said. "Back to the Lakota. Come with me,* chikala.*"*

I considered it, but in the end, I knew that as much as I cared for him, I would never be happy living in a hide lodge. Selfish creature that I was, I

*wanted to wear the latest fashions, not a buckskin
tunic and moccasins. The Dakota sky at night was
beautiful, but I wanted the bright lights of Paris.
The Great Plains were quiet, the Black Hills majes-
tic, but I favored tall buildings and city streets, all
the better to get lost in.*

*We made love one last time and he fell asleep in
my arms. Not wanting to say good-bye, I left him
while he slept. I saw him from time to time through
the years. I never blocked the blood link between us
as I did with so many others; instead, I kept it open
so that I would always know where he was . . .*

Thinking of him now was like losing him all over
again. With a sigh, she saved her work and closed the
document. She had been in Chicago in 1947, buying a
new wardrobe, when she felt Runs With Thunder's life
force fade and finally disappear. There was no way to
describe the feeling, but she had known when he drew
his last breath. It was a pain like nothing she had ever felt
before. Filled with sorrow, she had gone to ground for the
next ten years.

Runs With Thunder had been her last fledgling, until
Vince came along. She had turned no one since then.

And now she never would again, she thought with a
sigh of regret, but perhaps it was just as well.

Chapter Twenty

Lou McDonald leaned back in her chair, her feet propped on a corner of her desk as she listened to the latest update from Cindy.

"Mara had another appointment last night. According to her chart, the baby's growing and gaining weight and Ramsden isn't expecting any complications. Oh, one more thing. I overheard him tell Susan that he thinks Mara's either lost her powers or she's losing them."

"What do you mean, lost them?"

"I'm not sure. I didn't hear the whole conversation. Is it possible she isn't a vampire anymore?"

Lou grunted softly. "Who knows what's possible these days? Kind of makes sense, though." She drummed her fingertips on her thigh. "If she's not a vampire anymore, it would explain how she could get pregnant."

"True enough," Cindy agreed.

"Anything else new on that end?"

"Not really. What's going on with you? Made any kills lately?"

"Just one. It's not as easy as it once was, you know,

now that the vamps have gone back underground, so to speak."

"Underground," Cindy muttered. "That's a good one. Which one did you take out?"

"Travis Jackson. I caught him off guard in L.A. He went down hard."

"Chalk up one for the good guys," Cindy said, a smile in her voice.

"I'll get his grandmother one of these days, and that other old broad, too," Lou said in her best wicked Witch of the West voice.

"I can't believe those two old ladies are giving you so much trouble," Cindy said with a laugh. "I mean, come on, girl."

"Hey, if you can do better, go for it."

"Very funny."

"They're not as easy to corner as you might think. They used to be hunters, remember? They know all the tricks that hunters use, which makes them twice as hard to find. But I'll get 'em. Both of them. You wait and see."

"I know you will. Listen, I've got to go. Ramsden's calling me."

"All right. Talk at ya later." Lou tossed her cell phone on the desk, then gazed out her office window. Hunters had been trying to destroy Mara for centuries and they had all failed. But she wouldn't fail, and when it was a *fait accompli*, her customers would double and so would the price of her services.

She was about to leave her office when her business phone rang. She stared at it a moment, then decided to let the machine pick it up.

"Lou? This is Kyle Bowden. Dammit, where the hell have you been?"

"Avoiding you," she muttered, then swore softly when

her cell phone rang. Knowing she couldn't avoid him forever, she picked up the phone. "What can I do for you, Bowden?"

"You can do what I'm paying you for. I want to know where Mara is, now. No more games, no more evasions."

Lou considered a moment, then shrugged. What could it hurt if Kyle knew where Mara was, as long as Lou knew where they both were? "She's in Tyler, Nevada, just outside of Reno."

"What's she doing there?"

"Her doctor is there. Thomas A. Ramsden. He's not listed in the phone book, but his office is on Franklin, between the bank and the post office."

With a muttered "Thanks," Bowden ended the call.

Lou grunted softly. It might have been a mistake, telling Bowden where to find Mara, but what the hell? The guy was in love and the baby was due in a few weeks. Might as well let him spend a little time with the mother of his child while he could, since Mara's days were numbered one way or the other once the baby was born. If Ramsden didn't kill her, Lou would take her head, vampire or not.

With that thought in mind, Lou went home to pack a bag. Whatever went down when the baby was born, she intended to be there to see it all firsthand.

Chapter Twenty-one

Logan stared at Mara, a bemused expression on his face. "You want to learn how to drive a car, now?" He glanced at her ample girth.

"What's the matter?" she asked with a frown. "Don't you think I'll fit behind the wheel?"

His laughter thrilled her even as it irritated her. "Come on," he said, "there's nothing to it."

As it turned out, sitting behind the wheel, even with the seat all the way back, turned out to be a tight fit.

Mara glared at Logan. "Don't say a word."

He shrugged as he settled into the passenger seat. "I'm not the one who ate a whole pizza last night."

"I didn't eat the whole thing!" She hadn't eaten the crust.

He wisely refrained from making a comment. Instead, he spoke to the car and the engine revved to life.

"There's nothing to driving," he said. "You just tell the car where you want to go, and it'll take you there."

"That's not how you do it."

"Yeah, well, I like being in control."

"I want to drive, the old-fashioned way."

"Put your seat belt on."

"You don't wear yours."

He didn't say anything, just looked at her. She felt a rush of resentment. He was a vampire. He didn't need a seat belt. She did.

Logan spoke to the car, telling it to release control to the driver, then he looked at Mara. "Okay, that's the gas," he said, pointing. "That's the brake. Those are the headlights. Make sure the street is clear before you pull out of the driveway. Hey," he admonished as she stepped down hard on the gas pedal, "take it easy."

She backed out of the driveway, the car jerking crazily down the road until she got a feel for the gas pedal. She smiled, immensely pleased with herself when she managed to keep the car moving smoothly.

"Where should I go?" she asked.

"Turn left at the corner. There's a long stretch down Winter Ridge Drive that won't have much traffic this time of night. Don't forget to signal for the turn."

He clicked on the radio, then sat back, content to watch her while she got a feel for the car. He grinned. Her brow was furrowed in concentration, her lower lip caught between her teeth. He glanced at her abdomen. It still amazed him that she was pregnant. The fact that he wished the child was his was even more surprising, but there it was. He was one of the oldest vampires in existence, more powerful than any creature who walked the earth, and he was jealous of the puny human male who had sired her child.

"Pathetic," he muttered. "Just pathetic."

"What?"

"I said turn right."

"That's not what you said."

"Well, it's what I'm saying now."

She turned down the road he indicated, frowned as the road climbed higher and higher and got narrower and narrower until they ran out of road. A full moon shone down on a patch of tall grass surrounded by a stand of timber. Putting her foot on the brake, she looked at Logan and said, "Now what?"

Leaning forward, he switched off the engine and turned off the lights.

"What are you doing?" she asked.

He flicked a switch. The console between the seats disappeared. The steering wheel folded up and slid out of sight.

Mara lifted an inquisitive brow as Logan turned toward her, one arm stretched along the back of the seat. "Is this part of the lesson?" she asked.

"The best part. It used to be called 'parking.'"

"Parking?"

"Didn't you ever park in a car and neck?"

"No. Did you?"

"Sure, it was all the rage in the late fifties. Of course, kids don't do it much today. They just go to a motel."

"You weren't a kid when parking was popular."

Logan shrugged. "It was still fun," he said, moving closer. "Wanna give it a try?"

"Well, as long as it's part of the lesson," she said, trying not to grin.

"Radio," Logan said, "play some tunes from the fifties."

He put his arm around Mara and drew her up against him as Bonnie Guitar's voice came over the speaker and the words to "Dark Moon" wafted through the air.

"So," Mara said, her voice shaky as his tongue laved the sensitive skin beneath her ear. "Is this still part of lesson one?"

"Yes, and this is lesson two," he murmured, and claimed her lips with his.

Kissing Logan was like diving into a deep, warm pool. She felt weightless, breathless, as he deepened the kiss. Every nerve ending hummed to life as sensual heat flooded her being. The music faded into the distance as Logan became her whole world. He was the air she breathed, her reason for living. His mouth moved over hers, now as light and gentle as a summer breeze, now hard and demanding. His tongue dueled with hers while his hands moved over her body, his touch tender, almost reverent.

She shivered with pleasure as he whispered love words in her ear, soft sweet words that made her feel beautiful, desirable. When she was trembling with need, certain she would expire or explode, he lifted her out of the car. Holding her close, he opened the trunk and grabbed a blanket. Nuzzling her neck, he spread the blanket on a patch of grass, lowered her onto it, and dropped down beside her.

"You okay?" he asked.

"No."

"What's wrong?" he asked anxiously.

"You stopped kissing me, so I was wondering if that was the end of lesson two."

"What do you think?" he asked with a roguish grin.

She slipped her hand under his shirt. Her fingers rubbed back and forth across his belly, then slipped inside his trousers. "I think I'm ready for lesson three."

"You keep that up," he growled, "and we'll skip right to lesson four."

Closing her eyes, she flung her arms out to the side. "Teach me," she murmured. "Teach me everything."

"You asked for it."

He stretched out beside her, his arm sliding under her shoulders, drawing her body up against his, letting her feel the heat and strength of his arousal as he covered her mouth with his.

She moaned softly as his tongue tangled with hers. Caught up in his kisses, she hardly noticed the disappearance of their clothing until she felt his bare skin against hers.

She ran her hands over his back, his chest, loving the hard, muscular strength beneath her questing fingertips, the way his muscles quivered at her touch, the groan that rose in his throat as her hands caressed him.

Effortlessly, he rolled over, carrying her with him, so that she ended up on the top.

"Oh," she purred, "I like this."

He cupped her face in his hands. "I didn't want to squish you, or the little one," he said, and kissed her, slow and long and deep. "A taste?"

"You told me I tasted like poison," she said, pouting.

"You're human now, so . . ." He shrugged. "I'm willing to risk it."

She gazed up at the sky, her body quivering as his fangs brushed her skin. There was no pain, only a rush of sensual pleasure, a sense of satisfaction that came with knowing her life's blood was nourishing him.

"Logan, let me taste you."

He didn't argue, didn't question, merely made a slit in the pad of his thumb with his teeth and held it to her lips. His blood slid down her throat, hot and thick. It increased her desire, amplified her senses, heightened her pleasure as his body melded with hers.

It was, in a word, amazing. Drinking from humans had been wondrous beyond compare. Why had it never occurred to her that the opposite might also be true? If humans knew how wonderful a small drop of vampire blood tasted, how it magnified human senses, hunters would be seeking vampires more zealously than they did now, not for their heads, but for their blood.

Logan moved deep within her. Fulfillment came quickly and completely.

He kissed her gently, tenderly. "Thus endeth the lessons for tonight," he murmured, and rolled onto his side, taking her with him, so they lay face to face, their bodies still entwined.

"Logan . . ."

"What is it, love?"

"Tasting your blood." She gazed into his eyes, her own filled with wonder. "It made me feel . . . it was almost like being a vampire again! Did you know? Did you know it would make me feel like that?" Why hadn't she known how vampire blood affected humans? And why had it never occurred to her before?

"I've heard rumors to that effect."

"Why didn't you tell me?"

"Because it can be addicting." He ran his thumb over her lower lip. "And in the long run, it's dangerous."

"I want more."

"Maybe after the baby is born."

The baby. Mara slid her hand between her body and Logan's. Of course, concern for the baby had to come first. But after he was born . . . She smiled inwardly. If she couldn't be a vampire again, tasting Logan's blood would be the next best thing.

Chapter Twenty-two

Mara blew out a sigh as she smoothed her skirt over her hips. She was heartily tired of shapeless maternity clothes, swollen ankles, having to relieve herself every five minutes, and visits to the doctor, who now wanted to see her every week, and who had chided her, once again, for gaining too much weight.

Logan was waiting for her in the lobby of Ramsden's office. He looked up and smiled when he saw her.

Running into him at this time of her life had truly been a blessing, Mara thought as she walked toward him. He had been the one thing she could count on these past months, the only thing in her life that didn't change from day to day. At first, she hadn't planned to stay with him after the baby was born, but more and more she found herself wondering what she would ever do without him. As a vampire, she had been fearless, indomitable. As a mortal woman who would soon be responsible for a baby, she wasn't sure she could face the future alone. If not for Logan, she would now be dead by Rogen's hand. As much as she hated to admit it, she needed someone to protect her and her unborn child from her enemies.

And Logan was willing. Not only that, but he loved her. And she loved him. But was she in love with him? Only time would tell. Time, she thought. It was measured to her now, no longer infinite.

"So, how'd it go?" he asked.

"Ramsden said everything's fine. He's still going to induce me on the eighteenth, as planned."

"Is that a good idea? I don't know much about childbirth, but shouldn't he let the baby come when it's ready?"

She shrugged. "He said first babies often come early and he doesn't want to take a chance on my going into labor during the day, when he can't be there."

"I still think you should wait and see if you can't have it on the thirty-first."

Mara stuck her tongue out at him. "Sorry, you won't be getting a Halloween baby."

Logan made a clucking sound. "It would have been perfect."

"I guess so," Mara said.

"I can see the headlines now: EX-VAMPIRE GIVES BIRTH AT THE STROKE OF MIDNIGHT ON ALL-HALLOWS' EVE."

"Well, I'm sorry, but I'm glad I don't have to wait that extra two weeks."

Logan punched the button for the elevator, held the door for her while she stepped inside. She loved it that he was so polite, so protective of her. She admired his profile as they rode down to the first floor, curled her hands into fists to keep from reaching up to run her fingers through the hair at his nape, to stroke the firm line of his jaw, to run her thumb over his sultry lower lip. Lordy, the man seemed to get better looking every day.

Logan glanced at her. Quirking one brow, he smiled that insufferable knowing smile. And then he winked at her. "We'll be home soon."

"Doesn't matter. We're not supposed to make love anymore until after the baby's born." She grinned at his look of mock horror. The doctor had told her that, normally, he wouldn't have advised her to stop having sexual relations so soon, but, in this instance, he thought it would be a wise precaution, since her case was extremely unusual.

Logan grunted softly. "I guess it's a good thing we went parking when we did," he said with a wry grin.

The elevator doors slid open when they reached the main lobby. As Mara stepped outside, she said, "You know, the more I think about it, the more convinced I am that Ramsden is hiding something from me."

"What do you mean?"

"I'm not sure. He's been asking me an awful lot of questions about my past and about the baby's father . . ."

"What's the matter with that? Makes sense to me that he'd want to know everything he can."

"So, it doesn't seem strange to you? I mean, what possible difference can my past make? He's not asking about my health or my ancestors, but personal stuff, and . . ."

Her words trailed off as she reached the curb. Coming to an abrupt halt, she stared at the man standing a few feet away, unable to believe her eyes.

"What's wrong?" Logan glanced around, wondering what had put that stricken expression on her face.

"Kyle," she whispered. "It's Kyle."

Logan quickly stepped in front of her, ready to defend her, if necessary.

She couldn't stop staring at Kyle. He looked old and tired and endearingly familiar. She moved up beside Logan as Kyle closed the distance between them. "What are you doing here, Kyle?" she asked, keeping her tone deliberately cool.

He paid no attention to the man standing beside her. "Looking for you."

She couldn't stifle the rush of hope that filled her heart. "Why?"

"I should think that would be obvious. You're having my baby."

Mara lifted her chin, her heart pounding with trepidation. How had he found her? How did he know about the baby? She would have denied her pregnancy if it hadn't been so blatantly obvious. "What makes you think it's yours?"

Kyle glanced at Logan. "Are you going to tell me it's his?"

"Yes."

"I don't believe you."

"It doesn't matter what you believe."

"Dammit, Mara, I know it's mine. Can we talk for a few minutes?" Kyle glanced at Logan again. "Alone."

A muscle throbbed in Logan's jaw. "She's not going anywhere with you, alone or otherwise."

"It's all right, Logan," Mara said, laying her hand on his arm. "I'll meet you at the house."

Logan glared at Kyle. "I want her home in thirty minutes. Don't make me come looking for you."

"I'll bring her home when she's ready, and not one second before," Kyle retorted.

"Logan, I'll be all right." Standing on her tiptoes, Mara kissed his cheek. "I won't be long."

With a last warning look at Kyle, Logan got into his car and pulled away from the curb.

Kyle rubbed a hand over his jaw. "He's a vampire, isn't he?"

"Yes," she admitted. "A very old one."

"Why don't we go to the coffee shop across the street?" Kyle suggested. "We can talk there."

"All right."

Mara was as nervous as a cat in a thunderstorm as she sat in the booth facing Kyle. She couldn't stop staring at him, couldn't keep her heart from beating double-time whenever his gaze met hers. She had never been happier than when they were together, never been more miserable than when they were apart. And now he was here. She took a deep, calming breath. "What do you want to talk about?"

"I'm sorry for the way I behaved when you told me you were a . . ." He glanced around, lowering his voice. "When you told me what you are, but, dammit, you sprang it on me without any warning." He ran a hand through his hair, making her think he was as nervous as she. "I never told you, but my father was killed by a vampire. I know that doesn't excuse my behavior, but, maybe . . . maybe it explains why I reacted the way I did."

"I'm sorry about your father."

Kyle nodded. "If you'd just given me a little time to get used to the idea instead of taking off . . ."

"It's all water under the bridge now," she said, pleased that she sounded so cool and aloof.

"Is that what you think? I came to tell you . . ." He paused when a waitress approached their table. "A cup of coffee, please," he said.

With a nod, the waitress moved away.

"What did you come to tell me?" Mara asked.

"I want you to . . ." He took a deep breath, then said it all in a rush. "I want you to make me what you are."

Mara stared at him. "Are you saying that you want to be a vampire?"

"Hell, no," he exclaimed. "Who wants to be a vampire?"

"But you just said . . ."

"I'm willing to do whatever it takes for us to be together." He scrubbed his hands over his jaw. "The baby's mine, isn't it?"

"Yes." She glanced up in irritation when the waitress arrived with Kyle's order.

"Congratulations!" the waitress said, smiling expansively. "Can I get you anything else?"

"Just the check," Mara said.

The waitress knew how to take a hint. With a muttered "Yes, ma'am," she dropped the check on the table and hurried away.

Kyle stirred cream into his coffee, his expression thoughtful. "How can you be pregnant? Everybody knows that vampires can't reproduce."

Mara took a deep breath and let it out in a long, slow sigh. "I'm not a vampire anymore."

Kyle stared at her as though she had suddenly grown two heads and a tail. "What?"

She made a vague gesture with her hand. "It's true. I don't know how. I don't know why, but I've lost my powers."

"Are you telling me that you're mortal again?"

Nodding, she pulled his cup toward her, added sugar, and took a drink. "Now do you believe me?" she asked, pushing the cup away.

Kyle stared at her a moment longer, and then he grinned from ear to ear. "That's great!"

"I'm glad you think so."

"Don't you? Mara, think what it means. You're human again. We can be together now, as equals. I never stopped loving you. Even when I thought I hated you, I couldn't get you out of my mind." He reached across the table and took one of her hands in both of his. "Or my heart." He paused, his brow creasing in a frown. "That guy you were with, you're not . . . he's not . . ."

"He's just a good friend," she said, and wondered why it sounded like a lie. "I don't know what I would have done without him these last few months."

"You could have come to me."

"Do you really think I would have come back after what you said? The way you looked at me, as if I was some kind of monster?" She wasn't being entirely fair, and she knew it. To most humans, she had been a monster. There had been times when she had thought of herself that way. But she had expected more from the man who had vowed to love her as long as he lived.

"No, I guess not." He gave her hand a squeeze. "But that's all in the past. We're together now and that's the only thing that matters." He smiled at her. "We're together and we're going to have a baby. Call me old-fashioned, but I think we should get married."

"Married!" Now it was her turn to stare.

"Is that such a terrible idea?"

"No, but . . . married?"

"Don't you think our baby deserves a mother *and* a father?"

"Yes, but . . ." In all her years of existence, Mara had never once contemplated being a wife. Or a mother. Now both were there, within her grasp.

"I love you," Kyle said quietly. "I want to spend the rest of my life with you, grow old with you."

Mara frowned at him. What was so great about growing old, together or otherwise? Lovers in movies were always talking about growing old together, as if it was something wonderful, but for the life of her, she couldn't understand their reasoning. Why would anyone want to grow old, get sick, and die?

"Whether you're human or vampire," Kyle was saying, "it doesn't matter to me as long as we're together."

"Kyle, I don't like being human. When this baby is grown, I'm going to ask Logan to bring me over."

"Why the hell would you want to do that?"

"Because I liked being a vampire. Until this happened, I could scarcely remember what it was like to be mortal."

Mindful of others in the café, Kyle lowered his voice again. "You liked drinking blood?"

"Yes," she said, wanting to shock him without knowing why. "I liked that part, too."

Kyle looked at her as if seeing her for the first time. "I just can't believe this. I'd think you'd be thrilled to be human again. Grateful for the chance to have children and live an ordinary life."

"What's so great about being ordinary?"

With a sigh, Kyle drew his hands away from hers. "Nothing, I guess. I just thought . . ." He shook his head. "Never mind."

"What did you think?"

"I thought you loved me."

The hurt in his voice, the pain in his eyes, made her heart ache. "Kyle, I don't know how to be human anymore." Even that wasn't entirely true. She had finally mastered the art of cooking simple meals, she enjoyed working outside in the yard. She had even applied for a credit card using Logan's last name and address. She didn't like being human, but she was determined to make the best of it for as long as she had to, for the baby's sake.

"I'll help you," Kyle said. "I know we could be happy together if you'd just give us a chance."

Maybe he was right. If she sent him away now, she might never see him again. She had thought herself in love with him once. Perhaps she still was. Confused, she shook her head. She had been happy with Kyle in the past. When he'd left, she had been brokenhearted, certain she would never be happy again, and then Logan had entered her life again . . . Logan who loved her unconditionally. He would never turn his back on her. No matter what she did or what she said, she knew he would be there for her. In spite of Kyle's declaration of love, she wasn't sure she could depend on him.

She ran her finger around the rim of his coffee cup. Life would be so much easier if she wasn't pregnant. But she was, and Kyle was right—her baby deserved a mother and a father. So why was she hesitating? Being human wasn't all that bad. She might even grow to like it. She enjoyed mortal food. She liked being able to see her reflection in a mirror; in fact, she had spent far too much time admiring herself from every angle until she gained so much weight that she started avoiding anything that reflected her image.

She smiled inwardly. Fat or not, she was still a pretty woman; some said she was beautiful. Kyle was a strikingly handsome man. No doubt their baby would be adorable. But marriage . . . she just wasn't ready for that, not yet. She might never be ready.

"I'm sorry," Kyle said, "I don't mean to pressure you. Will you at least think about what I said?"

How could she refuse him when he had been willing to become a vampire—something he abhorred—just to be with her?

"Maybe we could move in together," Kyle suggested. "You know, sort of a trial marriage."

She had lived with Logan for several months. It seemed only fair to give Kyle equal time, and it would give her time to sort out her jumbled feelings.

* * *

Logan was less than thrilled with her decision. "So, you're going to move in with him, just like that?"

"Yes. He's waiting for me outside." She had decided to give Kyle another chance. He seemed sincere; otherwise, why would he have come looking for her? He had even been willing to join the ranks of the Undead. That couldn't have been an easy decision for him, especially in view of the fact that a vampire had killed his father. But, more than anything, she needed time away from Logan, time to figure out what—and who—she really wanted. Were all mortals this confused, or was it just her pregnancy that was causing her to change her mind every five minutes?

Logan crossed the floor in three long strides. He stopped in front of her, his face only inches from her own. "I love you," he declared. "I've loved you for centuries. I've taken care of you, given you shelter, and now you're turning your back on me for that . . . that mortal?"

Mara met Logan's angry gaze, unblinking. "I'm mortal, too, remember?" The fact that Kyle was also human had been the final, deciding factor in her decision to go with him.

"I can change that," Logan said flatly.

"No." Not liking the dark undercurrent in his voice or the ominous look in his eyes, Mara folded her arms protectively over her stomach. No matter how she felt about Logan, she had a baby to think of. And Kyle was right. Her baby needed a father. A mortal father. And no matter how she felt about Logan—and at the moment, she wasn't sure how she felt—her life and that of her child would be centered in the mortal world.

Logan's eyes narrowed. "What if I refuse to let you go?"

She lifted her chin defiantly. "You won't."

"No? What makes you so sure?"

"Because you love me," she said quietly, "and because you know I'll hate you forever if you keep me here against my will."

"Maybe I'll just kill him, then."

"Logan . . ." Mara cupped his cheek with her hand. "Please don't make this any harder than it is. I'm grateful for all of your help, and I do love you, but I'm mortal now. I can't stay with you." Tears stung her eyes and she blinked them back. "I can't bear the constant reminder of what I was, what I've lost." And that, at least, was true.

Logan blew out a breath, his anger routed by the unhappiness in her voice, the resignation in her eyes. "All right, have it your way." Like always, he thought.

"Will you help me pack?"

"Where are you going?"

"I'm not sure, but we can't very well stay here, with you." What a nightmare that would be! She could just imagine Logan and Kyle under the same roof, glaring at each other like two hungry wolves after the same prey.

"No need for you to move out," Logan said gruffly. "I'll go."

"That's sweet of you, but . . . I think Kyle and I are going back to California."

"Are you sure that's wise? I thought Ramsden wanted you close by."

"I know, but"—she bit down on the corner of her lip—"you remember I told you I thought he was acting suspicious? Well, it was even worse this last time. I can't put my finger on it, exactly, but . . . I don't know. I just don't trust him."

"Are you sure it's not because he's a vampire and you're not?"

"I don't know. Maybe that's it. But whatever the reason, I have a bad feeling about having the baby here, so I'm going back to California. Please don't tell Ramsden or anyone else where I've gone."

"Whatever you want," he said, his voice cool.

"Logan, I don't know how I'll ever be able to repay . . ."

He held up his hand. "Don't even go there! You don't owe me a damn thing," he said curtly. "Come on, I'll help you pack. The sooner you get out of here, the better."

"Logan . . ."

"You know where I live if it doesn't work out."

Without waiting to see if she followed or not, he turned on his heel and headed for the bedroom. He didn't want her to go, but he'd be damned if he would beg her to stay.

Chapter Twenty-three

Kyle shook his head as he stared at Mara's house. House! It was more like a mansion. Located in the Hollywood Hills, it rose up from the ground like a giant bird of prey about to take flight.

"This is yours?" he asked incredulously.

"Yes," Mara said, unlocking the front door. "Do you like it?"

"What's not to like? You didn't tell me you were rich."

She shrugged as she stepped over the threshold and switched on the lights. "It didn't occur to me."

Kyle followed her inside, pausing under the high arch that led into the spacious living room. The first thing he noticed was one of the paintings he had done of her hanging over the fireplace. He studied it for several moments. It was the best thing he had ever done. He glanced at Mara, then back at the painting. She looked the same as she had when he'd painted her portrait, and yet she didn't. Her skin was a little less translucent, her hair a little less lustrous. But it was more than that. He studied the painting a moment longer before he realized what it was. The vampire glamour she had once exuded was missing.

Moving into the room, he whistled softly. He had been in some swanky homes in his time, but nothing quite like this. The walls, carpets, and twin sofas were white. A tall, slender Egyptian vase was filled with red silk flowers. A couple of red throw pillows and a trio of red tapers in a wrought-iron candelabra added additional splashes of color to the room.

He crossed the floor to get a closer look at a glass-fronted curio cabinet that housed a variety of knickknacks, all with a decidedly Egyptian flavor. A large landscape that depicted the Nile River beneath a bloodred moon hung on the wall across from the cabinet.

"Mind if I light a fire?" he asked.

"That would be nice," Mara said, and tried not to remember that she had once been able to ignite a fire with a mere wave of her hand. "Make yourself at home," she said. "I'm going upstairs to change."

It was good to be back, Mara thought as she climbed the stairs. Of all the houses she owned, this was one of her favorites, the other being her hideaway in the mountains.

She would have to buy a mirror or two, she thought. Perhaps a gilt-edged one for the living room, a full-length one for her bedroom, and an oval one for the wall behind the sink in the bathroom.

She came to an abrupt halt when she opened her bedroom door. She wouldn't have to buy a mirror for this room, after all. The beautiful antique oak looking-glass that Logan had bought for her stood in the corner.

Blinking back her tears, she sank down on the edge of the bed. Murmuring, "Oh, Logan," she buried her face in her hands and wept. She cried because she didn't want to be human again, because she was afraid she would be a terrible mother, because Kyle loved her and she was afraid she didn't really love him. She cried because she missed Logan, because, of all the men she had known in her lengthy existence, he was the only one who truly understood her and loved her anyway.

Lifting a corner of the bedspread, she wiped the tears from her eyes. She had made her decision and she would live with it. She was mortal and pregnant and Kyle loved her. She had thought herself in love with him, but she knew now that it had only been infatuation. She was in love with Logan. Maybe she had always been in love with him, but once again, she had walked away from him, left him because she couldn't bear to live with a man who was now stronger and more powerful than she was. She was jealous of his preternatural powers. It was too painful to be with him, to be constantly reminded of the supernatural abilities she had once taken for granted and no longer possessed.

Shaking off her melancholy, she undressed and then, deciding a bath sounded relaxing, she slipped into her robe and went into the bathroom to fill the tub.

When it was full, she tossed her robe aside. Muttering, "You're as big as a whale," she stepped carefully into the water.

Closing her eyes, Mara rested her hands on her belly and tried to imagine what the baby looked like. She couldn't wait to hold her son in her arms. Perhaps she would name him after Cleopatra's one true love.

"Antony," she murmured. It was a nice name, a strong name, but one that held so many unhappy memories.

"You're frowning."

Opening her eyes, Mara looked up to see Kyle standing in the doorway. For centuries she had lived alone, bestowing her favors on those who pleased her, never giving away her heart, never letting anyone get close to her, running away whenever any of her lovers became too important or too demanding. Why was it that now, when she had lost her powers and apparently her ability to make a decision, she was attracted to two men? Men who were as different as night and day.

Her gaze moved over Kyle. He was almost as tall as Logan, though not as muscular. His hair was short and brown where Logan's was long and black. Kyle's eyes were gray, Logan's were dark brown. Each was handsome in his own way, although no mortal could hope to compete with a vampire's preternatural allure.

"I brought your suitcases upstairs in case you want to unpack later."

"Thank you."

He folded his arms over his chest, then rested one shoulder against the doorjamb. His gaze moved over her in a long, lingering glance filled with uncertainty and desire.

Mara blushed under his lustful gaze.

"Would you like me to wash your back?" he asked, his voice suddenly thick.

She hesitated a moment, then nodded. "If you like." Logan wouldn't have asked, she thought with a pang. He would have climbed into the tub with her.

She smiled inwardly as she watched Kyle walk toward her. One thing she loved about men was that they were unable to hide their lust. It was easy to see that Kyle was aroused by the sight of her reclining in a tub amid a froth of scented bubbles.

She grinned inwardly. Perhaps he had a thing for whales.

He dropped to his knees beside the bathtub and then,

taking up the soap, he washed her back, then her shoulders and her neck.

With a sigh, she closed her eyes as his soapy hands caressed her, easing the tensions of the day. Gradually, his hands moved lower, his touch turning from soothing to arousing.

His breath tickled her ear as he whispered, "Ever made love in a bathtub?"

"Not this one." In most tubs, it would have been uncomfortable if not impossible, but her bathtub was like a small pool, easily big enough for two. Or, in this case, three.

"I'm game if you are," he said, his voice husky.

She almost said yes, but then the baby moved, giving her the perfect excuse to say no without hurting Kyle's feelings.

"We shouldn't," she said, looking up at him. "This far along in my pregnancy . . . the doctor said it wouldn't be a good idea, given my history and all."

Kyle wasn't happy about her decision, but he accepted it with good grace.

"Would you hand me a towel, please?" she asked.

"Sure." Rising, he helped her out of the tub. "Motherhood agrees with you," he remarked, handing her a towel. "You're even more beautiful than when we met."

"I'm fat."

"You're not fat, you're pregnant. And it looks good on you."

Tears stung the backs of her eyes. Logan had said the same thing not so long ago. She dried off quickly, then wrapped herself in a fluffy white robe.

Coming up behind her, Kyle placed his hands on her shoulders and turned her to face him. "Kissing is still okay, isn't it?"

"Of course." She closed her eyes as he cupped her face in his hands and kissed her gently. She felt a rush of tenderness as his arms went around her, pulling her close. The baby chose that moment to give a lusty kick.

"I think the baby's jealous," Kyle remarked.

"Maybe you're squishing him."

Kyle grunted softly. "I'll be glad when he gets here."

She made a soft sound deep in her throat as he kissed her again, hard and quick, and then rained kisses along the curve of her neck. He nipped her earlobe, then nuzzled the sensitive skin behind her ear. She canted her head to the side, expecting the touch of fangs, and then felt a rush of disappointment. This wasn't Logan. It was Kyle.

The thought sobered her. Drawing away, she folded her arms over her middle.

"Is anything wrong?"

"No." She shook her head. "I'm just a little cold."

"How about some hot chocolate to warm you up? I don't know about you, but I'm kind of hungry. I make a mean tuna melt."

She forced a smile. "Thanks. That sounds good."

He laughed softly. "I never thought I'd be fixing you dinner."

Mara lay awake long after Kyle had fallen asleep. She had never expected to see him again and now he was here, lying close beside her, his legs tangled with hers. He was excited about the baby. He wanted to marry her. She still couldn't believe that he had found her, that he had been willing to become a vampire to be with her.

"Mrs. Kyle Bowden," she murmured. "And family." Lying beside him, with his breath warm upon her cheek, she told herself that she was happy, content. If she said it often enough, maybe she would begin to believe it. With each passing day, it was becoming easier to accept being human. Perhaps, in time, she would forget she had once been a vampire.

She placed her hand on her stomach and smiled as she felt the baby kick. Being a vampire had been wonderful, exciting, a high like nothing else, but this . . . being pregnant . . . could there be anything in all the world more amazing than creating a new life and feeling it move inside you? A new life with unlimited possibilities. She had been powerful as a vampire, but even that didn't compare to this. As a vampire she had only been able to take away life, not create it.

She felt the sting of tears behind her eyes as she imagined holding her son in her arms, counting each tiny finger and toe, pressing a kiss to baby-soft skin. In Biblical times, women had considered it a curse if they couldn't bear a child. Motherhood had been their reason for living. Elizabeth had borne a son to Zacharias in her old age and counted it a blessing. Rachel had envied her sister, Leah, because Rachel was barren. Modern women no longer felt it necessary to have children to prove their worth, but lying there, feeling her child move within her, Mara knew this was the reason for her existence.

Kyle stirred beside her, scattering her thoughts. He loved her. He would take care of her and the baby. Holding to that thought, she kissed his cheek.

"What's the matter?" he asked, slipping his arm around her shoulders. "Is the baby keeping you awake?"

"No, I was just lying here, feeling happy and maternal."

His arm tightened around her. "I intend to spend the rest of my life making you happy."

The rest of his life, she mused. How long would that

be? Forty years? Fifty? The blink of an eye in the life she had once known. She thrust the memory away, then frowned as a new thought occurred to her. "How did you find me?"

"I hired someone to look for you."

"Oh? Who?"

"Who else?" he asked with a grin. "A vampire hunter."

Heart pounding, Mara bolted upright and switched on the light. "A vampire hunter? You sent a vampire hunter after me?"

"Hey, take it easy. The contract was to find you, that's all."

"Are you mad? No hunter worth the name would keep a bargain like that. Who was it? What was his name?"

"Lou McDonald, and he's a she."

"McDonald!" Mara shook her head. Among the vampire community, Lou McDonald was a name to be reckoned with.

"She's the one who gave me your doctor's name. That's how I found you."

Mara blew out a sigh. Leaving Nevada had been the smartest thing she had ever done.

"I don't know why you're so upset," Kyle said, sitting up. "She's a vampire hunter, and you're not a vampire anymore."

"It doesn't matter. Don't you understand? If she finds me, she'll kill me." Mara wrapped her arms around her middle in a protective gesture that was as old as time. "And the baby, too."

Mara bit down on her lower lip. She had bought this house using an alias. She carried no credit cards in her name, had no driver's license. Her home phone was unlisted. There was no way for McDonald to find her.

Finding Kyle was another matter. And if McDonald found Kyle . . .

Mara shuddered. She had no desire to lose her head to a hunter's wicked blade.

"I'm sorry," Kyle said. "I didn't know how else to find you."

"You haven't told her you found me, have you?"

"No. We haven't talked in a while. Don't worry, I won't let her know where you are . . ." His voice trailed off, and then he swore softly. "She can find you through me, can't she?"

"Yes. You can't use any of your credit cards while we're here. We'll have to pay cash for everything. I bought this house under an assumed name, so I don't think she can find us that way. If she calls you, don't answer. It might be best if you got a new cell phone, a prepaid one like mine, so she can't trace it."

Kyle lay back on the bed and drew her down beside him. "Calm down, Mara. I won't let anything happen to you."

She rested her head against his shoulder, her heart still pounding. She'd be no match for any hunter now. And it wasn't just her life she had to worry about.

"Listen, sweetie, I don't know why you decided to leave Nevada, but . . ."

Something in his tone annoyed her. Maybe it was the condescending way he said "sweetie." Sitting up again, she put some space between them. "I left because I had a bad feeling about staying. Did I tell you that the doctor I was seeing is a vampire?"

Kyle shook his head ruefully. "No, you forgot to mention that."

"He seemed nice enough in the beginning, but the last few times I saw him . . ." She worried a lock of her hair.

"I can't put my finger on anything concrete, but, I don't know, he just creeped me out."

"So, who's going to deliver the baby?"

"I was thinking you would."

"Me?" He jackknifed into a sitting position, the color draining from his face. "Are you out of your mind? I'm not a doctor."

"I can't have the baby in a hospital. They'd want insurance forms and personal info. I don't have any identification."

"Why not?"

"I've rarely needed any, and when I did, I just made whoever wanted to see my ID believe they had. But I can't do that anymore. Besides, I can't risk having them take my blood or the baby's."

Kyle muttered an oath. She was right, of course. If the baby carried any trace of vampire blood, it would undoubtedly cause quite a stir among hospital personnel, especially when the mother was human.

"We could be in big trouble," he agreed. "What about your old vampire friends? Can't they help?"

Mara thought of Brenna and Cara and Savanah. Nice women, all of them. Cara and Savanah had both given birth. They would know what to do. But for some reason she didn't understand, she was reluctant to ask for their help, reluctant to admit to anyone, including herself, that she needed help, even though she had never needed it more. She had chosen to stay with Kyle because he was human and because he was the baby's father. She knew now that she would have been safer with Logan.

Mara yawned behind her hand. She was tired. Her back hurt, and she was getting a headache.

"We can talk about this tomorrow," Kyle said, turning off the light. "You should get some sleep."

She curled up against him and closed her eyes, but sleep was a long time coming. She wished fleetingly that it was Logan lying beside her. He would know what to do. She wouldn't be afraid to face McDonald or anyone else with Logan covering her back.

The next few days went by slowly, and yet all too fast. Kyle turned one of the bedrooms into a studio, and Mara turned another one into a nursery. They rarely left the house except for groceries. Most nights, they snuggled on the sofa watching TV and necking like teenagers, some nights they played cards. At other times, they went for walks in the moonlight.

One afternoon, Kyle suggested Mara pose for him before the baby came.

"Like this?" Mara glanced at her stomach. She was as big as a horse.

"You're beautiful."

"I'm sure no one else would think so," she muttered, and then smiled faintly. "But I'm glad you do."

"Come on," he coaxed. "I'm tired of watching TV."

"Oh, all right. What should I wear?"

"I was thinking of painting you in the buff."

"Nude? Are you serious?" She placed her hands on her stomach. "I don't think so."

"All right. Hang on a minute," he said, and left the room.

Mara stared after him. What was he up to? She shook her head. Naked, indeed. She must have gained fifty pounds if she had gained an ounce.

Kyle returned a few minutes later carrying a sheer panel from one of the bedroom windows.

She eyed the curtain suspiciously. "What are you going to do with that?"

"You'll see. Get undressed."

Minutes later, she was reclining on the sofa, her girth strategically camouflaged by the curtain, so that only her arms, legs, and shoulders were bare. A pot of greenery added a splash of color near her feet.

Kyle regarded his handiwork a moment and then pronounced it, "Perfect!"

Mara shook her head in amusement. "Only you would think so."

She watched his face as he worked, his brow furrowed in concentration, his brushes moving quick and sure over the canvas. After a time, she closed her eyes and Logan's image crept into her mind. She imagined she heard his voice, soft and silky and filled with longing as he whispered that he loved her. In her mind, she yearned toward him, her body aching for the touch of his hand in her hair, the pressure of his lips on hers. And then his voice again, low and seductive, reminding her of the nights they had spent together, the love they had shared.

"Mara? Hey, Mara, are you all right?"

Feeling disoriented, she opened her eyes, expecting to find Logan standing over her. It took her a moment to remember where she was. "Oh. Kyle."

"Are you all right?" he asked again.

"Of course. Why do you ask?"

"You were talking in your sleep."

"I was?" A rush of guilt swept through her. Had she called Logan's name? "What did I say?"

"I don't know. It was in a language I didn't understand."

"I must have been dreaming."

"Yeah. It must have been some dream. Your cheeks are

flushed." He smiled faintly. "Can I hope you were dreaming about me?"

"I . . . I don't remember."

He regarded her a moment, his brow furrowed. "I thought you might want to take a break."

"Yes, I would. Thank you."

He offered her his hand, and she let him pull her to her feet. "Can we continue this tomorrow?" she asked. "I'm tired. I think I'll go to bed."

"Sure, honey, if that's what you want. I'll be up in a little while."

"All right." She kissed him on the cheek and then left the room, her heart heavy with a load of guilt and remorse.

Chapter Twenty-four

"Gone? What do you mean, she's gone?" Lou stared at her sister. "Where would she go?"

"I don't know. She missed her last appointment. When I called to see if she was all right, I got a message saying the number had been disconnected. Ramsden went out to the house to check on her, but no one was home, and there was a For Rent sign on the front lawn."

Lou drummed her fingertips on the tabletop. "Why would she leave?" she asked, frowning. "And where would she go?"

Cindy shrugged. "Who knows why vampires do anything? I'm going to order dessert," she said as their waitress approached the table. "Do you want anything?"

"Apple pie a là mode and a cup of coffee, black."

Cindy ordered the same, then leaned forward, her arms crossed on the table. "Ramsden's going crazy. He's called everyone he can think of, but no one knows where Mara's gone, or why. He was supposed to induce her tomorrow night. He's got everything ready. Crib, blankets, diapers, even a wet nurse."

Lou grunted softly. Something about this whole thing

just didn't add up. Why would Mara take off now, when the baby was due? Had something spooked her? And if so, what? Had Bowden found her? Was he the one she was running from? Or had they taken off together? Maybe telling him where Mara was hadn't been such a great idea after all.

Lou raked her fingers through her hair. Maybe it was time to get in touch with Bowden. Digging her cell phone out of her pocket, she punched in his number and got a recording saying the number was no longer in service. Damn.

"Something wrong?" Cindy asked.

"Bowden's phone isn't working. Why do you suppose he'd cancel his service?"

"Maybe he lost his cell and got a new one."

"Maybe," Lou said thoughtfully. "Or maybe he found what he was looking for."

"You think he found Mara?"

"I'd say it was a definite possibility."

"Oh?"

"I gave him Ramsden's address."

"Why on earth did you do that?"

"I don't know," Lou muttered. "But it seemed like a good idea at the time."

"Well, pardon the pun," Cindy retorted, "but it sure sucks now."

Ramsden paced the floor of the delivery room he had painstakingly prepared. There was a hospital bed with tie-down straps for Mara, a crib for the baby, and a wet nurse waiting for his call.

A string of oaths emerged from his lips as he stared down at the bed. Here it was, the night before he was to induce her, and Mara had gone missing. Had something tipped her off? He went back over the times he had seen her and shook his head. He was certain he had never said or done anything to make her the least bit suspicious of his motives, and yet she had taken off without a word. Why? And what was he going to tell his wife? Janis had been wanting a baby for months, nagging, begging, crying for the child he couldn't give her. Mara had come along at just the right time. At the height of her powers, no one on Earth, living or Undead, could touch her, but she was helpless now. Helpless and pregnant, like the answer to a prayer.

In the beginning, he had only been interested in the child. He had intended to do some research on the baby before taking it home, hence the crib, changing table, and other items necessary for looking after a newborn. Who knew what could be learned from a child conceived by a mortal and a vampire that was thousands of years old? He hadn't decided what to do about Mara, whether to let her live or dispose of her after the baby was born. If he'd decided to let her live, he had planned to tell her that the baby had been born dead and deformed and that he had disposed of it.

As the months went by, he had grown more and more curious about Mara's condition, and he began to wonder what had caused her to revert. Had she found a cure for the vampire's kiss, and if so, what was it? Vampires, especially those newly made, often came to him looking for a cure that didn't exist. But if he could find one, there was a fortune to be made. One way or the other, he was certain something in Mara's DNA held the answers.

Of course, all his plans were useless without Mara.

Plucking a stuffed teddy bear from the crib, he stared at it a moment, then ripped it in half and threw the pieces across the room. He had never been one to give up without a fight. He wouldn't start now. He would find Mara. One way or another, he would find her.

Chapter Twenty-five

Edna Mae Turner pulled a pair of crystal wineglasses from the cupboard. She filled one for herself with O positive and after filling the second glass with AB negative, she handed it to her best friend, Pearl. She had met Pearl Jackson in a maternity ward in a Texas hospital decades ago. They had been friends, both as mortals and vampires, ever since. Shortly after they had been turned, they had bought this house and moved in together. Together, they had learned how to survive as vampires. She grinned inwardly. They were an odd couple. She was short, rather plump, and a trifle vain; Pearl was tall and angular. Edna dyed her hair red; Pearl's was as white as new-fallen snow. Their taste in furnishings was also disparate. Edna liked chrome and glass, Pearl liked antiques, which made for an interesting mix when they moved in together.

"To Travis," Edna said, lifting her glass.

"To Travis," Pearl echoed.

Grimacing, Edna sipped the contents of her glass. She was used to the taste, had, in fact, grown to love it, but sometimes she forgot that she was a vampire and that drinking blood was no longer repulsive.

"I miss him," Pearl said, wiping a crimson tear from her eye. "I can't believe he's gone."

Travis Jackson had been Pearl's grandson. Pearl had brought him across shortly after the Dark Gift had been forced upon her.

Pearl took another drink. "This is quite good. Have you found a new source?"

"Indeed, I have." They had discovered early on that they didn't like hunting. Instead, they had found a rather unsavory character named Josiah Hogg who sold blood to the vampire community. "Our new supplier's name is Pritkin. He's much more pleasant than Hogg ever was. Cheaper, too. And he smells better."

Pearl nodded, and took another drink.

"Do you know who destroyed Travis?" Edna asked, resuming her seat on the sofa.

"Some hunter based on the West Coast. Lee? Lou . . . ?"

"Not Lou McDonald!" Edna exclaimed, her eyes wide. "Tell me it wasn't McDonald."

"Yes, dear, that's the one," Pearl said, and then murmured, "Oh, my, that's not good, is it?"

"No." Edna took another sip from her glass. "I have some other, equally disturbing news," she said with a frown. "Or maybe it's good news. I heard that Mara has lost her powers."

Pearl stared at her friend over the rim of her wineglass. "You must have heard wrong, dear. That's impossible."

Edna shrugged. "Well, that's what I heard."

"Was the source reliable?" Pearl asked, her voice rising with excitement. "Maybe she's found a cure! Do you think she'd share it with us?"

"I don't know. I also heard she's somewhere in California. If we could find her, and ask her . . ."

"Yes," Pearl said. "And if she refuses . . ."

"Maybe we could get some of her blood . . ."

"And find a cure ourselves!" they finished in unison.

"Oh, to be human again," Pearl said wistfully. "To enjoy a lovely glass of iced tea on a warm summer day, or sip a nice cup of hot cocoa in front of the fire . . . chocolate!" she exclaimed. "Oh, Edna, do you remember the taste of chocolate?"

"Not really," Edna replied. She had forgotten so many things since becoming Nosferatu. Pearl remained the only constant in her life. She wouldn't have wished being a vampire on anyone, but she was forever grateful that Rafe Cordova, that self-righteous bloodsucker, had turned her and Pearl at the same time. She couldn't imagine what her life would be without her best friend. "Pearl . . . ?"

"Yes, dear?"

"I'm not sure I'd want to be mortal again."

Pearl stared at her in disbelief. "I don't believe what I'm hearing."

"Think about it, about what we'd be giving up. Do you want to go back to being a weak old lady? How many years would we have left if we were human again? I like feeling good all the time. I like not needing my glasses to read. And what about you? Your arthritis doesn't bother you anymore, does it? Except for the blood thing, I like being a vampire. And even that's not as bad as I thought it would be."

Pearl sat up straighter, a sudden sparkle in her eyes. "You're right, of course, dear."

"It doesn't mean we can't keep looking for a cure for

the werewolves," Edna said brightly. "After all, they're
nothing but a menace to human and Nosferatu alike."

"That's true."

"And the weather in California is much nicer than it is
here in Texas at this time of the year."

"And there's nothing to keep us here, now that Travis
is gone," Pearl added, warming to the idea.

"And McDonald is in California," Edna reminded her.
"We could kill two birds with one stone, so to speak."

"Yes," Pearl said, and then grinned. "Once we were
hunters hunting vampires. Now we're vampires hunting
hunters. I find that amusing, don't you?"

"Yes, indeed," Edna said. Draining her glass, she
threw it into the fireplace where it shattered against the
back wall, the tiny pieces of glass raining down on
the flames in a shower of rainbow-hued crystal. "Let's
go pack!"

After draining her own glass, Pearl tossed it into the
fire. "California, here we come!"

Chapter Twenty-six

Mara looked up from the magazine she had been reading, and frowned. "Kyle, you're staring at me again."

"Am I? I'm sorry, I can't seem to stop."

"Is something wrong?" she asked, laying the magazine aside. It was a silly question, she thought. She was pregnant. She had no friends, no doctor, and, in spite of the books she'd read, no idea how to take care of the infant once it arrived.

"What could be wrong?" Kyle asked with a wry grin. "You're expecting a baby any day now and the only help you've got is me."

She tried to think of something reassuring to say, but nothing came to mind. Hadn't she just been thinking the same thing? The baby would be here soon, she thought. She had been having contractions for the last couple of days. Braxton Hicks, her doctor had called them. She had gone online and looked up Braxton Hicks. The contractions had been named after an English doctor, John Braxton Hicks, back in 1872. Most of the time, the contractions were uncomfortable, but not painful. According to an article online, if she had more than four contractions in an hour, and if the pain escalated, it was probably time to call the doctor. She hadn't mentioned the contractions to Kyle. He was worried enough.

Kyle drummed his fingers on the arm of the sofa. Too worried to sit still any longer, he began to pace the floor. He didn't know a damn thing about childbirth, and neither did she. What if something went wrong? What if the baby was breach? What if Mara hemorrhaged? He swore softly. There were a hundred things that could go wrong during labor and delivery and he wasn't equipped to handle any of them. He was an artist, not a damned doctor.

"Go pack a bag," he said. "We're leaving."

"Where are we going?"

"To Porterville." He held up a hand to still her protest. "I know you don't want to go, but I don't care. We can't do this alone. There are just too many things that could go wrong. And since you're dead set against going to a hospital, Porterville's the only other option we've got."

"I don't want to . . ."

"Hey! We can do this the easy way, or the hard way. The easy way, you pack a bag and we go. The hard way, I stuff you into a bag and we go. It's your choice."

"Kyle . . ."

"I'm not kidding, sweetie. I can handle McDonald if she shows up. But what about that doctor? He's a frickin' vampire. If he comes looking for you, neither one of us stands a chance against him, and you know it."

In the end, that was the argument that swayed Mara.

Forty minutes later, their bags were packed and in the trunk of Kyle's car and they were on the road to Porterville.

* * *

Rane blew out a sigh of relief when he opened the door and saw Mara standing on the porch. He had been thinking about her, worrying about her, ever since he'd returned from Reno. He glanced at the man beside her, startled to see Kyle Bowden instead of Logan. Rane grunted softly, thinking that Kyle Bowden must have done some mighty fast talking to get back into Mara's good graces. As a vampire, she hadn't been really big on forgive and forget.

"It's good to see you," Rane said, opening the door wider. "You, too, Kyle. Come on in. So," Rane said when the three of them were seated in the living room, "what brings you up this way?"

"We need your help," Kyle said. "As you can see, Mara's pregnant."

"I hope you don't expect me to deliver the baby," Rane muttered.

"No," Kyle said, "but I think her life might be in danger. She's lost her powers . . ."

Rane looked at Mara, his senses probing the air around her. "You're human again," he murmured. He supposed that explained why Rafe hadn't been able to find her since they saw her in Nevada, and yet, it didn't, not really. Mara had shared blood with him and his brother. She had brought his father across. They should have been able to locate her no matter where she went. "How could it have happened? I mean, no one's ever heard of a vampire reverting. It's . . ." He shook his head. "Hell, I don't know what it is."

"I don't know how it happened." Mara folded her arms over her stomach. "No one knows."

Rane swore softly. She had told him she was changing,

but this was one change he hadn't considered. Human again. It was impossible, unthinkable.

"Hi, Mara, Kyle," Savanah said, coming into the room.

"Hello, Savanah," Mara said, forcing a smile.

Kyle nodded at Rane's wife.

Savanah sat on the arm of Rane's chair. "Kyle, did I hear you say Mara's life is in danger?" Savanah asked.

"We're not really sure," Kyle replied, "but Mara says she doesn't trust her doctor, even though he's a vampire . . ."

"Ramsden?" Rane asked.

Kyle nodded.

"Pregnant women get a lot of funny ideas as their due date approaches," Savanah remarked. "Maybe there's nothing to worry about."

"Better safe than sorry. Anyway," Kyle said, looking sheepish, "she's not just in danger from the doctor. When I couldn't find her, I hired a vampire hunter . . ."

"You did what?" Rane exclaimed.

"Yeah, I know, it was a dumb thing to do, but I didn't know how else to find her. I told the hunter I didn't want Mara hurt in any way, I just wanted to know where she was, and it worked. Only now . . ."

"Who was the hunter?" Rane asked, his voice grim.

"Lou McDonald."

"Damn! She's as hard as flint, that one. And her sister's not much better."

"Sister?" Kyle muttered, frowning. "She never mentioned a sister."

"Cindy Meloni."

"There was a Cindy working for Ramsden," Mara said. "Do you think that's her?"

"Could be. The McDonald sisters have made quite a name for themselves in the last few years," Rane said.

"They've racked up an impressive body count between them, although I don't think Meloni does much killing." Rane scrubbed a hand over his jaw. "You were right to bring Mara here. We'll take good care of her. I'll call Rafe and the old man and let them know what's going on."

"Hey, I didn't come here to drop her off," Kyle said, slipping his arm around Mara's shoulders. "We're in this together." He looked at Mara and smiled. "The three of us."

Rane looked at Mara. It was easy to see that Kyle was deeply in love with her. Who could blame him? Vampire or not, she was an incredibly beautiful woman, and softer, sweeter, somehow, now that she was mortal. He was less certain of Mara's feelings for Kyle. Had she really forgiven the man for the way he had behaved when she'd told him she was a vampire? Of course, now that she was human, Kyle's feelings on whether she was a vampire or not didn't really matter.

"The two of you are welcome to stay here, with us, of course," Rane said. "We've got plenty of room."

"Who's going to deliver the baby?" Savanah asked.

Mara shook her head. "I don't know. I don't want to go to a hospital where they might do tests. I don't know if the baby will be normal or not, human or not . . ."

"Well, you came to the right place," Savanah said with a smile. "I've taken the Lamaze classes."

Rane snorted softly. "Fat lot of good they did."

Savanah made a face at him. "Okay, so I didn't use the technique during the actual birth, but I still know what to do, and I think that, between myself and Cara, we've got enough experience to deliver a baby. And there's a hospital in town if anything goes wrong."

Later, while Kyle was getting their bags and Rane was calling his brother and his father, Savanah took

Mara upstairs to see Abbey, who was sleeping peacefully in her crib.

"She's beautiful," Mara said.

"Thank you."

"Why did you take the Lamaze classes and then not use what you learned?"

"It hurt too much. I used Rane instead."

"What do you mean?"

"He talked me through it." Savanah laid her hand on Mara's arm. "This must be so difficult for you."

"You have no idea."

"I hope you don't think this is rude, but I can't help wondering . . . how do you feel about being human again?" Savanah asked.

"I hated it at first, but now"—Mara placed her hand on her belly—"it's not so bad. I hope I have a little boy who'll be as handsome as your Abbey is pretty. Can I ask you something?"

"Sure."

"What's it like for you, being the only mortal in a family of vampires?"

"To tell you the truth, it was a little strange at first, even a little scary, but Rane's been wonderfully supportive. And I love the rest of his family, although Roshan can be a little intimidating at times."

"Yes, Roshan," Mara said thoughtfully. He was less than five hundred years old, and yet, even before she had given him her blood, he had been a powerful vampire. She wondered who had made him. Odd that she had never thought to ask. Of course, it didn't matter now.

Savanah bent over the crib to stroke her daughter's downy cheek, then turned and led the way back downstairs.

Rafe, Kathy, Cara, and Vince were sitting in the living

room with Rane and Kyle. Rafe gained his feet and gave Mara a hug; then, holding her at arm's length, he said, "It is good to see you."

"It's good to see you, too."

"Are you all right?" He glanced at her swollen belly and smiled. "This will take some getting used to."

"Don't tease her, Rafe," Cara said. "The last few weeks of any pregnancy are uncomfortable, at best."

"I am not teasing." Keeping hold of Mara's hand, Rafe led her to the sofa and gently drew her down beside him, so that she was sitting between himself and his wife.

"When's the baby due?" Kathy asked.

"Soon, I think. I've been having contractions all day."

"All day?" Kyle exclaimed. "Why didn't you say something sooner?"

"I didn't want to worry you. Besides, I've been having them for weeks. The doctor said they were just Braxton Hicks. Nothing to worry about." Mara bit down on her lower lip. "But they're coming harder now, and closer together." She groaned softly. "I think I'm in labor." She had no sooner spoken the words than she doubled over as a sharp pain threatened to cut her in two.

"Mara!" Kyle darted across the room and dropped to his knees in front of her. "What should I do?"

"Make it stop!"

"No!" Kyle shook his head in vigorous denial. "You can't be in labor. It's too early!"

Mara groaned as another contraction took her unawares. "Tell that to the baby."

"Maybe it's false labor," Cara suggested.

"I don't think so," Kathy said, coming up behind her mother-in-law. "Her water just broke."

"All right, everyone, just calm down," Savanah said, quickly taking charge. "Kyle, carry Mara into the guest room, last door on the left at the end of the hall. Kathy, find some clean towels. Cara, we'll need some hot water. Rane, you'd better call your grandparents. They might want to cut their vacation to Italy short. Rafe, we'll need something to cut the cord, and one of Abbey's blankets to wrap the baby in." She glanced around the room. "Now, people! Move!"

Mara groaned as Kyle picked her up and carried her down the hall.

"It'll be all right," he said. "I'll be right here beside you."

Savanah slipped into the guest room behind Kyle. She turned on the light and folded back the covers on the bed. "The contractions are coming pretty fast," she said. "I don't think this will be a long labor."

"It's already too long," Mara said, gasping. "It hurts!"

"It's supposed to hurt," Savanah said with a rueful smile.

Sitting on the edge of the bed, Kyle reached for Mara's hand, wincing as her fingers closed tightly around his.

Mara groaned again. The pains came hard and fast, more painful than anything she had imagined or expected, worse than anything she had ever known. She remembered staying out too late soon after Dendar had turned her. She had barely outrun the rising of the sun. She recalled the pain that had consumed her when the sun's light had touched her flesh. Even that hadn't been as bad as this. She choked back a cry, unable to imagine how any woman in her right mind, having endured the agony of childbirth once, would willingly go through it all again.

She clung to Kyle's hand as the contractions came, one hard upon the heels of the other. Was it always like this, she wondered. Maybe something was wrong . . . She groaned as another contraction threatened to split her in half.

"Try to breathe through the pain, like this," Savanah said, demonstrating the technique she had been taught in her Lamaze classes.

"Forget Lamaze," Rane said curtly. "Mara, look at me."

She followed the sound of Rane's voice and saw that he was standing beside the bed.

"That's right." He took a step closer. "Stay focused on me. Only me."

Nodding, Mara gazed into his eyes, eyes that burned with a dark inner fire.

"You can do this," Rane said, his voice low, hypnotic. "You don't feel the pain anymore, just the urge to push. Listen to your body and push when you need to."

"You can do it." Kyle's voice, filled with love and encouragement.

"That's right," Rane said quietly. "The pain is gone now. There's only pressure and the urge to push."

Miraculously, the pain receded. In a distant part of her mind, Mara knew he was using his preternatural power to mesmerize her, but she didn't care. Caught in the web of Rane's enchantment, she lost all track of time. There was only his voice holding the pain at bay, urging her to push when she felt the need, telling her that everything would be all right.

"We're almost there," Savanah said. "I can see the head. Lots of black hair. One more good push should do it."

"Come on, sweetie," Kyle urged, squeezing her hand. "You're almost through."

"Push, Mara," Rane said quietly. "You want to push, hard, now."

Helpless to resist his command, she gathered her strength, gritted her teeth, and pushed.

"Here it comes," Savanah said. "One more good push and you'll be holding your baby in your arms. Oh, my." Tears filled Savanah's eyes as the baby slid out of the birth canal and into her waiting hands. There was nothing in the whole world to equal the marvel of watching the birth of a new life. "It's a boy!" she exclaimed, cradling the infant in her hands. "A perfectly beautiful little boy. Kyle, do you want to cut the cord?"

"Uh, yeah, sure," he said.

There was a flurry of activity. Kyle cut the cord while Kathy wiped Mara's brow. Savanah bathed the baby and then wrapped him in a blanket.

Lifting her head, Mara looked at her son for the first time. One look, and she knew why women through the ages had been willing to endure the pains of childbirth. Her heart swelled with a rush of love such as she had never known existed.

"You did great," Kyle said, pressing a kiss to her forehead. "He's beautiful, but not as beautiful as you."

"Girls are beautiful," Mara murmured. "Boys are handsome."

"Well, this boy is beautiful," Kyle said proudly.

Mara smiled weakly, then groaned softly as Kathy pressed on her stomach to expel the afterbirth.

After that, everything passed in a blur until Savanah said, "Here's your son," and placed a tiny, blanket-wrapped bundle in Mara's waiting arms.

Mara looked up into a sea of smiling faces. "Thank you," she murmured. "All of you."

Amid a chorus of good wishes, Rane's family filed out of the room so that Kyle and Mara could be alone.

Mara looked at Kyle. "He is beautiful, isn't he?"

Kyle nodded, his expression tender as he glanced from Mara to their son and back again. "I love you."

She was supposed to say the words back to him. She knew it, but she couldn't seem to force them past her lips. And then she looked at the baby sleeping in her arms, and the words came easier. "I love you, too. Thank you . . . for this."

Mara brushed a kiss across the baby's cheek and then, her eyelids fluttering down, she fell asleep.

Kyle blew out a sigh as he gazed at Mara and his son. Life was very nearly perfect, he mused. Would, in fact, be perfect, if he could just silence the little voice in the back of his mind that wouldn't let him forget that his beautiful, perfect, newborn son could very well be a vampire.

Chapter Twenty-seven

"You promised me a baby, Tom. Where is it? Where's my baby?" Janis Ramsden stood in front of the fireplace, her hands fisted on her hips. A single blood-tinged tear slid down one cheek. She was a pretty woman, tall, with russet-colored hair, skin as pale as alabaster, and heavily lashed, light brown eyes. Even after a century of life as one of the Undead, Janis maintained an air of youthful innocence that was both endearing and annoying.

"Dammit, Janis, it's not my fault Mara took off," Ramsden replied heatedly. "How was I supposed to know she'd do such a stupid thing?"

"You must have done something, said something . . ."

"I didn't."

"You promised me a baby. My arms are empty, Tom. So empty."

The pleading note in Janis's voice stoked his anger. He had brought her across after he'd found her lying in the road, a victim of a hit-and-run. Even at the point of death, she'd had a fragile beauty that he had been unable to resist. He hadn't asked her permission. He had taken her blood and given it back to her, then carried her home.

He had been by her side when she succumbed to mortal death, been at her side when the change took place and she had awakened to a new world. She had been like a child, untouched, innocent, and he had been there to teach her, to guide her, to help her find her way in her new life.

For a time, knowing that Janis needed him, that she couldn't survive without him, had been an incredible high. Her presence in his life had added an element of freshness, an excitement that had been sorely lacking for over a century.

But in the last few years, Janis had taken it into her head that they needed a child to make their lives complete. Tom had been less than enthusiastic about the idea of adopting a baby until Mara came along. Mara, who had regained her humanity and lost her preternatural powers. The mystery of it had revitalized him.

Janis's sobs drew him back to the present. For a moment, he regretted having brought her across, but what was done was done. He had made her and he was responsible for her for as long as she lived . . .

Shaking off a sudden, unwelcome thought, Ramsden closed the distance between them and drew her into his arms. If . . . when . . . he found Mara's child, he would need Janis to look after it.

A baby! Ramsden swore softly. Why hadn't he thought of it before? If Janis was this desperate for a child of her own, there were probably others of their kind who yearned to experience parenthood. A cure for vampirism would undoubtedly make him rich, but finding a way for vampires to reproduce would make him richer still.

And Mara held the secret to both possibilities. Excitement spiraled through him. She could make him rich. Famous beyond his wildest dreams.

"I'll find her," he said. Even now, he had his people looking. Now that she had lost her preternatural powers, she couldn't hide from him forever.

And then he frowned. Perhaps it wasn't Mara who held the secret at all, but the human male who had planted his seed within her.

Chapter Twenty-eight

Mara stirred, frowning as the insistent cry of a baby reached her ears. For a moment, she thought it must be Rane's daughter. Grimacing, she flopped over onto her stomach and dragged a pillow over her head, only to come fully awake a few moments later. It wasn't Abbey Marie making that perfectly awful racket. It was her own beautiful baby boy.

Being careful not to wake Kyle, Mara eased out of bed, then padded barefoot across the floor to the cradle that Savanah had thoughtfully provided.

"Hush, now, my sweet angel," Mara crooned as she picked up her son and kissed his baby-smooth cheek. "You're much too tiny to make such a dreadful noise. If you're not careful, you'll wake everyone in the house."

Mara shook her head, bemused by the wave of motherly affection she felt for the infant in her arms. Did all new mothers feel this way? Had Eve been awed by the miracle of birth when she held Abel in her arms, amazed that she and Adam had created something so tiny, so perfect? Were all new mothers as terrified by the prospect of being wholly responsible for something so small and helpless? Had her own mother ever felt this wave of tender devotion? Probably not, Mara decided, or else her mother would not have abandoned her and left her to die.

Mara remembered that time in her life as clearly as if it had happened only days ago. She had been terrified when she woke up, alone in the dark. She had prayed to Bet, the protector of children, for help, but none had been forthcoming. She had cried for her mother, but no one had answered her cries. Frightened and hungry, she had wandered through the city, begging for food, stealing when necessary, afraid to close her eyes at night for fear someone would find her and sell her into slavery or worse. At a time when she should have been learning how to sew, cook, and keep house, she had been struggling to learn how to survive on the streets. Her dress, made of linen, soon grew dirty from sleeping on the ground. She'd had no shoes, but then most people had gone barefooted back then, although they had worn sandals on rare, special occasions. And then one night, one of Pharaoh's slaves had found her huddled beneath a tree. Mara had fought him as best she could, but her childish fists were no match for a man full-grown. Tucking her under one arm, he had taken her home to Pharaoh's house. She had spent the next ten years as a slave in the king's household. She hadn't liked being a slave. Even as a child, she had disliked taking orders, but she had been grateful to have a roof over her head, food to eat, clean clothes to wear.

Mara brushed a kiss across her son's cheek. "I'll never leave you," she whispered. "No one will ever abandon you, or hurt you. I swear it on my life. I'll see that you have everything you ever want, everything you need. Yes,

I will, you beautiful little boy, because your mother loves you very much."

He was such an adorable baby, with his dimpled hands and feet. She never tired of looking at him, holding him. His hair, as fine as down, was inky black. She wondered if his eyes would stay gray, like Kyle's.

Moving to the rocker in the corner, she sat down and put the baby to her breast. Nursing her son was both painful and pleasant. Savanah had assured her that, after a short time, the discomfort would go away.

Mara smiled faintly as she stroked her son's cheek. Had she known motherhood was this wonderful, she might have wished for a return to humanity centuries ago. Never had she ever felt so fulfilled, so needed, never experienced such love for anything or anyone else.

"Now there's a picture I've got to paint."

Mara glanced at the bed to find Kyle sitting up and watching her, his lips curved in a faint smile. He made quite a picture himself, she mused, with his hair tousled and the sheet pooled in his lap. For a moment, she wished it was Logan sitting there.

"I'm sorry," she murmured, looking down at the baby. "We didn't mean to wake you."

"No big deal." Kyle stretched his arms over his head, then rubbed the back of his neck. "I can't get over how beautiful you are." Indeed, he had never seen anything more stirring than the sight of Mara nursing their son. Faint rays of sunlight leaked into the room, bathing the two of them in a golden glow reminiscent of Old World paintings of the Madonna. "Both of you. Have you decided on a name for our boy?"

"No. I was thinking of Cleopatra if it was a girl."

"It's probably just as well that we had a boy then,"

Kyle said with a wry grin. "Can you imagine how the other kids would tease a girl with a name like that?"

She nodded absently. Odd that she had named Vince's twin sons, but she couldn't decide on a suitable name for her own child. "How about Derek?" Kyle suggested. "It's a bit old-fashioned, but it was my maternal grandfather's name. He was a wonderful old guy. Used to make me kites. I remember he taught me how to ride a bike, and how to fish and row a boat. He lived a good, long life."

"You don't want to name your son Kyle?"

"Maybe the next one."

"Derek," Mara murmured, trying the name on her tongue. It was a good name, a strong name. "Yes, I like that."

"So, now that we have a name for our son, don't you think it's time his mother married his father?" Rising, Kyle pulled on his jeans, then knelt in front of her. "Be my wife," he said, his dark eyes filled with tenderness. "I want to fall asleep at your side every night, and wake up in the morning with you in my arms. Say yes, Mara. Say you'll marry me, and I'll spend the rest of my life trying to make you happy."

Mara stared at him. She had made her decision to stay with Kyle weeks ago, so why was she hesitating now? Why did she suddenly hear Logan's voice in the back of her mind, thick with hurt and anger as he declared his love for her? Not for the first time, she found herself wondering if it was possible to be in love with two men at the same time.

Why had she let her foolish pride come between herself and Logan? And yet, even as the thought crossed her mind, she knew she had chosen Kyle because they were equals. Because she could control him in a way she would never be able to control Logan. But what did it matter now? She had walked out on Logan twice. He wasn't likely to take her back a third time.

"Mara?"

Kyle was looking up at her, waiting for her answer. "Yes," she said slowly. "I'll marry you."

Kyle smiled at her for a long moment, his throat too tight for words, and then, very gently, he kissed her. "I love you," he whispered hoarsely. "I'll love you for as long as I live."

She forced a smile, already regretting her decision.

"You're getting married!" Savanah exclaimed when Kyle made the announcement later that evening. "Oh, I think that's wonderful. Congratulations, you two! When's the happy occasion?"

"I'm not sure," Mara said. "Not for five or six weeks."

"Well, of course not," Savanah said with a knowing grin. "You're still recovering from having a baby. No sense getting married until you can have a real honeymoon."

"You've got that right!" Kyle exclaimed, then looked at Mara. "Hey, I'm kidding."

Mara smiled a bit self-consciously. Derek was living proof that they had already had the honeymoon.

"We haven't set a date yet," Kyle said, giving Mara's hand a squeeze, "but I'm ready whenever she is."

"What kind of wedding did you have in mind?" Rane asked.

Mara shook her head. "I really don't know." She looked at Kyle. "Do you?"

"Anything you want is fine with me."

Anything she wanted . . . In her time, there had been no formal marriage ceremony in front of a priest, although there was a written contract, which included the wedding date, the names of the bride and the groom, as well as the names of their parents. It was also customary to list the husband's profession, the name of the person who drew up the contract, and the names of three witnesses. When a young man and woman decided to wed, the man made a payment to the bride's father, and bestowed a gift of gold, silver, or other precious stones on the bride. Once an agreement was reached, the bride moved in with her future husband. Of course, back in those days, the woman might be as young as thirteen and the man only fifteen or sixteen. A wedding was naturally a festive occasion. There would be a lavish feast, with dancing and singing and toasts to the happy couple. When the bride and groom departed for their new home, it was customary for the guests to throw green wheat, the symbol of fertility, into the air. If the marriage didn't work out, a divorce was easily obtained by either party. Usually, the husband paid support of some kind to his ex-wife.

"I don't have any family," Mara said, "except for Rane's."

"My folks are gone, too," Kyle said, "so there won't be anyone on my side of the church."

"Small and intimate, then," Savanah said. "You know I'll be happy to help in any way I can, and I'm sure we can count on Cara and Kathy, too. Now, let's see, you'll need a dress, and a maid of honor and a best man . . . Rane and I would be happy to stand up with you, if you like."

"Slow down, Savanah," Rane said, grinning. "I think these are decisions that Mara and Kyle need to make on their own."

"I've no objections to having you as my best man," Kyle said.

"Savanah, you know I'd be pleased to have you as my maid of honor."

"That's settled, then," Savanah said, giving her husband a smug look. "When you're ready, we can go into town and look at dresses. Listen to me, running on like this. Rane's right. This is your wedding. Maybe you don't need a dress. I mean, if you don't want to get married in a church . . ." Savanah's voice trailed off.

"I'd like a church wedding," Kyle said, "if Mara has no objections."

"I guess it would be all right."

"Maybe we could have the baby baptized at the same time," Kyle said.

"I didn't know you were so religious," Mara remarked. She had been quite a believer, once upon a time, but that had been centuries ago.

"Well, I haven't been to Mass in years," Kyle admitted, "but marriage is a serious thing and should be done right. And baptism, well, it's important."

"You're Catholic, then?" Mara asked, thinking she still had a lot to learn about her future husband.

"More or less," Kyle said. "Is that a problem?"

"That means you'll need a priest," Rane said, glancing from Mara to Kyle.

Kyle nodded. "Definitely."

"Father Lanzoni," Rane and Savanah said in unison.

"Of course," Mara said, smiling.

"Lanzoni." Kyle looked at Rane. "He's the priest that married the two of you, isn't he?"

"And everyone else in the family," Rane said with a grin. "I'll get in touch with him, if you like."

That evening, while Kyle was rocking the baby to sleep and Rane was out hunting, Savanah took Mara aside. "I hope you two will think about moving up here with the rest of us," she said. "There's a lovely old house not far from here. It's for sale or lease."

"I'll mention it to Kyle," Mara said, although she wasn't sure she wanted to buy another house. Leasing would probably be best, at least for now.

"I hope he'll agree," Savanah remarked. "It would be nice to have some non-vampire friends close by."

"Does Rane's being a vampire ever bother you?" Mara asked. "I mean, it's none of my business, but . . . never mind."

"You're wondering how I could have fallen in love with a vampire when one killed my father."

"It's crossed my mind from time to time."

"Well, I didn't plan to fall in love with him," Savanah admitted with a faint smile. "I don't think we choose the one we fall in love with. It just happens. I didn't want to love him, but I do. I know he's done a lot of bad things in the past, but"—she shrugged—"who hasn't?"

Mara nodded. She was in no position to judge anyone. "It must get lonely sometimes," Mara said, "being the only mortal in the family."

"Not lonely, exactly," Savanah said. "Cara and Kathy are wonderful women, and I love Rafe and his dad. And, of course, Roshan and Brenna are terrific, although they don't spend much time here, but . . ." She blew out a sigh. "It'll be nice to have someone to go to lunch with, you know?"

Later that night, while nursing the baby, Mara thought about her conversation with Savanah. Mara had to admire her courage. In spite of what Rane's wife had said, it couldn't be easy for her, being the only human in a nest of vampires.

* * *

In the days that followed, Mara discovered what it was like to live in a house where people loved each other. She hadn't grown up in a home like Rane's. She had never known her father, hadn't spent much time with her mother. She had spent her early childhood in Pharaoh's palace. Later, she had been a slave in Shakir's household, and then, abruptly, Dendar had transformed her into a vampire and left her to fend for herself. Unlike most sires, he hadn't stayed around to tell her what to expect, or to help her adjust to her new lifestyle, and then in a rage, she had destroyed him. Turned and alone, she'd had no one to look after her, no one she dared trust.

One afternoon, at Kyle's insistence, they left the baby with Savanah and went to look at the house Savanah had told Mara about. It was, indeed, a lovely old place. The exterior paint, green with white trim, looked new. There was a wooden swing in a corner of the porch.

"The perfect place to rock the baby in the evening," Kyle remarked while the Realtor unlocked the front door.

The interior of the house had also been recently painted, and while Mara wasn't crazy about white walls, it was something she could live with, at least temporarily. The three bedrooms were all good sized; each had its own bathroom. The living room was large, with a stone fireplace in one corner. Though she hadn't spent much time in any kitchen, Mara fell in love with this one, which was large and sunny, with glass-fronted cabinets, lots of counter space, and a view of the backyard. She could already imagine a gazebo in the corner, and a swing for Derek.

"I think we should buy it," Kyle said, looking at Mara. "The Realtor said the seller is willing to knock ten grand off the price. That's a good deal. What do you think?"

"It is a nice house," she replied. Why was she so hesitant? "It's up to you."

"No, it's up to you," he said. "I can paint anywhere."

"All right." They couldn't stay with Rane and Savanah indefinitely, and it was a nice house.

After giving Mara a quick kiss, Kyle told the Realtor they would take it, with the stipulation that they could have a thirty-day escrow. "So we can spend our honeymoon in our new home," Kyle said.

After some not-so-subtle coaxing by Kyle, Mara set the date for the wedding. November 30.

On a Friday evening in mid-November, after giving Kyle detailed verbal and written instructions on caring for the baby, Mara accompanied Savanah, Kathy, and Cara on a trip into town to look at wedding gowns.

It was a new experience for Mara, shopping with other women. She'd never had any female friends. She had spent most of her mortal life as a slave; as a vampire, she had preferred the company of men.

She tried on a dozen dresses, each one beautiful, and yet none of them seemed right until she found a cream-colored, floor-length gown of brushed silk that fit as though it had been made for her. She had decided against wearing a veil. It wasn't as if she was some modest virgin, after all.

Savanah whistled softly when Mara stepped out of the dressing room. "Wow, you've got to buy that one!"

"We'll be lucky if he doesn't ravish you right there on the floor of the chapel," Kathy said.

"Are you sure you just had a baby almost six weeks ago?" Cara asked with a shake of her head. "It took me six months to get my figure back."

"Yes, but you had twins," Kathy reminded her with a grin.

"True enough. Enjoy your baby while you can, Mara," Cara said wistfully. "They grow up way too fast."

Mara nodded. She couldn't believe how much Derek had changed in just six short weeks. He was such a handsome, even-tempered little thing.

Turning, Mara looked at her reflection in the mirror. It was still something of a shock to look into a mirror and see herself staring back. She canted her head to the side. With all due modesty, she had to admit that she did look good. The gown clung to her figure, emphasizing her breasts, which, thanks to motherhood, were larger than ever, making her waist seem even smaller than it really was.

"You're going to be a beautiful bride," Cara said.

Mara smiled faintly. All brides were beautiful. Plain or pretty, wearing a wedding dress transformed them all.

"Yes, indeed," Kathy agreed. "Are you sure you don't want a veil?" She held up a froth of cream-colored lace.

"Oh, it's great!" Savanah snatched it from her sister-in-law's hand and placed it on Mara's head. "It's perfect!"

Mara looked at herself in the mirror again. The veil fell in graceful folds past her shoulders.

"What do you think?" Savanah asked.

"I'll take it," Mara decided. After all, she would only be a bride once. She might as well do it right. She just wished she was as excited about her upcoming nuptials as Cara and her daughters-in-law.

It was the end of November. For Mara, the days had passed all too quickly, and suddenly, the wedding was upon them. Mara stood in the small dressing room located in the rear of the church while Savanah and Kathy fussed over her hair and her gown. Cara sat in the corner, holding Derek.

"You look absolutely lovely," Savanah said, smoothing a wrinkle from Mara's veil.

"Thank you."

"I think that does it." Kathy gave Mara a hug. "Kyle's a lucky man."

Kathy and Cara moved toward the door, pausing when they realized Savanah wasn't behind them.

"Are you coming?" Kathy asked.

"Yes, I'll be right there."

Kathy and Cara exchanged glances, then left the room, closing the door behind them.

Savanah laid her hand on Mara's arm. "Is everything all right?"

"Of course," Mara said brightly, "why wouldn't it be?"

"Well, for one thing, brides are usually happy. I've seen corpses who didn't look so glum."

Mara started to say she was happy, but the words refused to come.

"It's not too late to change your mind," Savanah said quietly.

"I wish that was true," Mara said. "But there's no going back now." Lifting her chin, she left the dressing room, her footsteps heavy as she made her way to the chapel.

It was a lovely old church. The altar and the pews, carved from oak, carried the patina of their years. A shaft of bright silver moonlight filtered through the beautiful red, blue and gold stained glass window above the altar, a deep blue carpet covered the wooden floor. The chapel was nothing like the lavish temples of ancient Egypt and yet there was a sense of peace within these walls that she had felt nowhere else on Earth.

It was quiet in the chapel. Mara glanced at those already seated. Roshan and Brenna sat side by side, holding hands. They were a handsome couple. Roshan wore black, as always; Brenna wore a dress instead of her customary blouse and full skirt. Vince and Cara sat with Brenna and Roshan. Abbey Marie sat on Cara's lap, contentedly sucking her thumb. Rafe and Kathy sat in the second pew. Derek slept in Kathy's arms. Mara studied Rafe's wife, wondering if she ever regretted her decision to accept the Dark Gift so early in life. Did she ever long for children of her own?

Cordova family friends Susie and her were-tiger husband, Joe Cagin, sat behind Rafe and Kathy. Mara had been surprised to see them. She had never been particularly fond of Joe, though they had rubbed elbows from time to time during the War. Susie was a unique individual. Mara sometimes thought the other woman's life sounded like a paranormal soap opera. Susie had been an ordinary mortal until a werewolf bit her. She'd had a difficult time adjusting to being a werewolf, had been afraid her three sons wouldn't be safe around her. Susie had been swept up in Edna and Pearl's horrendous experiments during the War. She had been on the brink of death when Cagin and Kathy persuaded Rafe to bring her across. He had done so, reluctantly. To Mara's knowledge, no other were-creature had ever become a vampire.

Mara glanced at her watch, wondering what was keeping Father Lanzoni. The watch had been a wedding gift from Kyle. It was lovely, but only served to remind her that she was mortal, subject to the passage of time. Time. It was her enemy now.

"I'm sure Father Lanzoni will be here soon," Savanah said.

Mara nodded. Savanah looked lovely in a shimmery

gown of rose-colored silk. As best man, Rane stood beside Kyle.

Mara was beginning to think they would have to postpone the wedding when the double doors of the chapel flew open. But instead of Father Lanzoni, Logan stood there. Clad in black trousers, a black shirt, black leather boots, and a long black duster, he looked as handsome as the devil himself and equally dangerous.

The chapel suddenly hummed with tension as Roshan and the three Cordova men turned to stare at Logan.

Mara could almost smell the sudden increase in the testosterone level. She glanced at Roshan, who had gained his feet.

"It's all right," she said quietly. "He's a friend of mine, here at my invitation."

With a nod, Roshan resumed his seat, his expression wary.

"You invited him?" Kyle stared at Logan in disbelief as Logan took a seat across the aisle from the others.

For a moment, man and vampire glared at each other like wolves meeting for the first time. Then, with a lift of one brow, Logan inclined his head, and the tension in the room diminished.

"I called him a few days ago," Mara said. "I had to let him know."

"You should have told me," Kyle said, his voice tight.

"I know. I'm sorry, but he's my oldest friend, my only friend except for Rane's family." She lifted a hand to the ruby at her throat. "Please don't be angry."

A muscle ticked in Kyle's jaw. "I'm not mad, but you should have warned me."

The priest arrived then, putting an end to any further discussion. Father Giovanni Lanzoni was a man of medium height with warm hazel eyes and wavy black hair heavily laced with silver at his temples.

"I'm sorry I'm late," the priest said. "An old friend of mine needed last rites, may the Lord bless him." He smiled at Kyle and Mara, his expression turning to one of confusion as he took Mara's hand in his. "Mara . . . ?"

"Your senses don't deceive you, Father. I'm no longer Nosferatu." Even though she was no longer a vampire herself, she could feel the priest's preternatural power. It filled the room, an ancient power that, like fire, could be either beneficial or deadly. It occurred to her that Logan and Father Lanzoni were now the two oldest vampires in existence.

The priest was studying her carefully. "How did this happen? I don't understand."

"Neither do I."

"I heard rumors, of course, but I discounted them . . ."

"Please, Father," Mara said quietly. "Can we just get on with the ceremony?"

"Yes, of course." With a last worried glance in her direction, the priest took his place at the altar. "We are gathered here this evening to unite Kyle Bowden and Mara in the bonds of holy wedlock, an institution ordained by God for the blessing of His children. In the beginning, God joined Adam and Eve together and admonished them to cleave to one another, to be fruitful and multiply."

The priest turned his gaze on Mara. "And so I say to you, if you wish to have a happy marriage, then you must share your heart with no one else . . ."

Mara licked her lips. Had the priest somehow divined that she still had strong feelings for another man?

"For true happiness," Father Lanzoni continued, "you have only to put your loved one first and yourself second, to treat your spouse as you would be treated, to remember how much you love one another on this day, and on every day that follows, for as long as God grants you breath.

"I will say the words that legally bind you together, but the true marriage between the two of you must take place in your hearts."

Father Lanzoni glanced at those sitting in the audience. All were supernatural creatures, save for Savanah and the two infants. "If there is anyone here who knows why this man and this woman should not be joined together, let him speak now, or hereafter hold his peace."

Standing at the altar, with her back to the chapel, Mara could feel Logan's gaze boring into her back. Lifting a hand to the ruby pendant that seemed to be burning her skin, she held her breath as she waited for the words she longed to hear but hoped he wouldn't say.

"I object." Logan's voice pierced the silence.

"On what grounds?" Father Lanzoni asked.

"On the grounds that I love her, and I think she loves me."

Kyle whirled around, his hands clenched into tight fists at his sides. "Get the hell out of here, vampire!"

Vampire. The word hung in the air. Mara heard a stirring in the crowd, not because of the word itself, but because of the sneer in Kyle's voice when he said it.

"Mr. Bowden, that will be enough." Father Lanzoni's voice was quiet, calm, but there was steel underneath. "Mara, what have you to say?"

"Mara." Gaining his feet, Logan stepped into the aisle. "Look at me."

Slowly, her heart racing, she turned to face him. From the corner of her eye, she saw that Rafe and Rane had also gained their feet, ready to defend her if need be.

"Mara!" Kyle grabbed her hand. "Don't listen to him. He's a monster."

"Yes, he is," she admitted with a sad smile. "And I made him that way."

"I love you." Logan walked toward her, stopping when he was but an arm's length away. "If you don't love me, tell me so now."

"Please, Logan, don't make this any harder than it is. I'm doing what's best for the baby, what's best for all of us. If you think about it, you'll know I'm right."

"Fine, marry the bastard! I've waited for you this long. I can wait until the kid's grown," he said, his voice harsh, and with a low growl, he pulled her into his arms and kissed her, hard and quick, and then, in a swirl of ebony smoke, he was gone.

A heavy silence filled the room.

For one reckless moment, Mara was sorely tempted to follow her heart and go after Logan, but she couldn't do it.

She couldn't leave her son, couldn't take him away and deprive him of knowing his father.

Blinking back her tears, Mara turned to face the priest.

Kyle took her hand in his. "Please go on, Father."

The priest looked at Mara. At her nod, he continued with the ceremony. "Mara, do you promise to love and cherish Kyle Bowden, here present, for better or worse, in sickness and in health, for as long as you both shall live?"

"I do." They were, she thought, the hardest two words she had ever spoken.

"Kyle, do you promise to love and cherish Mara, here present, for better or worse, in sickness and in health, for as long as you both shall live?"

Kyle gazed deeply into her eyes, his own shining with love. "I do."

"Then, by the power vested in me, I now pronounce you husband and wife. You may kiss your bride."

Kyle was smiling broadly when he drew Mara into his arms. Never had she looked more beautiful than she did at that moment, her exquisite green eyes sparkling with unshed tears. And she was his, lawfully and legally his by all the laws of the land, and there was nothing Logan Blackwood could do about it.

"I love you," Kyle murmured. "I will always love you, in this life or the next." And so saying, he drew her closer and kissed her tenderly, and then he kissed her again.

He might have kissed her a third time if Derek hadn't chosen that moment to make his presence known.

Forcing herself to smile at Kyle, Mara slipped out of his arms, grateful for an excuse to pull away.

"There is nothing like the sound of new life," Father Lanzoni said with a grin. "Let us baptize the child before he gets any older, or any louder."

Leaving the altar, they gathered around the baptismal font. Mara held Derek as the priest dipped his fingers into the font, which Mara knew was filled with water that the priest himself had blessed, rendering it harmless to his touch. She listened to the words the priest spoke as he baptized her son, Derek Bowden, a child that might or might not be a vampire. She couldn't help smiling inwardly as she imagined how bizarre it would seem to an outsider—a vampire priest baptizing a human child while eight other vampires looked on.

Kyle took Mara's hand and gave it a squeeze as the priest made the sign of the cross on the baby's forehead. Derek had stopped crying and as Mara gazed lovingly into her son's eyes, she wondered why he needed to be baptized. Derek was young and innocent, incapable of sin or sinning. What need did he have for forgiveness?

She felt a twinge of conscience. If anyone needed forgiveness, it was she. She glanced at her new husband, wondering if he would still love her if he knew all of the horrible things she had done in ages past, the many lives she had taken to prolong her own, the lives she had ruined inadvertently or otherwise.

Father Lanzoni's resonant "Amen" drew her back to the present. When Kyle turned aside to speak to Roshan, Mara moved away from the others on the pretense of checking the baby's diaper when, in reality, she desperately needed a few minutes alone to come to terms with what she had done. For better or worse, she had joined her life with Kyle's.

Cuddling her baby close in her arms, she kissed his cheek and whispered, "I'd do it again, for you."

Chapter Twenty-nine

Logan sat on the sofa in front of the fireplace, a crystal goblet filled with Type O in one hand. So, she had married Kyle Bowden. He swore softly. It would have been so easy to wring the man's neck, to bring Mara here, where she belonged. But he hadn't done it because she would have hated him for it. And whether she was a vampire or not, he didn't want her hatred.

He wished fleetingly that he had brought her here anyway and to hell with the consequences. Enduring her hatred would have been better than the awful emptiness that burned inside him.

He sipped from the goblet as he stared at the fire, watched the flames burn hotter and brighter as his rage and his frustration grew. How long would it take him to get over her this time? How long to forget the sweetness of her lips, the pleasure of her exquisite body writhing in ecstasy beneath his, the sound of her voice crying his name as they reached for the stars?

Earlier, he had wandered into one of the bars on Hollywood Boulevard. Like most nightclubs, the interior was dark, intimate. Soft, sensual music flowed from hidden speakers, punctuated by the murmur of low-voiced conversation, the clink of glasses, an occasional burst of laughter.

Logan had perused the crowd inside, mostly young, unattached men and women hoping to get lucky. He had picked out a lovely young female, one as different from Mara as he could find. He had bought her a drink, made the requisite small talk, and accepted an invite to her place, only to find that, once he had her ready and eager, he had absolutely no desire for either her flesh or her blood. Not caring what she thought, he had vanished from her sight and walked home, hoping the exercise would help to alleviate his desire for the one woman he couldn't have.

It hadn't.

Muttering an oath, he hurled the empty goblet into the fireplace, watched as it shattered against the bricks, the shards of glass winking like diamonds in the fire's light before being swallowed up in the flames.

That didn't help, either, or change the fact that Mara was with Bowden. Maybe in bed with him. Making love to him. Letting him fondle her, kiss her.

The anger burned inside him, hotter and more corrosive than the flames crackling in the hearth. He knew why Mara had left him, knew it was her damnable pride that was keeping them apart. She had always had enough pride for ten vampires; he knew how difficult it was for her to be around him, to be around any vampire now that her own powers were gone. He could understand how she felt. He could even sympathize with her plight. But he couldn't forgive her.

Perhaps he would go to ground for a century or two. When he rose, she would be gone, returned to the earth whence she came. Yet even as he contemplated it, he knew he wouldn't do it, wouldn't hide himself away so long as she walked the earth. So long as there was a chance, however unlikely, that she might need him, or that, one day she would be his.

With a sigh, he leaned back and closed his eyes. It had taken him centuries to get over her the last time she left him. How long would it take to get her out of his mind and heart this time?

Chapter Thirty

Mara's days became a never-ending round of nursing the baby, bathing the baby, and rocking him to sleep. There were countless diapers to be changed, a husband to cook for, a house to clean, clothes to wash and fold and put away, trips to the store for food, more diapers, more meals, and endless nights spent walking the floor with a colicky infant.

There were times, when she paced the floor with her crying child, that Mara found it hard to believe that she had once been the world's oldest and most powerful vampire, a time when anything she had desired was hers for the taking. Days when a thought carried her anywhere she wished to go. How she longed for those days when she had been free to come and go as she pleased, when she'd had no responsibilities, no one to worry about or care for but herself, no demands on her time, or her affections. And always, hard on the heels of such selfish thoughts, came an overpowering sense of guilt, because, in spite of everything, she loved Derek with her whole heart and soul, loved him as she had never thought it possible to love another living creature.

And, deep in the farthest reaches of her heart where she dared not look, she knew she had been a fool to leave Logan, the first time, and the last.

And then there was Kyle. She was used to having men lust after her, adore her, plead for her favors, but no man had ever looked at her the way Kyle did, almost as if he worshiped her. It was disconcerting, all the moreso because she didn't deserve it. She knew now that what she had felt for him in Egypt wasn't love. She had been flattered by his attention, fascinated by his artistic talent. He had been both sexy and vulnerable, a combination she had found vastly appealing at the time. She had been ripe to fall in love and Kyle had been there, young and handsome and eager to please her.

And she didn't like being human. For a time, she had convinced herself that it wasn't too bad, but, again, she had been lying to herself in an effort to make her new life more palatable. She didn't know how she was going to get through the next eighteen years. She had considered asking Roshan or one of the Cordova men to turn her now, but she had no idea how it would affect her. Would she be a fledgling again, compelled to spend her days at rest, no longer able to endure the sun's light, ruled by the lust for blood? Or would she regain her full powers? There was no way to know. One thing she knew for certain, the day after Derek graduated from high school, she would seek the Dark Gift. She had hoped Logan would bring her across, but the way things stood between them now, that was no longer an option.

Mara glanced at her son, sleeping peacefully in her arms. For Derek, no sacrifice was too great. She would live and die for her son.

"Time enough to worry about the future," Mara murmured. When she had been a vampire, eighteen years had been little more than the blink of an eye. Now it seemed like forever.

As for Kyle . . . Mara blew out a sigh. She didn't know what she was going to do about Kyle.

Surprisingly, in the weeks and months that followed, Mara and Savanah became close friends. Then again, maybe it wasn't surprising, since they were the only two mortal females in a family of vampires.

They went shopping together, spent afternoons in the nearby park together, took walks together. Mara baby-sat Abbey Marie when Savanah went to the dentist; Savanah baby-sat Derek when Mara needed a few hours alone.

Today they were at the park, sitting on opposite sides of a blanket while Abbey and Derek napped between them.

Mara stared at Derek. Already six months old. How quickly the months had gone by. He was quite the active little guy now, always moving when he was awake. He could already sit up by himself, loved to suck his thumb, played with his ear when he was tired, and smiled whenever he saw her. She had started giving him a bottle at night, and baby food during the day. It was hard to believe he was growing so fast. He would be walking soon. Talking. Going to school. In a few short years, she would no longer be the center of his existence. The thought filled her with a strange melancholy. She was anxious for him to grow up, wasn't she? Anxious to return to her old life.

"It's beautiful here, isn't it?" Savanah remarked.

"What? Oh, yes." It was, indeed, a lovely spot, with a clear blue lake set in the middle of tall pines and stately oaks. Colorful flowers and shrubs lined the walkways, surrounded by white, wrought-iron fencing that was clearly intended to protect the blooms from small, curious hands.

A number of other mothers were gathered in small groups near the playground, chatting and laughing while boys and girls played on swings and slides or splashed in the kiddy pool. It seemed she and Savanah weren't the only ones who had decided to take advantage of the unusually warm weather.

Mara sighed heavily. How had she come to this? Maybe it wouldn't be so hard to bear if she just knew why it had happened to her.

"Is something wrong?" Savanah asked.

"Why do you ask?"

"You're wearing the same look you had at the wedding. Is it anything you want to talk about?" Leaning forward, Savanah placed her hand on Mara's arm. "I promise not to say anything to anyone else."

Mara lifted one shoulder and let it fall. "I miss my old life. I miss . . ." She folded her arms and gazed into the distance. She missed her preternatural vision and hearing. Living without her preternatural sight after so many centuries was like looking at the world through a filter. "I'm fine."

"It's Logan, isn't it? I saw the way he looked at you at the wedding. And the way you looked at him. Why did you marry Kyle?"

"Because he's my son's father. Because he's human. Because I couldn't live with Logan."

"Ah, I think I understand." Savanah sat back. "It's like being on a diet and living with someone who never gets fat. It's hard to feel his power and know you don't have it anymore, isn't it?"

"Yes, exactly," Mara said, surprised by Savanah's

perception. "I don't like feeling helpless. I know Logan would never abuse his power, never take advantage of me, and yet . . . I'm . . . embarrassed. I'm not making sense, am I?"

"You're making perfect sense. You're used to being powerful and in control, and now you're not. Of course you feel vulnerable, but . . ."

"Go on."

"Do you think it's fair to stay with Kyle when you're in love with someone else?"

"I don't know. I've thought about telling him the truth, but I don't want to hurt him. And I do love him, in a way."

"You're just not *in* love with him."

Leaning forward, Mara stroked her son's cheek. "I wish I knew what to do," she murmured. "I never used to be this way. I knew what I wanted, and I did it, but when I lost my powers, I seem to have lost"—she made a vague gesture with her hand—"everything."

"Give it time," Savanah said sympathetically. "I know it's got to be a big adjustment for you. I can't even begin to imagine what it must be like, but maybe it will get easier as time goes by."

"Easier! I was human for twenty years. I was a vampire for over two thousand! Maybe I should just leave Derek with Kyle and . . ." Mara shook her head in exasperation. "I can't do that. I can't leave my baby. I never knew I could feel like this." She stroked her son's cheek again. "I'm just feeling sorry for myself." Looking up, she met Savanah's gaze. "Thanks for listening."

"Anytime," Savanah said with a smile. "That's what friends are for."

* * *

Kyle was in his studio when Mara returned home. "How was your day?" he asked. "Did you have a good time with Savanah?"

"Yes." Mara settled Derek on her hip as she studied Kyle's current work-in-progress.

The painting had been commissioned by the mayor of the city. Kyle was working off of an old photograph of the town. When completed, the painting would hang in the foyer of Porterville's city hall.

"It's very good," she said, meaning it.

He shrugged. "The mayor stopped by to see it earlier today. He asked me to do a companion piece for his office, and maybe one for the post office."

"That's wonderful."

"Yeah." Giving her an affectionate swat on the backside, he said, "I'll be famous yet, wife, you just wait and see! Now, what's for dinner?"

Later that night, after Kyle and the baby were asleep, Mara went into the den and sat at the computer. Lately, when she couldn't sleep, she had taken to working on her life story, writing bits and pieces as they occurred to her. She supposed, at some point, she would have to arrange her journal in some sort of chronological order, but that could come later.

Sitting there, staring at the blinking cursor, she let her mind wander. It was amazing to remember the things she had seen, the places she had been, the advancements and inventions that everyone in this era took for granted. Communication between foreign countries had once taken months; now e-mails and text messages flew across the country or across the world with the click of a mouse. You could download music, videos, and movies on your phone, as well as send pictures and texts to anywhere in the world. A journey from one coast to the other that had once taken weeks, or even months, by horseback, could now be made in a matter of hours. She had once washed her clothes in a river and dried them on a rock in the sun. She had bathed in streams, relieved herself behind a bush. She wondered if the people of today had any idea how lucky they were to have washing machines and running water, indoor plumbing and toilet paper. At one time, an electric stove, a refrigerator, or a microwave would have been looked upon as miraculous; nowadays they were commonplace. Men flew to the moon, they walked on Venus, they lived on Mars, and yet, in spite of all the new inventions, new discoveries, and new explorations in space, Earth and its inhabitants remained basically the same. She wondered what miracles the future would hold, and regretted that she wouldn't be there to witness them.

She was contemplating how best to put her thoughts on paper when she heard the baby cry. Leaving the den, she went into the nursery.

"Hear now, young man," she murmured as she lifted her son from the crib. "Don't cry. Mama's here. Are you hungry? Or just lonely?"

Taking a seat in the rocking chair by the window, Mara rocked the baby. Sitting there in the dark, her thoughts again turned to Kyle. Her husband, for better or worse. She knew he was upset with her, and with good reason. He had been wanting to make love for the last week, but she kept putting him off, saying she wasn't ready, that she was too tired, or pleading that she had a headache, surely the oldest excuse in the world. She knew that, sooner or later, she would have to give in. She owed him that much. One thing for certain, she would be sure they both took precautions before they slept together again, because even though she loved Derek more than her own life, she didn't want any more babies.

Chapter Thirty-one

Thomas Ramsden stormed out of the house, afraid if he stayed another minute, he would do something he might regret. The sound of Janis's wailing followed him into the night. Damn the woman! Would she never shut up? For the last six months, she had talked of nothing but wanting a baby. She needed a baby. She didn't feel complete without a baby. She would never be happy until she had a baby.

Hell, maybe he should just go to the nearest hospital and grab one. He could be in and out of the maternity ward before anyone realized he had been there. The thing was, an ordinary baby wouldn't do. He wanted Mara's child, sired by a mortal man on a woman who had once been the most powerful vampire on Earth. Now, there was a child worth having.

Reluctant to go back home, Ramsden headed for his office. He had an emergency lair in the basement. Perhaps he would spend a day or two there. He could use the peace and quiet.

After letting himself into the office, he went downstairs to the lab and opened the refrigerator. He kept several packets of blood on hand for those times when he was too busy or simply not in the mood to hunt. He was reaching for the nearest container when he saw the vials filled with blood he had taken from Mara during her pregnancy. He had done several tests on her blood, hoping to find the secret of her transformation, but to no avail. What had wrought the change in her, he wondered yet again, and where in hell had she gone?

Grunting softly, he picked up one of the vials. Unlike vampire blood, which was dark, the blood inside the glass tube was bright red. Mara's blood. He removed the cork, his nostrils flaring as the rich coppery scent swirled through the air.

Had he preyed upon her when he'd had the chance, he would have been able to track her whereabouts with ease . . . He stared at the vial in his hand. This was her blood. He grunted thoughtfully. Perhaps there was a way to find her, after all.

Murmuring, "I wonder . . . ?" he tilted his head back and let the thick crimson liquid trickle down his throat.

Now, there was just one more thing he had to do.

Chapter Thirty-two

Kyle stared at the canvas in front of him, but instead of seeing Old Town Porterville, he saw Mara's face. She was beautiful, so beautiful, but the inner glow, the fire that had first attracted him, was gone. Her eyes were always sad now, except for those times when she held their son in her arms.

He had tried to be understanding and supportive, but how could any mortal truly understand what she was going through? Not long ago, she had been a monster who preyed on the innocent, and now she was human, with a fine, handsome son and a man who adored her, yet it wasn't enough. Why anyone would want to go back to being a vampire was beyond his comprehension. He had seen what vampires did the night the police drove him to the morgue to identify his father's body. Having seen that, he was somewhat amazed that he could love Mara, but love her he did. And she wasn't a vampire now. She was human, the mother of his child . . .

He raked a hand through his hair. A child that might very well be a vampire, something they might not know for years. In talking with Rane, he had learned that Rane and his brother had been like any other boys until they reached puberty, when their vampire natures overcame their humanity. Would that happen to his son? Hard to imagine that his pink-cheeked little boy might one day turn into a blood-drinking fiend. In all fairness, Rane and his brother didn't seem like monsters, yet he knew they preyed on humans, as did the rest of the family, save for Savanah. How long until she, too, joined the ranks of the Undead? Would she wait until Abbey was grown?

His son, a vampire. Kyle shook his head. He wouldn't think of that now. Until he knew otherwise, he would believe that Derek would grow up to be like any other child. He loved the boy beyond belief, knew that he would willingly lay down his life for his son. Not for the first time, Kyle thought of taking the boy and leaving his wife. He knew Mara would grieve for the child but he thought that, in the long run, she would be happier. If Derek was gone, Mara would have no reason to remain human. She could get her vampire lover to bring her across and go back to being one of the Undead . . .

Damn! If he lived to be a hundred, he would never forget the night she had told him what she was, shown him what she was. He didn't know what he had been expecting her to show him. Certainly not what he had seen. Not that she had looked like a monster. Even sprouting fangs and with a faint reddish glow in her eyes, she had been beautiful. No, the horror had been in knowing what she was, knowing that he had made love to the same kind of monster that had preyed upon his father and left his mother barely clinging to life.

Shaking off his morbid memories of the past, Kyle put brush to canvas, but the thought of taking his son far away lingered in the back of his mind.

Chapter Thirty-three

A week later, Savanah insisted on taking Mara out to lunch and a movie.

"I don't know about you," Savanah said, "but I need a little R and R. It's amazing, how exhausting motherhood can be. I don't know how women who have more than one kid manage to stay sane. Come on, my treat."

So it was that Mara reluctantly left Derek with Kyle, and Savanah left Abbey Marie with Rane.

"This was a good idea," Mara admitted over lunch.

"Do you feel any better about being human again?"

"The truth?"

"Of course." Savanah took a sip of her iced tea.

"I don't think I'll ever like it," Mara said. "Although I do like this." Using her fork, she gestured at her dessert, a large slice of seven-layer chocolate cake with chocolate fudge icing. "We never had anything like this when I was mortal the first time," she said, taking a bite.

"No doubt about it, chocolate is a woman's best friend," Savanah remarked, grinning. "I don't know how we'd get through life or PMS without it."

"So true." Mara closed her eyes, savoring the rich

taste. She might be able to survive being human, as long as there was chocolate. "I wonder if Kathy ever misses mortal food."

"I don't know, I've never asked." Savanah plucked the cherry off the top of her hot fudge sundae and popped it into her mouth. "I was surprised when she asked Rafe to bring her across. I mean, she was barely twenty-four. I thought she'd wait a few years, you know?"

"I guess so," Mara agreed. But it wasn't really hard for her to understand. Why get older if you didn't have to? Why take a chance on coming down with some horrible disease? Or being crippled? Or killed in an accident? After all, people died in cars and planes every day, and even a vampire couldn't bring the dead back to life.

"She's going to be a vampire for a very long time," Savanah went on. "I would have thought she'd want to enjoy being human a little, at least until she was closer to thirty, anyway. Oh, well, to each his own."

"I take it you're not looking forward to becoming a vampire, then," Mara remarked.

"Not really, although sometimes it appears very appealing. After all, no one wants to get old, or sick."

"And the other times?"

"I'm sure it's wrong, but there's no other way to stay with Rane. He says it doesn't matter, that he'll love me no matter what I do, but . . ."

"You don't believe him?"

"It's not that. I know he'll always love me, no matter what, but"—she leaned across the table—"I don't want to saddle him with an old woman. He's young and virile, and he always will be."

Mara nodded. Savanah didn't have to spell it out.

"Besides, I don't want people to see us together and think I'm his grandmother."

They went to the multiplex after lunch. Mara tried to enjoy the movie, but her thoughts kept wandering toward her son. She told herself there was nothing to worry about. She had left the baby with Kyle before, though not for this long. It was all she could do to keep from calling home. She was relieved when the end credits rolled and she and Savanah left the theater.

Outside, Savanah said, "It's a good thing it wasn't a double feature."

"What do you mean?"

Savanah shook her head. "I saw the way you kept glancing at your watch. I'll bet you don't have any idea who was in the movie or what it was even about."

Mara grinned sheepishly. "I guess I'm just being silly, but I worry every time I'm away from the baby."

"Trust me, you'll get over it. I'd suggest we do a little shopping, but I think I'd better get you home before you have a nervous breakdown."

They chatted amiably on the way home. This was what girlfriends did, Mara thought. They went to lunch, they exchanged recipes, they bragged about their children, complained about their husbands, and shared their dreams for the future. It was a good feeling, having someone to talk to, someone to confide in.

"We'll have to do this again soon," Mara said as Savanah pulled up in front of the house.

Savanah nodded. "I'll give you a call next week. Tell Kyle hello for me."

"Yes, I will. Give my love to Rane." Mara waved as Savanah backed out of the driveway, then stood on the porch for a few minutes, thinking how lucky she was to have Savanah for a friend. With Savanah's help, she just might get the hang of being human again after all.

Mara glanced around the front yard. Maybe she would

try her hand at gardening. She could plant some red roses on either side of the front porch, and maybe some daisies along the fence. She wanted to paint the inside of the house, too. All those white walls were driving her crazy. And since it seemed they were going to be here for a while, she might as well have some of the furniture from the Hollywood house shipped here. If this was going to be their home, it would be nice to have some of her favorite things around her.

Leaning against one of the porch uprights, she gazed into the distance. Unbidden, an image of Logan rose in her mind. What was he doing now? Was he still living in Hollywood, surrounded by beautiful starlets, or had he fled the country? The thought of never seeing him again sat like a heavy weight on her heart. Was he still angry? Did he truly hate her now? Could she blame him if he did?

Shaking his image from her mind, she opened the front door and went inside. Kicking off her shoes, she called, "Kyle, I'm home. Did the baby give you any trouble?" She frowned when there was no reply. "Kyle?"

Thinking he might be putting Derek down for a nap, Mara dropped her handbag on the sofa and made her way to the nursery, but Kyle wasn't there, and the crib was empty.

"Kyle?" She walked through the house calling his name, a tendril of fear expanding in her chest when each room she looked in proved to be empty.

Quickening her pace, she hurried outside. There was no one in the backyard. She breathed a sigh of relief when she saw that Kyle's car was in the garage. So, he hadn't gone far. It was such a nice day, he had probably decided to take the baby for a walk.

Chiding herself for overreacting, she went into the

kitchen for a drink of water, then went into the den and booted up the computer.

Calling up the file that held her life story, she read through what she had written the day before. It wasn't long before she was completely caught up in the past, her fingers flying over the keyboard as she wrote about a liaison she'd had with a handsome young Italian back in 1750. Lucian had courted her with music and poetry, sent her flowers every day. She had been contemplating bringing him across when he was killed by a highwayman.

Sitting back in her chair, Mara lifted her arms over her head and stretched her back and shoulders, only then noticing that night had fallen.

Rising to switch on the light, she glanced at the clock. It was after five.

Fear twisted her insides when she realized Kyle and the baby still hadn't come home. Where could they be?

Going out onto the front porch, she glanced up and down the street, surprised to see that a sudden storm had swallowed up the sunshine. She wrapped her arms around her midriff as lightning split the skies, followed by an ominous roar of thunder. Not long ago, she had been able to control the weather. She had called lightning from the skies. If only she had her powers now, she would be able to find Derek with no trouble at all.

Where were they? She rubbed her hands up and down her arms. It wasn't like Kyle to do something like this. He knew how she worried whenever the baby was out of her sight. Why didn't he call? Had he been in an accident? Was he lying hurt in a ditch somewhere? And what of her son? Was he hurt? Should she call the police?

Mara shivered as her imagination ran wild. Kyle could have been mugged and left for dead. Her son could be out there in the rain, crying and afraid.

She stood on the porch until the cold drove her back inside. She paced the living room floor, her worry increasing with every passing moment. Never had time moved so slowly. She told herself not to worry. Maybe Kyle had run into an old friend. Maybe he had holed up somewhere to wait out the storm. Maybe he was having an affair. Not that she could blame him. She hadn't been much of a wife, but even as the thought crossed her mind, she thrust it aside. A man having an affair didn't take a baby with him.

At eight o'clock, she picked up the phone and punched in Rane's phone number. He answered on the first ring.

She had barely finished asking for his help when he materialized in her living room.

Mara stared at him, overwhelmed by memories of her vampire life. She had once been able to will herself anywhere she wished to go. She had been able to dissolve into mist, move faster than the human eye could follow, drift on the wind. She had been lighter than air then. Now, her body felt heavy, earthbound.

"Mara?"

She blinked up at him. "Oh, Rane! Kyle's gone. He's taken the baby. I don't know where they are."

"Has he ever done this before? Taken the baby somewhere without telling you?"

"No. He was gone when I got home." She crossed her arms under her breasts, breasts now heavy with milk. "It's past Derek's feeding time. Where can they be?"

"I don't know. I'll go outside and sniff around, see what I can find."

With a nod, she followed him out the door, stood on the porch while he walked around the yard, then around the house. Lightning slashed through the clouds; thunder rolled across the skies.

Dripping wet, Rane returned to the porch a few minutes later.

"Did you find anything?" she asked anxiously.

"I'm not sure."

"What do you mean?"

"I followed his scent out the back door to the side gate. And then it just disappears."

"What do you mean, it disappears? That's impossible. What about my baby? Where's Derek?"

"His scent ends at the gate, the same as Kyle's. I don't want to pry into your private life, but did you and Kyle have a fight or anything?"

"No."

"Can you think of any reason why he'd leave?"

Her gaze slid away from his. She could think of a dozen reasons, and all of them her fault.

"Mara? This is no time for secrets."

"We haven't been intimate for a long time." The truth was, they hadn't been intimate since Derek was conceived. She took a deep breath. Might as well tell Rane the rest. "I think Kyle knows that I'm in love with Logan."

Rane scrubbed his hands over his face, then ran his fingers through his hair. "Women," he muttered. "If I live forever, I'll never understand them." He looked at her, his eyes filled with frustration. "If you're in love with Blackwood, why the devil did you marry Bowden?"

She lifted her chin defiantly. "You know why."

"Yes, I guess I do, but you must have seen this coming. Hell, it doesn't matter now. You stay here, by the phone. I'll get hold of Rafe and my old man and see if we can find anything. All right?"

Mara nodded. There was a faint shimmer in the air, and then Rane was gone.

Fighting back her tears, Mara went inside. She closed the door, then leaned back against it for a moment. If Kyle had left her, wouldn't he have packed a suitcase for himself and the baby? Wouldn't he have taken the car?

She went into their bedroom. Kyle's clothes were still in the closet, their suitcases were still on the shelf. She looked into the baby's room, but everything seemed to be in place.

Frowning, she ran out to the garage and checked the car. It was spotlessly clean, as always. Kyle's sunglasses were tucked away on the visor, the baby's car seat was in its usual place.

Returning to the house, she went into the living room and curled up on the sofa, feeling more alone than she ever had in her life. She hadn't prayed since Dendar forced the Dark Gift on her, but she prayed now, promising Heaven that she would be the best wife any man ever had if only Kyle would bring their son safely home.

Rafe and Vince showed up at Rane's house at the same time he did.

Savanah greeted her father-in-law with a smile, gave her brother-in-law a hug, and sent a questioning glance at her husband. "What's going on?"

"Bowden and the baby are gone."

"Gone?" Savanah asked. "Gone where?"

"I don't know." Rane ran his hand through his still-damp hair. "Neither does Mara. She thinks he's left her."

"And he took the baby?" Savanah asked incredulously.

"That's what Mara thinks."

"Sounds like a lover's quarrel to me," Vince remarked. "So, what are we doing here?"

"I just came from Mara's place. I didn't say anything to Mara, didn't want to worry her more than she was, but I don't think Bowden left of his own accord."

"What makes you think that?" Rafe asked.

"I walked around the house. Bowden's scent disappeared at the gate. I think someone took him. Someone who knew how to mask not only Bowden's scent, but his own, as well."

"A handy talent," Vince muttered. "But if whoever it was masked his scent, how do you know there was anyone else there?"

"It's hard to explain. It was more a sense of something out of place than anything else. I tried to follow the trail, but it disappeared once I got out of the yard."

"So, what do we do now?" Rafe asked. "If there's no trail . . ." He shrugged.

Rane shook his head. "I don't know. Put the word out on the street, I guess. Ask our people to keep an eye out for Bowden and the baby. Bowden's car was in the garage. If he intended to leave Mara, and he left under his own power, he wouldn't have left the car behind."

"Good point," Rafe remarked. "Doesn't make much sense to take off on foot lugging a six-month-old baby."

"That's true, but why would anyone kidnap Kyle and Derek?" Savanah asked.

Vince shoved his hands in his pants' pockets. "If we knew why, we might know who."

"Maybe we're worrying for nothing," Savanah suggested hopefully. "Maybe he just got caught out in the rain and he'll come home when it stops."

"Maybe, but Mara said he was gone when you dropped her off. That's been what, three hours ago?"

Savanah nodded.

"Besides," Rane added, "if that was true, I'd have been able to track him."

Rafe raked his hand through his hair. "Maybe we should call the police."

"Let's keep that as a last resort," Vince said, glancing from one son to the other.

Rafe shrugged. "It was just a thought."

"And not a very good one," Rane said, punching his brother on the arm. "When have the police ever been on our side?"

"I should go sit with Mara," Savanah said. "She must be worried sick."

"Good idea," Rane said. "You get Abbey. I'll bring the car around in case you need it while we're gone."

"I'll ride over with you," Vince said. "I want to have a look around."

Mara grew more frantic with each passing moment. She tried to tell herself that Kyle would return anytime now, but her mind constantly came up with new and more horrible possibilities—he had taken the baby for a walk and they had been hit by a bus; they had been abducted by aliens from outer space; they had been kidnapped by werewolves, by Gypsies, by a coven of dark witches who wanted to use Derek in some horrible Satanic ritual.

She was on the verge of hysterics when Savanah knocked on the door.

One look at Mara's face and Savanah set Abbey's car seat on the floor and took Mara into her arms.

"It'll be all right," Savanah said reassuringly. "Our men will find them."

Mara nodded, then dissolved into tears.

Murmuring words of comfort, Savanah held Mara until her tears ebbed; then, after settling Mara on the sofa, Savanah went into the kitchen to fix two cups of hot chocolate, though she feared this was one instance when all the chocolate in the world wouldn't be enough.

Mara was drying her eyes when Savanah returned to the living room. Taking a seat on the sofa, she handed one of the cups to Mara.

"Where can they be?" Mara stared into her cup as though she might find the answer to her question inside.

"I don't know, but I'm sure they're all right."

Mara took a deep breath and released it in a long, shuddering sigh. "I've made a mess of everything."

"Stop that! This isn't your fault."

"Of course it is." She looked at Savanah. "I just want my baby back."

"I know. I know. Rane and the men are out looking for them, even now. I'm sure they'll find Kyle and Derek. I just know they will."

Mara nodded. She had to believe it. If she didn't, she would surely go insane.

Mara paced the floor in front of the fireplace. Each tick of the mantel clock sounded like a death knell to her ears. Where was Kyle? Hours had passed, with no word from Rane or Vince or Rafe.

As the hours passed, she found herself hoping that Kyle had kidnapped Derek. At least then, her son would be safe. That scenario was far better than the ones her imagination continued to spew up in living color, not the worst of which was the very real possibility that Kyle and Derek had been kidnapped by a vampire carrying a grudge and hoping to get even with her by hurting those she loved.

She glanced at Savanah, who was asleep on the sofa, with Abbey cradled in her arms. Looking at Abbey made Mara's arms ache to hold her son.

She sank down in a chair, only to rise again a few minutes later. She couldn't rest, couldn't sleep, until she knew her baby was safe.

Rane appeared in the living room just after dawn.

One look at his face, and Mara knew he hadn't found anything.

"I'm sorry," he said. "There's just no trail to follow." He kissed Savanah, who had just finished nursing the baby. Sitting on the sofa, he took Abbey in his arms and gave her a hug.

Vince and Cara appeared ten minutes later. Again, there was no good news.

Mara sat on the chair in front of the hearth, her arms crossed under her breasts. Rafe was her last hope.

He arrived a few minutes after seven, along with Kathy. Rafe glanced at his father and his brother, then went to kneel in front of Mara. Taking her hands in his, he said, "It's like they've vanished from the face of the earth, but we won't stop looking."

"Maybe we should contact Roshan," Vince suggested. "He's the oldest member of the family. Maybe he'll have some ideas."

"No." Easing her hands from Rafe's, Mara gained her feet. "I want to thank you for what you've done, all of you, but there's only one man who can help me now."

Vince and his sons exchanged knowing looks.

"Blackwood," Rane said quietly.

"Yes. He's the oldest of our . . . of your . . . kind. If anyone can find my son, he can."

She was grateful that no one tried to talk her out of it. She couldn't just sit here and wait. She had to feel that she was doing something to help.

"I'll take you," Rane said.

She smiled, grateful for his offer. Today's airplanes were fast, but vampire transportation was faster, and safer.

She just hoped that, after the way she had treated Logan, he wouldn't slam the door in her face.

Chapter Thirty-four

Shivering uncontrollably, Kyle Bowden paced the narrow confines of his cage. The cement floor was bitterly cold beneath his bare feet. There was no chair, no bed in his prison, nothing but a rough wool blanket for a bed, and a covered chamber pot in one corner. Six steps carried him from one end of his gloomy cell to the other.

A glance at his watch told him it was a little after seven, but he didn't know if it was morning or evening, didn't know where in the hell he was, or how he had gotten there. But his biggest concern was his son's whereabouts. He didn't know if Derek was dead or alive.

Damn. The last thing he remembered before waking up here, wherever the hell here was, was sitting in the nursery, giving the baby a bottle. Had that been hours ago, or days? He had no way of knowing, hadn't seen anyone since he'd regained consciousness.

Knowing it was useless, he wrapped his hands around the steel bars and gave a hard yank. Nothing happened. The bars, set in concrete, were thick and solid. His hands tightened on the bars as he gazed at his surroundings. It didn't take long; there wasn't much to see. The room was a twelve by twelve foot square. The walls and floor were cement; there were no windows, and no furnishings save for a battered desk, a brown leather chair, and a small lamp that held the dark at bay. His gaze lingered on what looked like a doctor's bag on a stainless-steel table. Visions of illegal experiments flashed through his mind.

Sliding down into a sitting position with his back against the wall, he cradled his head in his hands. "Think, Bowden." How long had he been there? He scrubbed a hand over his jaw. It was scratchy with stubble. His stomach growled, reminding him that lunch had been his last meal. So, as near as he could figure, it was morning. Mara must be frantic with worry by now. He would have demanded to know where he was, where his son was, if there had been anyone to ask. Not that he was in any position to make demands.

He muttered an oath as a horrible thought insinuated itself into his mind. What if this was all Mara's doing? He wasn't blind. He knew she wasn't happy living with him, that she regretted their marriage. Had she arranged for . . .

No! He slammed his fist against the floor. He wouldn't believe she had planned this. But what if she had? What if she had arranged for someone to dispose of him, permanently?

Damn. The thought made him break out in a cold sweat, but once acknowledged, it burrowed deeper into his mind. Getting rid of one human male was probably no big deal to a woman who had once been a vampire. In her time, she had undoubtedly dispatched any number of lovers once she tired of them. Poor lovesick fool. He was probably just one more in a long line of men she had used and discarded.

Chapter Thirty-five

Logan swore softly as a knock on the front door roused him from a deep, dreamless sleep. His internal clock told him it was late afternoon. Rolling onto his side, he pulled a pillow over his head and closed his eyes. Whoever the hell was pounding on his door could just come back later.

He bolted upright as Mara's scent reached his nostrils. What the devil was she doing here? For a moment, one fleetingly foolish moment, he thought of ignoring her. And then he threw the covers aside and hurried down the stairs.

Heedless of the fact that he was stark naked, he opened the door.

He took one look at her face, drew her into the house, and closed the door. "Here, now," he said, "it can't be as bad as all that."

"It's worse."

He didn't ask questions, just wrapped his arms around her and held her tight.

The touch of his hand in her hair unleashed the flood

of tears she had been holding back and she collapsed against him, sobbing.

Swinging her into his arms, Logan carried her into the living room. Still cradling her against his chest, he sat down on the sofa. "All right," he said quietly, "tell me all about it."

"It's Derek . . . he's . . . he's gone. Kyle took him."

"Took him? You mean he's kidnapped him?"

"Yes, and we can't find either one of them." She sniffed noisily. "Rane and Rafe and Vince looked everywhere. They couldn't . . . couldn't find any trace of him or . . . or the baby."

"What do you mean, they couldn't find any trace of them?"

"No tracks, no scent. Nothing." She took a deep breath. "They searched the house, the yard, everywhere, but there was no trail to follow. It's like Kyle and the baby just disappeared into thin air."

"I've never heard of a mortal being able to disappear into thin air, or into anything else, for that matter," Logan said dryly.

"I know, but he did it. And he took Derek." A fresh spate of tears flooded her eyes and dripped down her cheeks. "Logan, where can he be?"

"I don't know." Unable to help himself, he brushed a kiss across her brow. "Do you remember during the War? Some of the vampires were able to mask their scent, not only from the werewolves, but from other vampires, as well."

"I remember," Mara said, wiping away her tears with her fingertips, "but no one ever figured out how they did it."

"Yeah."

She sniffed again. "You know you're naked, right?"

"Yes, ma'am, but it was nice of you to notice."

How could she help it when he stood there, all his masculine glory on display?

He grinned impudently.

"Will you help me find Derek? I won't blame you if you refuse, but, please, Logan, I'm so worried about him. As far as I can tell, Kyle didn't take anything for the baby with him—no diapers, no bottles, no warm clothes, nothing."

"Are you sure Bowden's the one who took him?"

"Yes, of course. I mean, they're both gone . . . Who else would have taken the baby? And why?"

"I don't know. All I'm saying is that maybe someone else took the kid and Kyle's out looking for him."

"Oh." She had never considered that, but what if Logan was right? "I should call Rane and see if they've heard anything."

"Good idea. In the meantime, I'll get dressed and go see what I can find out."

Mara nodded, though she couldn't help thinking it seemed a shame to clothe such a gorgeous hunk of man. Chiding herself for her wayward thoughts at such a time, she called Rane, listened intently as he told her that Rafe and Kathy were staying at her house on the off chance that Logan was right, and Kyle was out looking for Derek.

"My mom and dad are checking all the towns and cities hereabouts," Rane said. "I was just getting ready to go give them a hand. Once we cover Oregon, we'll head down the coast. Roshan and Brenna will be here later tonight. Don't worry, Mara, we'll find them."

After thanking Rane and bidding him good-bye, Mara curled up on the sofa. She comforted herself with the knowledge that they were doing everything they could, but all she could think about was Derek. Was her baby crying for her, even now? Was he in the hands of strangers, hungry and frightened? If Logan was right and her son had been kidnapped, maybe she should go back home in case the kidnapper called or sent a note demanding ransom. Yet even as the thought crossed her mind, she dismissed the idea. As far as she knew, only a handful of vampires even knew she had a baby, and they were all friends. Still, she couldn't ignore the possibility that the word had leaked out, that her enemies had learned she had lost her powers. Kidnapping her son would be the perfect way for her enemies to avenge themselves on her.

Fresh tears stung her eyes. She should have put the baby up for adoption, given him to a nice normal couple . . . She groaned low in her throat. She hated waiting, hated depending on others.

Rising, she paced the floor, her feet sinking into the thick carpet. Where was Logan? Where was Kyle? And where, oh where, was her son?

Mara was dozing on the sofa when Logan returned an hour later. "Did you find out anything?" she asked.

"No." Sitting beside her, he shrugged out of his jacket, then kicked off his shoes. "I went to Hells' Hollow and asked around." Hell's Hollow was a club that catered to vampires. Preternatural glamour hid it from human eyes. "No one's heard anything. As for vampires being able to mask their scent from other vampires, someone mentioned witchcraft."

"Witchcraft?" Mara asked, frowning. Witches and vampires rarely intermingled. Some believed the blood of witches was poison to vampires, but it was just a myth that reared its head every hundred years or so. Had it been true, Roshan DeLongpre would have been dead years ago because his wife was a practicing witch.

Logan shrugged. "Maybe some witch has come up with a spell or potion or something else that's effective."

"Maybe." Except for Brenna, Mara didn't remember any other witches being active in the War between the Vampires and the Werewolves, but in this day and age, anything was possible. "Do you know of any vampires who are currently involved with witches?"

"Other than DeLongpre? No. Anthony Loken's dead. His son is dead. That crazy woman, Serafina, is dead, and so are most of the members of her coven. I don't know of any other practicing witches hereabouts. Brenna might know."

Mara nodded. To the best of her recollection, Brenna had never mentioned knowing any other witches. But then, most witches, like most vampires, preferred to remain in the shadows.

Logan ran a hand through his hair. "You don't think . . . ?"

"Think what?" Mara asked.

"You don't think Ramsden's in on this, do you? You never did trust the guy."

Ramsden, she thought. Of course. "Remember I told you he seemed overly curious about the baby's father?"

"Yeah. Did you ever figure out why?"

"No."

"Well, let's put the good doctor at the top of the list. I'll call him first, but if he's in on this, he's probably in hiding somewhere. If I can't get ahold of him, I'll put the word out that I'm looking for him."

"And for Kyle, too."

"Right."

She nodded, her throat suddenly tight, her heart

swelling with gratitude. In spite of the awful way she had treated Logan in the past, he was right there by her side when she needed him the most. No recriminations, no bitterness in his eyes when he looked at her. How could she have been so blind all those years ago? Not only was he gorgeous and sexy, but he loved her as no other man ever had. Why had it taken her so long to realize that she loved him, too? She could have saved herself a world of grief and loneliness if she had only admitted she cared for him. They could have explored centuries together; now she would be lucky to live for another fifty or sixty years.

"I'm sorry," she murmured. "So sorry."

He didn't have to ask what she was apologizing for. He knew. "Forget it. It's yesterday's news."

"You've always been so good to me, and I . . ."

"I said forget it."

She looked at him, her heart breaking for all the lost years, for the pain she had caused him. She was hurting inside, aching for her son, filled with frustration and fear. She looked at Logan, and wanted nothing more than to be in his arms, to forget everything, if only for a little while. "Logan . . ."

He read it all in her eyes, her pain, her loneliness, her fear. Her desire for him. He could have taken her there and then, but cutting in on another man's territory was where he drew the line.

Rising, he said, "I asked you not to marry him." He held up his hand when she started to protest. "You don't have to explain anything to me. I know why you went with him, maybe better than you do yourself."

"Don't you want me?"

"You know damn well that I do. I wanted you the first

ime I saw you, and every night since then. I'll want you
or as long as I draw breath."

"I love you."

"I'm going to go make those calls. Why don't you try
and get some sleep?"

She stared after him as he walked out of the room,
and then she put her face in her hands and wept for
everything she had lost, everything she had thought-
essly thrown away.

Chapter Thirty-six

Kyle sprang to his feet as the door across the way opened and a tall man with graying brown hair and dark eyes entered the room. He wore a white lab coat and carried a notebook in one hand and a tray holding half a dozen bottles and vials in the other. A stethoscope hung from his neck. He placed the tray on the metal table before he approached the cage.

"So, Mr. Bowden, how are we feeling this evening?"

"I don't know about you, but I'm feeling like a rat in a trap."

"An apt description," the man agreed with a faint smile. "I'll need some information."

"Who are you? Where the hell am I? What do you want with me?"

"All in good time. For now, for your own good, I suggest you answer my questions."

"And if I don't?"

The man let out an aggrieved sigh. "I can promise you that you'll regret it."

Looking into the other man's eyes, Kyle had no doubt

that he spoke the truth. "What kind of information do you want?"

"Let's start with your age."

Kyle hesitated a moment, but could think of no good reason not to answer. "I was twenty-eight last November."

"Any childhood illnesses?"

"No."

"Have you been sexually promiscuous?"

"What the hell does that have to do with anything?"

"Just answer the question."

Kyle shrugged. "No moreso than most men my age."

"Ever had a blood transfusion?"

"No."

"Any sexually transmitted diseases?"

"No."

"Ever been bitten by a vampire?"

At the word *vampire*, alarm bells went off in Kyle's head. Was this guy one of the Undead?

"Mr. Bowden?"

Kyle shook his head. "No."

"Are you sure?"

"Hell, yes, I wouldn't forget something like that." But even as he said the words, he wondered if it was true. Could Mara have bitten him without his knowledge?

"Do you know where Mara is?"

Kyle gripped the bars in both hands, his earlier suspicions surfacing once again. "What does she have to do with any of this?"

"All in good time."

Kyle's hands tightened on the bars. "Where's my son?"

"I need to draw some blood."

"Go to hell."

"Bowden." The man's voice wrapped around him like

liquid iron, holding him immobile. "You will do as I say. Roll up your sleeve, then sit down on the floor and make a fist."

In spite of his desire to refuse, Kyle discovered he was helpless to disobey. When he was sitting on the floor, the man retrieved the tray from the table, unlocked the door to the cage, and stepped inside.

Kyle glanced at the open door. He willed himself to lunge at the man, but again his body refused to obey. Unable to move, Kyle watched as the man filled several vials with his blood and then, to Kyle's horror, the man forced Kyle's head to one side and sank his fangs into his throat.

And everything went black.

Chapter Thirty-seven

Lou McDonald held the phone to her ear with one hand while she tapped the end of her pencil on the desktop with the other.

"Anyway," Cindy said, "he told me I was fired and that he was closing up the office."

"Why would he do that?" Lou asked, frowning.

"I don't know, but I forgot to take my suede jacket with me when I left, and when I went to get it the next night, the place was locked up tight. I called Ramsden at home, and his wife answered. She doesn't know where he is, either, or if she does, she's not telling."

"That's really strange."

"Yeah," Cindy muttered. "Anyway, I'm out of a job and that jacket cost me five-hundred credits. I'll bet his nurse took it with her. Anyway, I was thinking about coming to stay with you, if that's all right."

"Sure, I've got room. Do you think this has anything to do with Mara?"

"I don't know," Cindy said, her frown evident in her tone. "Why?"

"I called Kyle sometime back to remind him that he

still owes me a few hundred credits, and his number's been disconnected."

"So? Do you think he skipped out on you?"

"I doubt it. He's too much of a Boy Scout to pull a fast one. Seems an odd coincidence, though. Ramsden and Bowden both having links to Mara and both of them disappearing like that."

"Well, you know what Dad always said."

"Yeah, that there's no such thing as coincidence. Mara would have had the baby by now," Lou said, sorting things out in her mind. "She's missing. Kyle's missing. Ramsden's missing. I think if we find one, we'll find them all, and . . . holy crap!"

"What is it?" Cindy asked. "Lou? Lou, are you all right?"

"You'll never believe who just walked in the door. I've gotta go."

"Lou . . ."

"Call ya later." Disconnecting the call, Lou gained her feet, one hand delving into the pocket of her slacks, her fingers curling around the bottle of holy water she was never without as a male vampire and a woman entered her office. Lou had never seen Mara before, but she recognized her immediately from the various descriptions she had heard in the past. The ex-vampire was as beautiful as everyone had said. "Mara." The name whispered past Lou's lips.

Mara inclined her head, but said nothing.

It was true, Lou thought. The one-time Queen of the Vampires had lost her powers. Lou took a deep breath, careful not to look the male in the eyes. Preternatural power radiated from him like thick black smoke from a forest fire. He was old, centuries old.

"Can I help you?" she asked, pleased that her voice didn't betray her fear.

"Only time will tell," the male said.

"What do you want?"

"I want you to find a vampire for me."

"I'd think you'd be better at that than I am," Lou said dryly.

"Ordinarily, you'd be right, but this one has found a way to mask his presence from our kind."

Lou grunted softly. She had heard rumors that some of the vampires had accomplished that during the War. She hadn't believed it at the time. She'd have to look into it, now that it appeared to be true. "Who are you looking for?"

"Dr. Thomas Ramsden."

Lou glanced at Mara, then back at the male. "I see. Any idea where he might be?"

"If I knew that, I wouldn't be here."

Lou shrugged. "Do you want him dead?"

"Not now, but you may have him when I'm done with him. I'm also looking for Kyle Bowden."

Lou glanced at Mara, then back at the vampire, careful, again, not to meet his gaze. She was dying to know exactly what kind of relationship Bowden had with Mara, and how the male vampire fit into the mix. Instead, she said, "I don't come cheap."

"Name your own price."

"Six hundred a day and expenses."

Logan nodded. "Now that you're working for me, do you know anything I should know?"

"Perhaps. My sister works for Ramsden, or she did until a few days ago when he fired her and closed his office."

Mara looked at Logan. Though she didn't say anything

out loud, he knew what she was thinking. Somehow, Ramsden had discovered her whereabouts. When she wasn't home, he had taken Derek and Kyle and gone into hiding. There was no other answer that made sense.

Lou's gaze settled on Mara's trim figure. She had to know. "Did the baby live? Was it normal?"

"Yes." Mara's voice was little more than a whisper.

The look in the vampire's eyes warned Lou not to ask any more questions about the birth or the baby.

Resting her hip on the edge of her desk, Lou said, "I'm thinking it's probably not a coincidence that the doctor and Kyle both went missing about the same time."

"Agreed," Logan said.

Lou nodded. "And I think I know why he wants Kyle."

"Because he got Mara pregnant while she was still a vampire," Logan said impatiently. "Any idiot could figure that out."

A flush crawled up Lou's neck and heated her cheeks. Ignoring the jibe, she said, "I imagine there are a lot of vampires who would pay any price he asked to be able to reproduce. Of course, this is all speculation at this point." She looked at Mara. "Is there any reason why Kyle would take off without telling you?"

Mara hesitated a moment, then said, "We haven't been getting along very well lately."

Lou slid a glance at the vampire, wondering if he was the cause of the rift between Mara and Kyle. Although Lou loathed vampires, she couldn't help thinking that, Undead or not, Mara's companion was one of the sexiest men she had ever seen. Annoyed with herself, she said, "I'll need a number where I can reach you."

"I'll contact you," the vampire said.

"Are you at least going to give me your name?"

"Sure," he said with an easy smile. "Which one would you like?"

"Whichever one you're using now."

"Logan."

"No last name?"

"We'll be in touch," Logan said, taking Mara's hand in his.

Before Lou could ask any more questions, the two of them vanished from her sight.

"Wish I could do that," Lou muttered.

Dropping down into her chair, she tapped her fingertips on the edge of her desk. There was more going on here than Logan had told her. But what? Kyle had apparently run off, maybe with another woman. Ramsden had closed his office and no one knew where he was. Was the baby also missing?

Lou slammed her hand on the desktop. Of course it was. Why else would Mara be looking for Kyle? He hadn't run off with another woman. He had run off with the baby. But why was Mara looking for the doctor? Surely Kyle and Ramsden weren't in this together. Or maybe they were. Stranger things had happened.

Grabbing her cell phone, Lou punched in her sister's number.

Cindy answered on the first ring.

"Hey, Cin, you're never going to believe who just hired us."

Chapter Thirty-eight

Thomas Ramsden glanced at the women standing on either side of him as he stepped away from the microscope. He had contacted Pearl and Edna the day before and asked them to join him at his hideaway in an abandoned laboratory near Area 51. A witch's clever spell, combined with his own preternatural wards, effectively cloaked the building and its occupants from both humans and supernatural creatures alike.

Ramsden had met the two elderly vampires shortly after the end of the War. Neither of them had any fondness for Mara or for the Cordova family, which was neither here nor there. What was important was their knowledge of genetics. He knew their proposed supernatural cure had failed, but that wasn't important. Had they pursued it, they might have eventually come up with a serum to restore humanity to the vampires and the werewolves, although he doubted such a thing was possible. The women had, in fact, continued their search for a cure for a short time after the War but then, as so often happened to those who had been turned against their will, they had learned to embrace their new lifestyle and eventually abandoned their search for a way to regain their lost humanity.

No one, looking at them, would ever guess the two elderly women were vampires. Pearl was tall and angular with shoulder-length white hair. She wore designer jeans, a gaudy red silk shirt, and a pair of white leather boots. Edna was short and a trifle plump; her curly red hair was obviously dyed. She wore a green sweater and comfortable sneakers; a green patchwork skirt swirled around her ankles.

Ramsden gestured at the microscope. "Take a look and tell me what you think."

Pearl smiled at the other woman. "After you, dear."

Edna peered through the eyepiece for several moments, nodded once, and moved to the side so that Pearl could have a look.

"Well?" Ramsden asked impatiently.

"It seems impossible," Pearl said, "but the proof is right there. Don't you agree, Edna?"

Edna nodded, then looked into the microscope again. "You know, if we'd had these samples to work with during the War, I'll bet our serum would have worked."

"Yes, I think you're right, dear."

Ramsden shook his head. "It doesn't make sense. Why would a dormant werewolf gene produce fertility in a vampire?"

"I have no idea," Edna said, moving away from the microscope, "but there it is."

Ramsden peered through the microscope again. "Do you think mating with a werewolf had anything to do with her reverting to mortality?"

Edna and Pearl exchanged glances, then Edna shook her head. "No. It's our opinion that her reverting to mortality was just a result of her long existence. To my knowledge, no vampire has ever survived as long as she has. With the passage of time, she gradually overcame her aversion to sunlight. She needed to feed less often, and her need for blood waned until she was able to digest mortal food."

"Yes," Pearl said, nodding. "After a great deal of study, we've come to the conclusion that all vampires, if they exist long enough, will gradually revert to mortality and die. Of course, for the lucky ones, reverting may take thousands of years. But no creatures, not even vampires, are truly immortal."

"An interesting hypothesis, ladies." Ramsden dragged a hand over his jaw. "Bowden seems completely unaware of the fact that he carries the werewolf gene. How do you account for that?"

Edna tapped her finger against her lips for a moment. "You said he's never shown any symptoms. If that's true, he'd have no reason to suspect he was infected."

"That's true." Pearl picked up one of the other slides and studied it through the microscope. "Have you taken the baby's blood? Was the gene passed on?"

Ramsden shook his head. "I've tested his blood, but the baby appears to be normal."

"I don't see how that could be possible," Edna said, frowning. "With a vampire for a mother, even one now mortal, and a father who carries the werewolf gene, even a dormant one . . . What do you think, Pearl?"

"Look at the Cordova twins," Pearl said. "They appeared to be normal until they reached puberty, and then all hell broke loose."

"Of course," Edna said, "but as far as we know, no blood tests were ever taken. We don't know if abnormalities in their blood would have shown up sooner . . ."

Ramsden swore softly. "Are you saying we'll have to wait until the baby reaches puberty to find out if he has any preternatural powers?"

"I'm afraid so, Doctor," Pearl said. "Although there's no way to know for certain. An abnormality could surface at any time."

Edna clapped her hands together. "Won't it be exhilarating to see which way he goes?" she asked, her voice rising with excitement. "Will he become a vampire or a werewolf? Fanged or furry?"

"Or perhaps a combination of the two, dear," Pearl mused. "Wouldn't that be remarkable?"

"That's all we need," Ramsden muttered irritably. "Hairy vampires!"

"Hairy vampires," Edna repeated, and burst out laughing.

"You know," Pearl remarked, "if Bowden's sperm is effective in impregnating other vampires . . ."

"We could make a fortune!" Edna exclaimed, finishing Pearl's thought.

"My idea exactly," Ramsden said. "I plan to use his sample to artificially inseminate my wife just as soon as she gets here."

Janis Ramsden arrived at her husband's secret lair the following night. She was not in a good mood.

"What's going on, Tom?" she asked, tossing her fur coat over a chair. "Why did you want me to come here?" She glanced around, her nose wrinkling in distaste as she took in her surroundings. The walls were gray stone and cement. There were no lights; a black leather couch and a wooden table were the room's only concessions to comfort. "This is where you've been hiding?" she asked disdainfully. "It certainly isn't the Ritz."

"Janis, shut up."

At his tone, her head snapped back as if he had slapped her. "How dare you . . ."

"I said shut up. I brought you here for a couple of reasons, and I think you'll like both of them."

"I'm listening."

"One, I've got a baby that needs looking after . . ."

"A baby!" she squealed. "Is it here? Is it ours? Can we keep it?"

"Yes, to all three questions. You can see him in a minute."

She clapped her hands in delight. "It's a boy!"

"Janis." The warning in his tone stilled her tongue. "Secondly, I want you to be part of an experiment I'm conducting."

"What kind of an experiment?" she asked warily.

"I want to see if you can get pregnant."

Her eyes widened. "Pregnant? Me? How?"

"You don't need to know the details. We'll do the procedure tomorrow night and every night for a week. For now, I want you to get some rest."

"Not until I've seen the baby. Where is it?"

Ramsden jerked his head toward a closed door. "Be quiet. He's asleep."

Janis hurried across the room. She paused at the door, then opened it quietly before stepping inside. This room, too, was made of stone and cement. A quick glance showed a crib standing alongside a king-sized bed.

Tiptoeing across the floor, she gazed down at the sleeping baby. When Tom came up behind her, she murmured, "He's adorable, isn't he?"

"Yeah. His name's Derek, but you can call him anything you want."

"Derek." Janis smoothed the baby's silky hair, then turned to face her husband. "Thank you, Tom. I'm sorry I've been such a shrew . . ."

Pulling her roughly into his arms, Ramsden said, "Let's go to bed and you can show me how sorry you are."

Chapter Thirty-nine

Like a restless tiger, Kyle paced the floor of his cage. Back and forth. Back and forth, until his legs ached. He rested a few minutes, and then he paced some more. His life had become an endless, waking nightmare. Trying to resist the vampire's commands was futile. If Kyle refused to do what he was told, the creature simply compelled him to obey. The vampire took his blood every night, his semen and tissue samples a couple of times a week. No matter how many times Kyle begged to know why he was there or what the vampire was doing, the blood-thirsty monster refused to answer.

There were three women on the premises now, two elderly females, and a rather pretty woman with russet-colored hair, and light brown eyes that carried a hint of madness. Kyle was certain that his son was somewhere nearby. There had been times when he'd heard a baby's cry, times when he was certain it was Derek. He had to get out of here, had to get his son away from this place, away from the monsters who kept them in captivity.

He paused in his endless pacing to stare at the door across the way. If only he had something he could use to pick the lock on his cage. He never saw the vampire or the three women during the day; no doubt the creatures slept when the sun was up. If he could only manage to escape the cage, he could find Derek and get the hell out of there.

He glanced at the tray that had held his nightly meal. There was nothing on it that he could use as a weapon, nothing he could use to pick the lock. The plates and cup were paper, the utensils plastic, the food uninspired.

Kyle swore a vile oath. He had to get Derek out of here. There was no telling what those creatures were doing to his child, no telling what they were doing with all the blood and tissue samples they had taken from him. Were they doing the same to his son? The thought of Derek being poked and prodded made Kyle's stomach churn.

Mired in a pit of despair, he sank down onto the floor, his head cradled in his hands. He wondered what Mara was doing. No doubt she thought he had kidnapped the baby and run away. Was she looking for them? Kyle slammed his fist on the floor. No doubt she was glad to be rid of him. He had seen the way she looked at Blackwood, seen the way Blackwood looked at her.

Kyle sighed heavily. Even if Mara didn't give a damn about what happened to him, she loved their son. She would be looking for Derek; he had no doubt of that. To consider anything else would surely drive him over the edge. He just hoped that when she came for the baby, she wouldn't leave him behind.

Chapter Forty

"If you don't stop pacing like that, darlin', you're gonna wear a hole in my brand-new carpet."

"I can't help it," Mara said irritably. "It's been over a month. Shouldn't that hunter have heard something by now?"

"You should know better than most that if a vampire doesn't want to be found, it's damned hard to find him. And if Ramsden's discovered a way to mask his presence"— Logan shrugged—"it'll take even longer."

Logan had called Lou McDonald every few days, but the news was always the same. Nothing to report. Roshan and the Cordova men weren't having any better luck. Between the four of them, they had covered every vampire hangout in the country, questioned every vampire they knew, and that was an impressive number. But no one in the Undead community had seen or heard from Thomas Ramsden in weeks. It was as if the doctor, Kyle, and the baby had vanished from the face of the earth.

Shoulders slumped, Mara sank down on the sofa beside Logan. "If I just knew my baby was all right . . ."

"I know." He slipped his arm around her shoulders

and gave her a squeeze. "We've been cooped up in this house too long. What do you say we go out for an hour or two? I'll take you to dinner . . ."

"I'm not hungry."

"You've got to eat something." She had lost a good twenty pounds in the last month. There were dark shadows under her eyes, hollows in her cheeks. And she was pale, so pale. "You're wasting away."

"Logan . . ."

"Dammit, Mara, you've got to keep your strength up. That kid of yours will need you to be at your best when we find him."

She nodded. He was right, of course. This was no time to let herself get mired in depression. She needed to keep her wits about her, to be strong for Derek.

"That's my girl. Where do you want to go?"

"I don't care."

Rising, Logan took Mara by the hand and pulled her to her feet. "Let's go."

He took her to Spago in Beverly Hills. It was a lovely place. A patio graced the center of the restaurant, shaded by graceful pepper trees. A bubbling fountain stood next to two imported one-hundred-year-old olive trees. The kitchen could be seen through a colorful glass wall. The dining room was delightful with its stained-glass windows, brightly colored tiles, and flamboyant carpets.

Mara glanced at the menu. Risotto with lobster and sweet shrimp, sweet English pea soup, wild black sea bass, Hong Kong-style steamed salmon, roasted rack and loin of Sonoma lamb, salmon and crème fraîche pizza, ricotta-stuffed agnolotti studded with black truffles. She frowned. She had no idea what agnolotti was, or what crème fraîche might be.

She wasn't hungry, but knowing she had to eat

something, and to please Logan, she ordered the grilled
lobster and summer vegetables with spicy herbed butter.
Logan ordered a bottle of red wine.

While waiting for her dinner to arrive, Mara glanced
around the restaurant. It was one of the few places she
had never been and as she looked around, she wondered
if any movie stars or celebrities were dining there that
night. It was well-known that, at one time or another,
most of Hollywood's rich and famous had dined at
Spago, stars like Tom Cruise, Russell Crowe, Jamie Lee
Curtis, and Tom Hanks. It was said to have been First
Lady Nancy Reagan's favorite eatery.

Mara sighed when her dinner arrived. It looked
wonderful. Too bad it was going to go to waste. She supposed the least she could do was take a bite or two. To
her surprise, she ate every bite, and then she ordered
everything chocolate on the dessert menu.

Logan grinned at her over the rim of his wineglass.
"Not hungry, eh?"

"So, maybe I was, a little."

"A little?" He snorted softly. "I thought you were
going to eat the plates, too."

"Well, the food was excellent. Don't you ever miss
eating?"

"I thought I did, until you made me try that roast
beef," he said, grimacing. "I'll stay with what I'm used
to." His gaze lingered on the pulse in her throat. "Do you
want anything else?"

"No, I don't think so." She was so full, she didn't think
she would ever need to eat again.

Logan paid the check and then, because it was a beautiful night, they decided to go for a walk.

They walked in silence for a time before Mara asked,
"Do you think he's all right?"

"Yeah, I do. I think you'd know if he wasn't."

"I miss him so much," Mara said with a wistful smile. "I never thought it was possible to love anyone so much."

Logan nodded. He doubted if there was any bond in all the world as strong as that between a mother and a child. He recalled his own mother. He hadn't thought of her in a long time. She had been a warm gentle woman who had brought nine healthy children into the world, and died all too soon. His father had mourned her until the day he took his last breath.

Logan blew out a sigh, wondering, for the first time in a long time, if his father's line still survived. He supposed it was highly unlikely after all these years. Still, it was possible. Maybe he'd look into it one of these days.

"Logan, what if it wasn't Ramsden who took the baby? What if we never find out what happened to Derek? Or to Kyle?" Mara looked up at him through haunted eyes. "I don't think I can go on living without knowing what happened to my son. Even if . . . if he's . . . I just have to know."

Her words, the tears shining in her eyes, filled Logan with a sadness he had not known in centuries. He yearned to sweep her into his arms and comfort her, to take her to his bed and make her forget her heartache, if only for an hour or so. But he couldn't suggest it now, not after refusing her when she'd said she loved him. Damn his honor! What had he been thinking?

"Logan, please take me home."

With a nod, he wrapped his arms tightly around her and willed them to his house. He would come back later, after she was asleep, and pick up his car.

Materializing inside the living room, Logan continued to hold her, his brow resting lightly on the top of her head. Her warmth engulfed him. The flowery scent of her skin tickled his nostrils with every breath. The way her body molded to his reminded him of all the lusty nights they had shared. The rich coppery scent of her blood and the steady beat of her heart only served to arouse him more. Hard with wanting her, he cursed himself again for having refused her.

She stirred in his arms and he drew back a little so he could see her face.

"What can I do?" he asked, thinking he would do anything she requested to erase the sorrow from her eyes.

"I want you to turn me."

"What?"

"I've been giving it a lot of thought the last few days. I think it's the only way I'll ever find him."

"Forget it! You know what the doctor said. It could kill you."

"He doesn't know that for a fact. No one does. Anyway, it's a risk I'm willing to take."

"Well, I'm not." Muttering an oath, Logan paced away from her to stare out into the night.

"Please, Logan."

He whirled around to face her, his eyes blazing. "Dammit, I said no!"

She took a step toward him. "Listen to me. There's a blood link between a mother and her child. I can't sense it now, but if I was a vampire, I'd be able to follow it. I know I would."

"DeLongpre and the Cordova family haven't been able to penetrate whatever spell is shielding Ramsden. What makes you think you can do any better?"

"I don't know," she said in a voice filled with anguish. "Maybe I won't be able to. Maybe I'll die in the attempt. But I have to try."

Logan shook his head. "No. There's got to be another

way." As much as he longed for her to be Nosferatu once again, the risk involved was too great.

"The longer it takes us to find him, the less of a chance we have. Surely you can see that."

"It's too dangerous."

She looked up at him, her green eyes narrowed, her hands fisted at her sides. "If you won't bring me across, then I'll find someone who will!"

"Yeah, who?"

"I'll ask Roshan or one of the Cordova men."

"And if they refuse?"

"Then I'll find someone else!" Closing the distance between them, she placed her hand on his arm. "I'd rather it was you."

She wasn't bluffing and he knew it, just as he knew that he would never let anyone else turn her. He couldn't abide the thought of another vampire being her master.

With a sigh of resignation, he said, "Let me call McDonald first and see if she's heard anything."

"And if she hasn't, you'll bring me across. Now, tonight. You promise?"

With a nod, he reached for his cell phone.

Mara listened intently as Logan talked to Lou. There had been a time when she would have been able to hear both sides of the conversation. Hopefully, that time would come again.

"Right," Logan said, and ended the call.

"What?" Mara asked. "What did she say?"

"Same as always. She says she's checked with every hunter and undercover agent she knows, and none of them have any idea where Ramsden might be. They've checked all his known hangouts, his last known residence." Logan shrugged. "His house is closed up tight, his wife's not home."

"Then it's up to us," Mara said quietly. "It's up to me."

"Give it one more day," Logan said.

"No, I've already waited too long."

"You've been planning to do this all day, haven't you?" he asked, and then he grunted softly. "I guess that explains all that chocolate for dessert."

She didn't deny it, only continued to look up at him, a silent plea in her eyes.

He tried to think of some way to dissuade her, to make her wait, but he drew a blank. Mortal or vampire, once she took hold of an idea, there was no changing her mind. He had never been able to deny her anything, but this . . . He raked a hand through his hair. "Don't let me take too much."

She nodded as he took her hand and led her over to the sofa. Sitting, he drew her down beside him.

"Are you sure you want to do this? I'd say there was no going back once it's done, but with you . . ." He grinned wryly. "With you, it might not be true."

"Just do it." A sudden attack of nerves made her voice sharp. What if Ramsden was right? What if attempting to become a vampire again proved fatal? If she died, who would find Derek? Who would look after him?

"You're having second thoughts, aren't you?"

"Of course not." She told herself it was what she wanted, that it was the only way to find Derek and Kyle. She reminded herself that she hated being human, despised being weak and vulnerable. And yet she knew, deep in her heart, that once it was done, her son would be lost to her in so many ways. She could do what Roshan and Brenna had done. They had lied to Cara, hired a nanny to look after her during the day, let Cara grow up believing that her parents' aversion to the sun was due to some rare illness. Did she want to do the same? Did she

want to let Derek grow up believing that his mother was
something she wasn't? Even as the thought crossed her
mind, she knew she couldn't live a lie like that. Her son,
the only child she would ever have, deserved a normal
life, and Kyle could give it to him.

"You don't have to do this," Logan said quietly. "Not
right now."

"Logan, please, just get it over with."

His jaw tightened as he brushed her hair away from
her slender neck. There was no fear in her eyes, yet her
heart beat erratically as she gazed up at him. He had
never worked the Dark Trick on anyone. He had been
tempted on more than one occasion. He had been un-
derstandably curious to see what it would be like to sire
a fledgling of his own, but having been turned against his
will, he had never been able to bring himself to do it to
anyone else. Not that he regretted being a vampire. He
enjoyed the benefits, the supernatural powers, his long
existence. But it was a life against nature, not for the faint
of heart. It took a good deal of courage and stamina to
exist for a thousand years or more. Many vampires grew
weary of their existence. After a century or two, they lost
the will to go on and walked out into the sunlight. Others
went mad and had to be destroyed. Some, like Logan,
reinvented themselves every fifty years or so.

"Wait," Mara said. "Promise me something?"

"Whatever you want."

"If I don't survive, promise me you'll keep looking for
Derek and Kyle, and that you'll protect them as long as
they live."

Logan stared at her. "Do you know what you're asking?"

"I know. Promise me?"

"All right, dammit, I promise."

She smiled at him. "Let's do it, then."

He took a deep breath in an effort to steady his nerves. Though he had never turned anyone, he knew how it was done. His only fear was that he would get caught up in the moment, lose himself in her sweetness, and take too much. If Mara died in his arms, his own life would no longer be worth living.

Tension coiled deep within Mara's belly as Logan drew her into his embrace. It had been centuries since Dendar had brought her across. All she remembered from that encounter was her mind-numbing fear of the unknown as she stared into his hell-red eyes, the unrelenting pain that had twisted through her being as her mortal life was slowly drained away.

She wasn't afraid with Logan. If his vampire nature took over and he drank too much, so be it. At least she would die in the arms of a man who loved her.

Logan caressed her cheek, kissed her lightly, and then, murmuring, "Forgive me," he sank his fangs into the soft, warm skin beneath her ear.

Her blood, bitter before she had turned completely human, was now hot and sweet as it flowed over his tongue. Would she hate him for what he had done once her son had been found? Would she regret the loss of her humanity? Most troubling of all was the fear that, when she was Nosferatu again and no longer needed him, she would go back to Kyle.

Her heart was beating in rhythm with his now, her memories were his, and then, as he continued to drink, her heartbeat grew slower, heavier, weaker.

When her heartbeat was no more than a whisper, when she lay across his lap like a pale rag doll, he bit into his wrist and held the bleeding wound to her lips. The rest was up to her.

"Drink, Mara," he murmured, his tears falling like crimson rain onto her ashen cheeks. "Drink and live."

For a moment, he feared he had taken too much, but then, after a few drops of his blood had dripped onto her tongue, her mouth fastened onto the wound. Logan closed his eyes in ecstasy as his blood revived her. Her heartbeat grew stronger, steadier.

Looking down at her, he saw that the dark shadows had faded from beneath her eyes, color bloomed in her cheeks.

Murmuring, "Enough," he tried to draw his arm away, but she held on tightly, greedily. "Enough, Mara!" he said, and wrenched his arm from her grasp. In her present condition, she would drain him dry if given the chance.

After sealing the wounds in her neck, he carried her upstairs to his bedroom, held her in his arms through the last dark hours before dawn as her body sloughed off its humanity.

As she writhed in pain, it reminded him all too clearly of his own mortal death, something he hadn't thought of in centuries. Mara had stayed at his side, talking him through the worst of it, assuring him that it was normal, that it would pass, that there was nothing to fear.

And so he held her now, murmuring to her in his native tongue, telling her that he loved her. Whether she heard him or not, he didn't know. Had he taken too much? Perhaps he hadn't given her enough of his blood to sustain life.

Just before dawn, she surrendered to the Dark Sleep.

As gently as he could, he removed her clothing and put her to bed. After stripping off his own attire, he slipped under the covers and gathered her into his arms. All he could do now was wait.

Would she rise as a newly made vampire with the setting of the sun, or would death steal her away from him forever?

Chapter Forty-one

Ramsden examined his wife a second time, a vile oath escaping his lips as he turned away from the bed and stalked out of the room. She wasn't pregnant. Why hadn't it worked? Bowden had impregnated Mara. Why had his sperm failed to impregnate Janis? It had to be because Mara had been reverting to humanity when she became pregnant. It was the only answer that made sense. Why hadn't he realized it sooner?

Maybe it was time to give up. Bowden was growing weaker, but that was to be expected, what with the amount of blood Ramsden had been taking from him. In addition to what he took for experimental purposes, Edna and Pearl had fed from the man a few times, as had Janis. Bowden no longer objected; no longer demanded to know where his son was, no longer paced for hours on end. He just sat in a corner of his cage, his face gaunt, his expression blank, a beaten man on the brink of death.

Aside from that, Edna and Pearl hadn't had any success in learning why Bowden carried the werewolf gene but didn't transform during the full moon. Few werewolves were born; most were infected by the bite of another. Either way, they were compelled to change when the moon was full, but the lunar cycle had no effect on Bowden.

Then there was the baby. The child should have been growing; instead, it grew weaker and more listless with every passing day. And now Janis was harassing Tom again, accusing him of bringing her an inferior baby, nagging him to find her another child, one that was older, stronger. Ramsden wasn't sure, but he thought the cause of the baby's declining health was because Janis was feeding off the baby. She had denied it, of course.

Going into the lab, he closed and locked the door. In spite of all the tests, he hadn't been able to determine if the child carried the werewolf gene, nor had he been able to detect any indication that it was likely to become a vampire. As far as he could tell, the baby was just a normal male. Given the brat's heritage, that didn't make any sense at all.

Filled with frustration, he hurled a tray of empty test tubes against the wall. "All for nothing," he muttered. "All that time wasted, and for what?"

He was fed up with Janis, sick and tired of Edna and Pearl and their infernal chatter, weary of being cooped up with a crying baby and a half-dead mortal. He hadn't survived this long by being stupid. It was time to admit defeat and call it quits.

Tomorrow night, he would get rid of his shrew of a wife, then drain the man and the child. As for Pearl and Edna . . . He grunted softly. He doubted they would cause him any trouble in the future, but it was better to make sure now, while he had the chance. When all the loose ends were tied up, he would leave here and reinvent himself in a new city. Rome, perhaps, or Cairo, or maybe Rio. He would sever all his ties in the States, sell his property, buy a new wardrobe, pick a new name, obtain the necessary documents, and leave the country for a century or two.

The thought cheered him. He had been tied to one woman and one identity for too long. Why had he wasted his time and energy trying to find a way to impregnate female vampires? What did he care if there were female vampires who felt unfulfilled because they couldn't bear children? Or if there were vampires who wished to regain their humanity? True, had he accomplished those goals, he could have amassed a great deal of wealth, but he didn't need the money. He was already rich. Nor had he conducted his experiments for any altruistic reasons, but simply out of sheer boredom with Janis and his current way of life. Tomorrow night he would put it all behind him.

Whistling softly, he left the lab and went out in search of prey, something warm and fresh and overflowing with the elixir of youth.

A new life awaited him. It was time to celebrate.

Chapter Forty-two

Mara woke feeling sluggish. For a time, she lay there, wondering what was wrong. Was she sick? Had she come down with a bad case of the flu? She felt strange, almost as if she was in someone else's body.

Sitting up, she glanced around. She was in Logan's room, in his bed. Naked. She frowned. Had they made love? Surely she would have remembered if they had.

She blinked, suddenly realizing that she saw everything clearly even though the room was pitch black. And then she remembered. Logan had brought her across last night.

Flinging the covers aside, she threw back her head and let her senses expand. Laughter bubbled up inside her. She was Nosferatu!

The colors in the room were crystal clear and bright. She could hear the tick-tick of the mantel clock downstairs, the low hum of Logan's computer, the drip of a faucet in the bathroom. She took a deep breath and her nostrils filled with a myriad of scents—the soap used to wash the sheets, the faint fragrance of Logan's cologne, the promise of rain in the air, and overall, the rich, musky scent of Logan himself.

Leaping from the bed, she twirled around, her arms outstretched, her body humming with preternatural power. Oh, how she had missed it! She felt alive again, strong again. Lighter than air, now that she had shed the weight of mortality. But, most of all, she felt like Mara again. And how hungry she was. Not for bacon and eggs, but for the warm, rich blood of life itself.

She dressed quickly, then hurried downstairs.

She found Logan in the living room, staring out the window at the gathering storm.

He turned as soon as she entered the room, his gaze moving over her, his expression one of relief.

She smiled at him, a brilliant smile filled with happiness, and a hint of fang. "You did it!" she said exuberantly, and throwing herself into his arms, she kissed him soundly. "Thank you!"

"You don't hate me then?"

"Hate you? Why would I hate you?"

He shrugged. "In spite of what you said to the contrary, you seemed to like being human, eating, drinking . . ." His gaze searched hers. "No regrets?"

"No." She lifted her arms over her head. "I feel like me again! And I need to hunt!"

Anticipation rose up within her at the thought. She remembered how it had been when she had been turned the first time. The hunger had been insatiable, uncontrollable. With no one to teach her, no one to guide her, she'd had no way of knowing that she could feed without killing. She had hunted among rich and poor alike, untroubled by guilt. She was a vampire. Humans were her natural prey. It was only later that she had discovered she could satisfy her hunger by feeding from many instead of illing one; only later that she had learned she didn't ave to hunt them down at all. No, it was far more leasant to seduce them, to give them pleasure and find deeper pleasure in return. But tonight, ah, tonight she vasn't interested in seducing her prey; she wanted to xperience the excitement of the hunt, feel her prey's fear s she closed in, hear the frantic beating of a human eart, and feed. Feed until she was sated.

She glanced at Logan then, a smile of anticipation on er lips as she left the house, certain he would follow.

Logan trailed after her, hanging back as she prowled 1e dark alleys of the city, and it was as if she had never een human, never been anything but the Queen of the /ampires. She stalked her first victim, trapped him in the veb of her stare, and took what she wanted. Logan feared he would drain the man dry, but she took only a little, nd moved on.

She called the second man to her, quick and confident, ook what she needed, and moved on.

Logan couldn't stop watching her—the glow in her yes, the way she moved, like liquid silver. The sound f her laughter warmed his heart and yet he waited on enterhooks, waited for her to say she was leaving him. she made no mention of the baby or Kyle. Had she orgotten them completely, or only for the moment?

She fed and fed again, until she was drunk on the aste of the crimson nectar. With her hunger satisfied, he left the city and returned to her home in the hills of Iollywood.

And Logan followed her, as he had always fol-owed her.

Mara stood in the front yard, her gaze searching the larkness, jubilation filling her as she reveled in her re-tored powers. It was dark, but nothing was hidden from her. She saw and heard everything clearly, the delicate veins in the leaf of a tree, the rustle of feathers as a bird stirred in a nest overhead. A deep breath filled her nostrils with the scent of earth and foliage and the stink of an animal long dead.

A thought, and she transformed herself into swirling mist. She floated over Logan for a moment before resuming her own form, laughter again bubbling from her throat as her feet touched the ground.

Logan's laughter joined hers. Bound by blood, he knew what she was feeling, thinking. Like a proud parent, he watched her test her powers. She changed into a beautiful black wolf with startling green eyes. Resuming her own form once again, she held her arms out at her sides, palms up, and rose into the air. She hovered there a moment, then drifted slowly to the ground, her eyes glowing with delight.

"Oh, how I've missed this!" She twirled around, arms outstretched, spinning faster and faster, until she would have been a blur to any eyes but his.

She was like a woman reborn, he thought. Venus rising from the sea. Eternally young, eternally beautiful.

She lifted her face toward the heavens, her eyes closed as she communed with the darkness, as she became one with the night. He could feel her summoning her power, drawing it around her like an invisible cloak. It lifted the hair along his nape.

Thick black clouds gathered overhead. Bolts of jagged yellow lightning slashed through the darkened skies. Thunder rolled across the heavens and shook the earth.

Logan watched in awe. She was a newly made vampire. Most were weak, uncertain. But not Mara. He knew he was responsible for her strength, at least in part, because he had never bequeathed the Dark Gift to another.

Never weakened his power by sharing it. He was an old vampire, and his blood was ancient and powerful. Had anyone else turned her, she wouldn't be as strong as she was, but his blood was her blood, older than any other.

She continued to draw on her power, reveling in it. It hummed through the air, vibrant and alive, a physical force manifested in the elements. The wind whipped around them, seeming to gather its strength from her presence.

She looked like an ancient goddess standing there, her long black hair blowing in the wind, her skin translucent, her arms lifted over her head.

He yearned to go to her, to pull her into his arms and make love to her, there in the grass, with the storm raging all around them. But his honor forbade it. Undead or mortal, she still had a husband, even though she seemed to have forgotten both Kyle and the child, at least for the moment.

He didn't know how long they stood there. An hour, a year. Time lost its meaning as he stared at her, his mind replaying every night, every moment, they had shared. He had known, from the instant she had turned him, that he would never love anyone else. He had made love to women, countless women, beautiful women, but he had loved none of them. Only Mara. Always Mara.

Slowly, she lowered her arms to her sides. When she opened her eyes, the thunder grew quiet, the lightning ceased, the wind stilled.

"I know where they are." Her voice was like smooth velvet over steel, her eyes as deep and cold as the grave. "We have to hurry."

Chapter Forty-three

"Why, Tom?" Eyes wide and scared, Janis Ramsden backed away from her husband. "Why are you doing this?"

She bolted for the door as he came after her, murder in his eyes, but he was too quick for her. She screamed as his hand closed around her arm, his grip like iron.

Like any wild animal, she fought viciously for her life. Crying with despair, she used every ounce of strength and power she possessed, but she was no match for her husband. He wrestled her down to the floor, his eyes blazing with an unholy light as he straddled her hips, one of his hands grasping both of hers.

She rolled her head back and forth, sobbing, "Tom, please don't do this!" as he pulled a wooden stake from under his coat. "No! No!" She screamed as he drove the stake deep into her heart, murmured, "Why, Tom?" as the light slowly went out of her eyes.

Ramsden left her body where it lay. He felt no regret for what he had done, no remorse at her death. He had made her; now that he was tired of her, it was his right to destroy her.

Taking a deep breath, Ramsden glanced at the child

asleep in the crib. Some near-forgotten hint of compassion refused to let him leave the child in the same room with a dead woman. Dragging a blanket from the bed, Ramsden wrapped it around his wife's body, then carried it outside and dumped it by the back door where it would disintegrate in the morning.

The two old women were next on his list. One thing he had always been careful to do was tie up all the loose ends from his old life when he was about to embark on a new one.

A quick search of their rooms and he knew Edna and Pearl had packed up and gone. How had they known? He smiled faintly. They might be old women and relatively new vampires, but they were smarter than they looked. They must have sensed that something was in the air. Deciding to err on the side of caution, they had fled without a word. Smart, he thought. Last night, he hadn't quite made up his mind about whether or not to destroy them. Had he found them now, when his bloodlust was running hot, they wouldn't have stood a chance. Smart, he thought again. Having gained his admiration, he decided to let them live, at least for the time being.

As soon as he disposed of the man and the child, he would be on his way. Although he had not yet decided on a destination, he was leaning toward Italy. It had been too long since he had walked among the ruins of the Colosseum, or viewed the beauty of the Pantheon, a remarkable building the Romans had built to honor the gods. Yes, he mused, far too long since he had ridden a gondola through the canals, admired the frescoes in the Sistine Chapel, made love to a hot-blooded Italian woman. Yes, Italy, he decided, suddenly anxious to see Rome.

But first he had to get rid of the man and the child.

Walking down the corridor toward the lab, he smiled faintly. Nothing like a good meal before bedtime.

Chapter Forty-four

Edna's hands were shaking visibly as she lifted the crystal wineglass to her lips and took a long drink. Pearl sat beside her on the sofa, her whole body trembling. Such a close call. Another few minutes, and they might have met the same fate as Janis Ramsden.

Thank goodness for preternatural hearing, Edna thought. She hadn't meant to eavesdrop on Ramsden and his wife. She had gone looking for the doctor to ask him a question, only to pause outside the door when she heard Janis sobbing and begging for her life.

Grateful for preternatural speed and power, Edna had hurried back to warn Pearl that their lives might be in danger. Deciding it was better to be safe than sorry, they had grabbed what was at hand and quickly transported themselves back to their home in Texas.

"I feel bad about leaving the baby," Edna remarked, her hands tightly clasped around her wineglass in an effort to still their trembling.

"I know, dear, but what else could we have done?"

"Nothing, I guess," Edna said, "since the baby was in Ramsden's room."

"I'm going to miss the little guy," Pearl remarked. "He was such a dear. It would have been interesting to watch him grow up."

Edna pursed her lips, then blew out a sigh. "I have something to tell you."

"Oh? Something juicy?"

"I was thinking the same thing as you, that it would be interesting to watch the baby grow, to see how he'd turn out . . ."

Pearl leaned forward. "Go on."

"So, I drank from him. Just a little," she said quickly, "but enough so that I'll be able to find him if we ever want to check up on him."

"You drank from the baby?" Pearl exclaimed.

"It was wrong of me, I know."

Pearl clapped her hands together. "I think it was brilliant! I thought of it, too, but I never had the opportunity." She took a deep breath. "Do you think Ramsden will come after us?"

"I don't know. Maybe we shouldn't have left. Doing so only proves we know what he did."

"You're right. I didn't stop to think."

"That's always been your problem, dear."

Edna stuck her tongue out at her friend. "I guess you think we should have stayed and given him a chance to stake us."

"Of course not."

Edna sipped her drink, and then sighed heavily. "I'm just sorry we never made it to California."

"There's always tomorrow, dear," Pearl said cheerfully. "After all, we haven't avenged Travis's death yet."

"Now, why didn't I think of that?" Edna said, her mood lifting.

Pearl raised her glass. "Here's to tomorrow. And to all the tomorrows to follow."

Chapter Forty-five

Kyle grabbed the bars and pulled himself to his feet when the vampire entered the room. He had known this night was coming. He had felt it, deep in his bones. So be it. If he was to die, it would not be cowering on the floor. Gathering his courage, Kyle met the monster's gaze.

Ramsden cocked his head to the side as he regarded the pitiful mortal. He could smell the man's fear. It rolled off him in waves, yet he stood tall and straight, his eyes filled with hatred and defiance. You had to admire that kind of grit, but then, mortal men were often at their best in the face of unbeatable odds.

For a moment, Ramsden regretted having to kill the man, and then he shrugged. The destruction of one more human meant nothing to him. He had seen death in all its ugliness far too often to feel either queasiness or remorse at the thought of taking a human life.

Still, the man had courage.

Feeling generous, Ramsden said, "I'll make this as quick and painless as I can."

"I won't."

At the sound of her voice, Ramsden whirled around, his eyes going wide with disbelief. "Mara!"

Kyle's voice echoed her name as he sank to his knees. Thank God, the cavalry had arrived just in the nick of time.

Mara swept into the room, her bearing that of a queen paying a call on a peasant. "I've come for my son, Doctor," she said imperiously. "For your sake, I hope he's well."

Ramsden shrugged. "He was fine, last I saw him." He moved away from the cage, putting his back to the far wall. "If you'll excuse me, I was just leaving."

Mara glanced at Kyle. She breathed in his scent, and knew he was dying. "I'm sorry, Doctor, but you're not going anywhere."

Ramsden's eyes narrowed. "How did you find me?"

"I followed my son's heartbeat. All the witchcraft in the world will not save you now."

Ramsden looked past her to where Logan stood in the doorway. "Two against one? Not very sporting of you."

"Logan won't interfere."

"And if I win?"

Mara smiled, baring her fangs. "Then I won't be here to stop him."

"Can't we talk this over?" Ramsden asked, his hands outstretched in a gesture of goodwill. "The brat's fine."

It was the wrong thing to say.

Her eyes narrowing with rage, Mara flew at him, her fangs fully extended, her hands like claws.

Logan watched the battle impassively. Ramsden fought valiantly, but Mara was a mother defending her young. Almost, Logan could pity the doctor. Ramsden was as helpless as a fledgling to defend himself against Mara's wrath. His claws and teeth savaged her flesh, but, thanks to Logan's ancient blood, her wounds healed almost instantly.

Like a cat with a mouse, she toyed with Ramsden until she tired of the game, and then she slammed him against the wall with such force, it shattered the plaster. Eyes blazing with hell's own fury, she pulled a stake from her skirt pocket, the very same stake she had pulled from Janis's body outside.

A harsh cry of denial rose in the doctor's throat as she plunged the stake deep into his heart and gave it a sharp twist.

Ramsden slid helplessly to the floor. He clutched weakly at the stake protruding from his chest, but only for a moment. With a sigh, his eyes glazed over. His hand fell away from the stake. It was over.

Inside the cage, Kyle smiled faintly, then toppled onto his side and lay still. Mara was there. She would rescue their son. He could stop fighting. Help had arrived at last, he thought dully, only it had arrived too late for him.

Mara was at Kyle's side in an instant. Ripping the door off the cage, she ducked inside and dropped to her knees. Murmuring Kyle's name, she cradled his head in her lap. Guilt rose up within her. It was her fault he was here, her fault he was dying. Ramsden had fed off him. And not just Ramsden, she thought, scenting the air, but Edna and Pearl as well. They would pay for that, she vowed. Sooner or later, she would find the old biddies and she would make them pay dearly for what they had done.

"Kyle, hold on." She stroked his brow. "You can't die. Our son needs you, now more than ever."

At the sound of her voice, his eyelids fluttered open. "I always loved you," he said, his voice little more than a whisper. "Even when I hated you."

"Save your strength. Let me bring you across." There

was no time to lose. His life force was ebbing away with each breath he took, each beat of his heart.

Kyle glanced at Logan, who stood a few feet away. "He turned you back."

"Yes, that's how I found you. It isn't so bad, being what we are."

"No . . . no. One kiss . . ." he murmured weakly. "One kiss . . . of farewell . . . to send me on my way."

She thought briefly of bringing him across against his will, but she knew in her heart he would hate her for it; knew that Kyle, like Jeffrey Dunston before him, would destroy himself the first chance he got.

With tears in her eyes, Mara gathered him into her arms. Lightly pressing her lips to his, she swallowed his last breath. His body went limp as his life ebbed away. Her fault, she thought, all her fault. He would never have been involved in any of this if not for her.

She sat there a moment, lightly stroking his hair, until, from somewhere down the hall, she heard a baby's cry.

"Derek!" Sliding out from under Kyle's lifeless body, Mara gained her feet and flew out of the room and down the hallway. "Derek!" Bending over the crib, she gathered her son into her arms and held him close. "Oh, my sweet baby boy," she wailed. "What have they done to you?"

"Is he all right?"

Turning, Mara looked at Logan over the baby's head. "They fed off of him!" she exclaimed, her eyes flashing with anger as she kissed her son's cheek. Her baby, once plump and pink, was now pale and thin, so thin. "Don't worry, my love," she cooed. "I've come to take you home."

"Mara."

"What?"

"You go on ahead. I'll take care of the bodies."

Mara nodded. In her joy at seeing her son, she had forgotten about Ramsden and his wife. It would never do for their bodies to be found. It would lead to too many questions about why they had been killed, and who had killed them. "Bring Kyle home with you."

Logan stared at her a moment, then nodded.

Mara hugged her son tighter. Tomorrow night, she would bury Kyle in the tiny graveyard up in the mountains. But for now, she needed to take her baby home, to wash him and feed him and hold him close, to breathe in his sweet baby scent, to kiss each tiny finger and toe, to assure herself that no permanent damage had been done to her child, the only child she would ever have.

Logan prowled the living room of the house Mara had shared with Kyle. He had expected her to go back to her house in the Hollywood Hills, but the baby's things were here. Watching her with her son, seeing the love in her eyes, her tenderness as she gave the baby a bottle, her gentleness as she rocked the boy to sleep, stirred a never-before-felt emotion deep within him. He wasn't sure what it was. Jealousy, perhaps, that he would never sire a child, never experience the unbreakable bond that existed between a parent and a child.

He and Mara had spoken little since leaving Ramsden's lab. Seeing her with the baby, Logan wondered again if Mara was regretting her decision to accept the Dark Trick, and yet she had been convinced it was the only way to find her son. No doubt she had been right. After seeing what Ramsden had done to his wife, Logan had no doubt that the doctor had planned to dispose of the kid and Kyle, as well. And what of the other two vampires who had been there? Logan had detected their scents though he hadn't recognized them. But Mara had.

"Edna and Pearl," she'd said. "They were vampire hunters until Rafe turned them some years ago. Troublesome creatures."

Bored and impatient, Logan went down the hall to the nursery and peered through the half-open door. Mara sat in a rocking chair near the window, the baby cradled in her arms.

Sensing his presence, she looked up. "Is something wrong?"

"No, I just wondered what was keeping you."

"I can't bear to put him down."

Logan nodded. No doubt it would be weeks, maybe months, before she felt comfortable letting the baby out of her sight.

She glanced around the nursery. "We'll have to leave here as soon as I get everything packed up."

He nodded. Now that Edna and Pearl knew about the house in Porterville, moving was the smart thing to do. Not that Mara couldn't handle the two old broads, but she had the baby to think about, and it was better to be safe than sorry.

Returning to the living room, Logan gazed at the painting of Mara and Derek hanging over the fireplace. Bowden's signature was in the lower right-hand corner. Logan had no doubt that, in spite of everything, Kyle Bowden had loved Mara dearly. It was evident in every brush stroke.

Muttering an oath, Logan began to pace again. He didn't belong here, in this house. Maybe he didn't belong in Mara's life, either. She had planned to give the baby to Kyle, but that was no longer an option. There was always the chance that she would let Savanah raise the boy; they had discussed it before, but now . . . He shook his head. After everything that had happened, he doubted that Mara would let anyone else raise her son.

Selfish creature that he was, he couldn't help wondering where that left him. He didn't like admitting, even to himself, that he was jealous of every minute Mara spent with the boy. But he was. And how sick was that, to be envious of an infant?

He was muttering to himself, calling himself a worthless, useless, fool, when he realized he was no longer alone. Feeling like an idiot, he turned to face her.

Looking amused, she met his gaze.

Had he been capable of it, he would have blushed.

"Why are you a worthless, useless fool?" she asked, closing the distance between them.

"You make me that way."

"Do I?" She ran her fingertips down his cheek.

"I'm jealous of every minute you spent with Bowden, and every second you spend with your son. I love you, and I don't want to share you with anyone. If that doesn't make me a fool, I don't know what else to call it."

"I can't help loving him. He's mine."

"Am I?"

With a sigh, Mara said, "I can't talk about this right now. It's too soon. Too much has happened." She glanced at the picture over the fireplace, remembering the night Kyle had painted it. And now he was dead, and it was her fault. If she had never cared for him, never married him, he would still be alive. In all her years as a vampire, she had rarely experienced remorse or guilt, but now both emotions weighed heavily on her conscience.

Moving past Logan, she sat on the sofa. Tomorrow night, she would bury Kyle. And after that, what? She considered asking Rane and Savanah to take care of

Derek. Not long ago, she had been convinced that she didn't want her son to grow up the way Cara had, not knowing the truth about her parents until she was grown, but now . . . now she wasn't sure she could let someone else raise her son. Did she really want her baby to call another woman Mama? Did she want to miss out on watching her son take his first step, miss hearing him speak his first word? Was she being selfish to want to keep Derek? Would it be better to let Savanah raise him, or should she perhaps give him to a mortal couple who could raise him in a normal home? But what if Derek wasn't a normal child? What if, like Rafe and Rane, he carried vampire blood that manifested itself when he reached puberty? Human parents would be ill-equipped to handle such a thing.

Mara blew out a sigh. She didn't know what to do, didn't know which decision would be best.

She glanced at Logan as he sat down beside her.

"It's a hard decision, isn't it?" he asked.

"Yes. I want to do what's best for Derek, but I don't know what that is. Would it be selfish of me to keep him?"

"He's your son," Logan said quietly. "He belongs with you."

He belongs with you. Four words that sank deep into Mara's heart, and in that instant, she knew she could never let her baby go.

The following night, Mara laid Kyle to rest in the small graveyard located in the woods behind her house in the mountains. It was an old cemetery, surrounded by a white wrought-iron fence with an arched gate. A wooden sign, carved with the words, REST YE IN PEACE, hung from the top of the gate. No one had been buried there in over fifty years.

A full moon shone down on the mourners, splashing the tops of the trees with silver. Standing there, with her son cradled in her arms, Mara couldn't help thinking that the scene at the graveside looked like something out of an old horror movie, but instead of humans digging up a vampire to destroy it, vampires were burying a human who had died too soon.

Brenna and Roshan were there to comfort her, along with Vince and Cara, their sons and their daughters-in law. Logan stood at Mara's side. She held a quietly crying Derek in her arms. Did the baby somehow know that his father was dead? Was that why he cried?

Father Lanzoni presided. He glanced at the mourners, his gaze briefly touching each one. "I wish that we were meeting under happier circumstances this evening," he said with quiet reverence. "Though we do not like to think of it, we know that death eventually comes to us all. Mortal or vampire, sooner or later death comes. At this time, we mourn the loss of our friend, Kyle, who was taken from us too soon. Even so, he will not be forgotten. He will live on in our memories, and in the life of his son, Derek."

Pausing, the priest lowered his head a moment, as if in prayer, before going on.

"At this time, we lay the body and soul of Kyle Bowden to rest, confident that he will rise in the resurrection of the just. Amen."

Mara hugged her son as the men lowered the casket into the ground. Overcome with guilt, she turned away as they began to shovel dirt into the hole. She should have been a better wife. She should never have married Kyle at all.

Later, they gathered at Mara's house. After Mara and Savanah put their children to bed, Logan opened a bottle of wine and offered a toast. "To Mara, welcome back to the fold."

Rane lifted his glass in agreement.

"And to Derek's safe return," Rafe added.

Mara smiled at each of them in turn. They were good friends, something she had never truly appreciated before.

Later, Cara took Mara aside. "Is everything all right?"

"What do you mean?"

"You look troubled."

"Can I ask you something?"

"Of course."

"Did it upset you, when you learned your parents were vampires?"

"Yes, at first. It came as quite a shock, learning that they weren't human. Of course, it explained a lot, like why they didn't age, and why they never attended any of the school functions that were held during the day, and why I never saw them eat. But the real shock was learning that I had been adopted. It's a hard thing, learning that your own mother didn't want you."

"When did they tell you that you were adopted?"

"I think I was seven or eight at the time."

"Does it still bother you?"

"Not now, but it troubled me for a long while. I don't know anything about my natural mother except that she gave birth to me in an alley, and then gave me away." Cara laid her hand on Mara's arm. "You're thinking about Derek, aren't you? Savanah told me you had talked to her about raising him."

"It seemed like a good idea at the time, but now . . ."

Mara shook her head. "He belongs with me," she said, repeating Logan's words.

"I think you're right. Have you tried going out in daylight since Logan turned you?"

"No," Mara admitted, frowning. "I just assumed that, being newly made, I wouldn't be able to."

"You're unique among our kind," Cara said. "You were *Nosferatu* far longer than any other vampire we know of, and you are far stronger than any of us."

"Yes, but that was before. Ramsden thought accepting the Dark Gift again would kill me."

"Well, he was wrong about that, wasn't he?"

Mara nodded. She felt as strong and capable as she had before she'd lost her powers. She was able to be awake during the day to look after the baby, so why did she still hesitate to go outside when the sun was up? Because of Ramsden, she thought. Instead of trusting her own instincts, she was letting a dead man influence her.

"I think you'll be just fine," Cara said. "You're a survivor. You've proved that."

Cara was right, Mara thought. She was being foolish. She was no longer human. She was her old self again, as strong and powerful as she had ever been. There was nothing to fear. She would walk in the sun's light. She would be a good mother to Derek. She would spend the rest of her existence with the man she loved. She smiled inwardly as a wave of self-confidence routed the last of her doubts and fears.

Later, after everyone had left for home, she went down to her lair to check on Derek. She would have to redecorate, she thought as she leaned over the side of the crib. Get rid of her Egyptian art collection and replace it with something more youthful and cheerful. Or maybe not. She could decorate one of the rooms upstairs for the baby. Paint the walls blue, buy a pretty oak crib and a matching changing table and rocking chair. The baby could use the upstairs room during the day, then sleep in his bed in her lair at night until he was a little older.

Pleased with the idea, Mara leaned over the edge of the crib and kissed her son's cheek. "I'll never leave you," she murmured. "I'll never let anyone or anything hurt you again, I promise."

Warmth filled her heart as her son smiled in his sleep, almost as if he understood what his mother had said.

"Sweet little boy," Mara whispered. "Do you know how much I love you?"

"I'm sure he does."

Mara glanced over her shoulder as Logan entered the room.

He came to stand beside her, his expression guarded. "So, you've made your decision."

"Yes." She kissed Derek's cheek, then moved away from the crib. "You were right. He belongs here, with me."

"What about me?" Logan asked. "Where do I belong?"

"What do you mean?"

"Mara, don't play games with me. You know how I feel about you, how I've always felt. There's nothing to stop us from being together now, if that's what you want."

"Logan." Taking his hand in hers, Mara lifted it to her lips and kissed his palm. "I love you, Logan. I don't think I ever stopped. I'm not sure what I've been running away from all these years. But I know what I want now. And it's you, by my side, forever."

"Mara!"

He reached for her, but she held up her hand, keeping him at bay. "It's not that easy. I know how you feel about having a baby in the house, how difficult it is for you. And I've sensed your jealousy."

"I won't deny it. As idiotic and petty as it sounds, I've been jealous of the boy. I told you that before. I did some research, and it's quite common for men to be jealous of a new baby. But Derek is your son, and I'll love him for that reason alone. As for his being here"—he shrugged—"it's getting easier having him around. Okay?"

"Okay."

Drawing her into his arms, he held her close, content, for the moment, just to hold her and then, tilting her head back, he claimed her lips with his in a kiss that held nothing back. Mara, Queen of the Vampires, was his, for now and forever.

"Mara?"

Breathless from the intensity of his kiss, she met his gaze. "More."

He brushed a kiss across the top of her head. "Derek should have a father," he said. "I always wanted it to be me, so, will you marry me?"

"Yes."

"Is tomorrow night too soon?"

She frowned. Was he serious?

Logan blew out a sigh. "I guess we should wait a while."

"Perhaps." Had she still been human, people would have expected her to mourn before contemplating marriage. But she wasn't human anymore. Still, it was customary to have a period of mourning for the dead. Jewish people observed shivah, which lasted seven days. Parents mourned the death of a child for a year. In old England, a widow was expected to dress in mourning for as long as four years. Black was the traditional color for mourning in most parts of the world, although queens in medieval Europe and Spain had worn white.

If she married so soon, there were those who would

call her callous, unfeeling, but those who knew her would understand. It wasn't indifference to Kyle's death. She grieved for his loss, but nothing would bring him back. She had offered him a chance at a new life, and he had rejected it. "I don't want to wait too long."

"Just you and me and the priest, okay?"

"No one else?" she asked, thinking of the Cordova family.

"Just our son."

Mara caressed his cheek, thinking that she had never loved Logan Blackwood more than she did at that moment. As for Vince and his family, she hoped they would understand.

Mara contacted Father Lanzoni later that night, and he agreed to come to her house in the Hollywood Hills the following week to perform the ceremony.

After hanging up the phone, Mara found herself again having second thoughts. Was she doing the right thing? She had just buried her first husband. Was she being disrespectful to Kyle's memory? Maybe she should have told Logan they needed to wait a few months, she thought, and then shook her head. She was Nosferatu, no longer bound by the customs and mores of ordinary people. She had nothing to prove to anyone. Perhaps it was wrong of her to marry Logan so soon after Kyle's demise, but it didn't feel wrong. In fact, nothing had ever felt so right.

Chapter Forty-six

The next week passed quickly. With Logan's help, Mara moved her belongings from the house in Porterville to the house in the Hollywood Hills. Before they left, they spent one night visiting Vince and Cara, another with Rane and Rafe and their wives. It felt good to be with them again, to know she was again their equal and not an outsider.

"We're going to miss you," Savanah said. "I'm going to miss you. Promise me you'll keep in touch."

"She'd better," Rane said with mock severity.

"You know I will," Mara promised. "And you're always welcome to come for a visit. I'd like Derek and Abbey to be friends."

"Of course," Savanah said, smiling.

On the ride home, Mara couldn't help feeling a little guilty for not telling the Cordova family about her upcoming marriage.

She slid a glance at Logan. They had agreed not to sleep together until after the wedding. Mara found it endearing that Logan wanted to wait. On one hand, it seemed a little silly; after all, they had made love many times before. But Logan had insisted this was different. They were starting a new life together, and he wanted to start it right.

The night of the wedding, Father Lanzoni arrived with the setting sun.

"So," he said, taking Mara's hand in his. "What I sensed the other night is true. You are one of us again."

"Yes, thanks to Logan."

"I sense no weakening in your powers," the priest remarked, "but then, I suppose that was to be expected. You turned Logan, after all. His blood is yours. And so . . . no regrets?"

"No. This is who I am."

The priest nodded. "Are you ready?"

"Yes, Logan went downstairs to get the baby."

"The child is well after his ordeal?"

"Yes."

"And you've decided to raise him yourself?"

Mara nodded. "Since I'm not bound by the Dark Sleep, I can look after him day and night."

"And Logan? How does he feel about having a child in the house?"

"He's adjusting," Mara said. She knew Logan had a weakness for infants, knew there were times when it was difficult for him to be around Derek, and yet he genuinely cared for her son. "He loves Derek because he's mine, and because, well, who wouldn't love him?" She made light of the question, but she knew about Logan's past, knew how he felt about children.

Logan arrived with the baby just then. Father Lanzoni grinned at the sight of the tall rugged-looking vampire lovingly cradling a baby in his arms. It was a sight he didn't see every day, a sight rarely seen in their world.

"Are we ready then?" the priest asked.

Logan took Mara's hand in his. "Yes, Father."

"It pleases me to be here," Father Lanzoni said. "I can feel the love you have for one another, and for the child. There are those of us who have turned our backs on our humanity, those who prey on mortals like savage beasts. And then there are others, like the Cordova family, who have managed to rise above their instincts.

"Mara, I sense a change in you, a softening, a gentling, if you will, brought about perhaps by your recent experiences not only as a mortal, but as a mother. And so it gives me great pleasure to join the two of you in marriage.

"Mara, will you take Logan, here present, to be your lawfully wedded husband for as long as you both shall live?"

"I will."

"Logan, will you take Mara, here present, to be your lawfully wedded wife for as long as you both shall live?"

Logan gazed into Mara's eyes as he murmured, "I will."

"Then, by the power vested in me, I now pronounce you husband and wife and child, bound together by your love for one another, and by the laws of the land, from this night forward." The priest smiled at Logan. "You may kiss your bride."

Logan wrapped his free arm around Mara's waist and drew her close to his side. "I love you, wife, now and forever," he murmured, his voice husky.

"And I love you," Mara said, "now and forever."

Logan smiled at her and then, careful not to crush the baby between them, he bestowed his first husbandly kiss on his bride while their son and an ancient priest looked on, smiling.

Epilogue

One week later

Lou McDonald sat with her feet propped on a corner of her desk. Weeks had passed and she'd had no word from Mara or her companion. The baby would be several months old by now and she was dying to know if it was a boy or a girl, if it was normal or vampire. Or perhaps some bizarre combination of both.

She had contacted everyone she could think of who might have a clue as to Mara's whereabouts, but to no avail. Either her snitches didn't know, or they just weren't talking. Cindy wasn't having any luck on her end, either.

Lou was about to close up shop and call it a day when her computer notified her she had a new e-mail. She didn't recognize the screen name.

Dropping her feet to the floor, she opened the message.

McDonald, your fee has been credited to your bank. FYI, Bowden is dead. Ramsden and his wife

are dead. Mara has regained her powers. Logan
Blackwood

Lou read the message a second time. Scowling, she
muttered, "The least he could have done was let me
know if the baby was a boy or a girl."

Two weeks later

Savanah Cordova sat on the sofa, her mother's black
book open on her lap as she brought the journal up to
date, noting that Travis Jackson had been destroyed
by hunter Louise McDonald. She added the names of
Dr. Thomas Ramsden and his wife, Janis Leigh Ramsden,
noting that the former had been destroyed by Mara, and
the latter by her own husband.

Turning the page, she added the names of Ed Rogen
and Sasha (no known last name), noting that both had
been killed in Reno, Nevada, by Logan Blackwood.

And the battle raged on, she thought as she closed the
book, and wondered what kind of world her daughter
would inherit. Would Abbey be a hunter? It was in her
blood, after all. And what of Derek? Had he inherited his
mother's vampire heritage?

Would Derek become Nosferatu when he reached
puberty, the way Rane and Rafe had?

Would Derek and Abbey Marie be friends?

Or enemies.

Only time would tell.

* * *

Six weeks later

Mara sat in the nursery, quietly rocking her son. In the last few weeks, Derek had regained the weight he had lost while in Ramsden's custody. His cheeks were rosy with good health. His appetite was excellent. He slept through the night, and rarely cried.

And every now and then, after the sun had set, his deep blue eyes shone with a faint red glow, proving that he was, indeed, his mother's son.

Dear Readers,

I'm excited and relieved that Mara's story, *Night's Mistress*, is finally a reality. She's an amazing character. As many of you know, she started out as a minor player in *Night's Kiss*. I never had any plans for her to be in the subsequent Children of the Night books. But there was something about her that captivated me . . . and my readers, also.

I wrote the first draft of her story quite some time ago and even announced in the back of *Night's Pleasure* that her book would be coming soon. But then . . . it didn't. I began to have doubts about the story, which is unusual for me. And I began to get letters—lots of letters—asking where her story was and wanting to know more about this ancient vampire. With so many people writing to tell me how much they liked her and how eager they were for her story, I began to wonder if anything I wrote would live up to my readers' expectations. Not a good place for a writer to be!

But, a promise is a promise, so I went through the manuscript again. And again. And finally, at long last, I'm happy with Mara's journey. I hope my readers will be, too.

I almost forgot. Congratulations to Linda Lattimer, Ingeborg Deyaert, and Farrah Pettis for winning my Name the Hero contest.

Best,
Amanda
www.amandaashley.net
DarkWritr@aol.com

*Read all of Amanda Ashley's
Children of the Night series,
available now from your
local bookseller and online.*

It all begins with

NIGHT'S KISS

HE HAS FOUND HIS SOUL'S DESIRE . . .

The Dark Gift has brought Roshan DeLongpre a lifetime
of bitter loneliness—until, by chance, he comes across a
picture of Brenna Flanagan. There is something haunt-
ingly familiar in Brenna's fiery red hair and sensual
body, something that compels him to travel into the past,
save the beautiful witch from the stake, and bring her
safely to his own time. Now, in the modern world,
Brenna's seductive innocence and sense of wonder are ut-
erly bewitching the once-weary vampire, blinding him
to a growing danger. For there is one whose dark magick
is strong . . . one who knows who they both are and won't
stop till their powers are his . . . and they are nothing
more than shadows through time . . .

Eternal passion continues . . .
Enter the lush, sensual world of
bestselling author Amanda Ashley . . . a place
where vampires indulge their appetites,
but find they can fall prey to love and desire.

NIGHT'S TOUCH

ONE KISS CAN SEAL YOUR FATE . . .

Cara DeLongpre wandered into the mysterious Nocturne club looking for a fleeting diversion from her sheltered life. Instead she found a dark, seductive stranger whose touch entices her beyond the safety she's always known and into a heady carnal bliss . . .

A year ago, Vincent Cordova believed that vampires existed only in bad movies and bogeyman stories. That was before a chance encounter left him with unimaginable powers, a hellish thirst, and an aching loneliness he's sure will never end . . . until the night he meets Cara DeLongpre. Cara's beauty and bewitching innocence call to his mind, his heart . . . his blood. For Vincent senses the Dark Gift shared by Cara's parents, and the lurking threat from an ancient and powerful foe. And he knows that the only thing more dangerous than the enemy waiting to seek its vengeance is the secret carried by those Cara trusts the most . . .

Fall prey to the ultimate seduction . . .

NIGHT'S MASTER

PASSION HAS A DARKER SIDE . . .

Kathy McKenna was sure that the little Midwestern town of Oak Hollow would be isolated enough for safety, but the moment the black-clad stranger walked into her bookstore, she knew she was wrong. Raphael Cordova exudes smoldering power, and his sensual touch draws Kathy into a world of limitless pleasure and unimaginable dangers.

Oak Hollow was supposed to be neutral territory for supernatural beings. Instead it has become home to an evil force determined to destroy them—and kill any mortal who gets in the way. As leader of the North American vampires, Raphael has always put duty first, but then, no woman ever enthralled him the way Kathy does. And as the enemy's terrifying plan is revealed, Raphael's desire could be a fatal distraction for all of his kind, and for the woman he has sworn to love forever . . .

NIGHT'S PLEASURE

DESIRE CASTS A DARK SPELL . . .

Savanah Gentry's life was so much simpler when she was a reporter for the local newspaper. That was before her father's sudden death drew her into a mysterious new world she was just beginning to understand. A vampire hunter by birth, Savanah has been entrusted with a legacy that puts everyone she cares for in danger—including the seductive, sensual vampire who unleashes her most primal desires . . .

Rane Cordova has always been alone, half hating himself for his Dark Gift even as he relishes its extraordinary power. But one look at Savanah fills him with the need to take everything she has to give and carry her to heights of unimagined ecstasy. And though he never intended their relationship to go this far, now Savanah is in more danger than she knows—and facing a relentless enemy determined to eliminate Rane and all his kind . . .